PENGUIN CLASSICS

THE PRIVATE MEMOIRS AND
CONFESSIONS OF A JUSTIFIED SINNER

JAMES HOGG (1770–1835) was a Scottish Borderer who became
a celebrated poet and the author of one of the great novels of
Romanticism. He was born in Ettrick, and spent many years
herding sheep and cattle. His schooling suffered, but he was
writing poems by the mid 1790s, and was to help Walter Scott
with material for his collection of ballads, the *Minstrelsy of the
Scottish Border*. He moved to Edinburgh in 1810, where he
launched his year-long magazine the *Spy*. *The Queen's Wake*, a
miscellany of narrative poems, including 'Kilmeny', made his
name. He was given, by the fourth Duke of Buccleuch, the lease
of a cottage at Altrive, near St Mary's Loch, where his later life
was spent. In 1816 a brilliant book of verse parodies appeared,
and the year after that *Blackwood's Edinburgh Magazine* began
with a no less brilliant biblical parody, the 'Chaldee Manuscript',
initiated by Hogg: an account of Edinburgh's magazine wars. For
the journal's symposium feature, the 'Noctes Ambrosianae', his
conversation was scripted by his enemy friends, his 'devils', John
Wilson and John Gibson Lockhart. His relations with these men
have been detected in his novel the *Confessions of a Justified
Sinner*, published anonymously in 1824. Long hidden from view,
it was read again in the 1940s, and is now generally seen as his
masterpiece.

KARL MILLER founded the *London Review of Books*, which he
edited for many years. Before this, he was literary editor of the
Spectator and the *New Statesman* and editor of the *Listener*. He
was also, from 1974 to 1992, Lord Northcliffe Professor of
Modern English Literature at University College London. His
Cockburn's Millennium received the James Tait Black Memorial
Prize. Other books of his include *Doubles*, *Authors*, and two
works of autobiography, *Rebecca's Vest* and *Dark Horses*. A
study of James Hogg, *Electric Shepherd*, was published in 2003.

Contents

Acknowledgements

I am indebted to the editors of Hogg's *Collected Works*, who have brought a new depth to Hogg studies, and I am grateful in particular to one of them, Gillian Hughes, for good advice and the benefit of her immense knowledge of the field. Her three volumes of his letters are now in the process of publication. Meiko O'Halloran's doctoral thesis on Hogg (Oxford University, 2004) refers to his 'kaleidoscopic art', and I am obliged to her for the arguments she presents. Passages of the Introduction formed part of a lecture, 'Who wrote James Hogg?', given at the University of Stirling on 4 May 2005.

Chronology

1770 Born at Ettrickhall farmhouse in the Scottish Borders and baptized on 9 December. Son of a farmer, Robert Hogg, and his wife Margaret (née Laidlaw). Soon put to the herding of cattle and sheep, and to an acquaintance with hunger and fatigue. His early education was restricted to two spells of some six months in all. At the age of sixteen he served at the farm of Willenslee, where there was a library.

1790 To the farm of Blackhouse, where the master's son was the poet William Laidlaw, who became his closest friend. Around 1793 he started to write poems. A poem was taken by the *Scots Magazine* the following year, and his first book of verse, *Scottish Pastorals*, crept out in Edinburgh in 1801.

1800 Moved to run Ettrickhouse farm for his father, and presently met Walter Scott, to whose *Minstrelsy of the Scottish Border* he contributed ballad material, together with his mother, and who became his friend and mentor. From the turn of the century he paid visits to the Highlands and Western Isles, and in 1803 he offered for a farm in Harris. The venture fell through for legal reasons.

1807 A book of poems, *The Mountain Bard*, and an essay on the care of sheep, *The Shepherd's Guide*, were brought out by Constable. Having herded ewes on Queensbury Hill in Nithsdale, he acquired two Dumfriesshire farms, Corfardin and Locherben, which failed. Bankrupt. Love affairs with two Border girls produced one daughter, and perhaps a second. The kirk session took note of this 'uncleanness', and Hogg was summoned for rebuke.

1810 And so, for several years, to Edinburgh, where he

launched and largely wrote a literary magazine, the *Spy*, a testing-ground for themes and preoccupations that were to remain with him. A mild attention to sexual matters affronted his precarious readership. The *Forest Minstrel* of this year was an anthology of poems by himself and others. In 1811 he climbed and slid down Ben More in the Western Highlands, from whose summit he surveyed the haunts of Scott's *Lady of the Lake* and much of Hogg's beloved Scotland.

1813 *The Queen's Wake* – a series of narrative poems, which are set within the framework of a literary competition ordained by Mary Queen of Scots – was published by George Goldie. Among these are his most celebrated poem, which tells of the maid Kilmeny's translation to Heaven, and the fine ballad 'The Witch of Fife'. Goldie then went bankrupt. William Blackwood, a trustee for the ensuing settlement, purchased surviving copies of the third edition, and went on, for good and ill, to become Hogg's publisher-in-chief.

1814 Having been introduced to Wordsworth in Edinburgh that summer, he travelled with him about the Borders and visited his house of Rydal Mount in the Lake District, where, beneath a brilliant night sky, he experienced a snub at the hand of his 'superior being'. Hogg served for three years as secretary of the Forum, a debating society, which he saw as completing his belated education.

1815 The fourth Duke of Buccleuch leased him rent-free the cottage of Altrive Lake, where he was to spend the rest of his life. The following year he brought out his remarkable book of verse parodies, *The Poetic Mirror*, in which Wordsworth is mocked. It had been hoped that Scott and Hogg's new friend Byron would contribute to the project in its original form.

1817 Drawn into Edinburgh's magazine wars, where Constable and Blackwood were contending potentates, rival 'bibliopoles'. In October 1817 *Blackwood's Edinburgh Magazine* started to appear. The inaugural number carried 'The Chaldee Manuscript', an explosive Biblical parody, initiated by Hogg, and charged with politico-religious provocation, in which these wars were evoked. Blackwood laughed at it, while removing it from the number in perfect fear of the consequences: but it was to make the journal's name. Hogg worked on the paper with John Wilson and John Gibson Lockhart, who presently enrolled him as a star of its serial feature, the 'Noctes Ambrosianae', imaginary conversations sited in Ambrose's tavern. Hogg's words were, for the most part, scripted for him by these two, and his equivocal relations with them were to dominate the rest of his life. His Covenanter novel, *The Brownie of Bodsbeck*, was published in 1818.

1820 Married Margaret Phillips, a pious woman from a wealthy south-west farming family. Her dowry failed when her father's finances did. Margaret's parents came to live with the Hoggs at Altrive, where a son and four daughters were born. A collection of country pieces, evolved from earlier work, *Winter Evening Tales*, was published in the same year. In 1821 he obtained from the Buccleuchs the nine-year lease of the adjacent farm of Mount Benger. His *Poetic Works* was issued in four volumes by Constable the year after that, while his phantasmagoric medieval romance, *The Three Perils of Man*, was published by Longman in London. This was followed by *The Three Perils of Woman*. Both of these wild and busy works have found a niche in post-modernist taste.

1823 Wrote the *Confessions of a Justified Sinner*, which would one day be reckoned his principal achievement. Published, anonymously, by Longman, in 1824, it made no stir at the time. Nor did his mock-epic poem *Queen Hynde*, whose Dark Age Argyllshire projects a foundation myth, a Scots cosmogony.

1827 Inaugural meeting, at Innerleithen, of the St Ronan's Games. He was a leading light of these 'Scottish Olympics' and a lifelong sportsman: a runner, fisherman and curler, captain of the Bowmen of the Border.

1832 To London for three months, to promote a collected edition of his prose fiction, which got no farther than *Altrive Tales*, and to be fêted by the Anglo-Scottish aristocracy and literati. He was led to think that he might be in mind for a knighthood, an honour presaged in his writings but distinctly unacceptable to his wife. A Scottish fête was later held at the Tontine Hotel in Peebles, where he reviewed his career and was reported to say of his 'literary fame': 'I hae got it at last.' While curling on Duddingston Loch, he fell through the ice and felt he would never be the same again. He no longer cut the famous figure he had once done on the streets of Edinburgh. In 1832 there appeared *A Queer Book*, ballads done in his 'ancient style'.

1834 There appeared, in two versions, his anecdotes of Scott, mortally offensive to Scott's biographer, Lockhart.

1835 Died calmly, in poverty, at Altrive. Born again a century later, when his literary fame acquired a new lease of life.

Introduction

In the summer of 2003, a friend of mine murmured that he'd read the first three chapters of *Electric Shepherd*, a book I'd published on James Hogg, and still didn't understand how this man could have written the novel, the *Confessions of a Justified Sinner*. Shortly afterwards, James Buchan brought out his book, *Capital of the Mind*, an account of Enlightenment Edinburgh in which Hogg keeps a low profile, and in which the novel is said to have been, not by, but merely attributed to Hogg.[1]

The *Confessions* is a book about uncertainty which is itself uncertain, and whose very authorship has sometimes been questioned – with John Gibson Lockhart nominated, at times, as a contender for the title; and there are questioners who may or must have felt that a poor man from the country, a man of simplicities, slips and inequalities, or that a graduate of the school of nature, an 'inspired', untutored lyric poet, could not have written it. Hogg belonged, moreover, to a coterie of writers – those responsible for *Blackwood's Magazine* – whose tricks, mysteries, attributions, denials, joint authorship, anonymity and pseudonymity became, for a while, habitual. So why is it now generally and confidently believed that he wrote the novel? Well, he did claim it, despite publishing it anonymously, and the publishers dealt with him as its author. He was not, or not for long, its hidden or absent author, in the way that Walter Scott, at this same time, was the 'Great Unknown' of the Waverley novels. It has in it his native scenes, his shepherd places. And he discussed it, as his, with Mary Ann Hughes, the Scott-adoring, true-blue Tory wife of a canon of St Paul's Cathedral.[2]

Mrs Hughes is one of the very few of his contemporaries who is on record as appreciating it.

Visiting the Borders in 1824, the year the *Confessions* was published, Mrs Hughes talked to Hogg's uncle, William Laidlaw, an old shepherd who had deserted his ballads for religion, and who observed in his forthright Ettrick way that his nephew had shown no 'particular indication of talent', as she phrased it, when he was young: 'Na, na he was e'en like other laddies, but na ill chiel' and 'ready at his bible – the readiest ever I saw'. Not a bad lad, but a book by him was 'full of lees', which was not the only time that Hogg was blamed for lying. Four years later she met the man himself, at Scott's baronial country house of Abbotsford, catching him at the centre of that part of his life which revolved round his relations with the friend, mentor, fellow artist and semi-feudal superior who lived there. 'Hogg,' she thought, 'is a very simple-mannered, pleasant person, much less rough in exterior than I expected, and has an open, good-humoured face which must prepossess every one in his favour.'

He and Scott are noticed, in her recollections of the two, laughing over a local worthy known as 'the daft Laird', who once called to his servant: 'Jock, I saw an Otter in yon Pool.' Jock splashed about for it, until the laird let fall that the sighting was thirty-two years ago. Hogg the song-writer and 'proficient' fiddler is remembered talking 'very eagerly' in the drawing-room at Abbotsford. Of a woman's rendering of Venetian ballads in the library he says: 'Oh this is just Etawlian singing which I canna understand ... if it had na been a thing of ceveelity I had far rather sat and had our cracks here.' But he, too, gets to sing for his supper. Mistaken for Hogg the writer, Mrs Hughes learns, his brother, the master of Scott's sheep, was embraced by a daft French count, who was elegantly advised: 'I'm wae to think ye'll be sorry to ken I hae na manner of right to receive' the Count's compliments. Hogg's brother reckoned that he paid undue attention to those poems of his, neglecting his flock.

During her 1828 visit to the North she discussed the novel with Hogg, who reported: 'Mrs Hughes insists on the Confessions of a Sinner being republished with my name as she says it is positively the best story of that frightful kind that was ever written.' She had found in Scotland a genial, storytelling man who had written a sovereign Gothic novel.

Given the tricks of the time, it may not be decisive, for a confirmation of his authorship, that a manuscript of the novel in Hogg's hand was formerly known to exist; nor is it impossible that other hands may have helped with its composition. But there are many different reasons for believing it to be his. Those which are internal to the novel itself, and to which I shall turn in a moment, are reasons which help one to understand it, and to enjoy its uncertainty. Writers' lives, which create their works of art, can be read there, difficult as such readings may often prove, and the attempt can certainly be made with Hogg's work of art.

Its sinner predicts that his adventures will puzzle the readers of the future, and they did so. But posterity came round to his adventures: the tide began to turn in favour of the book when an edition appeared in 1947 with the endorsement of the French novelist André Gide. In earlier times Hogg could be thought a strange compound of sense and nonsense, coarseness and delicacy, and his writings had lain open to the condescension and contempt which have been directed at the simple soul from the country who has had the nerve to write a book. '*Him* write a book? I kent his faither.' Scotland's proverbial mockery of an ancient prejudice. The history of Hogg's contested claim to the novel commemorates a view of his writings which has now been subdued by a new regard for his achievement.

Hogg was born in 1770 at the heart of the Border lands, by the parallel streams of Yarrow and Ettrick, and spent his youth as a farm labourer and then as a shepherd, denied the schooling earlier available to Robert Burns. His so-called 'wilderness', rough and tough as it was for the poor, was also 'elegant and agreeable' – his words for it – and convivial, richly customary and legendary. It had more than its share of likely lads whose energies could surmount educational slow starts and a rigorous, a visceral class distinction. The Borders were a history and a civilization, in which violence, songs and sport had long been pursued, and in which hardship and hunger had survived the

agricultural revolution of the eighteenth century and the prosperity it delivered to the enterprising. Hogg was never to be
financially secure, and more than once became insolvent – a fate
that also overtook Walter Scott and other eminent Scotsmen of
the day.

In his mid-thirties this friend and neighbour of Scott was still
to be found in a hole in the ground, his hillside bothy. Soon
after this, having fathered a child, or two perhaps, Hogg set off
for Edinburgh, travelling the thirty-seven miles to arrive in the
metropolis at starvation point, and, nothing loth, to launch a
literary magazine, the *Spy*. Seven years later he took up with
the Tory publisher William Blackwood and his rising stars,
Lockhart and John Wilson. Three years later still, in 1820, he
got married to a pious woman from a well-to-do farming family
in Nithsdale, who bore him four daughters and a son. His life
was divided between Ettrick and Edinburgh, and suspended
between social classes. It can be said of him that this was his
world, the one world he inhabited. It can also be said of him
that he inhabited two worlds, which made two and more of the
man in his book, the author of the *Confessions*.

He wrote poems and stories for Blackwood's journal for
the rest of his life, falling out with it at intervals, and he took
part, mostly by proxy, in its series of published conversations,
the 'Noctes Ambrosianae', where literary cronies, in various
stages of disguise, mingled with outright *messieurs de l'imagination*'. Wilson, alias Christopher North, was the principal
Ambrosianist, and Wilson and Lockhart, in the main, were
Hogg's scriptwriters, his ghosts. He was dramatized by his
'madcap Tories', who would also write or rewrite material
published in his name. They were both his cronies and his
enemies. '*O sus, quando te aspiciam?*' they asked. 'When shall
I see you, you swine?' This is the voice of friendship, which is
rarely unequivocal. But his grand young friends effected a
betrayal of the man they liked, and meant to celebrate, and
they were sometimes to 'banish' him, as he put it, from their
brotherhood. An affinity with Shakespeare's Falstaff makes an
appearance in the record. Falstaff was 'banished', as Shakespeare put it, from the society of the young friend who became

king, and, like James Hogg, he was both witty and the cause of wit in others. And there is another affinity to speak of.

In the Classical world, the upstart musician Marsyas was punished for his temerity by the god Apollo. Titian painted his picture, and so did the Ambrosians, in their treatment of Hogg. Nor did they omit to mention the flaying of Marsyas in their discussions. Hogg wasn't proof to the pain inflicted by this mockery and masquerading. There were failures of confidence which left their mark in the course of his later years. Marsyas had the last word, though, a hundred years later.[3]

Hogg's urban experience encompassed conflicts in the province of ideas. Enlightenment values shared a sky with the crescent moon of Romance, and there were magazines which fought on opposite sides of the dispute that emerged between the two, with the matter of supremacy and succession by no means free from doubt in generations to come. The Scottish Enlightenment did not disappear with the eighteenth century; it can be caught, along with its flamboyant negation, in the *Blackwood's Magazine* of this time. Neither of these lights was to leave the sky, and they have survived as a living duality, a rivalry and mutuality, for readers of the present time. The contest of Whig and Tory over the extension of the franchise achieved by the Reform Bill of 1832 was a further feature of his urban experience, as was the return of evangelical religion personified by his wife. Meanwhile the wisdom and superstition of the countryside, and of the oral tradition, continued to command the sympathy of the Ettrick Shepherd, as he became known to his public.

He was a watcher of the skies, and this contest and confluence of forces was written there by what transpired on his way from the Borders to Edinburgh in 1801. He passed the night at the inn in the village of Straiton, which afforded, for his contemplation, a romantic scene. The landlord's disturbed son had been baying at the moon, telling it off, as it hung in its splendour over the Pentland Hills. Conscious, perhaps, of Wordsworth's recent lyric about his 'idiot boy', there was to be a poem of Hogg's, 'Sandy Tod', about this Midlothian lad and about himself. Benighted in Straiton, Hogg shared the moon, as you might say, with its detractor, his eyes to the hills, his back to the shepherds, lairds, weavers, wizards and fairies of his wilderness, with its now treeless Ettrick Forest. Below him in the moonlight lay Edinburgh, 'Capital of the Mind', alias the 'metropolis of mind' seriously and satirically so called by the novelist John Galt at the time of Hogg's *Confessions*.

At about the time of this episode the Ettrick Shepherd made it to the moon, according to Hogg's extravaganza, 'Dr David Dale's Account of a Grand Aerial Voyage', published much later, in 1830. The flight is fuelled by hydrogen gas, and its Ettrick Shepherd, 'this thirsty and ravenous son of the mountains', talks of scientific calculation, rather as Hogg refers, elsewhere in his writings, to the optics of his friend Sir David Brewster. This Hogg reveals a serio-comic acquaintance with the principles both of geometry (logarithms, tangents, 'the parabolic and the hyperbolic curves', crop up) and of poetry. Poetry is called 'a kind o' representation o' things by similitude' – which forms part of a Wordsworthian definition employed in Hogg's verse parodies. Enlightenment science made it to the moon in fact, eventually, and there could be no more graphic illustration of the, for some, scandalous proposition that we live in a world where the scientific mind has worked with the romantic imagination, several of whose hypotheses came true. Not only did Edgar Allan Poe, with his balloonist Hans Pfaall, emulate Hogg's lunar flight. Science did.

There was a familiar term of the time which bore a special resonance for Hogg. He and his friends Lockhart and Wilson were 'printers' devils' of a kind. He could see these friends as two devils, with himself as a third, feeling for Wilson a mixture of 'terror, admiration and jealousy'. Such was the intimacy and ambivalence of their relationship, of the *Blackwood's* collective, in which they copied one another, rewrote each other's stuff, impersonated each other, in a welter of false names, parody, imposture, sport. The welter was referred to in the 'Noctes' as a 'universal plagiarism', which can be considered an aspect of the universal mystery and uncertainty imagined by the inner circle of these writers. An astonishing jamboree, all this, and a test of Hogg's integrity. He feared that his integrity might be compromised if he went in for too much in the way of revising his work. But the ruthless brilliance of *Blackwood's* journalism was a greater hazard for him than the ordeal of revision. His integrity is best expressed in the duality that invests the *Confessions*, where his life was spoken in ways impossible for most forms of autobiography.

An age of reason encountered what Coleridge called 'an age of personality'. Hogg became a personality, both in the Borders and at *Blackwood's*, where the word 'personality' became a pun. It could mean both an *ad hominem* insult and an individual human being, whether one person or two, *homo simplex* or *homo duplex*. And it was on its way to meaning, as in his case, a celebrity or star. The romantic reaction which had come about in this quarter of Edinburgh swore by personality and its uncertainties, and by error, and by nation and imagination, the nation being both Scotland and Britain, together with their empire, on which, as Wilson has been thought to have been the first to say, the sun never set.

The views of these writers, not least their views on the proximity or identity of truth and error, yield anticipations of Post-Modernist theory, while embodying a displayed adherence to the truths of Christianity. 'There never was a baseless fiction,' said the 'Noctes' diners, whose talk carried a message that was to recur in the writings of the modern American philosopher Richard Rorty. For Rorty, truth is made, rather than found or given. Like Rorty, the diners were in favour of nonsense, hero-worship, greatness and romance, and of Wordsworth. It isn't clear how far the real Hogg would have gone with the more subversive propositions put into his mouth, for all the unsettling tendency of his novel, for all its theory of relativity, for all its placing in a state of indeterminacy contrasting versions of the same events. But it does seem clear that the novel can't be thought irrelevant to the philosophizings heard at Ambrose's tavern, that it makes sense to ask if the errors at issue in the novel can be associated with the love of error professed in the magazine, where error and accident can appear to offer an escape from the certainty of God's will.

In the pages of the magazine, at certain times, romantic indeterminacy and indifferentism teach – and tease – that error is beautiful and truthful, and most things much the same. The 'Noctes' Shepherd is made to reflect: 'Ae thing's just as good as anither. It's nae matter what ane pits in a book; my warst things aye sell best, I think. I'm resolved, I'll try and write some awfu' ill thing this winter.' The real Hogg once said that he'd lost the ability to tell which of his things would 'take'.[4] This was expressed as a matter of regret, and it would be a mistake to suppose that he lost himself in the worship of error. But he was very interested in it, nowhere more than in the *Confessions*. The novel is a tragi-comedy of errors.

The *Confessions* consists of an editor's story of the sinner's life, followed by the sinner's own word for what happened to him. An editorial postscript, which supplies an extract from a letter of Hogg's published in the magazine, describes the opening up of a suicide's grave on a hilltop near his house at Altrive in Ettrick. The participants in this gruesome souvenir hunt include the unnamed editor himself, Lockhart, and Hogg's and Walter Scott's friend Laidlaw – another William Laidlaw, a poet and a Whig sympathizer, whose brother James, said to have been helped with his lessons by Hogg, became a powerful Highland sheep-farmer and improver. The postscript is a corridor to the historical reality of Hogg's personal relationships.

E. T. A. Hoffmann's novel *The Devil's Elixirs* came out at this point, in 1824, having been translated for Blackwood from the German by Hogg's friend R. P. Gillies, and may well have encouraged Hogg to write a book which implies that a person can be two persons or more; the double of the time owed much to Germany. Hogg was himself more men than one, and the idea of the double stands here in allegorical relation to the opposites and self-belyings perceptible in the story of his life, as in the lives of others. It's possible to plead authority for this generic claim, alleging allegory. With Bunyan in mind, perhaps, Hogg spoke of certain of his fictions as allegories, while also making use of Bunyan's and Wordsworth's word 'similitude'. Puritan election and predestination, puritan abhorrence of morals, merit, 'filthy works', in contradistinction to God's grace, and gift of faith, are at stake in Hogg's novel. They belong to the dualistic 'involute' of the novel, to use an expression coined by De Quincey, whose likeness takes part in the 'Noctes'; and they have been seen in general, by Yvor Winters, as 'a long step towards the allegorization of experience'.[5] Hogg's novel might well be seen as an allegory which confronts the allegory of justification by faith, whereby, as for the seventeenth-century Covenanter, salvation goes, foreordained and irreversible, to the true believer.

Hogg's sinner is a Whig and a 'fanatic of old', as the enlightened and as Episcopalians tended to think of the Covenanters and their commemorators. The novel is dominated by its exposure of ultra-Calvinism's antinomian excesses, of the errors that flow from the conviction that God's chosen few are infallible, and will not be forsaken by their dualizing maker, with his sheep and his goats. Hogg had a cousin who felt that way, who hated the idea that a man may be saved and yet fall from it tomorrow. But there are other main meanings here too.

The novel is a response to the rival Christianities of the time – a blow for charity and tolerance. But it's also an outcome of Hogg's experience of the double life of poet and peasant, and of the multiple personality of the *Blackwood's* collective. I can imagine the retort that he may have been no more double than the next man or woman, but I don't see how anyone could deny that he was a man of contradictions. To make much of these contradictions has been thought to risk failing to convey what he was like as a person: but this is what persons are like. Their contradictions do not efface them, and to deny that this can be so is as much as to say that the novel has been written in vain, and that many subsequent novels have been written in vain. The *Confessions* is the work of someone who believed that personality and its appearances are uncertain, and his explorations fed into a variety of later approaches to the problem of human identity, including the psychoanalytic approach. A stress on the fragmentary, the momentary, on the multiple, mutual and mutable, on splitting and sharing and merging, on transference, and on performance, is now in widest commonalty spread. Edward St Aubyn has recently pointed, in one of his novels, to the possibility that identity may be 'a series of

impersonations held together by a central intelligence', a condition which abolishes the distinction between action and acting, and which he distinguishes from disintegration.[6]

Hogg's novel tells, in its two different ways, of a young man,
Robert Wringhim, whose real father is a predestinarian divine,
and whose nominal father, a jolly laird, has a son, handsome
and chivalrous George, as the editor portrays him. Robert takes
up with a princely tempter and impersonator, Gil-Martin, who
becomes his intimate friend and who tells him what he already
knows about the immunity of the elect. Such a plot gives scope
for uncertainty. Nevertheless, the novel has an expoundable
aim, which has a great deal to do with its dislike of religious
intolerance, with the 'be not angry' scornfully identified as the
sum of Hogg's morality by angry Thomas Carlyle. It's a book
about 'the effects of puritanical superstition in destroying the
moral feelings'. These are not Hogg's words, but he would have
responded to their purport. They are those of Lockhart, whose
novel of the same time, *Matthew Wald*, has in it an antinomian
fanatic, a justified sinner, who had been 'permitted to make a
sore stumble', words that Hogg might have written. The novel's
objections to puritanical superstition are opposed by its diary
of a madman. They are assisted by affirmations of a benign
piety, of what Hogg referred to, in his novel *The Three Perils
of Woman*, as 'the religion of the heart'.[7]

Lockhart may have influenced Hogg's interest in religious
fanaticism. But they were very different people. Hogg's novel
is concerned with the troubles of an outcast, with banishment
and betrayal, and with the seductions of rank and power. Lockhart was not indifferent to these seductions, but his experience
of them was hardly Hogg's: it is easier to think of him inflicting,
rather than suffering, the attentions of Gil-Martin, and he could
be evoked by his friends in a way that caused him to resemble
this dark spirit. Of the two men, Hogg is the more likely author
of the *Confessions*, and the canvassing of alternative authors
comes to look like an intervention of the class police, like
the punishment of an intruder among 'better men', as one
twentieth-century critic characterized his Edinburgh friends. He
felt that he was regarded as an intruder, and was aware that

there was a school of thought which had difficulty in accepting that a poor man, without a degree and with supposed
deficiencies in respect of sensitivity and self-discipline, could be
a writer. They could also think, at times, as some others did,
that there were poor men who made especially good writers.
These poor men were inspired. Heaven helped them.

The novel's concern with likeness furnishes another way of
saying that it is by Hogg. Evidence of its being his includes the
presence in the novel of passages which correspond to material
in previous writings by him which have gone unchallenged as
to authorship, and its treatment of likeness is a case in point.
Robert follows his brother George about in the novel, and the
demon Gil-Martin, who has the knack of looking like whoever
he pleases, does the same for Robert. The real Hogg, a mimic,
like Walter Scott and other choice spirits of the time, may be
said to have possessed the knack too. In 1810, in the opening
number of his magazine, he spoke, in the character of the Spy,
of his 'abominable propensity' to look at other people and to
take them over, become them. Fourteen years on, whether or
not Hogg really regretted the propensity, which has the air of
a supernatural gift, Gil-Martin was awarded it in his novel,
where it frankly resembles the evil eye.

Looking ensures likeness, Gil-Martin explains, and, by
assuming someone's likeness, 'I attain to possession of his most
secret thoughts.' He does not have 'full control' over this propensity, but it enables him to control and invade others. Lockhart took part in the vigilance of his circle, his frightening eye
well known to his friends. So you could say that both he and
Hogg shared Gil-Martin's gift. This does not mean that Lockhart wrote the novel. And when Hogg began, as it were, to
write it, with the likeness passage in the *Spy*, it was seven years
before he and Lockhart first met.[8]

The editorial essays in the *Spy* borrow from other writers,
notably from Samuel Johnson. Could the likeness passage have
been derived from or instigated by some eighteenth-century
periodical essay, the work of some stroller in the city and
observer of its citizens? The ploys and preoccupations of Joseph
Addison's *Spectator* were responded to, played with, in the *Spy*,

and the *Spectator* had more eyes than Argus, who is himself present there. It has the notorious jealous eye; it has the eye that penetrates, to the soul, the eye of others. Unlike Addison's surrogate or persona, the Spectator, the Spy is not a club-man: the club came later, for Hogg, in *Blackwood's*, whose Ambrosians were no less affected than the editor of the *Spy* by the performance of Addison, Steele and their imaginaries. The material recycled by Hogg for his journal was not all of importance to his developing literary purposes. This can't be said, however, of the occasions when he recycled himself, as in the case of the likeness passage, taken for his novel from his own journalism, with or without some prompting from the journalism of an earlier time. Likeness, and imitation, continued to matter to him over the most productive years of his writing life, as did the uncertain self and the uncertain son.

His was an age of personality, of mimicry, and of physiognomy, with his own plaided person much spectated. Body and soul could each of them be invaded and hallucinated, mistaken, as Hogg's brother was mistaken for Hogg. Identities could be shared and confused. 'Like is an ill mark,' said the marvellous maid Bessy Gillies in Hogg's novel, meaning that it's an unreliable sign, or a bad sign – hers was a society in which the Devil left his mark on people. 'Like' is a major preoccupation of the novel, and a function of its duality. It takes two to produce a likeness.

Hogg's own doubleness includes the gaps between the subtlety and power of his best work and the more run-of-the-mill of his magazine pieces, his first-draft effusions, some of his tales of horror and of humour, his deplored lapses of taste and judgement. These disparities may be more marked than any that can be noticed in most writers of comparable worth, but they are scarcely an ill mark, and present no case for dispossessing him of his masterpiece.

A self-expressive, a personally revealing, an authorially revealing interest in the subject of duality is evident elsewhere in his work. His story 'John Gray o' Middleholm' was published in 1820, four years before the *Confessions*. It's a very funny fabliau, a folk tale which has in it the sophistication of Allemagne – the Germany of the Gothic imagination – and Edinburgh. Poor John is a hungry weaver who goes in search of treasure, who dreams of a cobbler no less zealous for treasure than himself, and who meets up with him in the town of Kelso. The two men conduct a dialogue of doubles on the uncertainties of personality and of what one person can know about another. 'This is *me*,' says the cobbler, 'as sure as that is *you*; but wha either you or me is, I fancy me or you disna very weel ken.'

There must be few more resolute expressions, or exhibitions, of human indeterminacy than the one in a ballad of his done in the antique style he adopted from time to time. The ballad is about Robin Reid, athlete and star, with more in him than meets the eye. In this respect, as in some others, a portrait of the artist is implied. Robin's father and mother are daft, and he's hardly right himself. But he will yield to none that breathes beneath the heaven.

> For I haif ane knolege at myne herte
> From quhare I cannot telle
> That I am double – I'm Rob Reidde
> And I'm besyde myselle.

A further involvement on Hogg's part in the drama of human indeterminacy has seen the light of publication in the last few months. 'Jock Armstrong'[9] is a study in likeness where a Scots-speaking Cumbrian family, the Wightmans, discovers that deer-stealing Jock has murdered his enemy half-brother, the nasty laird Fletcher, a Jacobite and a 'rascal' (for Walter Scott, Reform Whigs were 'rascals'). 'The squire it seems has lost his life and that by his own brother, his very image an' likeness, and but two years and twenty days older than himself.' Jock's mother had been a maid in Fletcher's house, and he himself had grown up, in other accommodation, as a wild devil. By now he is a Government man, a Whig poacher. What do the Wightmans then do but persuade Jock to go into the forest, change clothes with the corpse, and take over as the laird? Every man should live for his own benefit, thinks farmer Wightman – who may, the story sometimes seems to hint, be Jock's real father. The new laird carries off the masquerade and marries Miss Sarah Wightman – his Byronic sister, if you follow me, and if you take the hint – while reverting to his old self, one moonlight night, on a trip to the greenwood. Two lads, deer-stalkers themselves, spy him as he seems to 'eye a feeding deer', one of the new laird's own herd. A fine sentence states what happens next: 'The surprised poacher turned his pale face quietly round toward them and said in a calm voice that chilled their hearts, "Weel callants I suppose you think ye hae me safe at last."' The lads head off, mistaking him for a ghost.

The tale rustles like any greenwood with intimations of Hogg. It offers a union of opposites and a divided self, and an illegitimate child. Jock never learns that he is (or may be) a blood relation of the bad proprietor, while an interpreter might want to say that he *is* the proprietor, on the grounds that Hogg's equivocal rise in the world, and his suspension between Ettrick and Edinburgh, are pictured in the story. Jock is a James Hogg, that is to say, and the story also suggests that James Hogg is the author of the *Confessions*. John Wightman testifies before a judge that the dead body is very like the body of Jock Armstrong, 'but he would not swear to the identity' of the body and its belongings, *'for like was but an ill mark'*. Bessie Gillies of the *Confessions* said the same about her mistress's belongings. And Wightman's words may be felt to bear on the question of Jock's paternity.

It's hard to be quite right or quite sure about Hogg, and there are writings of his which seem intended to prevent this. He was a man who was interested in error and who made mistakes and who was the cause of mistakes in others. The *Confessions* is a devil of a book to write about. But it's not hard to be moved by it. It has the energy, pathos and delusion of the human struggle, and it makes a virtue of its lifelike uncertainty. It is a work expressive of the life of a man who has met his double in the pages of a magazine, and been attacked by those in whom he has confided, who has moved among the warring outlooks, the warring religions and philosophies, of his time, and who has moved from one environment to another, and back again.

It's hard to be quite right about what might seem obvious enough – this move from one corner of his society to another, a translation which contained reversions and a return, and was at no point a desertion. Like Jock Armstrong, he was held to be a poacher, towards the end of a life during which he became both a celebrity and an elder of the kirk. There is very much more to the Hogg enigma than the matter of his two environments, of the country boy, the child of nature, who fell among sophisticates. The Border lands of his lifetime were well stocked with men and women of talent, some of whom left their cottages in pursuit of their callings, just as the explorer Mungo Park left the region for the heart of darkness, for 'Africa sae dreary oh', as Hogg was to describe the continent. Moves, with their features of betrayal and hurt, their accidents of acquaintance, their strokes of luck and of the pen, their writing of books and sitting of exams, their seeking of asylum, are in most places ancient and frequent. Writers have been writers partly *because* they have moved off the hill and out of the country cottages to which there can now be a need for them to return. Nevertheless, there can be little doubt that Hogg's inhabiting of two worlds, at once a liberation for him and a trouble, played a part in creating what we may feel there is in him of the elusive, the mutable, the mutual and the multiple.

Nor should we make light of the human interest of his flourishing at an interface between the old rural order and a metropolitan world of the clever and the well-off and the ambitious, of 'factory publishing' and 'reviewer bitterness' – terms of the time – of the rise of the media star, of personality and of 'the personality', in something like the modern sense of these expressions. His early pastoral poems can sound the note of a beautiful and ideal Borders, and can appear to define themselves in contrast with a magnetic urban excitement, to which he was finally drawn in 1810. His persona 'Sandy' sounds the note in addressing one of his two native streams:[10]

> Flow, my Ettrick, it was thee
>   Into life wha first did drap me:
> Thee I've sung, an' when I dee
>   Thou wilt lend a sod to hap me.

And yet his early world remained with him, for all the excitement of Edinburgh – here once more is the syntax of duality, with its 'for alls' and its 'and yets'. He returned to Selkirkshire after his years away, and died there. The Ettrick lent its sod. His first friends, his thrilling landscapes, his songs and his fiddle, his fireside stories, his sports, never became a paradise lost. During his later years he sponsored the Border Games, his 'Scottish Olympics', as they were christened in the press.

The thought of those two worlds of his which were also one suggests the workings of what I've been talking of, and has been talked of since the nineteenth century, as duality, where one thing can be seen as two and two things can be seen as one – as in the case of the Hogg who must often have felt himself to be leading the one life, for all his Ettrick and Edinburgh, for all the rival attractions of his precipitous class-divided Scotland. Duality promotes treacherous, though also advantageous, attitudes of mind. Among the quicksands is a suspension or slippage between the literal and the figurative, the true and the false, earnest and fun. But it's an idea which has to be applied both to this novel and to the author of the novel, and which is brought to life in the novel. Hogg was supposed by some to be the simple soul who may or may not have written a deep book. But he was not that simple, to say the least. This was not the *sancta simplicitas*, the holy simplicity, of the religious past, an attribute which may nevertheless have contributed to the period understanding of who he was. His complex book was written by a complex man, who might remind you of a story about another Jock. Jock Gray was a member, as he felt, of a 'stiff-necked and rebellious' Border congregation, and he defied the minister whose pulpit he had invaded and who ordered him to come down. No, said Jock to the minister: 'Come ye up. It'll tak us baith.' Two Hoggs and more were needed for the

Confessions, which was written by just the one, an acute responder to the people and to the talent around him.

Duality and heredity, both of them prone to pairs and like-nesses, and to imitation, sometimes coincide in the literature of the double. One of the most compelling events in the chequered history of the reception of Hogg's writings in this country has been the news that the Canadian writer Alice Munro is a collateral descendant of his. She was born Alice Laidlaw and is of the blood of his grandfather Will o' Phaup, the last man in the region to converse with the fairies, and is also related to Hogg's antinomian cousin, who blamed him for writing fiction, blamed him, as his uncle did, for writing lies, and who blamed the Methodists of North America, where he moved, for showing an insufficient respect for the privileges of the elect. Munro's writing does not resemble Hogg's, but it refers to his concerns, to the embattled Early Modern Borders and to elective privilege, and she is 'proud' of the connection. The Victorian term 'heredi-tary genius' comes to mind. Alice Munro is arguably what Hogg is – one of Scotland's greatest writers.

It took a century or more for Hogg's stature to sink in, despite the prominence he enjoyed in mid-life. Over the last few decades, as the Ambrosians foretold, he has been dug up, like his sinner, and the editors of his *Collected Works* have now been seeing to it that these works will be accessible to the reader as they have never been before. This is a great deed, which will inspire a wide variety of thoughts about Hogg. One of mine is that his writings should continue to be assessed in terms of an appropriate literary criticism: assigning his principal book to a ghost writer was a threat to Hogg, and there would be another threat if he were to be canonized, with each of his things seen to be as good as the other, each exalted by an equal ingenuity on the part of commentators. He should be known both for all he did and for what he did best. But it's also true that there are things of his which were to remain in the dark after the rise to fame of the *Confessions* in the 1940s, and which deserve to be known. His two hunger tales, 'John Gray o' Middleholm' and 'Marion's Jock', are examples: the first a dualistic comedy of starvation, the second a dynamic escape from the hill.

Alice Munro will in future seldom be treated as a housewife from darkest Ontario who wrote books. But it happened to her in Canada when she was young, and in this country there's an urban bias which has also been capable of such estimates. They may help to explain why a neglect of Hogg can sometimes seem to have survived his rediscovery, and his re-invention as a modern writer. There's a British ignorance for which Scott, Burns and Stevenson are the only Scottish writers, for which there is no Hogg, no Galt. The English theatre director Richard Eyre raised this question the other day, in speaking up for Hogg. The other day too, however, one of Scotland's finest writers, Hogg's contemporary Henry Cockburn, a denouncer of the hanging judge Lord Braxfield, was described in the *Guardian* as the 'famous hanging judge'.

On 13 September 1814 Hogg wrote to Byron, from John Wilson's house in the Lake District, to say that he and his host had been engaged in 'a serious perusal of *Wordsworth's Excursion* together and no little laughter and some parodying'. Like the *Confessions*, the parodies of Wordsworth attributed to Hogg have been denied to him on occasion, and the letter to Byron might suggest that collaboration occurred here. There is no comparable reason to doubt that Hogg's novel, like his sinner's testament, was 'written by himself'.

He would say that he couldn't help certain things. He would say that he was like a meteor: a meteor is 'nature's error', and 'so am I.'[11] And the man who sometimes spoke in this way can be heard in the polyphony of the *Confessions*, which found a voice for human error, and for the duality of man. Among the ironies that lay in store for the novel are the suggestions of those who have doubted whether – in this way, or others, or in any way – Hogg is present there. Here is a great work of history, mystery and imagination which feels for delusion and compulsion, which brings together the two halves of a human life, and of a civilization – comprised of Scotland's Romantic Enlightenment and religious quarrel – and which can be read in the light of the efforts made to evacuate it of the James Hogg we take to be its author.

NOTES

1. Except where other sources are provided, quotations from writings by Hogg, and about him, come from the *Collected Works* edition now in progress (*CW*, in abbreviation), and from the biography of Hogg, *Electric Shepherd*, by the present writer.

2. *Letters and Recollections of Sir Walter Scott*, 1904, Mrs Hughes of Uffington (ed. Horace Hutchinson), pp. 152, 289–92.

3. See *Electric Shepherd*, pp. 138, 171, 271.

4. Ibid., pp. 203, 175.

5. *In Defence of Reason*, 1960, p. 158.

6. *Some Hope*, 1994, p. 70.

7. For Carlyle's opinion of Hogg's morality, see *Anecdotes of Scott*, *CW*, p. xiii. For Lockhart's various words, see *Electric Shepherd*, p. 235. For 'the religion of the heart', see Hogg's novel, *CW*, p. 174.

8. *Electric Shepherd*, pp. 226–7.

9. *Studies in Hogg and His World*, 14:2003. Douglas Mack and Gillian Hughes are responsible for its discovery. The story dates from after 1827.

10. The poem in question, 'By a Bush', written in 1802, appears in the second volume of Thomas Thomson's edition of Hogg's works, 1865.

11. See Hogg's long poem, *Queen Hynde*, *CW*, p. 31.

Further Reading

HOGG'S WRITINGS

The Collected Works of James Hogg (general editors Gillian Hughes and Douglas Mack) consist, to date, of *The Shepherd's Calendar* (1995), *The Three Perils of Woman* (1995), *A Queer Book* (1995), *Tales of the Wars of Montrose* (1996), *Lay Sermons* (1997), *Queen Hynde* (1998), *Anecdotes of Scott* (1999), *The Spy* (2000), *Confessions of a Justified Sinner* (2001), *The Jacobite Relics of Scotland*, First Series (2002), *Winter Evening Tales* (2002), *Altrive Tales* (2003), *The Queen's Wake* (2004), and *The Letters of James Hogg*, Vol. I, 1800 to 1819 (2004).

Scottish Pastorals, 1801, 1988 (ed. Elaine Petrie)
The Mountain Bard, 1807
The Shepherd's Guide, 1807
The Forest Minstrel, 1810
The Poetic Mirror, 1816
Dramatic Tales, 2 vols, 1817
The Brownie of Bodsbeck, 1818, 1976 (ed. Douglas Mack)
The Poetical Works of James Hogg, 4 vols, 1822
The Three Perils of Man, 1822, 1972 (ed. Douglas Gifford)
Songs, 1831
Altrive Tales, 1832
The Works of the Ettrick Shepherd, 2 vols, 1865 (ed. Thomas Thomson)
James Hogg: Selected Poems, 1970 (ed. Douglas Mack)
Memoir of the Author's Life and *Familiar Anecdotes of Sir Walter Scott*, 1972 (ed. Douglas Mack)

James Hogg: Selected Poems and Sketches, 1982 (ed. Douglas Mack)
Tales of Love and Mystery, 1985 (ed. David Groves)
A Shepherd's Delight, 1985 (ed. Judy Steel)
James Hogg: Selected Poems and Songs, 1986 (ed. David Groves)

BOOKS ON HOGG

Memorials of James Hogg the Ettrick Shepherd, Mary Garden, 1885
James Hogg, Sir George Douglas, 1899
The Ettrick Shepherd, Edith Batho, 1927
The Life and Letters of James Hogg, Vol. I, 1770–1825, Alan Strout, 1946
James Hogg, Douglas Gifford, 1976
James Hogg at Home, Norah Parr, 1980
Doubles, Karl Miller, 1985
James Hogg: The Growth of a Writer, David Groves, 1988
The Tavern Sages, a selection from the 'Noctes Ambrosianae', 1992 (ed. J. H. Alexander)
Electric Shepherd, Karl Miller, 2003
Studies in Hogg and his World, published annually (ed. Gillian Hughes)

Textual Note

James Hogg's justified sinner places a curse on anyone who might try to 'alter or amend' his testament. The *Confessions of a Justified Sinner*, which incorporates that testament, has not been spared the interference of editors. But it entered the world in excellent condition. Published by Longman in London and printed in Edinburgh by James Clarke, the first edition of 1824 is a beautiful and careful book – textually, it would appear, in close accord with the writer's wishes. The present edition is based on the first; a few printing errors were corrected in the bowdlerized version of 1837, and these corrections have been adopted. Recent editions, also based on the first, have been consulted: the Cresset Library edition of 1947, with a preface by André Gide, which helped at long last to make the novel widely known, John Carey's edition of 1969, John Wain's Penguin Classic of 1983, and the *Collected Works* edition of 2001 (hardback), and 2002 (paperback), edited by P. D. Garside.

The 'facsimile' on p. xxxiv forms the frontispiece of the first edition: see pp. 197 and 209 of the present edition.

In the case of all three of the texts carried in this book, the first-publication spellings and punctuation have been retained, save for a few small adjustments and some easing of the over-punctuation of the period, with regard to dashes and to the system for parenthesis. Points of difficulty are registered in the notes.

'Marion's Jock' figured as the Laird of Peatstacknowe's tale in Hogg's novel of 1822, *The Three Perils of Man*, and was reissued, more or less intact, as one of the *Altrive Tales* of 1832.

The present text follows that of Gillian Hughes's *Collected Works* edition of the stories, which is based on that of the first edition of *Altrive Tales*.

'John Gray o' Middleholm' first appeared in Hogg's collection of 1820, *Winter Evening Tales*. The present text follows that of Ian Duncan's *Collection Works* edition of 2002, which is derived from the first edition, as 'conservatively' corrected with reference to changes introduced in the second edition of 1821.

September 8. — My first night of trial in this place is overpast! Would that it were the last that I should ever see in this detested world! If the horrors of hell are equal to those I have suffered, eternity will be of short duration there, for no creative energy can support them for one single month, or week. I have been buffeted as never living creature was. My vitals have all been torn and every faculty and feeling of my soul racked, and tormented into callous insensibility. I was even hung by the locks over a yawning chasm to which I could perceive no bottom, and then — not till then, did I repeat the tremendous prayer! — I was instantly at liberty; and what I now am, the Almighty knows! Amen.

THE PRIVATE MEMOIRS
AND CONFESSIONS
OF A JUSTIFIED SINNER:

WRITTEN BY HIMSELF:

WITH A DETAIL OF CURIOUS
TRADITIONARY FACTS, AND
OTHER EVIDENCE, BY THE EDITOR

THE EDITOR'S NARRATIVE

It appears from tradition, as well as some parish registers still extant, that the lands of Dalcastle[1] (or Dalchastel, as it is often spelled) were possessed by a family of the name of Colwan, about one hundred and fifty years ago, and for at least a century previous to that period. That family was supposed to have been a branch of the ancient family of Colquhoun, and it is certain that from it spring the Cowans that spread towards the Border. I find, that in the year 1687, George Colwan succeeded his uncle of the same name, in the lands of Dalchastel and Balgrennan; and this being all I can gather of the family from history, to tradition I must appeal for the remainder of the motley adventures of that house. But of the matter furnished by the latter of these powerful monitors,[2] I have no reason to complain: It has been handed down to the world in unlimited abundance; and I am certain, that in recording the hideous events which follow, I am only relating to the greater part of the inhabitants of at least four counties of Scotland, matters of which they were before perfectly well informed.

This George was a rich man, or supposed to be so, and was married, when considerably advanced in life, to the sole heiress and reputed daughter of a Baillie Orde, of Glasgow. This proved a conjunction any thing but agreeable to the parties contracting. It is well known, that the Reformation principles[3] had long before that time taken a powerful hold of the hearts and affections of the people of Scotland, although the feeling was by no means general, or in equal degrees; and it so happened that this married couple felt completely at variance on the subject. Granting it to have been so, one would have thought that the

laird, owing to his retired situation, would have been the one
that inclined to the stern doctrines of the reformers; and that
the young and gay dame from the city would have adhered to
the free principles cherished by the court party, and indulged
in rather to extremity, in opposition to their severe and carping
contemporaries.

The contrary, however, happened to be the case. The laird
was what his country neighbours called 'a droll, careless chap',
with a very limited proportion of the fear of God in his heart,
and very nearly as little of the fear of man. The laird had not
intentionally wronged or offended either of the parties, and
perceived not the necessity of deprecating their vengeance. He
had hitherto believed that he was living in most cordial terms
with the greater part of the inhabitants of the earth, and with
the powers above in particular: but woe be unto him if he was
not soon convinced of the fallacy of such damning security! for
his lady was the most severe and gloomy of all bigots to the
principles of the Reformation. Hers were not the tenets of the
great reformers, but theirs mightily overstrained and deformed.
Theirs was an unguent hard to be swallowed; but hers was
that unguent embittered and overheated until nature could not
longer bear it. She had imbibed her ideas from the doctrines of
one flaming predestinarian divine alone; and these were so rigid,
that they became a stumbling-block to many of his brethren,
and a mighty handle for the enemies of his party to turn the
machine of the state against them.

The wedding festivities at Dalcastle partook of all the gaiety,
not of that stern age, but of one previous to it. There was
feasting, dancing, piping, and singing: the liquors were handed
around in great fulness, the ale in large wooden bickers, and
the brandy in capacious horns of oxen. The laird gave full scope
to his homely glee. He danced, he snapped his fingers to the
music, clapped his hands and shouted at the turn of the tune.
He saluted every girl in the hall whose appearance was any
thing tolerable, and requested of their sweethearts to take the
same freedom with his bride, by way of retaliation. But there
she sat at the head of the hall in still and blooming beauty,
absolutely refusing to tread a single measure with any gentle-

man there. The only enjoyment in which she appeared to partake, was in now and then stealing a word of sweet conversation
with her favourite pastor about divine things; for he had accompanied her home after marrying her to her husband, to see her
fairly settled in her new dwelling. He addressed her several
times by her new name, Mrs Colwan; but she turned away her
head disgusted, and looked with pity and contempt towards
the old inadvertent sinner, capering away in the height of his
unregenerated mirth. The minister perceived the workings of
her pious mind, and thenceforward addressed her by the courteous title of Lady Dalcastle, which sounded somewhat better,
as not coupling her name with one of the wicked: and there is
too great reason to believe, that for all the solemn vows she
had come under, and these were of no ordinary binding,
particularly on the laird's part, she at that time depised, if not
abhorred him, in her heart.

The good parson again blessed her, and went away. She took
leave of him with tears in her eyes, entreating him often to visit
her in that heathen land of the Amorite, the Hittite, and the
Girgashite[4]: to which he assented, on many solemn and qualify-
ing conditions – and then the comely bride retired to her
chamber to pray.

It was customary, in those days, for the bride's-man and
maiden, and a few select friends, to visit the new married couple
after they had retired to rest, and drink a cup to their healths,
their happiness, and a numerous posterity. But the laird delighted not in this: he wished to have his jewel to himself; and,
slipping away quietly from his jovial party, he retired to his
chamber to his beloved, and bolted the door. He found her
engaged with the writings of the Evangelists, and terribly
demure. The laird went up to caress her; but she turned away
her head, and spoke of the follies of aged men, and something
of the broad way that leadeth to destruction. The laird did not
thoroughly comprehend this allusion; but being considerably
flustered by drinking, and disposed to take all in good part, he
only remarked, as he took off his shoes and stockings, 'that
whether the way was broad or narrow, it was time that they
were in their bed'.

'Sure, Mr Colwan, you won't go to bed to-night, at such an important period of your life, without first saying prayers for yourself and me.'

When she said this, the laird had his head down almost to the ground, loosing his shoe-buckle; but when he heard of *prayers*, on such a night, he raised his face suddenly up, which was all over as flushed and red as a rose, and answered –

'Prayers, Mistress! Lord help your crazed head, is this a night for prayers?'

He had better have held his peace. There was such a torrent of profound divinity poured out upon him, that the laird became ashamed, both of himself and his new-made spouse, and wist not what to say: but the brandy helped him out.

'It strikes me, my dear, that religious devotion would be somewhat out of place to-night,' said he. 'Allowing that it is ever so beautiful, and ever so beneficial, were we to ride on the rigging of it at all times, would we not be constantly making a farce of it: It would be like reading the Bible and the jest-book, verse about, and would render the life of man a medley of absurdity and confusion.'

But against the cant of the bigot or the hypocrite, no reasoning can aught avail. If you would argue until the end of life, the infallible creature must alone be right. So it proved with the laird. One Scripture text followed another, not in the least connected, and one sentence of the profound Mr Wringhim's sermons after another, proving the duty of family worship, till the laird lost patience, and, tossing himself into bed, said, carelessly, that he would leave that duty upon her shoulders for one night.

The meek mind of Lady Dalcastle was somewhat disarranged by this sudden evolution. She felt that she was left rather in an awkward situation. However, to show her unconscionable spouse that she was resolved to hold fast her integrity, she kneeled down and prayed in terms so potent, that she deemed she was sure of making an impression on him. She did so; for in a short time the laird began to utter a response so fervent, that she was utterly astounded, and fairly driven from the chain of her orisons. He began, in truth, to sound a nasal bugle of no

ordinary calibre, the notes being little inferior to those of a
military trumpet. The lady tried to proceed, but every returning
note from the bed burst on her ear with a louder twang, and a
longer peal, till the concord of sweet sounds became so truly
pathetic, that the meek spirit of the dame was quite overcome;
and after shedding a flood of tears, she arose from her knees,
and retired to the chimney-corner with her Bible in her lap,
there to spend the hours in holy meditation till such time as the
inebriated trumpeter should awaken to a sense of propriety.

The laird did not awake in any reasonable time; for, he being
overcome with fatigue and wassail, his sleep became sounder,
and his Morphean measures more intense. These varied a little
in their structure; but the general run of the bars sounded
something in this way – 'Hic-hoc-wheew!' It was most pro-
foundly ludicrous; and could not have missed exciting risibility
in any one, save a pious, a disappointed, and humbled bride.

The good dame wept bitterly. She could not for her life go
and awaken the monster, and request him to make room for
her: but she retired somewhere; for the laird, on awaking next
morning, found that he was still lying alone. His sleep had been
of the deepest and most genuine sort; and all the time that it
lasted, he had never once thought of either wives, children, or
sweethearts, save in the way of dreaming about them; but as
his spirit began again by slow degrees to verge towards the
boundaries of reason, it became lighter and more buoyant from
the effects of deep repose, and his dreams partook of that
buoyancy, yea, to a degree hardly expressible. He dreamed of
the reel, the jig, the strathspey, and the corant; and the elasticity
of his frame was such, that he was bounding over the heads of
the maidens, and making his feet skimmer against the ceiling,
enjoying, the while, the most extatic emotions. These grew too
fervent for the shackles of the drowsy god to restrain. The nasal
bugle ceased its prolonged sounds in one moment, and a sort
of hectic laugh took its place. 'Keep it going – play up, you
devils!' cried the laird, without changing his position on the
pillow. But this exertion to hold the fiddlers at their work, fairly
awakened the delighted dreamer; and though he could not
refrain from continuing his laugh, he at length, by tracing out

a regular chain of facts, came to be sensible of his real situation. 'Rabina, where are you? What's become of you, my dear?' cried the laird. But there was no voice, nor any one that answered or regarded. He flung open the curtains, thinking to find her still on her knees, as he had seen her; but she was not there, either sleeping or waking. 'Rabina! Mrs Colwan!' shouted he, as loud as he could call, and then added, in the same breath, 'God save the king – I have lost my wife!'

He sprung up and opened the casement: the day-light was beginning to streak the east, for it was spring, and the nights were short, and the mornings very long. The laird half dressed himself in an instant, and strode through every room in the house, opening the windows as he went, and scrutinizing every bed and every corner. He came into the hall where the wedding festival had held[5]; and, as he opened the various window-boards, loving couples flew off like hares surprised too late in the morning among the early braird. 'Hoo-boo! Fie, be frightened!' cried the laird. 'Fie, rin like fools, as if ye were caught in an ill turn!' His bride was not among them: so he was obliged to betake himself to farther search. 'She will be praying in some corner, poor woman,' said he to himself. 'It is an unlucky thing this praying. But, for my part, I fear I have behaved very ill; and I must endeavour to make amends.'

The laird continued his search, and at length found his beloved in the same bed with her Glasgow cousin, who had acted as bride's maid. 'You sly and malevolent imp,' said the laird; 'you have played me such a trick when I was fast asleep! I have not known a frolic so clever, and, at the same time, so severe. Come along, you baggage you!'

'Sir, I will let you know, that I detest your principles and your person alike,' said she. 'It shall never be said, Sir, that my person was at the controul of a heathenish man of Belial, a dangler among the daughters of women, a promiscuous dancer, and a player at unlawful games. Forego your rudeness, Sir, I say, and depart away from my presence and that of my kinswoman.'

'Come along, I say, my charming Rab. If you were the pink of all puritans, and the saint of all saints, you are my wife, and must do as I command you.'

'Sir, I will sooner lay down my life than be subjected to your godless will; therefore, I say, desist, and begone with you.'

But the laird regarded none of these testy sayings: he rolled her in a blanket, and bore her triumphantly away to his chamber, taking care to keep a fold or two of the blanket always rather near to her mouth, in case of any outrageous forthcoming of noise.

The next day at breakfast the bride was long in making her appearance. Her maid asked to see her; but George did not choose that any body should see her but himself: he paid her several visits, and always turned the key as he came out. At length breakfast was served; and during the time of refreshment the laird tried to break several jokes; but it was remarked, that they wanted their accustomed brilliancy, and that his nose was particularly red at the top.

Matters, without all doubt, had been very bad between the new-married couple; for in the course of the day the lady deserted her quarters, and returned to her father's house in Glasgow, after having been a night on the road; stage-coaches and steam-boats having then no existence in that quarter. Though Baillie Orde had acquiesced in his wife's asseveration regarding the likeness of their only daughter to her father, he never loved or admired her greatly; therefore this behaviour nothing astounded him. He questioned her strictly as to the grievous offence committed against her; and could discover nothing that warranted a procedure so fraught with disagreeable consequences. So, after mature deliberation, the baillie addressed her as follows:

'Ay, ay, Raby! An' sae I find that Dalcastle has actually refused to say prayers with you when you ordered him; an' has guidit you in a rude indelicate manner, outstepping the respect due to my daughter – as my daughter. But wi' regard to what is due to his own wife, of that he's a better judge nor me. However, since he has behaved in that manner to *my daughter*, I shall be revenged on him for aince; for I shall return the obligation to ane nearer to him: that is, I shall take pennyworths of his wife, an' let him lick at that.'

'What do you mean, Sir?' said the astonished damsel.

'I mean to be revenged on that villain Dalcastle,' said he, 'for what he has done to my daughter. Come hither, Mrs Colwan, you shall pay for this.'

So saying, the baillie began to inflict corporal punishment on the runaway wife. His strokes were not indeed very deadly, but he made a mighty flourish in the infliction, pretending to be in a great rage only at the Laird of Dalcastle. 'Villain that he is!' exclaimed he, 'I shall teach him to behave in such a manner to a child of mine, be she as she may; since I cannot get at himself, I shall lounder her that is nearest to him in life. Take you that, and that, Mrs Colwan, for your husband's impertinence!'

The poor afflicted woman wept and prayed, but the baillie would not abate aught of his severity. After fuming, and beating her with many stripes, far drawn, and lightly laid down, he took her up to her chamber, five stories high, locked her in, and there he fed her on bread and water, all to be revenged on the presumptuous Laird of Dalcastle; but ever and anon, as the baillie came down the stair from carrying his daughter's meal, he said to himself, 'I shall make the sight of the laird the blithest she ever saw in her life.'

Lady Dalcastle got plenty of time to read, and pray, and meditate; but she was at a great loss for one to dispute with about religious tenets; for she found, that without this advantage, about which there was a perfect rage at that time, her reading, and learning of Scripture texts, and sentences of intricate doctrine, availed her nought; so she was often driven to sit at her casement and look out for the approach of the heathenish Laird of Dalcastle.

That hero, after a considerable lapse of time, at length made his appearance. Matters were not hard to adjust; for his lady found that there was no refuge for her in her father's house; and so, after some sighs and tears, she accompanied her husband home. For all that had passed, things went on no better. She *would* convert the laird in spite of his teeth: The laird would not be converted. She *would* have the laird to say family prayers, both morning and evening: The laird would neither pray morning nor evening. He would not even sing psalms, and kneel beside her, while she performed the exercise; neither would he converse at all times, and in all places, about the sacred mysteries of religion, although his lady took occasion to contradict flatly every assertion that he made, in order that she might spiritualize him by drawing him into argument.

The laird kept his temper a long while, but at length his patience wore out; he cut her short in all her futile attempts at spiritualization, and mocked at her wire-drawn degrees of faith, hope, and repentance. He also dared to doubt of the great standard doctrine of absolute predestination, which put the crown on the lady's christian resentment. She declared her helpmate to be a limb of Antichrist, and one with whom no regenerated person[6] could associate. She therefore bespoke a separate establishment, and before the expiry of the first six months, the arrangements of the separation were amicably adjusted. The upper, or third story of the old mansion-house, was awarded to the lady for her residence. She had a separate door, a separate stair, a separate garden, and walks that in no instance intersected the laird's; so that one would have thought the separation complete.[7] They had each their own parties, selected from their own sort of people; and though the laird never once chafed himself about the lady's companies, it was not long before she began to intermeddle about some of his.

'Who is that fat bouncing dame that visits the laird so often, and always by herself?' said she to her maid Martha one day.

'O dear, mem, how can I ken? We're banished frae our acquaintances here, as weel as frae the sweet gospel ordinances.'

'Find me out who that jolly dame is, Martha. You, who hold communion with the household of this ungodly man, can be at no loss to attain this information. I observe that she always casts her eye up toward our windows, both in coming and going; and I suspect that she seldom departs from the house empty-handed.'

That same evening Martha came with the information, that this august visitor was a Miss Logan, an old and intimate acquaintance of the laird's, and a very worthy respectable lady, of good connections, whose parents had lost their patrimony in the civil wars.[8]

'Ha! very well!' said the lady; 'very well, Martha! But, never-theless, go thou and watch this respectable lady's motions and behaviour the next time she comes to visit the laird, and the next after that. You will not, I see, lack opportunities.'

Martha's information turned out of that nature, that prayers were said in the uppermost story of Dalcastle-house against the Canaanitish woman, every night and every morning; and great discontent prevailed there, even to anathemas and tears. Letter after letter was dispatched to Glasgow; and at length, to the lady's great consolation, the Rev. Mr Wringhim arrived safely and devoutly in her elevated sanctuary. Marvellous was the conversation between these gifted people. Wringhim had held in his doctrines that there were eight different kinds of FAITH, all perfectly distinct in their operations and effects. But the lady, in her secluded state, had discovered other five, making twelve[9] in all: the adjusting of the existence or fallacy of these five faiths served for a most enlightened discussion of nearly seventeen hours; in the course of which the two got warm in their argu-ments, always in proportion as they receded from nature, utility, and common sense. Wringhim at length got into unwonted fervour about some disputed point between one of these faiths and TRUST; when the lady, fearing that zeal was getting beyond its wonted barrier, broke in on his vehement asseverations with the following abrupt discomfiture: 'But, Sir, as long as I remember, what is to be done with this case of open and avowed iniquity?'

The minister was struck dumb. He leaned him back on his chair, stroked his beard, hemmed – considered, and hemmed again; and then said, in an altered and softened tone, 'Why, that is a secondary consideration; you mean the case between your husband and Miss Logan?'

'The same, Sir. I am scandalized at such intimacies going on under my nose. The sufferance of it is a great and crying evil.'

'Evil, madam, may be either operative, or passive. To them it is an evil, but to us none. We have no more to do with the sins of the wicked and unconverted here, than with those of an infidel Turk; for all earthly bonds and fellowships are absorbed and swallowed up in the holy community of the Reformed

Church. However, if it is your wish, I shall take him to task, and reprimand and humble him in such a manner, that *he* shall be ashamed of his doings, and renounce such deeds for ever, out of mere self-respect, though all unsanctified the heart, as well as the deed, may be. To the wicked, all things are wicked; but to the just, all things are just and right.'

'Ah, that is a sweet and comfortable saying, Mr Wringhim! How delightful to think that a justified person can do no wrong! Who would not envy the liberty wherewith we are made free? Go to my husband, that poor unfortunate, blindfolded person, and open his eyes to his degenerate and sinful state; for well are you fitted to the task.'

'Yea, I will go in unto him, and confound him. I will lay the strong holds of sin and Satan as flat before my face, as the dung that is spread out to fatten the land.'

'Master, there's a gentleman at the fore-door wants a private word o' ye.'

'Tell him I'm engaged: I can't see any gentleman to-night. But I shall attend on him to-morrow as soon as he pleases.'

'He's coming straight in, Sir. – Stop a wee bit, Sir, my master is engaged. He cannot see you at present, Sir.'

'Stand aside, thou Moabite!¹⁰ my mission admits of no delay. I come to save him from the jaws of destruction!'

'An that be the case, Sir, it maks a wide difference; an', as the danger may threaten us a', I fancy I may as weel let ye gang by as fight wi' ye, sin' ye seem sae intent on't. – The man says he's comin' to save ye, an' canna stop, Sir. Here he is.'

The laird was going to break out into a volley of wrath against Waters, his servant; but before he got a word pronounced, the Rev. Mr Wringhim had stepped inside the room, and Waters had retired, shutting the door behind him.

No introduction could be more *mal-a-propos*: it is impossible; for at that very moment the laird and Arabella Logan were both sitting on one seat, and both looking on one book, when the door opened. 'What is it, Sir?' said the laird fiercely.

'A message of the greatest importance, Sir,' said the divine, striding unceremoniously up to the chimney, turning his back to the fire, and his face to the culprits. 'I think you should know

me, Sir?' continued he, looking displeasedly at the laird, with
his face half turned round.

'I think I should,' returned the laird. 'You are a Mr
How's-tey-ca'-him, of Glasgow, who did me the worst turn
ever I got done to me in my life. You gentry are always ready
to do a man such a turn. Pray, Sir, did you ever do a good job
for any one to counterbalance that? for, if you have not, you
ought to be –'

'Hold, Sir, I say! None of your profanity before me. If I do
evil to any one on such occasions, it is because he will have it
so; therefore, the evil is not of my doing. I ask you, Sir – before
God and this witness, I ask you, have you kept solemnly and
inviolate the vows which I laid upon you that day? Answer
me?'

'Has the partner whom you bound me to, kept hers inviolate?
Answer me that, Sir? None can better do so than you, Mr
How's-tey-ca'-you.'

'So, then, you confess your backslidings, and avow the
profligacy of your life. And this person here, is, I suppose, the
partner of your iniquity, she whose beauty hath caused you to
err! Stand up, both of you, till I rebuke you, and show you
what you are in the eyes of God and man.'

'In the first place, stand you still there, till I tell you what *you*
are in the eyes of God and man: You are, Sir, a presumptuous,
self-conceited pedagogue, a stirrer up of strife and commotion
in church, in state, in families, and communities. You are one,
Sir, whose righteousness consists in splitting the doctrines of
Calvin into thousands of undistinguishable films, and in setting
up a system of justifying-grace against all breaches of all laws,
moral or divine. In short, Sir, you are a mildew, a canker-worm
in the bosom of the Reformed Church, generating a disease of
which she will never be purged, but by the shedding of blood.
Go thou in peace, and do these abominations no more; but
humble thyself, lest a worse reproof come upon thee.'

Wringhim heard all this without flinching. He now and then
twisted his mouth in disdain, treasuring up, mean time, his
vengeance against the two aggressors; for he felt that he had
them on the hip, and resolved to pour out his vengeance and

indignation upon them. Sorry am I, that the shackles of modern decorum restrain me from penning that famous rebuke; fragments of which have been attributed to every divine of old notoriety throughout Scotland. But I have it by heart; and a glorious morsel it is to put into the hands of certain incendiaries. The metaphors were so strong, and so appalling, that Miss Logan could only stand them a very short time: she was obliged to withdraw in confusion. The laird stood his ground with much ado, though his face was often crimsoned over with the hues of shame and anger. Several times he was on the point of turning the officious sycophant to the door; but good manners, and an inherent respect that he entertained for the clergy, as the immediate servants of the Supreme Being, restrained him.

Wringhim, perceiving these symptoms of resentment, took them for marks of shame and contrition, and pushed his reproaches farther than ever divine ventured to do in a similar case. When he had finished, to prevent further discussion, he walked slowly and majestically out of the apartment, making his robes to swing behind him in a most magisterial manner; he being, without doubt, elated with his high conquest. He went to the upper story, and related to his metaphysical associate his wonderful success; how he had driven the dame from the house in tears and deep confusion, and left the backsliding laird in such a quandary of shame and repentance, that he could neither articulate a word, nor lift up his countenance. The dame thanked him most cordially, lauding his friendly zeal and powerful eloquence; and then the two again set keenly to the splitting of hairs, and making distinctions in religion where none existed.

They being both children of adoption, and secured from falling into snares, or any way under the power of the wicked one, it was their custom, on each visit, to sit up a night in the same apartment, for the sake of sweet spiritual converse; but that time, in the course of the night, they differed so materially on a small point, somewhere between justification and final election, that the minister, in the heat of his zeal, sprung from his seat, paced the floor, and maintained his point with such ardour, that Martha was alarmed, and, thinking they were going to fight, and that the minister would be a hard match for her mistress, she put on some clothes, and twice left her bed and stood listening at the back of the door, ready to burst in should need require it. Should any one think this picture over-strained, I can assure him that it is taken from nature and from truth; but I will not likewise aver, that the theologist was neither crazed nor inebriated. If the listener's words were to be relied on, there was no love, no accommodating principle manifested between the two, but a fiery burning zeal, relating to points of such minor importance, that a true Christian would blush to hear them mentioned, and the infidel and profane make a handle of them to turn our religion to scorn.

Great was the dame's exultation at the triumph of her beloved pastor over her sinful neighbours in the lower parts of the house; and she boasted of it to Martha in high-sounding terms. But it was of short duration; for, in five weeks after that, Arabella Logan came to reside with the laird as his house-keeper, sitting at his table, and carrying the keys as mistress-substitute of the mansion. The lady's grief and indignation were now raised to a higher pitch than ever; and she set every agent to work, with whom she had any power, to effect a separation between these two suspected ones. Remonstrance was of no avail: George laughed at them who tried such a course, and retained his house-keeper, while the lady gave herself up to utter despair; for though she would not consort with her hus-band herself, she could not endure that any other should do so.

But, to countervail this grievous offence, our saintly and afflicted dame, in due time, was safely delivered of a fine boy, whom the laird acknowledged as his son and heir, and had him christened by his own name, and nursed in his own premises. He gave the nurse permission to take the boy to his mother's presence if ever she should desire to see him; but, strange as it may appear, she never once desired to see him from the day that he was born. The boy grew up, and was a healthful and happy child; and, in the course of another year, the lady pre-sented him with a brother. A brother he certainly was, in the eye of the law, and it is more than probable that he was his brother in reality. But the laird thought otherwise; and, though he knew and acknowledged that he was obliged to support and provide for him, he refused to acknowledge him in other respects. He neither would countenance the banquet, nor take the baptismal vows on him in the child's name; of course, the poor boy had to live and remain an alien from the visible church for a year and a day; at which time, Mr Wringhim, out of pity and kindness, took the lady herself as sponsor for the boy, and baptized him by the name of Robert Wringhim, that being the noted divine's own name.

George was brought up with his father, and educated partly at the parish-school, and partly at home, by a tutor hired for the purpose. He was a generous and kind-hearted youth; always ready to oblige, and hardly ever dissatisfied with any body. Robert was brought up with Mr Wringhim, the laird paying a certain allowance for him yearly; and there the boy was early inured to all the sternness and severity of his pastor's arbitrary and unyielding creed. He was taught to pray twice every day, and seven times on Sabbath days; but he was only to pray for the elect, and, like David of old, doom all that were aliens from God to destruction. He had never, in that family into which he had been as it were adopted, heard ought but evil spoken of his reputed father and brother; consequently he held them in utter abhorrence, and prayed against them every day, often 'that the old hoary sinner might be cut off in the full flush of his iniquity, and be carried quick into hell; and that the young stem of the corrupt trunk might also be taken from a world that he disgraced, but that his sins might be pardoned, because he knew no better'.

Such were the tenets in which it would appear young Robert was bred. He was an acute boy, an excellent learner, had ardent and ungovernable passions, and withal, a sternness of demeanour from which other boys shrunk. He was the best grammarian, the best reader, writer, and accountant in the various classes that he attended, and was fond of writing essays on controverted points of theology, for which he got prizes, and great praise from his guardian and mother. George was much behind him in scholastic acquirements, but greatly his superior in personal prowess, form, feature, and all that constitutes gentility in deportment and appearance. The laird had often manifested to Miss Logan an earnest wish that the two young men should never meet, or at all events that they should be as little conversant as possible; and Miss Logan, who was as much attached to George as if he had been her own son, took every precaution, while he was a boy, that he should never meet with his brother; but as they advanced towards manhood, this became impracticable. The lady was removed from her apartments in her husband's house to Glasgow, to her great content; and all to prevent the young laird being tainted with the company of her and her second son; for the laird had felt the effects of the principles they professed, and dreaded them more than persecution, fire, and sword. During all the dreadful times that had overpast, though the laird had been a moderate man, he had still leaned to the side of the kingly prerogative, and had escaped confiscation and fines, without ever taking any active hand in suppressing the Covenanters. But after experiencing a specimen of their tenets and manner in his wife, from a secret favourer of them and their doctrines, he grew alarmed at the prevalence of such stern and factious principles, now that there was no check nor restraint upon them; and from that time he began to set himself against them, joining with the cavalier party of that day in all their proceedings.

It so happened, that, under the influence of the Earls of Seafield and Tullibardine, he was returned for a Member of Parliament in the famous session that sat at Edinburgh, when the Duke of Queensberry was commissioner, and in which party spirit ran to such an extremity.[11] The young laird went with his father to the court, and remained in town all the time that the session lasted; and as all interested people of both factions flocked to the town at that period, so the important Mr Wringhim was there among the rest, during the greater part of the time, blowing the coal of revolutionary principles with all his might, in every society to which he could obtain admission. He was a great favourite with some of the west country gentlemen of that faction, by reason of his unbending impudence. No opposition could for a moment cause him either to blush, or retract one item that he had advanced. Therefore the

Duke of Argyle and his friends made such use of him as sports-
men often do of terriers, to start the game, and make a great
yelping noise to let them know whither the chace is proceeding.
They often did this out of sport, in order to tease their opponent;
for of all pesterers that ever fastened on man he was the most
insufferable: knowing that his coat protected him from manual
chastisement, he spared no acrimony, and delighted in the
chagrin and anger of those with whom he contended. But he was
sometimes likewise *of real use* to the heads of the presbyterian
faction, and therefore was admitted to their tables, and of
course conceived himself a very great man.

His ward accompanied him; and very shortly after their
arrival in Edinburgh, Robert, for the first time, met with the
young laird his brother, in a match at tennis.[12] The prowess
and agility of the young squire drew forth the loudest plaudits
of approval from his associates, and his own exertion alone
carried the game every time on the one side, and that so far as
all along to count three for their one. The hero's name soon
ran round the circle, and when his brother Robert, who was
an onlooker, learned who it was that was gaining so much
applause, he came and stood close beside him all the time that
the game lasted, always now and then putting in a cutting
remark by way of mockery.

George could not help perceiving him, not only on account
of his impertinent remarks, but he, moreover, stood so near
him that he several times impeded him in his rapid evolutions,
and of course got himself shoved aside in no very ceremonious
way. Instead of making him keep his distance, these rude shocks
and pushes, accompanied sometimes with hasty curses, only
made him cling the closer to this king of the game. He seemed
determined to maintain his right to his place as an onlooker, as
well as any of those engaged in the game, and if they had tried
him at an argument, he would have carried his point: or perhaps
he wished to quarrel with this spark of his jealousy and aversion, and draw the attention of the gay crowd to himself by
these means; for, like his guardian, he knew no other pleasure
but what consisted in opposition. George took him for some
impertinent student of divinity, rather set upon a joke than

any thing else. He perceived a lad with black clothes, and a methodistical face, whose countenance and eye he disliked exceedingly, several times in his way, and that was all the notice he took of him the first time they two met. But the next day, and every succeeding one, the same devilish-looking youth attended him as constantly as his shadow; was always in his way as with intention to impede him, and ever and anon his deep and malignant eye met those of his elder brother with a glance so fierce that it sometimes startled him.

The very next time that George was engaged at tennis, he had not struck the ball above twice till the same intrusive being was again in his way. The party played for considerable stakes that day, namely, a dinner and wine at the Black Bull tavern; and George, as the hero and head of his party, was much interested in its honour; consequently, the sight of this moody and hellish-looking student affected him in no very pleasant manner. 'Pray, Sir, be so good as keep without the range of the ball,' said he.

'Is there any law or enactment that can compel me to do so?' said the other, biting his lip with scorn.

'If there is not, they are here that shall compel you,' returned George: 'so, friend, I rede you to be on your guard.'

As he said this, a flush of anger glowed in his handsome face, and flashed from his sparkling blue eye; but it was a stranger to both, and momently took its departure. The black-coated youth set up his cap before, brought his heavy brows over his deep dark eyes, put his hands in the pockets of his black plush breeches, and stepped a little farther into the semi-circle, immediately on his brother's right hand, than he had ever ventured to do before. There he set himself firm on his legs, and, with a face as demure as death, seemed determined to keep his ground. He pretended to be following the ball with his eyes; but every moment they were glancing aside at George. One of the competitors chanced to say rashly, in the moment of exultation, 'That's a d—d fine blow, George!' On which the intruder took up the word, as characteristic of the competitors, and repeated it every stroke that was given, making such a ludicrous use of it, that several of the on-lookers were compelled to laugh immoderately; but the players were terribly nettled at it, as he really contrived, by dint of sliding in some canonical terms, to render the competitors and their game ridiculous.

But matters at length came to a crisis that put them beyond sport. George, in flying backward to gain the point at which the ball was going to light, came inadvertently so rudely in contact with this obstreperous interloper, that he not only over-threw him, but also got a grievous fall over his legs; and, as he arose, the other made a spurn at him with his foot, which, if it had hit to its aim, would undoubtedly have finished the course of the young laird of Dalcastle and Balgrennan. George, being irritated beyond measure, as may well be conceived, especially at the deadly stroke aimed at him, struck the assailant with his racket, rather slightly, but so that his mouth and nose gushed out blood; and, at the same time, he said, turning to his cronies, 'Does any of you know who the infernal puppy is?'

'Do you not know, Sir?' said one of the on-lookers, a stranger: 'The gentleman is your own brother, Sir – Mr Robert Wringhim Colwan!'

'No, not Colwan, Sir,' said Robert, putting his hands in his pockets, and setting himself still farther forward than before, 'not a Colwan, Sir; henceforth I disclaim the name.'

'No, certainly not,' repeated George: 'My mother's son you may be, but *not a Colwan!* There you are right.' Then turning round to his informer, he said, 'Mercy be about us, Sir! is this the crazy minister's son from Glasgow?'

This question was put in the irritation of the moment; but it was too rude, and too far out of place, and no one deigned any answer to it. He felt the reproof, and felt it deeply; seeming anxious for some opportunity to make an acknowledgment, or some reparation.

In the meantime, young Wringhim was an object to all of the uttermost disgust. The blood flowing from his mouth and nose he took no pains to stem, neither did he so much as wipe it away; so that it spread over all his cheeks, and breast, even off at his toes. In that state did he take up his station in the middle of the competitors; and he did not now keep his place, but ran about, impeding every one who attempted to make at the ball.

They loaded him with execrations, but it availed nothing; he seemed courting persecution and buffetings, keeping stedfastly to his old joke of damnation. and marring the game so completely, that, in spite of every effort on the part of the players, he forced them to stop their game, and give it up. He was such a rueful-looking object, covered with blood, that none of them had the heart to kick him, although it appeared the only thing he wanted; and as for George, he said not another word to him, either in anger or reproof.

When the game was fairly given up, and the party were washing their hands in the stone fount, some of them besought Robert Wringhim to wash himself; but he mocked at them, and said, he was much better as he was. George, at length, came forward abashedly toward him, and said, 'I have been greatly to blame, Robert, and am very sorry for what I have done. But, in the first instance, I erred through ignorance, not knowing you were my brother, which you certainly are; and, in the second, through a momentary irritation, for which I am ashamed. I pray you, therefore, to pardon me, and give me your hand.'

As he said this, he held out his hand toward his polluted brother; but the froward predestinarian took not his from his breeches pocket, but lifting his foot, he gave his brother's hand a kick. 'I'll give you what will suit such a hand better than mine,' said he, with a sneer. And then, turning lightly about, he added, 'Are there to be no more of these d—d fine blows, gentlemen? For shame, to give up such a profitable and edifying game!'

'This is too bad,' said George. 'But, since it is thus, I have the less to regret.' And, having made this general remark, he took no more note of the uncouth aggressor. But the persecution of the latter terminated not on the play-ground: he ranked up among them, bloody and disgusting as he was, and, keeping close by his brother's side, he marched along with the party all the way to the Black Bull. Before they got there, a great number of boys and idle people had surrounded them, hooting and incommoding them exceedingly, so that they were glad to get into the inn; and the unaccountable monster actually tried to get in alongst with them, to make one of the party at dinner. But the innkeeper and his men, getting the hint, by force prevented him from entering, although he attempted it again and again, both by telling lies and offering a bribe. Finding he could not prevail, he set to exciting the mob at the door to acts of violence; in which he had like to have succeeded. The landlord had no other shift, at last, but to send privately for two officers, and have him carried to the guard-house; and the hilarity and joy of the party of young gentlemen, for the evening, was quite spoiled, by the inauspicious termination of their game.

The Rev. Robert Wringhim was now to send for, to release his beloved ward. The messenger found him at table, with a number of the leaders of the Whig faction, the Marquis of Annandale being in the chair; and the prisoner's note being produced, Wringhim read it aloud, accompanying it with some explanatory remarks. The circumstances of the case being thus magnified and distorted, it excited the utmost abhorrence, both of the deed and the perpetrators, among the assembled faction. They declaimed against the act as an unnatural attempt on the character, and even the life, of an unfortunate brother, who had been expelled from his father's house. And, as party spirit was the order of the day, an attempt was made to lay the burden of it to that account. In short, the young culprit got some of the best blood of the land to enter as his securities, and was set at liberty. But when Wringhim perceived the plight that he was in, he took him, as he was, and presented him to his honourable patrons. This raised the indignation against the young laird and his associates a thousand fold, which actually roused the party to temporary madness. They were, perhaps, a little excited by the wine and spirits they had swallowed; else a casual quarrel between two young men, at tennis, could not have driven them to such extremes. But certain it is, that from one at first arising to address the party on the atrocity of the offence, both in a moral and political point of view, on a sudden there were six on their feet, at the same time, expatiating on it; and, in a very short time thereafter, every one in the room was up, talking with the utmost vociferation, all on the same subject, and all taking the same side in the debate.

In the midst of this confusion, some one or other issued from the house, which was at the back of the Canongate, calling out, 'A plot, a plot! Treason, treason! Down with the bloody incendiaries at the Black Bull!'

The concourse of people that were assembled in Edinburgh at that time was prodigious; and as they were all actuated by political motives, they wanted only a ready-blown coal to set the mountain on fire. The evening being fine, and the streets thronged, the cry ran from mouth to mouth through the whole city. More than that, the mob that had of late been gathered to the door of the Black Bull, had, by degrees, dispersed; but, they being young men, and idle vagrants, they had only spread themselves over the rest of the street to lounge in search of farther amusement: consequently, a word was sufficient to send them back to their late rendezvous, where they had previously witnessed something they did not much approve of.

The master of the tavern was astonished at seeing the mob again assembling; and that with such hurry and noise. But his inmates being all of the highest respectability, he judged himself sure of protection, or, at least, of indemnity. He had two large parties in his house at the time; the largest of which was of the Revolutionist faction. The other consisted of our young tennis-players, and their associates, who were all of the Jacobite order; or, at all events, leaned to the Episcopal side. The largest party were in a front-room; and the attack of the mob fell first on their windows, though rather with fear and caution. Jingle went one pane; then a loud hurra; and that again was followed by a number of voices, endeavouring to restrain the indignation from venting itself in destroying the windows, and to turn it on the inmates. The Whigs, calling the landlord, inquired what the assault meant: he cunningly answered, that he suspected it was some of the youths of the Cavalier, or High-Church party, exciting the mob against them. The party consisted mostly of young gentlemen, by that time in a key to engage in any row; and, at all events, to suffer nothing from the other party, against whom their passions were mightily inflamed.

The landlord, therefore, had no sooner given them the spirit-rousing intelligence, than every one, as by instinct, swore his own natural oath, and grasped his own natural weapon. A few of those of the highest rank were armed with swords, which they boldly drew; those of the subordinate orders immediately flew to such weapons as the room, kitchen, and scullery afforded – such as tongs, pokers, spits, racks, and shovels; and breathing vengeance on the prelatic party, the children of Antichrist and the heirs of d–n–t–n! the barterers of the liberties of their country, and betrayers of the most sacred trust – thus elevated, and thus armed, in the cause of right, justice, and liberty, our heroes rushed to the street, and attacked the mob with such violence, that they broke the mass in a moment, and dispersed their thousands like chaff before the wind. The other party of young Jacobites, who sat in a room farther from the front, and were those against whom the fury of the mob was meant to have been directed, knew nothing of this second uproar, till the noise of the sally made by the Whigs assailed their ears; being then informed that the mob had attacked the house on account of the treatment they themselves had given to a young gentleman of the adverse faction, and that another jovial party had issued from the house in their defence, and was now engaged in an unequal combat, the sparks likewise flew to the field to back their defenders with all their prowess, without troubling their heads about who they were.

A mob is like a spring-tide in an eastern storm, that retires only to return with more overwhelming fury. The crowd was taken by surprise, when such a strong and well-armed party issued from the house with so great fury, laying all prostrate that came in their way. Those who were next to the door, and were, of course, the first whom the imminent danger assailed, rushed backward among the crowd with their whole force. The Black Bull standing in a small square half way between the High Street and the Cowgate, and the entrance to it being by two closes, into these the pressure outward was simultaneous, and thousands were moved to an involuntary flight they knew not why.

But the High Street of Edinburgh, which they soon reached, is a dangerous place in which to make an open attack upon a mob. And it appears that the entrances to the tavern had been somewhere near to the Cross, on the south side of the street; for the crowd fled with great expedition, both to the east and west, and the conquerors, separating themselves as chance directed, pursued impetuously, wounding and maiming as they flew. But, it so chanced, that before either of the wings had followed the flying squadrons of their enemies for the space of a hundred yards each way, the devil an enemy they had to pursue! the multitude had vanished like so many thousands of phantoms! What could our heroes do? Why, they faced about to return toward their citadel, the Black Bull. But that feat was not so easily, nor so readily accomplished, as they divined. The unnumbered alleys on each side of the street had swallowed up the multitude in a few seconds; but from these they were busy reconnoitring; and, perceiving the deficiency in the number of their assailants, the rush from both sides of the street was as rapid, and as wonderful, as the disappearance of the crowd had been a few minutes before. Each close vomited out its levies, and these better armed with missiles than when they sought it for a temporary retreat. Woe then to our two columns of victorious Whigs! The mob actually closed around them as they would have swallowed them up; and, in the meanwhile, shower after shower of the most abominable weapons of offence were rained in upon them. If the gentlemen were irritated before, this inflamed them still farther; but their danger was now so apparent, they could not shut their eyes on it, therefore, both parties, as if actuated by the same spirit, made a desperate effort to join, and the greater part effected it; but some were knocked down, and others were separated from their friends, and blithe to become silent members of the mob.

The battle now raged immediately in front of the closes leading to the Black Bull; the small body of Whig gentlemen was hardly bested,[13] and it is likely would have been overcome and trampled down every man, had they not been then and there joined by the young Cavaliers; who, fresh to arms, broke from the wynd, opened the head of the passage, laid about them manfully, and thus kept up the spirits of the exasperated Whigs, who were the men in fact that wrought the most deray among the populace.

The town-guard was now on the alert; and two companies of the Cameronian regiment,[14] with the Hon. Captain Douglas, rushed down from the Castle to the scene of action; but, for all the noise and hubbub that these caused in the street, the combat had become so close and inveterate, that numbers of both sides were taken prisoners fighting hand to hand, and could scarcely be separated when the guardsmen and soldiers had them by the necks.

Great was the alarm and confusion that night in Edinburgh; for every one concluded that it was a party scuffle, and, the two parties being so equal in power, the most serious consequences were anticipated. The agitation was so prevailing, that every party in the town, great and small, was broken up; and the lord-commissioner thought proper to go to the council-chamber himself, even at that late hour, accompanied by the sheriffs of Edinburgh and Linlithgow, with sundry noblemen besides, in order to learn something of the origin of the affray.

For a long time the court was completely puzzled. Every gentleman brought in exclaimed against the treatment he had received, in most bitter terms, blaming a mob set on him and his friends by the adverse party, and matters looked extremely ill, until at length they began to perceive that they were examining gentlemen of both parties, and that they had been doing so from the beginning, almost alternately, so equally had the prisoners been taken from both parties. Finally, it turned out, that a few gentlemen, two-thirds of whom were strenuous Whigs themselves, had joined in mauling the whole Whig population of Edinburgh. The investigation disclosed nothing the effect of which was not ludicrous; and the Duke of Queensberry, whose aim was at that time to conciliate the two factions, tried all that he could to turn the whole *fracas* into a joke – an unlucky frolic, where no ill was meant on either side, and which yet had been productive of a great deal.

The greater part of the people went home satisfied; but not so the Rev. Robert Wringhim. He did all that he could to inflame both judges and populace against the young Cavaliers, especially against the young Laird of Dalcastle, whom he represented as an incendiary, set on by an unnatural parent to slander his mother, and make away with a hapless and only brother; and, in truth, that declaimer against all human merit[15] had that sort of powerful, homely, and bitter eloquence, which seldom missed affecting his hearers: the consequence at that time was, that he made the unfortunate affair between the two brothers appear in extremely bad colours, and the populace retired to their homes impressed with no very favourable opinion of either the Laird of Dalcastle or his son George, neither of whom were there present to speak for themselves.

As for Wringhim himself, he went home to his lodgings, filled with gall and with spite against the young laird, whom he was made to believe the aggressor, and that intentionally. But most of all was he filled with indignation against the father, whom he held in abhorrence at all times, and blamed solely for this unmannerly attack made on his favourite ward, namesake, and adopted son; and for the public imputation of a crime to his own reverence, in calling the lad *his* son, and thus charging him with a sin against which he was well known to have levelled all the arrows of church censure with unsparing might.

But, filled as his heart was with some portion of these bad feelings, to which all flesh is subject, he kept, nevertheless, the fear of the Lord always before his eyes so far as never to omit any of the external duties of religion, and farther than that, man hath no power to pry. He lodged with the family of a Mr Miller, whose lady was originally from Glasgow, and had been a hearer, and, of course, a great admirer of Mr Wringhim. In that family he made public worship every evening; and that night, in his petitions at a throne of grace, he prayed for so many vials of wrath to be poured on the head of some particular sinner, that the hearers trembled, and stopped their ears. But that he might not proceed with so violent a measure, amounting to excommunication, without due scripture warrant, he began the exercise of the evening by singing the following verses,[16] which it is a pity should ever have been admitted into a Christian psalmody, being so adverse to all its mild and benevolent principles:

Set thou the wicked over him,
  And upon his right hand
Give thou his greatest enemy,
  Even Satan, leave to stand.
And when by thee he shall be judged,
  Let him remembered be;
And let his prayer be turned to sin,
  When he shall call on thee.
Few be his days; and in his room
  His charge another take;
His children let be fatherless;
  His wife a widow make:
Let God his father's wickedness
  Still to remembrance call;
And never let his mother's sin
  Be blotted out at all.
As he in cursing pleasure took,
  So let it to him fall;
As he delighted not to bless,
  So bless him not at all.
As cursing he like clothes put on,
  Into his bowels so,
Like water, and into his bones
  Like oil, down let it go.

Young Wringhim only knew the full purport of this spiritual song: and went to his bed better satisfied than ever, that his father and brother were cast-aways, reprobates, aliens from the church and the true faith, and cursed in time and eternity.

The next day George and his companions met as usual – all who were not seriously wounded of them. But as they strolled about the city, the rancorous eye and the finger of scorn was pointed against them. None of them was at first aware of the reason; but it threw a damp over their spirits and enjoyments, which they could not master. They went to take a forenoon game at their old play of tennis, not on a match, but by way of improving themselves; but they had not well taken their places till young Wringhim appeared in his old station, at his brother's right hand, with looks more demure[17] and determined than ever. His lips were primmed so close that his mouth was hardly discernible, and his dark deep eye flashed gleams of holy indignation on the godless set, but particularly on his brother. His presence acted as a mildew on all social intercourse or enjoyment; the game was marred, and ended ere ever it was well begun. There were whisperings apart – the party separated; and, in order to shake off the blighting influence of this dogged persecutor, they entered sundry houses of their acquaintances, with an understanding that they were to meet on the Links for a game at cricket.

They did so; and, stripping off part of their clothes, they began that violent and spirited game. They had not played five minutes, till Wringhim was stalking in the midst of them, and totally impeding the play. A cry arose from all corners of 'O, this will never do. Kick him out of the play-ground! Knock down the scoundrel; or bind him, and let him lie in peace.'

'By no means,' cried George: 'it is evident he wants nothing else. Pray do not humour him so much as to touch him with either foot or finger.' Then turning to a friend, he said in a whisper, 'Speak to him, Gordon; he surely will not refuse to let us have the ground to ourselves, if you request it of him.'

Gordon went up to him, and requested of him, civilly, but ardently, 'to retire to a certain distance, else none of them could or would be answerable, however sore he might be hurt.'

He turned disdainfully on his heel, uttered a kind of pulpit hem! and then added, 'I will take my chance of that; hurt me, any of you, at your peril.'

The young gentlemen smiled, through spite and disdain of the dogged animal. Gordon followed him up, and tried to remonstrate with him; but he let him know that 'it was his pleasure to be there at that time; and, unless he could demonstrate to him what superior right he and his party had to that ground, in preference to him, and to the exclusion of all others, he was determined to assert his right, and the rights of his fellow-citizens, by keeping possession of whatsoever part of that common field he chose'.

'You are no gentleman, Sir,' said Gordon.

'Are you one, Sir?' said the other.

'Yes, Sir, I will let you know that I am, by G–!'

'Then, thanks be to Him whose name you have profaned, I am none. If *one* of the party be a gentleman, *I do hope in God I am not!*'

It was now apparent to them all that he was courting obloquy and manual chastisement from their hands, if by any means he could provoke them to the deed; and, apprehensive that he had some sinister and deep-laid design in hunting after such a singular favour, they wisely restrained one another from inflicting the punishment that each of them yearned to bestow, personally, and which he so well deserved.

But the unpopularity of the Younger George Colwan could no longer be concealed from his associates. It was manifested wherever the populace were assembled; and his young and intimate friend, Adam Gordon, was obliged to warn him of the circumstance, that he might not be surprised at the gentlemen of their acquaintance withdrawing themselves from his society, as they could not be seen with him without being insulted. George thanked him; and it was agreed between them, that the former should keep himself retired during the day-time while he remained in Edinburgh, and that at night they should always meet together, along with such of their companions as were disengaged.

George found it every day more and more necessary to adhere to this system of seclusion; for it was not alone the hisses of the boys and populace that pursued him – a fiend of more malignant aspect was ever at his elbow, in the form of his brother. To whatever place of amusement he betook himself, and however well he concealed his intentions of going there from all flesh living, there was his brother Wringhim also, and always within a few yards of him, generally about the same distance, and ever and anon darting looks at him that chilled his very soul. They were looks that cannot be described; but they were felt piercing to the bosom's deepest core. They affected even the on-lookers in a very particular manner, for all whose eyes caught a glimpse of these hideous glances followed them to the object toward

which they were darted: the gentlemanly and mild demeanour
of that object generally calmed their startled apprehensions; for
no one ever yet noted the glances of the young man's eye in the
black coat, at the face of his brother, who did not at first
manifest strong symptoms of alarm.

George became utterly confounded; not only at the import
of this persecution, but how in the world it came to pass that
this unaccountable being knew all his motions, and every intention of his heart, as it were intuitively. On consulting his own
previous feelings and resolutions, he found that the circumstances of his going to such and such a place were often the
most casual incidents in nature – the caprice of a moment had
carried him there, and yet he had never sat or stood many
minutes till there was the self-same being, always in the same
position with regard to himself, as regularly as the shadow is
cast from the substance, or the ray of light from the opposing
denser medium.

For instance, he remembered one day of setting out with the
intention of going to attend divine worship in the High Church,
and when within a short space of its door, he was overtaken by
young Kilpatrick of Closeburn, who was bound to the Grey-
Friars[18] to see his sweetheart, as he said; 'and if you will go
with me, Colwan,' said he, 'I will let you see her too, and then
you will be just as far forward as I am.'

George assented at once, and went; and after taking his seat,
he leaned his head forward on the pew to repeat over to himself
a short ejaculatory prayer, as had always been his custom on
entering the house of God. When he had done, he lifted his eyes
naturally toward that point on his right hand where the fierce
apparition of his brother had been wont to meet his view: there
he was, in the same habit, form, demeanour, and precise point
of distance, as usual! George again laid down his head, and his
mind was so astounded, that he had nearly fallen into a swoon.
He tried shortly after to muster up courage to look at the
speaker, at the congregation, and at Captain Kilpatrick's sweetheart in particular; but the fiendish glances of the young man
in the black clothes were too appalling to be withstood – his
eye caught them whether he was looking that way or not: at

length his courage was fairly mastered, and he was obliged to look down during the remainder of the service.

By night or by day it was the same. In the gallery of the Parliament House, in the boxes of the play-house, in the church, in the assembly, in the streets, suburbs, and the fields; and every day, and every hour, from the first rencounter of the two, the attendance became more and more constant, more inexplicable, and altogether more alarming and insufferable, until at last George was fairly driven from society, and forced to spend his days in his own and his father's lodgings with closed doors. Even there, he was constantly harassed with the idea, that the next time he lifted his eyes, he would to a certainty see that face, the most repulsive to all his feelings of aught the earth contained. The attendance of that brother was now become like the attendance of a demon on some devoted being that had sold himself to destruction; his approaches as undiscerned, and his looks as fraught with hideous malignity. It was seldom that he saw him either following him in the streets, or entering any house or church after him; he only appeared in his place, George wist not how, or whence; and, having sped so ill in his first friendly approaches, he had never spoken to his equivocal attendant a second time.

It came at length into George's head, as he was pondering, by himself, on the circumstances of this extraordinary attendance, that perhaps his brother had relented, and, though of so sullen and unaccommodating a temper that he would not acknowledge it, or beg a reconciliation, it might be for that very purpose that he followed his steps night and day in that extraordinary manner. 'I cannot for my life see for what other purpose it can be,' thought he. 'He never offers to attempt my life; nor dares he, if he had the inclination; therefore, although his manner is peculiarly repulsive to me, I shall not have my mind burdened with the reflection, that my own mother's son yearned for a reconciliation with me, and was repulsed by my haughty and insolent behaviour. The next time he comes to my hand, I am resolved that I will accost him as one brother ought to address another, whatever it may cost me; and, if I am still flouted with disdain, then shall the blame rest with him.'

After this generous resolution, it was a good while before his gratuitous attendant appeared at his side again; and George began to think that his visits were discontinued. The hope was a relief that could not be calculated; but still George had a feeling that it was too supreme to last. His enemy had been too pertinacious to abandon his design, whatever it was. He, however, began to indulge in a little more liberty, and for several days he enjoyed it with impunity.

George was, from infancy, of a stirring active disposition, and could not endure confinement; and, having been of late much restrained in his youthful exercises by this singular persecutor, he grew uneasy under such restraint, and, one morning, chancing to awaken very early, he arose to make an excursion to the top of Arthur's Seat, to breathe the breeze of the dawning, and see the sun arise out of the eastern ocean. The morning was calm and serene; and as he walked down the south back of the Canongate, toward the Palace, the haze was so close around him that he could not see the houses on the opposite side of the way. As he passed the lord-commissioner's house, the guards were in attendance, who cautioned him not to go by the Palace, as all the gates would be shut and guarded for an hour to come, on which he went by the back of St Anthony's gardens, and found his way into that little romantic glade adjoining to the Saint's chapel and well. He was still involved in a blue haze, like a dense smoke, but yet in the midst of it the respiration was the most refreshing and delicious. The grass and the flowers were loaden with dew; and, on taking off his hat to wipe his forehead, he perceived that the black glossy fur of which his chaperon was wrought, was all covered with a tissue of the most delicate silver – a fairy web, composed of little spheres, so minute that no eye could discern any one of them; yet there they were shining in lovely millions. Afraid of defacing so beautiful and so delicate a garnish, he replaced his hat with the greatest caution, and went on his way light of heart.

As he approached the swire at the head of the dell, that little delightful verge from which in one moment the eastern limits and shores of Lothian arise on the view – as he approached it, I say, and a little space from the height, he beheld, to his astonishment, a bright halo in the cloud of haze, that rose in a semi-circle over his head like a pale rainbow. He was struck motionless at the view of the lovely vision; for it so chanced that he had never seen the same appearance before, though common at early morn. But he soon perceived the cause of the phenomenon, and that it proceeded from the rays of the sun from a pure unclouded morning sky striking upon this dense vapour which refracted them. But the better all the works of nature are understood, the more they will be ever admired. That was a scene that would have entranced the man of science with delight, but which the uninitiated and sordid man would have regarded less than the mole rearing up his hill in silence and in darkness.[19]

George did admire this halo of glory, which still grew wider, and less defined, as he approached the surface of the cloud. But, to his utter amazement and supreme delight, he found, on reaching the top of Arthur's Seat, that this sublunary rainbow, this terrestrial glory, was spread in its most vivid hues beneath his feet. Still he could not perceive the body of the sun, although the light behind him was dazzling; but the cloud of haze lying dense in that deep dell that separates the hill from the rocks of Salisbury, and the dull shadow of the hill mingling with that cloud, made the dell a pit of darkness. On that shadowy cloud was the lovely rainbow formed, spreading itself on a horizontal plain, and having a slight and brilliant shade of all the colours of the heavenly bow, but all of them paler and less defined. But this terrestrial phenomenon of the early morn cannot be better delineated than by the name given of it by the shepherd boys, 'The little wee ghost of the rainbow.'

Such was the description of the morning, and the wild shades of the hill, that George gave to his father and Mr Adam Gordon that same day on which he had witnessed them; and it is necessary that the reader should comprehend something of their nature, to understand what follows.

He seated himself on the pinnacle of the rocky precipice, a little within the top of the hill to the westward, and, with a light and buoyant heart, viewed the beauties of the morning, and inhaled its salubrious breeze. 'Here,' thought he, 'I can converse with nature without disturbance, and without being intruded on by any appalling or obnoxious visitor.' The idea of his brother's dark and malevolent looks coming at that moment across his mind, he turned his eyes instinctively to the right, to the point where that unwelcome guest was wont to make his appearance. Gracious Heaven! What an apparition was there presented to his view! He saw, delineated in the cloud, the shoulders, arms, and features of a human being of the most dreadful aspect. The face was the face of his brother, but dilated to twenty times the natural size. Its dark eyes gleamed on him through the mist, while every furrow of its hideous brow frowned deep as the ravines on the brow of the hill. George started, and his hair stood up in bristles as he gazed on this horrible monster. He saw every feature, and every line of the face, distinctly, as it gazed on him with an intensity that was hardly brookable. Its eyes were fixed on him, in the same manner as those of some carnivorous animal fixed on its prey; and yet there was fear and trembling, in these unearthly features, as plainly depicted as murderous malice. The giant apparition seemed sometimes to be cowering down as in terror, so that nothing but its brow and eyes were seen; still these never turned one moment from their object – again it rose imperceptibly up, and began to approach with great caution; and as it neared, the dimensions of its form lessened, still continuing, however, far above the natural size.

George conceived it to be a spirit. He could conceive it to be nothing else; and he took it for some horrid demon by which he was haunted, that had assumed the features of his brother in every lineament, but in taking on itself the human form, had miscalculated dreadfully on the size, and presented itself thus to him in a blown-up, dilated frame of embodied air, exhaled from the caverns of death or the regions of devouring fire. He was farther confirmed in the belief that it was a malignant spirit, on perceiving that it approached him across the front of a precipice, where there was not footing for thing of mortal frame. Still, what with terror and astonishment, he continued rivetted to the spot, till it approached, as he deemed, to within two yards of him: and then, perceiving that it was setting itself to make a violent spring on him, he started to his feet and fled distractedly in the opposite direction, keeping his eye cast behind him lest he had been seized in that dangerous place. But the very first bolt that he made in his flight he came in contact with a *real* body of flesh and blood, and that with such violence that both went down among some scragged rocks, and George rolled over the other. The being called out 'Murder'; and, rising, fled precipitately. George then perceived that it was his brother; and, being confounded between the shadow and the substance, he knew not what he was doing or what he had done; and there being only one natural way of retreat from the brink of the rock, he likewise arose and pursued the affrighted culprit with all his speed towards the top of the hill. Wringhim was braying out 'Murder! murder!' at which George being disgusted, and his spirits all in a ferment from some hurried idea of intended harm, the moment he came up with the craven he seized him rudely by the shoulder, and clapped his hand on his mouth. 'Murder, you beast!' said he; 'what do you mean by roaring out murder in that way? Who the devil is murdering you, or offering to murder you?'

Wringhim forced his mouth from under his brother's hand, and roared with redoubled energy, 'Eh! Egh! murder! murder!' &c. George had felt resolute to put down this shocking alarm, lest some one might hear it and fly to the spot, or draw inferences widely different from the truth; and, perceiving the terror of this elect youth to be so great that expostulation was vain, he seized him by the mouth and nose with his left hand, so strenuously, that he sunk his fingers into his cheeks. But the poltroon still attempting to bray out, George gave him such a stunning blow with his fist on the left temple, that he crumbled, as it were, to the ground, but more from the effects of terror than those of the blow. His nose, however, again gushed out blood, a system of defence which seemed as natural to him as that resorted to by the race of stinkards. He then raised himself on his knees and hams, and raising up his ghastly face, while the blood streamed over both ears, he besought his life of his brother, in the most abject whining manner, gaping and blubbering most piteously.

'Tell me then, Sir,' said George, resolved to make the most of the wretch's terror – 'tell me for what purpose it is that you thus haunt my steps? Tell me plainly, and instantly, else I will throw you from the verge of that precipice.'

'Oh, I will never do it again! I will never do it again! Spare my life, dear, good brother! Spare my life! Sure I never did you any hurt?'

'Swear to me, then, by the God that made you, that you will never henceforth follow after me to torment me with your hellish threatening looks; swear that you will never again come into my presence without being invited. Will you take an oath to this effect?'

'O yes! I will, I will!'

'But this is not all: you must tell me for what purpose you sought me out here this morning?'

'Oh, brother! for nothing but your good. I had nothing at heart but your unspeakable profit, and great and endless good.'

'So then, you indeed knew that I was here?'

'I was told so by a friend, but I did not believe him; a–a–at least I did not know it was true till I saw you.'

'Tell me this one thing, then, Robert, and all shall be forgotten and forgiven – Who was that friend?'

'You do not know him.'

'How then does he know me?'

'I cannot tell.'

'Was he here present with you to-day?'

'Yes; he was not far distant. He came to this hill with me.'

'Where then is he now?'

'I cannot tell.'

'Then, wretch, confess that the devil was that friend who told you I was here, and who came here with you. None else could possibly know of my being here.'

'Ah! how little you know of him! Would you argue that there is neither man nor spirit endowed with so much foresight as to deduce natural conclusions from previous actions and incidents but the devil? Alas, brother! But why should I wonder at such abandoned notions and principles? It was fore-ordained that you should cherish them, and that they should be the ruin of your soul and body, before the world was framed. Be assured of this, however, that I had no aim in seeking you *but your good!*'

'Well, Robert, I will believe it. I am disposed to be hasty and passionate: it is a fault in my nature; but I never meant, or wished you evil; and God is my witness that I would as soon stretch out my hand to my own life, or my father's, as to yours.' At these words, Wringhim uttered a hollow exulting laugh, put his hands in his pockets, and withdrew a space to his accustomed distance. George continued: 'And now, once for all, I request that we may exchange forgiveness, and that we may part and remain friends.'

'Would such a thing be expedient, think you? Or consistent with the glory of God? I doubt it.'

'I can think of nothing that would be more so. Is it not consistent with every precept of the Gospel? Come, brother, say that our reconciliation is complete.'

'O yes, certainly! I tell you, brother, according to the flesh: it is just as complete as the lark's is with the adder; no more so, nor ever can. Reconciled, forsooth! To what would I be reconciled?'

As he said this, he strode indignantly away. From the moment that he heard his life was safe, he assumed his former insolence and revengeful looks – and never were they more dreadful than on parting with his brother that morning on the top of the hill. 'Well, go thy ways,' said George; 'some would despise, but I pity thee. If thou art not a limb of Satan, I never saw one.'

The sun had now dispelled the vapours; and the morning being lovely beyond description, George sat himself down on the top of the hill, and pondered deeply on the unaccountable incident that had befallen to him that morning. He could in nowise comprehend it; but, taking it with other previous circumstances, he could not get quit of a conviction that he was haunted by some evil genius in the shape of his brother, as well as by that dark and mysterious wretch himself. In no other way could he account for the apparition he saw that morning on the face of the rock, nor for several sudden appearances of the same being, in places where there was no possibility of any foreknowledge that he himself was to be there, and as little that the same being, if he were flesh and blood like other men, could always start up in the same position with regard to him. He determined, therefore, on reaching home, to relate all that had happened, from beginning to end, to his father, asking his counsel and his assistance, although he knew full well that his father was not the fittest man in the world to solve such a problem. He was now involved in party politics, over head and ears; and, moreover, he could never hear the names of either of the Wringhims mentioned without getting into a quandary of disgust and anger; and all that he would deign to say of them was, to call them by all the opprobrious names he could invent.

It turned out as the young man from the first suggested: old Dalcastle would listen to nothing concerning them with any patience. George complained that his brother harassed him with his presence at all times, and in all places. Old Dal asked why he did not kick the dog out of his presence, whenever he felt him disagreeable? George said, he seemed to have some demon for a familiar. Dal answered, that he did not wonder a bit at that, for the young spark was the third in a direct line who had all been children of adultery; and it was well known that all such were born half deils themselves, and nothing was more likely than that they should hold intercourse with their fellows.[20] In the same style did he sympathize with all his son's late sufferings and perplexities.

In Mr Adam Gordon, however, George found a friend who entered into all his feelings, and had seen and knew every thing about the matter. He tried to convince him, that at all events there could be nothing supernatural in the circumstances; and that the vision he had seen on the rock, among the thick mist, was the shadow of his brother approaching behind him. George could not swallow this, for he had seen his own shadow on the cloud, and, instead of approaching to aught like his own figure, he perceived nothing but a halo of glory round a point of the cloud, that was whiter and purer than the rest. Gordon said, if he would go with him to a mountain of his father's, which he named, in Aberdeenshire, he would show him a giant spirit of the same dimensions, any morning at the rising of the sun, provided he shone on that spot. This statement excited George's curiosity exceedingly; and, being disgusted with some things about Edinburgh, and glad to get out of the way, he consented to go with Gordon to the Highlands for a space. The day was accordingly set for their departure, the old laird's assent obtained; and the two young sparks parted in a state of great impatience for their excursion.

One of them found out another engagement, however, the instant after this last was determined on. Young Wringhim went off the hill that morning, and home to his upright guardian again, without washing the blood from his face and neck; and there he told a most woful story indeed: How he had gone out to take a morning's walk on the hill, where he had encountered with his reprobate brother among the mist, who had knocked him down and very near murdered him; threatening dreadfully, and with horrid oaths, to throw him from the top of the cliff.

The wrath of the great divine was kindled beyond measure. He cursed the aggressor in the name of the Most High; and bound himself, by an oath, to cause that wicked one's transgressions return upon his own head sevenfold. But before he engaged farther in the business of vengeance, he kneeled with his adopted son, and committed the whole cause unto the Lord, whom he addressed as one coming breathing burning coals of juniper, and casting his lightnings before him, to destroy and root out all who had moved hand or tongue against the children of the promise.[21] Thus did he arise confirmed, and go forth to certain conquest.

We cannot enter into the detail of the events that now occurred, without forestalling a part of the narrative of one who knew all the circumstances – was deeply interested in them, and whose relation is of higher value than any thing that can be retailed out of the stores of tradition and old registers; but, his narrative being different from these, it was judged expedient to give the account as thus publicly handed down to us. Suffice it, that, before evening, George was apprehended, and lodged in jail, on a criminal charge of an assault and battery, to the shedding of blood, with the intent of committing fratricide. Then was

the old laird in great consternation, and blamed himself for
treating the thing so lightly, which seemed to have been gone
about, from the beginning, so systematically, and with an intent
which the villains were now going to realize, namely, to get the
young laird disposed of, and then his brother, in spite of the
old gentleman's teeth, would be laird himself.

Old Dal now set his whole interest to work among the noblemen and lawyers of his party. His son's case looked exceedingly
ill, owing to the former assault before witnesses, and the unbe-
coming expressions made use of by him on that occasion, as
well as from the present assault, which George did not deny,
and for which no moving cause or motive could be made to
appear.

On his first declaration before the sheriff, matters looked no
better: but then the sheriff was a Whig. It is well known how
differently the people of the present day, in Scotland, view the
cases of their own party-men, and those of opposite political
principles. But this day is nothing to that in such matters,
although, God knows, they are still sometimes barefaced
enough. It appeared, from all the witnesses in the first case, that
the complainant was the first aggressor – that he refused to
stand out of the way, though apprised of his danger; and when
his brother came against him inadvertently, he had aimed a
blow at him with his foot, which, if it had taken effect, would
have killed him. But as to the story of the apparition in fair
day-light – the flying from the face of it – the running foul of
his brother – pursuing him, and knocking him down, why
the judge smiled at the relation; and saying, 'It was a very
extraordinary story', he remanded George to prison, leaving
the matter to the High Court of Justiciary.

When the case came before that court, matters took a different turn. The constant and sullen attendance of the one brother
upon the other excited suspicions; and these were in some
manner confirmed, when the guards at Queensberry-house
deponed, that the prisoner went by them on his way to the hill
that morning, about twenty minutes before the complainant,
and when the latter passed, he asked if such a young man
had passed before him, describing the prisoner's appearance to

them; and that, on being answered in the affirmative, he mended his pace and fell a-running.

The Lord Justice, on hearing this, asked the prisoner if he had any suspicions that his brother had a design on his life.

He answered, that all along, from the time of their first unfortunate meeting, his brother had dogged his steps so constantly, and so unaccountably, that he was convinced it was with some intent out of the ordinary course of events; and that if, as his lordship supposed, it was indeed his shadow that he had seen approaching him through the mist, then, from the cowering and cautious manner that it advanced, there was too little doubt that his brother's design had been to push him headlong from the cliff that morning.

A conversation then took place between the Judge and the Lord Advocate; and, in the mean time, a bustle was seen in the hall; on which the doors were ordered to be guarded – and, behold, the precious Mr R. Wringhim was taken into custody, trying to make his escape out of court. Finally it turned out, that George was honourably acquitted, and young Wringhim bound over to keep the peace, with heavy penalties and securities.

That was a day of high exultation to George and his youthful associates, all of whom abhorred Wringhim; and the evening being spent in great glee, it was agreed between Mr Adam Gordon and George, that their visit to the Highlands, though thus long delayed, was not to be abandoned; and though they had, through the machinations of an incendiary, lost the season of delight, they would still find plenty of sport in deer-shooting. Accordingly, the day was set a second time for their departure; and, on the day preceding that, all the party were invited by George to dine with him once more at the sign of the Black Bull of Norway. Every one promised to attend, anticipating nothing but festivity and joy. Alas, what short-sighted improvident creatures we are, all of us; and how often does the evening cup of joy lead to sorrow in the morning!

The day arrived – the party of young noblemen and gentlemen met, and were as happy and jovial as men could be. George was never seen so brilliant, or so full of spirits; and exulting to see so many gallant young chiefs and gentlemen about him, who all gloried in the same principles of loyalty (perhaps this word should have been written *disloyalty*), he made speeches, gave toasts, and sung songs, all leaning slily to the same side, until a very late hour. By that time he had pushed the bottle so long and so freely, that its fumes had taken possession of every brain to such a degree, that they held Dame Reason rather at the staff's end, overbearing all her counsels and expostulations; and it was imprudently proposed by a wild inebriated spark, and carried by a majority of voices, that the whole party should adjourn to a bagnio for the remainder of the night.

They did so; and it appears from what follows, that the house to which they retired, must have been somewhere on the opposite side of the street to the Black Bull Inn, a little farther to the eastward. They had not been an hour in that house, till some altercation chanced to arise between George Colwan and a Mr Drummond, the younger son of a nobleman of distinction. It was perfectly casual, and no one thenceforward, to this day, could ever tell what it was about, if it was not about the misunderstanding of some word, or term, that the one had uttered. However it was, some high words passed between them; these were followed by threats; and in less than two minutes from the commencement of the quarrel, Drummond left the house in apparent displeasure, hinting to the other that they two should settle that in a more convenient place.

The company looked at one another, for all was over before any of them knew such a thing was begun. 'What the devil is the matter?' cried one. 'What ails Drummond?' cried another. 'Who has he quarrelled with?' asked a third.

'Don't know.' – 'Can't tell, on my life.' – 'He has quarrelled with his wine, I suppose, and is going to send it a challenge.'

Such were the questions, and such the answers that passed in the jovial party, and the matter was no more thought of.

But in the course of a very short space, about the length of which the ideas of the company were the next day at great variance, a sharp rap came to the door: It was opened by a female; but there being a chain inside, she only saw one side of the person at the door. He appeared to be a young gentleman, in appearance like him who had lately left the house, and asked, in a low whispering voice, 'if young Dalcastle was still in the house?' The woman did not know. 'If he is,' added he, 'pray tell him to speak with me for a few minutes.' The woman delivered the message before all the party, among whom there were then sundry courteous ladies of notable distinction, and George, on receiving it, instantly rose from the side of one of them, and said, in the hearing of them all, 'I will bet a hundred merks that is Drummond.' – 'Don't go to quarrel with him, George,' said one. – 'Bring him in with you,' said another. George stepped out; the door was again bolted, the chain drawn across, and the inadvertent party, left within, thought no more of the circumstance till the next morning, that the report had spread over the city, that a young gentleman had been slain, on a little washing-green at the side of the North Loch, and at the very bottom of the close where this thoughtless party had been assembled.

Several of them, on first hearing the report, hasted to the dead-room in the old Guard-house, where the corpse had been deposited, and soon discovered the body to be that of their friend and late entertainer, George Colwan. Great were the consternation and grief of all concerned, and, in particular, of his old father and Miss Logan; for George had always been the sole hope and darling of both, and the news of the event para-lysed them so as to render them incapable of all thought or exertion. The spirit of the old laird was broken by the blow, and he descended at once from a jolly, good-natured, and active man, to a mere driveller, weeping over the body of his son, kissing his wound, his lips, and his cold brow alternately; denouncing vengeance on his murderers, and lamenting that he himself had not met the cruel doom, so that the hope of his race might have been preserved. In short, finding that all further motive of action and object of concern or of love, here below, were for ever removed from him, he abandoned himself to despair, and threatened to go down to the grave with his son.

But although he made no attempt to discover the murderers, the arm of justice was not idle; and it being evident to all, that the crime must infallibly be brought home to young

Drummond, some of his friends sought him out, and compelled him, sorely against his will, to retire into concealment till the issue of the proof that should be led was made known. At the same time, he denied all knowledge of the incident with a resolution that astonished his intimate friends and relations, who to a man suspected him guilty. His father was not in Scotland, for I think it was said to me that this young man was second son to a John, Duke of Melfort,[22] who lived abroad with the royal family of the Stuarts; but this young gentleman lived with the relations of his mother, one of whom, an uncle, was a Lord of Session: these having thoroughly effected his concealment, went away, and listened to the evidence; and the examination of every new witness convinced them that their noble young relative was the slayer of his friend.

All the young gentlemen of the party were examined, save Drummond, who, when sent for, could not be found, which circumstance sorely confirmed the suspicions against him in the minds of judges and jurors, friends and enemies; and there is little doubt, that the care of his relations in concealing him, injured his character, and his cause. The young gentlemen, of whom the party was composed, varied considerably, with respect to the quarrel between him and the deceased. Some of them had neither heard nor noted it; others had, but not one of them could tell how it began. Some of them had heard the threat uttered by Drummond on leaving the house, and one only had noted him lay his hand on his sword. Not one of them could swear that it was Drummond who came to the door, and desired to speak with the deceased, but the general impression on the minds of them all, was to that effect; and one of the women swore that she heard the voice distinctly at the door, and every word that voice pronounced; and at the same time heard the deceased say, that it was Drummond's.

On the other hand, there were some evidences on Drummond's part, which Lord Craigie, his uncle, had taken care to collect. He produced the sword which his nephew had worn that night, on which there was neither blood nor blemish; and above all, he insisted on the evidence of a number of surgeons, who declared that both the wounds which the deceased had received, had been given behind. One of these was below the left arm, and a slight one; the other was quite through the body, and both evidently inflicted with the same weapon, a two-edged sword, of the same dimensions as that worn by Drummond.

Upon the whole, there was a division in the court, but a majority decided it. Drummond was pronounced guilty of the murder; outlawed for not appearing, and a high reward offered for his apprehension. It was with the greatest difficulty that he escaped on board of a small trading vessel, which landed him in Holland, and from thence, flying into Germany, he entered into the service of the Emperor Charles VI. Many regretted that he was not taken, and made to suffer the penalty due for such a crime, and the melancholy incident became a pulpit theme over a great part of Scotland, being held up as a proper warning to youth to beware of such haunts of vice and depravity, the nurses of all that is precipitate, immoral, and base, among mankind.

After the funeral of this promising and excellent young man, his father never more held up his head. Miss Logan, with all her art, could not get him to attend to any worldly thing, or to make any settlement whatsoever of his affairs, save making her over a present of what disposable funds he had about him. As to his estates, when they were mentioned to him, he wished them all in the bottom of the sea, and himself along with them. But whenever she mentioned the circumstance of Thomas Drummond having been the murderer of his son, he shook his head, and once made the remark, that 'It was all a mistake, a gross and fatal error; but that God, who had permitted such a flagrant deed, would bring it to light in his own time and way.' In a few weeks he followed his son to the grave, and the notorious Robert Wringhim took possession of his estates as the lawful son of the late laird, born in wedlock, and under his father's roof. The investiture was celebrated by prayer, singing of psalms, and religious disputation. The late guardian and adopted father, and the mother of the new laird, presided on the grand occasion, making a conspicuous figure in all the work of the day; and though the youth himself indulged rather more freely in the bottle, than he had ever been seen to do before, it

was agreed by all present, that there had never been a festivity
so sanctified within the great hall of Dalcastle. Then, after due
thanks returned, they parted rejoicing in spirit; which thanks,
by the by, consisted wholly in telling the Almighty what he was;
and informing him, with very particular precision, what *they*
were who addressed him; for Wringhim's whole system of
popular declamation consisted it seems in this – to denounce
all men and women to destruction, and then hold out hopes to
his adherents that they were the chosen few, included in the
promises, and who could never fall away. It would appear that
this pharisaical doctrine is a very delicious one, and the most
grateful of all others to the worst characters.

But the ways of heaven are altogether inscrutable, and soar
as far above and beyond the works and the comprehensions of
man, as the sun, flaming in majesty, is above the tiny boy's
evening rocket. It is the controller of Nature alone, that can
bring light out of darkness, and order out of confusion. Who
is he that causeth the mole, from his secret path of darkness, to
throw up the gem, the gold, and the precious ore? The same, that
from the mouths of babes and sucklings can extract the perfec-
tion of praise, and who can make the most abject of his creatures instrumental in bringing the most hidden truths to light.

Miss Logan had never lost the thought of her late master's
prediction, that Heaven would bring to light the truth concerning the untimely death of his son. She perceived that some
strange conviction, too horrible for expression, preyed on his
mind from the moment that the fatal news reached him, to the
last of his existence; and in his last ravings, he uttered some
incoherent words about justification by faith alone, and absolute and eternal predestination having been the ruin of his
house. These, to be sure, were the words of superannuation,
and of the last and severest kind of it; but for all that, they sunk
deep into Miss Logan's soul, and at last she began to think with
herself, 'Is it possible the Wringhims, and the sophisticating
wretch who is in conjunction with them, the mother of my
late beautiful and amiable young master, can have effected his
destruction? if so, I will spend my days, and my little patrimony,
in endeavours to rake up and expose the unnatural deed.'

In all her outgoings and incomings, Mrs Logan (as she was now styled) never lost sight of this one object. Every new disappointment only whetted her desire to fish up some particulars concerning it; for she thought so long, and so ardently upon it, that by degrees it became settled in her mind as a sealed truth. And as woman is always most jealous of her own sex in such matters, her suspicions were fixed on her greatest enemy, Mrs Colwan, now the Lady Dowager of Dalcastle. All was wrapt in a chaos of confusion and darkness; but at last by dint of a thousand sly and secret inquiries, Mrs Logan found out where Lady Dalcastle had been, on the night that the murder happened, and likewise what company she had kept, as well as some of the comers and goers; and she had hopes of having discovered a cue,[23] which, if she could keep hold of the thread, would lead her through darkness to the light of truth.

Returning very late one evening from a convocation of family servants, which she had drawn together in order to fish something out of them, her maid having been in attendance on her all the evening, they found on going home, that the house had been broken, and a number of valuable articles stolen therefrom. Mrs Logan had grown quite heartless before this stroke, having been altogether unsuccessful in her inquiries, and now she began to entertain some resolutions of giving up the fruitless search.

In a few days thereafter, she received intelligence that her clothes and plate were mostly recovered, and that she for one was bound over to prosecute the depredator, provided the articles turned out to be hers, as libelled in the indictment, and as a king's evidence had given out. She was likewise summoned, or requested, I know not which, being ignorant of these matters, to go as far as the town of Peebles on Tweedside, in order to survey these articles on such a day, and make affidavit to their identity before the Sheriff. She went accordingly; but on entering the town by the North Gate, she was accosted by a poor girl in tattered apparel, who with great earnestness inquired if her name was not Mrs Logan? On being answered in the affirmative, she said that the unfortunate prisoner in the tolbooth requested her, as she valued all that was dear to her in

life, to go and see her before she appeared in court, at the hour
of cause, as she (the prisoner) had something of the greatest
moment to impart to her. Mrs Logan's curiosity was excited,
and she followed the girl straight to the tolbooth, who by the
way said to her, that she would find in the prisoner a woman
of a superior mind, who had gone through all the vicissitudes
of life. 'She has been very unfortunate, and I fear very wicked,'
added the poor thing, 'but she is my mother, and God knows,
with all her faults and failings, she has never been unkind to
me. You, madam, have it in your power to save her; but she
has wronged you, and therefore if you will not do it for her
sake, do it for mine, and the God of the fatherless will reward
you.'

Mrs Logan answered her with a cast of the head, and a hem!
and only remarked, that 'the guilty must not always be suffered
to escape, or what a world must we be doomed to live in!'

She was admitted to the prison, and found a tall emaciated
figure, who appeared to have once possessed a sort of masculine
beauty in no ordinary degree, but was now considerably advanced in years. She viewed Mrs Logan with a stern, steady
gaze, as if reading her features as a margin to her intellect; and
when she addressed her it was not with that humility, and
agonized fervor, which are natural for one in such circumstances to address to another, who has the power of her life
and death in her hands.

'I am deeply indebted to you, for this timely visit, Mrs Logan,'
said she. 'It is not that I value life, or because I fear death, that
I have sent for you so expressly. But the manner of the death
that awaits me, has something peculiarly revolting in it to a
female mind. Good God! when I think of being hung up,[24] a
spectacle to a gazing, gaping multitude, with numbers of which
I have had intimacies and connections, that would render the
moment of parting so hideous, that, believe me, it rends to
flinders a soul born for another sphere than that in which it has
moved, had not the vile selfishness of a lordly fiend ruined all
my prospects, and all my hopes. Hear me then: for I do not ask
your pity: I only ask of you to look to yourself, and behave
with womanly prudence. If you deny this day, that these goods

are yours, there is no other evidence whatever against my life, and it is safe for the present. For as for the word of the wretch who has betrayed me, it is of no avail; he has prevaricated so notoriously to save himself. If you deny them, you shall have them all again to the value of a mite, and more to the bargain. If you swear to the identity of them, the process will, one way and another, cost you the half of what they are worth.'

'And what security have I for that?' said Mrs Logan.

'You have none but *my word*,' said the other proudly, 'and that never yet was violated. If you cannot take that, I know the worst you can do – But I had forgot – I have a poor helpless child without, waiting, and starving about the prison door – Surely it was of her that I wished to speak. This shameful death of mine will leave her in a deplorable state.'

'The girl seems to have candour and strong affections,' said Mrs Logan; 'I grievously mistake if such a child would not be a thousand times better without such a guardian and director.'

'Then will you be so kind as come to the Grass Market, and see me put down?' said the prisoner. 'I thought a woman would estimate a woman's and a mother's feelings, when such a dreadful throw was at stake, at least in part. But you are callous, and have never known any feelings but those of subordination to your old unnatural master. Alas, I have no cause of offence! I have wronged you; and justice must take its course. Will you forgive me before we part?'

Mrs Logan hesitated, for her mind ran on something else: On which the other subjoined, 'No, you will not forgive me, I see. But you will pray to God to forgive me? I know you will *do that*.'

Mrs Logan heard not this jeer, but looking at the prisoner with an absent and stupid stare, she said, 'Did you know my late master?'

'Ay, that I did, and never for any good,' said she. 'I knew the old and the young spark both, and was by when the latter was slain.'

This careless sentence affected Mrs Logan in a most peculiar manner. A shower of tears burst from her eyes ere it was done, and when it was, she appeared like one bereaved of her mind.

She first turned one way and then another, as if looking for something she had dropped. She seemed to think she had lost her eyes, instead of her tears, and at length, as by instinct, she tottered close up to the prisoner's face, and looking wistfully and joyfully in it, said, with breathless earnestness, 'Pray, mistress, what is your name?'

'My name is Arabella Calvert,' said the other: 'Miss, mistress, or widow, as you chuse, for I have been all the three, and that not once nor twice only – Ay, and something beyond all these. But as for you, you have never been any thing!'

'Ay, ay! and so you are Bell Calvert? Well, I thought so – I thought so,' said Mrs Logan; and helping herself to a seat, she came and sat down close by the prisoner's knee. 'So you are indeed Bell Calvert, so called once. Well, of all the world you are the woman whom I have longed and travailed the most to see. But you were invisible; a being to be heard of, not seen.'

'There have been days, madam,' returned she, 'when I *was* to be seen, and when there were few to be seen like me. But since that time there have indeed been days on which I was not to be seen. My crimes have been great, but my sufferings have been greater. So great, that neither you nor the world can ever either know or conceive them. I hope they will be taken into account by the Most High. Mine have been crimes of utter desperation. But whom am I speaking to? You had better leave me to myself, mistress.'

'Leave you to yourself? That I will be loth to do, till you tell me where you were that night my young master was murdered?'

'Where the devil would, I was! Will that suffice you? Ah, it was a vile action! A night to be remembered that was! Won't you be going? I want to trust my daughter with a commission.'

'No, Mrs Calvert, you and I part not, till you have divulged that mystery to me.'

'You must accompany me to the other world, then, for you shall not have it in this.'

'If you refuse to answer me, I can have you before a tribunal, where you shall be sifted to the soul.'

'Such miserable inanity! What care I for your threatenings of a tribunal? I who must so soon stand before my last earthly one? What could the word of such a culprit avail? Or if it could, where is the judge that could enforce it?'

'Did you not say that there was some mode of accommodating matters on that score?'

'Yes, I prayed you to grant me my life, which is in your power. The saving of it would not have cost you a plack, yet you refused to do it. The taking of it will cost you a great deal, and yet to that purpose you adhere. I can have no parley with such a spirit. I would not have my life in a present from its motions, nor would I exchange courtesies with its possessor.'

'Indeed, Mrs Calvert, since ever we met, I have been so busy thinking about who you might be, that I know not what you have been proposing. I believe, I meant to do what I could to save you. But once for all, tell me every thing that you know concerning that amiable young gentleman's death, and here is my hand there shall be nothing wanting that I can effect for you.'

'No, I despise all barter with such mean and selfish curiosity; and, as I believe *that* passion is stronger with you, than fear is with me, we part on equal terms. Do your worst; and my secret shall go to the gallows and the grave with me.'

Mrs Logan was now greatly confounded, and after proffering in vain to concede every thing she could ask in exchange, for the particulars relating to the murder, she became the suppliant in her turn. But the unaccountable culprit, exulting in her advantage, laughed her to scorn; and finally, in a paroxysm of pride and impatience, called in the jailor and had her expelled, ordering him in her hearing not to grant her admittance a second time, on any pretence.

Mrs Logan was now hard put to it, and again driven almost to despair. She might have succeeded in the attainment of that she thirsted for most in life so easily, had she known the character with which she had to deal – had she known to have soothed her high and afflicted spirit: but that opportunity was past, and the hour of examination at hand. She once thought of going and claiming her articles, as she at first intended; but then, when she thought again of the Wringhims swaying it at Dalcastle, where she had been wont to hear them held in such contempt, if not abhorrence, and perhaps of holding it by the most diabolical means, she was withheld from marring the only chance that remained of having a glimpse into that mysterious affair.

Finally, she resolved not to answer to her name in the court, rather than to appear and assert a falsehood, which she might be called on to certify by oath. She did so; and heard the Sheriff give orders to the officers to make inquiry for Miss Logan from Edinburgh, at the various places of entertainment in town, and to expedite her arrival in court, as things of great value were in dependence. She also heard the man who had turned king's evidence against the prisoner, examined for the second time, and sifted most cunningly. His answers gave any thing but satisfaction to the Sheriff, though Mrs Logan believed them to be mainly truth. But there were a few questions and answers that struck her above all others.

'How long is it since Mrs Calvert and you became acquainted?'

'About a year and a half.'

'State the precise time, if you please; the day, or night, according to your remembrance.'

'It was on the morning of the 28th of February, 1705.'

'What time of the morning?'

'Perhaps about one.'

'So early as that? At what place did you meet then?'

'It was at the foot of one of the north wynds of Edinburgh.'

'Was it by appointment that you met?'

'No, it was not.'

'For what purpose was it then?'

'For no purpose.'

'How is it that you chance to remember the day and hour so minutely, if you met that woman, whom you have accused, merely by chance, and for no manner of purpose, as you must have met others that night, perhaps to the amount of hundreds, in the same way?'

'I have good cause to remember it, my lord.'

'What was that cause? No answer? You don't choose to say what that cause was?'

'I am not at liberty to tell.'

The Sheriff then descended to other particulars, all of which tended to prove that the fellow was an accomplished villain, and that the principal share of the atrocities had been committed by him. Indeed the Sheriff hinted, that he suspected the only share Mrs Calvert had in them, was in being too much in his company, and too true to him. The case was remitted to the Court of Justiciary; but Mrs Logan had heard enough to convince her that the culprits first met at the very spot, and the very hour, on which George Colwan was slain; and she had no doubt that they were incendiaries set on by his mother, to forward her own and her darling son's way to opulence. Mrs Logan was wrong, as will appear in the sequel; but her antipathy to Mrs Colwan made her watch the event with all care. She never quitted Peebles as long as Bell Calvert remained there, and when she was removed to Edinburgh, the other followed. When the trial came on, Mrs Logan and her maid were again summoned as witnesses before the jury, and compelled by the prosecutor for the Crown to appear.

The maid was first called; and when she came into the witnesses' box, the anxious and hopeless looks of the prisoner were manifest to all: But the girl, whose name, she said, was Bessy Gillies, answered in so flippant and fearless a way, that the auditors were much amused. After a number of routine questions, the depute-advocate asked her if she was at home on the morning of the fifth of September last, when her mistress's house was robbed?

'Was I at hame, say ye? Na, faith-ye, lad! An I had been at hame, there had been mair to dee. I wad hae raised sic a yelloch!'

'Where were you that morning?'

'Where was I, say you? I was in the house where my mistress was, sitting dozing an' half sleeping in the kitchen. I thought aye she would be setting out every minute, for twa hours.'

'And when you went home, what did you find?'

'What found we? Be my sooth, we found a broken lock, an' toom kists.'

'Relate some of the particulars, if you please.'

'O, sir, the thieves didna stand upon particulars: they were halesale dealers in a' our best wares.'

'I mean, what passed between your mistress and you on the occasion?'

'What passed, say ye? O, there wasna muckle: I was in a great passion, but she was dung doitrified a wee. When she gaed to put the key i' the door, up it flew to the fer wa'. "Bess, ye jaud, what's the meaning o' this?" quo she. "Ye hae left the door open, ye tawpie!" quo she. "The ne'er o' that I did," quo I, "or may my shakel bane never turn another key." When we got the candle lightit, a' the house was in a hoad-road. "Bessy, my woman," quo she, "we are baith ruined and undone creatures." "The deil a bit," quo I; "that I deny positively. H'mh! to speak o' a lass o' my age being ruined and undone! I never had muckle except what was within a good jerkin, an' let the thief ruin me there wha can."'

'Do you remember ought else that your mistress said on the occasion? Did you hear her blame any person?'

'O, she made a great deal o' grumphing an' groaning about the *misfortune*, as she ca'd it, an' I think she said it was a part o' the ruin wrought by the Ringans, or some sic name – "they'll hae't a'! they'll hae't a'!" cried she, wringing her hands; "they'll hae't a', an' hell wi't, an' they'll get them baith." "Aweel, that's aye some satisfaction," quo I.[25]

'Whom did she mean by the Ringans, do you know?'

'I fancy they are some creatures that she has dreamed about, for I think there canna be as ill folks living as she ca's them.'

'Did you never hear her say that the prisoner at the bar there, Mrs Calvert, or Bell Calvert, was the robber of her house; or that she was one of the Ringans?'

'Never. Somebody tauld her lately, that ane Bell Calvert robbed her house, but she disna believe it. Neither do I.'

'What reasons have you for doubting it?'

'Because it was nae woman's fingers that broke up the bolts an' the locks that were torn open that night.'

'Very pertinent, Bessy. Come then within the bar, and look at these articles on the table. Did you ever see these silver spoons before?'

'I hae seen some very like them, and whaever has seen siller spoons, has done the same.'

'Can you swear you never saw them before?'

'Na, na, I wadna swear to ony siller spoons that ever war made, unless I had put a private mark on them wi' my ain hand, an' that's what I never did to ane.'

'See, they are all marked with a C.'

'Sae are a' the spoons in Argyle, an' the half o' them in Edinburgh I think. A C is a very common letter, an' so are a' the names that begin wi't. Lay them by, lay them by, an' gie the poor woman her spoons again. They are marked wi' her ain name, an' I hae little doubt they are hers, an' that she has seen better days.'

'Ah, God bless her heart!' sighed the prisoner; and that blessing was echoed in the breathings of many a feeling breast.

'Did you ever see this gown before, think you?'

'I hae seen ane very like it.'

'Could you not swear that gown was your mistress's once?'

'No, unless I saw her hae't on, an' kend that she had paid for't. I am very scrupulous about an oath. *Like* is an ill mark. Sae ill indeed, that I wad hardly swear to ony thing.'

'But you say that gown is *very like* one your mistress used to wear.'

"I never said sic a thing. It is like one I hae seen her hae out airing on the hay raip i' the back green. It is very like ane I hae seen Mrs Butler in the Grass Market wearing too; I rather think it is the same. Bless you. sir, I wadna swear to my ain forefinger, if it had been as lang out o' my sight, an' brought in an' laid on that table.'

'Perhaps you are not aware, girl, that this scrupulousness of yours is likely to thwart the purposes of justice, and bereave your mistress of property to the amount of a thousand merks?' (*From the Judge.*)

'I canna help that, my lord: that's her lookout. For my part, I am resolved to keep a clear conscience, till I be married, at any rate.'

'Look over these things and see if there is any one article among them which you can fix on as the property of your mistress.'

'No ane o' them, sir, no ane o' them. An oath is an awfu'

thing, especially when it is for life or death. Gie the poor woman her things again, an' let my mistress pick up the next she finds: that's my advice.'

When Mrs Logan came into the box, the prisoner groaned, and laid down her head. But how she was astonished when she heard her deliver herself something to the following purport! – That whatever penalties she was doomed to abide, she was determined she would not bear witness against a woman's life, from a certain conviction that it could not be a woman who broke her house. 'I have no doubt that I may find some of my own things there,' added she, 'but if they were found in her possession, she has been made a tool, or the dupe, of an infernal set, who shall be nameless here. I believe she *did not* rob me, and for that reason I will have no hand in her condemnation.'

The Judge. 'This is the most singular perversion I have ever witnessed. Mrs Logan, I entertain strong suspicions that the prisoner, or her agents, have made some agreement with you on this matter, to prevent the course of justice.'

'So far from that, my lord, I went into the jail at Peebles to this woman, whom I had never seen before, and proffered to withdraw my part in the prosecution, as well as my evidence, provided she would tell me a few simple facts; but she spurned at my offer, and had me turned insolently out of the prison, with orders to the jailor never to admit me again on any pretence.'

The prisoner's counsel, taking hold of this evidence, addressed the jury with great fluency; and finally, the prosecution was withdrawn, and the prisoner dismissed from the bar, with a severe reprimand for her past conduct, and an exhortation to keep better company.

It was not many days till a caddy came with a large parcel to Mrs Logan's house, which parcel he delivered into her hands, accompanied with a sealed note, containing an inventory of the articles, and a request to know if the unfortunate Arabella Calvert would be admitted to converse with Mrs Logan.

Never was there a woman so much overjoyed as Mrs Logan was at this message. She returned compliments: Would be most happy to see her: and no article of the parcel should be looked at, or touched, till her arrival. It was not long till she made her

appearance, dressed in somewhat better style than she had yet
seen her; delivered her over the greater part of the stolen property, besides many things that either never had belonged to Mrs
Logan, or that she thought proper to deny, in order that the
other might retain them.

The tale that she told of her misfortunes was of the most
distressing nature, and was enough to stir up all the tender, as
well as abhorrent feelings in the bosom of humanity. She had
suffered every deprivation in fame, fortune, and person. She
had been imprisoned; she had been scourged, and branded as
an impostor; and all on account of her resolute and unmoving
fidelity and truth to *several* of the very worst of men, every one
of whom had abandoned her to utter destitution and shame.
But this story we cannot enter on at present, as it would perhaps
mar the thread of our story, as much as it did the anxious
anticipations of Mrs Logan, who sat pining and longing for the
relation that follows.

'Now I know, Mrs Logan, that you are expecting a detail of
the circumstances relating to the death of Mr George Colwan;
and in gratitude for your unbounded generosity, and disin-
terestedness, I will tell you all that I know, although, for causes
that will appear obvious to you, I had determined never in life
to divulge one circumstance of it. I can tell you, however, that
you will be disappointed, for it was not the gentleman who was
accused, found guilty, and would have suffered the utmost
penalty of the law, had he not made his escape. *It was not he*,
I say, who slew your young master, nor had he any hand in it.'

'I never thought he had. But, pray, how do you come to
know this?'

'You shall hear. I had been abandoned in York, by an artful
and consummate fiend; found guilty of being art and part concerned in the most heinous atrocities, and, in his place, suffered
what I yet shudder to think of. I was banished the county –
begged my way with my poor outcast child up to Edinburgh,
and was there obliged, for the second time in my life, to betake
myself to the most degrading of all means to support two
wretched lives. I hired a dress, and betook me, shivering, to the
High Street, too well aware that my form and appearance would

soon draw me suitors enow at that throng and intemperate
time of the parliament. On my very first stepping out to the
street, a party of young gentlemen was passing. I heard by the
noise they made, and the tenor of their speech, that they were
more than mellow, and so I resolved to keep near them, in
order, if possible, to make some of them my prey. But just as
one of them began to eye me, I was rudely thrust into a narrow
close by one of the guardsmen. I had heard to what house the
party was bound, for the men were talking exceedingly loud,
and making no secret of it: so I hasted down the close, and
round below to the one where their rendezvous was to be; but
I was too late, they were all housed and the door bolted. I
resolved to wait, thinking they could not all stay long; but I
was perishing with famine, and was like to fall down. The moon
shone as bright as day, and I perceived, by a sign at the bottom
of the close, that there was a small tavern of a certain description
up two stairs there. I went up and called, telling the mistress of
the house my plan. She approved of it mainly, and offered me
her best apartment, provided I could get one of these noble
mates to accompany me. She abused Lucky Sudds, as she called
her, at the inn where the party was, envying her huge profits,
no doubt, and giving me afterward something to drink, for
which I really felt exceedingly grateful in my need. I stepped
down stairs in order to be on the alert. The moment that I
reached the ground, the door of Lucky Sudds' house opened
and shut, and down came the Honourable Thomas Drummond,
with hasty and impassioned strides, his sword rattling at his
heel. I accosted him in a soft and soothing tone. He was taken
with my address; for he instantly stood still and gazed intently
at me, then at the place, and then at me again. I beckoned him
to follow me, which he did without farther ceremony, and we
soon found ourselves together in the best room of a house
where every thing was wretched. He still looked about him,
and at me; but all this while he had never spoken a word. At
length, I asked if he would take any refreshment? 'If you please,'
said he. I asked what he would have? but he only answered,
'Whatever you choose, madam.' If he was taken with my
address, I was much more taken with his; for he was a complete

gentleman, and a gentleman will ever act as one. At length, he began as follows:

'"I am utterly at a loss to account for this adventure, madam. It seems to me like enchantment, and I can hardly believe my senses. An English lady, I judge, and one, who from her manner and address should belong to the first class of society, in such a place as this, is indeed matter of wonder to me. At the foot of a close in Edinburgh! and at this time of the night! Surely it must have been no common reverse of fortune that reduced you to this?" I wept, or pretended to do so; on which he added, "Pray, madam, take heart. Tell me what has befallen you; and if I can do any thing for you, in restoring you to your country or your friends, you shall command my interest."

'I had great need of a friend then, and I thought now was the time to secure one. So I began and told him the moving tale I have told you. But I soon perceived that I had kept by the naked truth too unvarnishedly, and thereby quite overshot my mark. When he learned that he was sitting in a wretched corner of an irregular house, with a felon, who had so lately been scourged, and banished as a swindler and impostor, his modest nature took the alarm, and he was shocked, instead of being moved with pity. His eye fixed on some of the casual stripes on my arm, and from that moment he became restless and impatient to be gone. I tried some gentle arts to retain him, but in vain; so, after paying both the landlady and me for pleasures he had neither tasted nor asked, he took his leave.

'I showed him down stairs; and just as he turned the corner of the next land, a man came rushing violently by him; exchanged looks with him, and came running up to me. He appeared in great agitation, and was quite out of breath; and, taking my hand in his, we ran up stairs together without speaking, and were instantly in the apartment I had left, where a stoup of wine still stood untasted. "Ah, this is fortunate!" said my new spark, and helped himself. In the mean while, as our apartment was a corner one, and looked both east and north, I ran to the easter casement to look after Drummond. Now, note me well: I saw him going eastward in his tartans and bonnet, and the gilded hilt of his claymore glittering in the moon; and, at the very same time, I saw two men, the one in black, and the other likewise in tartans, coming toward the steps from the opposite bank, by the foot of the loch; and I saw Drummond and they eying each other as they passed. I kept view of *him* till he vanished towards Leith Wynd, and by that time the two strangers had come close up under our window. This is what I wish you to pay particular attention to. I had only lost sight of Drummond (who had given me his name and address) for the short space of time that we took in running up one pair of short stairs; and during that space he had halted a moment, for, when I got my eye on him again, he had not crossed the mouth of the next entry, nor proceeded above ten or twelve paces, and, *at the same time*, I saw the two men coming down the bank on the opposite side of the loch, at about three hundred paces distance. Both he and they were distinctly in my view, and never within speech of each other, until he vanished into one of the wynds leading toward the bottom of the High Street, at which precise time the two strangers came below my window; so that it was quite clear he neither could be one of them, nor have any communication with them.

'Yet, mark me again; for of all things I have ever seen, this was the most singular. When I looked down at the two strangers, *one of them was extremely like Drummond*. So like was he, that there was not one item in dress, form, feature, nor voice, by which I could distinguish the one from the other. I was certain it was not he, because I had seen the one going and the other approaching at the same time, and my impression at the moment was, that I looked upon some spirit, or demon, in his likeness. I felt a chillness creep all round my heart, my knees tottered, and, withdrawing my head from the open casement that lay in the dark shade, I said to the man who was with me, 'Good God, what is this!'

'"What is it, my dear?" said he, as much alarmed as I was.

'"As I live, there stands an apparition!" said I.

'He was not so much afraid when he heard me say so, and peeping cautiously out, he looked and listened a-while, and then drawing back, he said in a whisper, "They are both living men, and one of them is he I passed at the corner."

'"That he is not," said I, emphatically. "To that I will make oath."

'He smiled and shook his head, and then added, "I never then saw a man before, whom I could not know again, particularly if he was the very last I had seen. But what matters it whether it be or not? As it is no concern of ours, let us sit down and enjoy ourselves."

'"But it *does* matter a very great deal with me, sir," said I. "Bless me, my head is giddy – my breath quite gone, and I feel as if I were surrounded with fiends. Who are you, sir?"

'"You shall know that ere we two part, my love," said he: "I cannot conceive why the return of this young gentleman to the spot he so lately left, should discompose you? I suppose he got a glance of you as he passed, and has returned to look after you, and that is the whole secret of the matter."

'"If you will be so civil as to walk out and join him then, it will oblige me hugely," said I, "for I never in my life experienced such boding apprehensions of evil company. I cannot conceive how you should come up here without asking my permission? Will it please you to begone, sir?" I was within an ace of prevailing. He took out his purse – I need not say more – I was bribed to let him remain. Ah, had I kept by my frail resolution of dismissing him at that moment, what a world of shame and misery had been evited! But that, though uppermost still in my mind, has nothing ado here.

'When I peeped over again, the two men were disputing in a whisper, the one of them in violent agitation and terror, and the other upbraiding him, and urging him on to some desperate act. At length I heard the young man in the Highland garb say indignantly, "Hush, recreant! It is God's work which you are commissioned to execute, and it must be done. But if you positively decline it, I will do it myself, and do you beware of the consequences."

'"Oh, I will, I will!" cried the other in black clothes, in a wretched beseeching tone. "You shall instruct me in this, as in all things else."

'I thought all this while I was closely concealed from them, and wondered not a little when he in tartans gave me a sly nod,

as much as to say, "What do you think of this?" or, "Take note
of what you see," or something to that effect, from which I
perceived, that whatever he was about, he did not wish it to be
kept a secret. For all that, I was impressed with a terror and
anxiety that I could not overcome, but it only made me mark
every event with the more intense curiosity. The Highlander,
whom I still could not help regarding as the evil genius of
Thomas Drummond, performed every action, as with the quick-
ness of thought. He concealed the youth in black in a narrow
entry, a little to the westward of my windows, and as he was
leading him across the moonlight green by the shoulder, I perceived, for the first time, that both of them were armed with
rapiers. He pushed him without resistance into the dark shaded
close, made another signal to me, and hasted up the close to
Lucky Sudds' door. The city and the morning were so still, that
I heard every word that was uttered, on putting my head out a
little. He knocked at the door sharply, and after waiting a
considerable space, the bolt was drawn, and the door, as I
conceived, edged up as far as the massy chain would let it. "Is
young Dalcastle still in the house?" said he sharply.

'I did not hear the answer, but I heard him say, shortly after,
"If he is, pray tell him to speak with me for a few minutes." He
then withdrew from the door, and came slowly down the close,
in a lingering manner, looking oft behind him. Dalcastle came
out; advanced a few steps after him, and then stood still, as if
hesitating whether or not he should call out a friend to accompany him; and that instant the door behind him was closed,
chained, and the iron bolt drawn; on hearing of which, he
followed his adversary without farther hesitation. As he passed
below my window, I heard him say, "I beseech you, Tom, let
us do nothing in this matter rashly"; but I could not hear the
answer of the other, who had turned the corner.

'I roused up my drowsy companion, who was leaning on the
bed, and we both looked together from the north window. We
were in the shade, but the moon shone full on the two young
gentlemen. Young Dalcastle was visibly the worse of liquor,
and his back being turned toward us, he said something to

the other which I could not make out, although he spoke a
considerable time, and, from his tones and gestures, appeared
to be reasoning. When he had done, the tall young man in the
tartans drew his sword, and his face being straight to us, we
heard him say distinctly, "No more words about it, George, if
you please; but if you be a man, as I take you to be, draw your
sword, and let us settle it here."

'Dalcastle drew his sword, without changing his attitude; but
he spoke with more warmth, for we heard his words, "Think
you that I fear you, Tom? Be assured, sir, I would not fear ten
of the best of your name, at each other's backs: all that I want
is to have friends with us to see fair play, for if you close with
me, you are a dead man."

'The other stormed at these words. "You are a braggart, sir,"
cried he, "a wretch – a blot on the cheek of nature – a blight
on the Christian world – a reprobate – I'll have your soul, sir –
You must play at tennis, and put down elect brethren in another
world to-morrow." As he said this, he brandished his rapier,
exciting Dalcastle to offence. He gained his point: The latter,
who had previously drawn, advanced in upon his vapouring
and licentious antagonist, and a fierce combat ensued. My
companion was delighted beyond measure, and I could not
keep him from exclaiming, loud enough to have been heard,
"that's grand! that's excellent!" For me, my heart quaked like
an aspen. Young Dalcastle either had a decided advantage over
his adversary, or else the other thought proper to let him have
it; for he shifted, and wore,[26] and flitted from Dalcastle's thrusts
like a shadow, uttering ofttimes a sarcastic laugh, that seemed
to provoke the other beyond all bearing. At one time, he would
spring away to a great distance, then advance again on young
Dalcastle with the swiftness of lightning. But that young hero
always stood his ground, and repelled the attack: he never gave
way, although they fought nearly twice round the bleaching
green, which you know is not a very small one. At length they
fought close up to the mouth of the dark entry, where the fellow
in black stood all this while concealed, and then the combatant
in tartans closed with his antagonist, or pretended to do so; but

the moment they began to grapple, he wheeled about, turning Colwan's back towards the entry, and then cried out, "Ah, hell has it! My friend, my friend!"

'That moment the fellow in black rushed from his cover with his drawn rapier, and gave the brave young Dalcastle two deadly wounds in the back, as quick as arm could thrust, both of which I thought pierced through his body. He fell, and rolling himself on his back, he perceived who it was that had slain him thus foully, and said, with a dying emphasis, which I never heard equalled, "Oh, dog of hell, is it you who has done this!"

'He articulated some more, which I could not hear for other sounds; for the moment that the man in black inflicted the deadly wound, my companion called out, "That's unfair, you rip! That's damnable! to strike a brave fellow behind! One at a time, you cowards! &c." to all which the unnatural fiend in the tartans answered with a loud exulting laugh; and then, taking the poor paralysed murderer by the bow of the arm, he hurried him into the dark entry once more, where I lost sight of them for ever.'

Before this time, Mrs Logan had risen up; and when the narrator had finished, she was standing with her arms stretched upward at their full length, and her visage turned down, on which were pourtrayed the lines of the most absolute horror. 'The dark suspicions of my late benefactor have been just, and his last prediction is fulfilled,' cried she. 'The murderer of the accomplished George Colwan has been his own brother, set on, there is little doubt, by her who bare them both, and her directing angel, the self-justified bigot. Aye, and yonder they sit, enjoying the luxuries so dearly purchased, with perfect impunity! If the Almighty do not hurl them down, blasted with shame and confusion, there is no hope of retribution in this life. And, by his might, I will be the agent to accomplish it! Why did the man not pursue the foul murderers? Why did he not raise the alarm, and call the watch?'

'He? The wretch! He durst not move from the shelter he had obtained – no, not for the soul of him. He was pursued for his life, at the moment when he first flew into my arms. But I did not know it; no, I did not *then* know him. May the curse of heaven, and the blight of hell, settle on the detestable wretch! He pursue for the sake of justice! No; his efforts have all been for evil, but never for good. But *I* raised the alarm; miserable and degraded as I was, I pursued and raised the watch myself. Have you not heard the name of Bell Calvert coupled with that hideous and mysterious affair?'

'Yes, I have. In secret often I have heard it. But how came it that you could never be found? How came it that you never appeared in defence of the Honourable Thomas Drummond; you, the only person who could have justified him?'

'I could not, for I then fell under the power and guidance of a wretch, who durst not for the soul of him be brought forward in the affair. And what was worse, his evidence would have overborne mine, for he would have sworn, that the man who called out and fought Colwan, was the same he met leaving my apartment, and there was an end of it. And moreover, it is well known, that this same man, this wretch of whom I speak, never mistook one man for another in his life, which makes the mystery of the likeness between this incendiary and Drummond the more extraordinary.'

'If it was Drummond, after all that you have asserted, then are my surmises still wrong.'

'There is nothing of which I can be more certain, than that it was not Drummond. We have nothing on earth but our senses to depend upon: if these deceive us, what are we to do. I own I cannot account for it; nor ever shall be able to account for it as long as I live.'

'Could you know the man in black, if you saw him again?'

'I think I could, if I saw him walk or run: his gait was very particular: He walked as if he had been flat-soled, and his legs made of steel, without any joints in his feet or ancles.'

'The very same! The very same! The very same! Pray will you take a few days' journey into the country with me, to look at such a man?'

'You have preserved my life, and for you I will do any thing. I will accompany you with pleasure: and I think I can say that I will know him, for his form left an impression on my heart not soon to be effaced. But of this I am sure, that my unworthy

companion *will* recognize him, and that he will be able to swear
to his identity every day as long as he lives.'

'Where is he? Where is he? O! Mrs Calvert, where is he?'

'Where is he? He is the wretch whom you heard giving me
up to the death; who, after experiencing every mark of affection
that a poor ruined being could confer, and after committing
a thousand atrocities of which she was ignorant, became an
informer to save his diabolical life, and attempted to offer up
mine as a sacrifice for all. We will go by ourselves first, and I
will tell you if it is necessary to send any farther.'

The two dames, the very next morning, dressed themselves
like country goodwives; and, hiring two stout ponies furnished
with pillions, they took their journey westward, and the second
evening after leaving Edinburgh they arrived at the village about
two miles below Dalcastle, where they alighted. But Mrs Logan,
being anxious to have Mrs Calvert's judgment, without either
hint or preparation, took care not to mention that they were so
near to the end of their journey. In conformity with this plan,
she said, after they had sat a while, 'Heigh-ho, but I am weary!
What suppose we should rest a day here before we proceed
farther on our journey?'

Mrs Calvert was leaning on the casement, and looking out
when her companion addressed these words to her, and by far
too much engaged to return any answer, for her eyes were
riveted on two young men who approached from the farther
end of the village; and at length, turning round her head, she
said, with the most intense interest, 'Proceed farther on our
journey, did you say? That we need not do; for, as I live, here
comes the very man!'

Mrs Logan ran to the window, and behold, there was indeed
Robert Wringhim Colwan (now the Laird of Dalcastle) coming
forward almost below their window, walking arm in arm with
another young man; and as the two passed, the latter looked
up and made a sly signal to the two dames, biting his lip,
winking with his left eye, and nodding his head. Mrs Calvert
was astonished at this recognizance, the young man's former
companion having made exactly such another signal on the
night of the duel, by the light of the moon; and it struck her,

moreover, that she had somewhere seen this young man's face before. She looked after him, and he winked over his shoulder to her; but she was prevented from returning his salute by her companion, who uttered a loud cry, between a groan and shriek, and fell down on the floor with a rumble like a wall that had suddenly been undermined. She had fainted quite away, and required all her companion's attention during the remainder of the evening, for she had scarcely ever well recovered out of one fit before she fell into another, and in the short intervals she raved like one distracted, or in a dream. After falling into a sound sleep by night, she recovered her equanimity, and the two began to converse seriously on what they had seen. Mrs Calvert averred that the young man who passed next to the window, *was* the very man who stabbed George Colwan in the back, and she said she was willing to take her oath on it at any time when required, and was certain if the wretch Ridsley saw him, that he would make oath to the same purport, for that his walk was so peculiar, no one of common discernment could mistake it.

Mrs Logan was in great agitation, and said, 'It is what I have suspected all along, and what I am sure my late master and benefactor was persuaded of, and the horror of such an idea cut short his days. That wretch, Mrs Calvert, is the born brother of him he murdered, sons of the same mother they were, whether or not of the same father, the Lord only knows. But, O Mrs Calvert, that is not the main thing that has discomposed me, and shaken my nerves to pieces at this time. Who do you think the young man was who walked in his company to-night?'

'I cannot for my life recollect, but am convinced I have seen the same fine form and face before.'

'And did not he seem to know us, Mrs Calvert? You who are able to recollect things as they happened, did he not seem to recollect us, and make signs to that effect?'

'He did, indeed, and apparently with great good humour.'

'O, Mrs Calvert, hold me, else I shall fall into hysterics again! Who is he? Who is he? Tell me who you suppose he is, for I cannot say my own thought.'

'On my life, I cannot remember.'

'Did you note the appearance of the young gentleman you saw slain that night? Do you recollect aught of the appearance of my young master, George Colwan?'

Mrs Calvert sat silent, and stared the other mildly in the face. Their looks encountered, and there was an unearthly amazement that gleamed from each, which, meeting together, caught real fire, and returned the flame to their heated imaginations, till the two associates became like two statues, with their hands spread, their eyes fixed, and their chops fallen down upon their bosoms. An old woman who kept the lodging-house, having been called in before when Mrs Logan was faintish, chanced to enter at this crisis with some cordial, and, seeing the state of her lodgers, she caught the infection, and fell into the same rigid and statue-like appearance. No scene more striking was ever exhibited; and if Mrs Calvert had not resumed strength of mind to speak, and break the spell, it is impossible to say how long it might have continued. 'It is he, I believe,' said she, uttering the words as it were inwardly. 'It can be none other but he. But, no, it is impossible! I saw him stabbed through and through the heart; I saw him roll backward on the green in his own blood, utter his last words, and groan away his soul. Yet, if it is not he, who can it be?'

'It *is* he!' cried Mrs Logan, hysterically.

'Yes, yes, it *is* he!' cried the landlady, in unison.

'It is who?' said Mrs Calvert; 'whom do you mean, mistress?'

'Oh, I don't know! I don't know! I was affrighted.'

'Hold your peace then till you recover your senses, and tell me, if you can, who that young gentleman is, who keeps company with the new Laird of Dalcastle?'

'Oh, it is he! it is he!' screamed Mrs Logan, wringing her hands.

'Oh, it is he! it is he!' cried the landlady, wringing hers.

Mrs Calvert turned the latter gently and civilly out of the apartment, observing that there seemed to be some infection in the air of the room, and she would be wise for herself to keep out of it.

The two dames had a restless and hideous night. Sleep came not to their relief; for their conversation was wholly about the dead, who seemed to be alive, and their minds were wandering and groping in a chaos of mystery. 'Did you attend to his corpse, and know that he positively died and was buried?' said Mrs Calvert.

'O, yes, from the moment that his fair but mangled corpse was brought home, I attended it till that when it was screwed in the coffin. I washed the long stripes of blood from his lifeless form, on both sides of the body – I bathed the livid wound that passed through his generous and gentle heart. There was one through the flesh of his left side too, which had bled most outwardly of them all. I bathed them, and bandaged them up with wax and perfumed ointment, but still the blood oozed through all, so that when he was laid in the coffin he was like one newly murdered. My brave, my generous young master! he was always as a son to me, and no son was ever more kind or more respectful to a mother. But he was butchered – he was cut off from the earth ere he had well reached to manhood – most barbarously and unfairly slain. And how is it, how can it be, that we again see him here, walking arm in arm with his murderer?'

'The thing cannot be, Mrs Logan. It is a phantasy of our disturbed imaginations, therefore let us compose ourselves till we investigate this matter farther.'

'It cannot be in nature, that is quite clear,' said Mrs Logan; 'yet how it should be that I should *think* so – I who knew and nursed him from his infancy – there lies the paradox. As you said once before, we have nothing but our senses to depend on, and if you and I believe that we see a person, why, we do see him. Whose word, or whose reasoning can convince us against our own senses? We will disguise ourselves, as poor women selling a few country wares, and we will go up to the Hall, and see what is to see, and hear what we can hear, for this is a weighty business in which we are engaged, namely, to turn the vengeance of the law upon an unnatural monster; and we will farther learn, if we can, who this is that accompanies him.'

Mrs Calvert acquiesced, and the two dames took their way to Dalcastle, with baskets well furnished with trifles. They did not take the common path from the village, but went about, and approached the mansion by a different way. But it seemed

as if some overruling power ordered it, that they should miss
no chance of attaining the information they wanted. For ere
ever they came within half a mile of Dalcastle, they perceived
the two youths coming, as to meet them, on the same path. The
road leading from Dalcastle toward the north-east, as all the
country knows, goes along a dark bank of brushwood called
the Bogle-heuch. It was by this track that the two women were
going; and when they perceived the two gentlemen meeting
them, they turned back, and the moment they were out of their
sight, they concealed themselves in a thicket close by the road.
They did this because Mrs Logan was terrified for being discovered, and because they wished to reconnoitre without being
seen. Mrs Calvert now charged her, whatever she saw, or
whatever she heard, to put on a resolution, and support it, for
if she fainted there and was discovered, what was to become
of her!

The two young men came on, in earnest and vehement conversation; but the subject they were on was a terrible one, and
hardly fit to be repeated in the face of a Christian community.
Wringhim was disputing the boundlessness of the true Christian's freedom, and expressing doubts, that, chosen as he knew
he was from all eternity, still it might be possible for him to
commit acts that would exclude him from the limits of the
covenant. The other argued, with mighty fluency, that the thing
was utterly impossible, and altogether inconsistent with eternal
predestination. The arguments of the latter prevailed, and the
laird was driven to sullen silence. But, to the women's utter
surprise, as the conquering disputant passed, he made a signal
of recognizance through the brambles to them, as formerly, and
that he might expose his associate fully, and in his true colours,
he led him backward and forward by the women more than
twenty times, making him to confess both the crimes that he
had done, and those he had in contemplation. At length he said
to him, 'Assuredly I saw some strolling vagrant women on this
walk, my dear friend: I wish we could find them, for there is
little doubt that they are concealed here in your woods.'

'I wish we *could* find them,' answered Wringhim; 'we would
have fine sport maltreating and abusing them.'

'That we should, that we should! Now tell me, Robert, if you found a malevolent woman, the latent enemy of your prosperity, lurking in these woods to betray you, what would you inflict on her?'

'I would tear her to pieces with my dogs, and feed them with her flesh. O, my dear friend, there is an old strumpet who lived with my unnatural father, whom I hold in such utter detestation, that I stand constantly in dread of her, and would sacrifice the half of my estate to shed her blood!'

'What will you give me if I will put her in your power, and give you a fair and genuine excuse for making away with her; one for which you shall answer at any bar, here or hereafter?'

'I should like to see the vile hag put down. She is in possession of the family plate, that is mine by right, as well as a thousand valuable relics, and great riches besides, all of which the old profligate gifted shamefully away. And it is said, besides all these, that she has sworn my destruction.'

'She has, she has. But I see not how she can accomplish that, seeing the deed was done so suddenly, and in the silence of the night?'

'It was said there were some on-lookers. But where shall we find that disgraceful Miss Logan?'

'I will show you her by and by. But will you then consent to the other meritorious deed? Come, be a man, and throw away scruples.'

'If you can convince me that the promise is binding, I will.'

'Then step this way, till I give you a piece of information.'

They walked a little way out of hearing, but went not out of sight; therefore, though the women were in a terrible quandary, they durst not stir, for they had some hopes that this extraordinary person was on a mission of the same sort with themselves, knew of them, and was going to make use of their testimony. Mrs Logan was several times on the point of falling into a swoon, so much did the appearance of the young man impress her, until her associate covered her face that she might listen without embarrassment. But this latter dialogue aroused different feelings within them; namely, those arising from imminent personal danger. They saw his waggish associate point out the

place of their concealment to Wringhim, who came toward
them, out of curiosity to see what his friend meant by what he
believed to be a joke, manifestly without crediting it in the least
degree. When he came running away, the other called after him,
'If she is too hard for you, call to me.' As he said this, he
hasted out of sight, in the contrary direction, apparently much
delighted with the joke.

Wringhim came rushing through the thicket impetuously, to
the very spot where Mrs Logan lay squatted. She held the
wrapping close about her head, but he tore it off and discovered
her. 'The curse of God be on thee!' said he: 'What fiend has
brought thee here, and for what purpose art thou come? But,
whatever has brought thee, *I have thee!*' and with that he seized
her by the throat. The two women, when they heard what
jeopardy they were in from such a wretch, had squatted among
the underwood at a small distance from each other, so that he
had never observed Mrs Calvert; but no sooner had he seized
her benefactor, than, like a wild cat, she sprung out of the
thicket, and had both her hands fixed at his throat, one of them
twisted in his stock, in a twinkling. She brought him back-over
among the brushwood, and the two, fixing on him like two
harpies, mastered him with ease. Then indeed was he wofully
beset. He deemed for a while that his friend was at his back,
and turning his bloodshot eyes toward the path, he attempted
to call; but there was no friend there, and the women cut short
his cries by another twist of his stock. 'Now, gallant and rightful
Laird of Dalcastle,' said Mrs Logan, 'what hast thou to say for
thyself? Lay thy account to dree the weird thou hast so well
earned. Now shalt thou suffer due penance for murdering thy
brave and only brother.'

'Thou liest, thou hag of the pit! I touched not my brother's
life.'

'I saw thee do it with these eyes that now look thee in the
face; ay, when his back was to thee too, and while he was hotly
engaged with thy friend,' said Mrs Calvert.

'I heard thee confess it again and again this same hour,' said
Mrs Logan.

'Ay, and so did I,' said her companion. 'Murder will out,

though the Almighty should lend hearing to the ears of the willow, and speech to the seven tongues of the woodriff.'

'You are liars, and witches!' said he, foaming with rage, 'and creatures fitted from the beginning for eternal destruction. I'll have your bones and your blood sacrificed on your cursed altars! O, Gil-Martin! Gil-Martin![27] where art thou now? Here, here is the proper food for blessed vengeance! Hilloa!'

There was no friend, no Gil-Martin there to hear or assist him: he was in the two women's mercy, but they used it with moderation. They mocked, they tormented, and they threatened him; but, finally, after putting him in great terror, they bound his hands behind his back, and his feet fast with long straps of garters which they chanced to have in their baskets, to prevent him from pursuing them till they were out of his reach. As they left him, which they did in the middle of the path, Mrs Calvert said, 'We could easily put an end to thy sinful life, but our hands shall be free of thy blood. Nevertheless thou art still in our power, and the vengeance of thy country shall overtake thee, thou mean and cowardly murderer, ay, and that more suddenly than thou art aware!'

The women posted to Edinburgh; and as they put themselves under the protection of an English merchant, who was journeying thither with twenty horses loaden, and armed servants, so they had scarcely any conversation on the road. When they arrived at Mrs Logan's house, then they spoke of what they had seen and heard, and agreed that they had sufficient proof to condemn young Wringhim, who they thought richly deserved the severest doom of the law.

'I never in my life saw any human being,' said Mrs Calvert, 'whom I thought so like a fiend. If a demon could inherit flesh and blood, that youth is precisely such a being as I could conceive that demon to be. The depth and the malignity of his eye is hideous. His breath is like the airs from a charnel house, and his flesh seems fading from his bones, as if the worm that never dies were gnawing it away already.'

'He was always repulsive, and every way repulsive,' said the other; 'but he is now indeed altered greatly to the worse. While we were hand-fasting him, I felt his body to be feeble and emaciated; but yet I know him to be so puffed up with spiritual pride, that I believe he weens every one of his actions justified before God, and instead of having stings of conscience for these, he takes great merit to himself in having effected them. Still my thoughts are less about him than the extraordinary being who accompanies him. He does every thing with so much ease and indifference, so much velocity and effect, that all bespeak him an adept in wickedness. The likeness to my late hapless young master is so striking, that I can hardly believe it to be a chance model; and I think he imitates him in every thing, for some purpose, or some effect on his sinful associate. Do you know that he is so like in every lineament, look, and gesture, that, against the clearest light of reason, I cannot in my mind separate the one from the other, and have a certain indefinable impression on my mind, that they are one and the same being, or that the one was a prototype of the other.'

'If there is an earthly crime,' said Mrs Calvert, 'for the due punishment of which the Almighty may be supposed to subvert the order of nature, it is fratricide. But tell me, dear friend, did you remark to what the subtile and hellish villain was endeavouring to prompt the assassin?'

'No, I could not comprehend it. My senses were altogether so bewildered, that I thought they had combined to deceive me, and I gave them no credit.'

'Then hear me: I am almost certain he was using every persuasion to induce him to make away with his mother; and I likewise conceive that I heard the incendiary give his consent!'

'This is dreadful. Let us speak and think no more about it, till we see the issue. In the meantime, let us do that which is our bounden duty – go and divulge all that we know relating to this foul murder.'

Accordingly the two women went to Sir Thomas Wallace of Craigie, the Lord Justice Clerk (who was, I think, either uncle or grandfather to young Drummond, who was outlawed, and obliged to fly his country on account of Colwan's death), and to that gentleman they related every circumstance of what they had seen and heard. He examined Calvert very minutely, and seemed deeply interested in her evidence – said he knew she was relating the truth, and in testimony of it, brought a letter of young Drummond's from his desk, wherein that young gentleman, after protesting his innocence in the most forcible terms, confessed having been with such a woman in such a house, after leaving the company of his friends; and that on going home, Sir Thomas's servant had let him in, in the dark, and from these circumstances he found it impossible to prove an *alibi*. He begged of his relative, if ever an opportunity offered, to do his endeavour to clear up that mystery, and remove the horrid stigma from his name in his country, and among his kin, of having stabbed a friend behind his back.

Lord Craigie, therefore, directed the two women to the proper authorities, and after hearing their evidence there, it was judged proper to apprehend the present Laird of Dalcastle, and bring him to his trial. But before that, they sent the prisoner in the tolbooth, he who had seen the whole transaction along with Mrs Calvert, to take a view of Wringhim privately; and his discrimination being so well known as to be proverbial all over the land, they determined secretly to be ruled by his report. They accordingly sent him on a pretended mission of legality to Dalcastle, with orders to see and speak with the proprietor, without giving him a hint what was wanted. On his return, they examined him, and he told them that he found all things at the place in utter confusion and dismay; that the lady of the place was missing, and could not be found, dead or alive. On being asked if he had ever seen the proprietor before, he looked astounded, and unwilling to answer. But it came out that he had; and that he had once seen him kill a man on such a spot at such an hour.

Officers were then despatched, without delay, to apprehend the monster, and bring him to justice. On these going to the mansion, and inquiring for him, they were told he was at home; on which they stationed guards, and searched all the premises, but he was not to be found. It was in vain that they overturned beds, raised floors, and broke open closets: Robert Wringhim Colwan was lost once and for ever. His mother also was lost; and strong suspicions attached to some of the farmers and house servants, to whom she was obnoxious, relating to her disappearance. The Honourable Thomas Drummond became a distinguished officer in the Austrian service, and died in the memorable year for Scotland, 1715; and this is all with which history, justiciary records, and tradition, furnish me relating to these matters.

I have now the pleasure of presenting my readers with an original document of a most singular nature, and preserved for their perusal in a still more singular manner. I offer no remarks on it, and make as few additions to it, leaving every one to judge for himself. We have heard much of the rage of fanaticism in former days, but nothing to this.

PRIVATE MEMOIRS AND
CONFESSIONS OF A SINNER

WRITTEN BY HIMSELF

PRIVATE MEMOIRS AND CONFESSIONS OF A SINNER

My life has been a life of trouble and turmoil; of change and vicissitude; of anger and exultation; of sorrow and of vengeance. My sorrows have all been for a slighted gospel, and my vengence has been wreaked on its adversaries. Therefore, in the might of heaven I will sit down and write: I will let the wicked of this world know what I have done in the faith of the promises, and justification by grace, that they may read and tremble, and bless their gods of silver and of gold, that the minister of heaven was removed from their sphere before their blood was mingled with their sacrifices.

I was born an outcast in the world, in which I was destined to act so conspicuous a part. My mother was a burning and a shining light, in the community of Scottish worthies,[1] and in the days of her virginity had suffered much in the persecution of the saints. But it so pleased Heaven, that, as a trial of her faith, she was married to one of the wicked; a man all over spotted with the leprosy of sin. As well might they have conjoined fire and water together, in hopes that they would consort and amalgamate, as purity and corruption: She fled from his embraces the first night after their marriage, and from that time forth, his iniquities so galled her upright heart, that she quitted his society altogether, keeping her own apartments in the same house with him.

I was the second son of this unhappy marriage, and, long ere ever I was born, my father according to the flesh disclaimed all relation or connection with me, and all interest in me, save what the law compelled him to take, which was to grant me a scanty maintenance; and had it not been for a faithful minister of the gospel, my mother's early instructor, I should have remained an outcast from the church visible. He took pity on me, admitting me not only into that, but into the bosom of his own household and ministry also, and to him am I indebted, under Heaven, for the high conceptions and glorious discernment between good and evil, right and wrong, which I attained even at an early age. It was he who directed my studies aright, both in the learning of the ancient fathers, and the doctrines of the reformed church, and designed me for his assistant and successor in the holy office. I missed no opportunity of perfecting myself particularly in all the minute points of theology in which my reverend father and mother took great delight; but at length I acquired so much skill, that I astonished my teachers, and made them gaze at one another. I remember that it was the custom, in my patron's house, to ask the questions of the Single Catechism[2] round every Sabbath night. He asked the first, my mother the second, and so on, every one saying the question asked, and then asking the next. It fell to my mother to ask Effectual Calling at me. I said the answer with propriety and emphasis. 'Now, madam,' added I, 'my question to you is, What is *In*effectual Calling?'

'Ineffectual Calling? There is no such thing, Robert,' said she.

'But there is, madam,' said I; 'and that answer proves how much you say these fundamental precepts by rote, and without any consideration. Ineffectual Calling is, *the outward call of the gospel* without any effect on the hearts of unregenerated and impenitent sinners. Have not all these the same calls, warnings, doctrines, and reproofs, that we have? and is not this Ineffectual Calling? Has not Ardinferry the same? Has not Patrick M'Lure the same? *Has not the Laird of Dalcastle and his reprobate heir* the same? And will any tell me, that *this is not In*effectual Calling?'

'What a wonderful boy he is!' said my mother.

'I'm feared he turn out to be a conceited gowk,' said old Barnet, the minister's man.

'No,' said my pastor, and *father* (as I shall henceforth denominate him). 'No, Barnet, he *is* a wonderful boy; and no marvel, for I have prayed for these talents to be bestowed on him from his infancy: and do you think that Heaven would refuse a prayer so disinterested? No, it is impossible. But my dread is, madam,' continued he, turning to my mother, 'that he is yet in the bond of iniquity.'

'God forbid!' said my mother.

'I have struggled with the Almighty long and hard,' continued he; 'but have as yet had no certain token of acceptance in his behalf. I have indeed fought a hard fight, but have been repulsed by him who hath seldom refused my request; although I cited his own words against him, and endeavoured to hold him at his promise, he hath so many turnings in the supremacy of his power, that I have been rejected. How dreadful is it to think of our darling being still without the pale of the covenant!³ But I have vowed a vow, and in that there is hope.'

My heart quaked with terror, when I thought of being still living in a state of reprobation, subjected to the awful issues of death, judgement, and eternal misery, by the slightest accident or casualty, and I set about the duty of prayer myself with the utmost earnestness. I prayed three times every day, and seven times on the Sabbath; but the more frequently and fervently that I prayed, I sinned still the more. About this time, and for a long period afterwards, amounting to several years, I lived in a hopeless and deplorable state of mind; for I said to myself, 'If my name is not written in the book of life from all eternity, it is in vain for me to presume that either vows or prayers of mine, or those of all mankind combined, can ever procure its insertion now.' I had come under many vows, most solemnly taken, every one of which I had broken; and I saw with the intensity of juvenile grief, that there was no hope for me. I went on sinning every hour, and all the while most strenuously warring against sin, and repenting of every one transgression, as soon after the commission of it as I got leisure to think. But O what a wretched state this unregenerated state is, in which every effort after righteousness only aggravates our offences! I found it vanity to contend; for after communing with my heart, the conclusion was as follows: 'If I could repent me of all my sins, and shed tears of blood for them, still have I not a load of original transgression pressing on me, that is enough to crush me to the lowest hell. I may be angry with my first parents for having sinned, but how I shall repent me of their sin, is beyond what I am able to comprehend.'

Still, in those days of depravity and corruption, I had some of those principles implanted in my mind, which were afterward to spring up with such amazing fertility among the heroes of the faith and the promises. In particular, I felt great indignation against all the wicked of this world, and often wished for the means of ridding it of such a noxious burden. I liked John Barnet, my reverend father's serving-man, extremely ill; but, from a supposition that he might be one of the justified, I refrained from doing him any injury. He gave always his word against me, and when we were by ourselves, in the barn or the fields, he rated me with such severity for my faults, that my heart could brook it no longer. He discovered some notorious lies that I had framed, and taxed me with them in such a manner that I could in nowise get off. My cheek burnt with offence, rather than shame; and he, thinking he had got the mastery of me, exulted over me most unmercifully, telling me I was a selfish and conceited blackguard, who made great pretences towards religious devotion to cloak a disposition tainted with deceit, and that it would not much astonish him if I brought myself to the gallows.

I gathered some courage from his over severity, and answered him as follows: 'Who made thee a judge of the actions or dispositions of the Almighty's creatures – thou who art a worm, and no man in his sight? How it befits thee to deal out judgments and anathemas! Hath he not made one vessel to honour, and another to dishonour, as in the case with myself and thee? Hath he not builded his stories in the heavens,[4] and laid the foundations thereof in the earth, and how can a being like thee judge between good and evil, that are both subjected to the workings of his hand; or of the opposing principles in the soul of man, correcting, modifying, and refining one another?'

I said this with that strong display of fervor for which I was remarkable at my years, and expected old Barnet to be utterly confounded; but he only shook his head, and, with the most

provoking grin, said, 'There he goes! sickan sublime and ridiculous sophistry I never heard come out of another mouth but
ane. There needs nae aiths to be sworn afore the session wha is
your father, young goodman. I ne'er, for my part, saw a son
sae like a dad, sin' my een first opened.' With that he went
away, saying, with an ill-natured wince, 'You made to honour
and me to dishonour! Dirty bow-kail thing that thou be'st!'

'I will have the old rascal on the hip for this, if I live,' thought
I. So I went and asked my mother if John was a righteous man?
She could not tell, but supposed he was, and therefore I got no
encouragement from her. I went next to my reverend father,
and inquired his opinion, expecting as little from that quarter.
He knew the elect as it were by instinct, and could have told
you of all those in his own, and some neighbouring parishes,
who were born within the boundaries of the covenant of
promise, and who were not.

'I keep a good deal in company with your servant, old Barnet,
father,' said I.

'You do, boy; you do, I see,' said he.

'I wish I may not keep too much in his company,' said I, 'not
knowing what kind of society I am in; is John a good man,
father?'

'Why, boy, he is but so, so. A morally good man John is, but
very little of the leaven of true righteousness, which is faith,
within. I am afraid old Barnet, with all his stock of morality,
will be a cast-away.'

My heart was greatly cheered by this remark; and I sighed
very deeply, and hung my head to one side. The worthy father
observed me, and inquired the cause? when I answered as
follows: 'How dreadful the thought, that I have been going
daily in company and fellowship with one, whose name is
written on the red-letter side[5] of the book of life; whose body
and soul have been, from all eternity, consigned over to everlasting destruction, and to whom the blood of the atonement can
never, never reach! Father, this is an awful thing, and beyond
my comprehension.'

'While we are in the world, we must mix with the inhabitants
thereof,' said he; 'and the stains which adhere to us by reason

of this admixture, which is unavoidable, shall all be washed away. It is our duty, however, to shun the society of wicked men as much as possible, lest we partake of their sins, and become sharers with them in punishment. John, however, is a morally good man, and may yet get a cast of grace.'[6]

'I always thought him a good man till to-day,' said I, 'when he threw out some reflections on your character, so horrible that I quake to think of the wickedness and malevolence of his heart. He was rating me very impertinently for some supposed fault, which had no being save in his own jealous brain, when I attempted to reason him out of his belief in the spirit of calm Christian argument. But how do you think he answered me? He did so, sir, by twisting his mouth at me, and remarking that such sublime and ridiculous sophistry never came out of another mouth but one (meaning yours), and that no oath before a kirk session was necessary to prove who was my dad, for that he had never seen a son so like a father as I was like mine.'

'He durst not for his soul's salvation, and for his daily bread, which he values much more, say such a word, boy; therefore take care what you assert,' said my reverend father.

'He said these very words, and will not deny them, sir,' said I.

My reverend father turned about in great wrath and indignation, and went away in search of John; but I kept out of the way, and listened at a back window; for John was dressing the plot of ground behind the house; and I hope it was no sin in me that I did rejoice in the dialogue which took place, it being the victory of righteousness over error.

'Well, John, this is a fine day for your delving work.'

'Ey, it's a tolerable day, sir.'

'Are you thankful in your heart, John, for such temporal mercies as these?'

'Aw doubt we're a' ower little thankfu', sir, baith for temporal an' speeritual mercies; but it isna aye the maist thankfu' heart that maks the greatest fraze wi' the tongue.'

'I hope there is nothing personal under that remark, John?'

'Gin the bannet fits ony body's head, they're unco welcome to it, sir, for me.'

'John, I do not approve of these innuendoes. You have an arch malicious manner of vending your aphorisms, which the men of the world are too apt to read the wrong way, for your dark hints are sure to have *one* very bad meaning.'

'Hout na, sir, it's only bad folks that think sae. They find ma bits o' gibes come hame to their hearts wi' a kind o' yerk, an' that gars them wince.'

'That saying is ten times worse than the other, John; it is a manifest insult: it is just telling me to my face, that you think me a bad man.'

'A body canna help his thoughts, sir.'

'No, but a man's thoughts are generally formed from observation. Now I should like to know, even from the mouth of a misbeliever, what part of my conduct warrants such a conclusion?'

'Nae particular pairt, sir; I draw a' my conclusions frae the haill o' a man's character, an' I'm no that aften far wrang.'

'Well, John, and what sort of general character do you suppose mine to be?'

'Yours is a Scripture character, sir, an' I'll prove it.'

'I hope so, John. Well, which of the Scripture characters do you think approximates nearest to my own?'

'Guess, sir, guess; I wish to lead a proof.'

'Why, if it be an Old Testament character, I hope it is Melchizedek,[7] for at all events you cannot deny there is one point of resemblance: I, like him, am a preacher of righteousness. If it be a New Testament character, I suppose you mean the Apostle of the Gentiles, of whom I am an unworthy representative.'

'Na, na, sir, better nor that still, an' fer closer is the resemblance. When ye bring me to the point, I maun speak. Ye are the just Pharisee, sir, that gaed up wi' the poor publican to pray in the Temple; an' ye're acting the very same pairt at this time, an' saying i' your heart, "God, I thank thee that I am not as other men are, an' in nae way like this poor misbelieving unregenerate sinner, John Barnet."'

'I hope I may say so indeed.'

'There now! I tauld you how it was! But, d'ye hear, maister: Here stands the poor sinner, John Barnet, your beadle an' servant-man, wha wadna change chances wi' you in the neist world, nor consciences in this, for ten times a' that you possess – your justification by faith an' awthegither.'

'You are extremely audacious and impertinent, John; but the language of reprobation cannot affect me: I came only to ask you one question, which I desire you to answer candidly. Did you ever say to any one that I was the boy Robert's natural father?'

'Hout na, sir! Ha – ha – ha! Aih, fie na, sir! I durstna say that for my life. I doubt the black stool, an' the sack gown, or maybe the juggs wad hae been my portion had I said sic a thing as that. Hout, hout! Fie, fie! Unco-like doings thae for a Melchizedek or a Saint Paul!'

'John, you are a profane old man, and I desire that you will not presume to break your jests on me. Tell me, dare you say, or dare you think, that I am the natural father of that boy?'

'Ye canna hinder me to think whatever I like, sir, nor can I hinder mysel.'

'But did you ever *say* to any one, that he resembled me, and fathered himself well enough?'

'I hae said mony a time, that he resembled you, sir. Naebody can mistake that.'

'But, John, there are many natural reasons for such likenesses, besides that of consanguinity. They depend much on the thoughts and affections of the mother; and, it is probable, that the mother of this boy, being deserted by her worthless husband, having turned her thoughts on me, as likely to be her protector, may have caused this striking resemblance.'

'Ay, it may be, sir. I coudna say.'

'I have known a lady, John, who was delivered of a blacka-moor child, merely from the circumstance of having got a start by the sudden entrance of her negro servant, and not being able to forget him for several hours.'

'It may be, sir; but I ken this – an I had been the laird, I wadna hae ta'en that story in.'

'So, then, John, you positively think, from a casual likeness, that this boy is my son?'

'Man's thoughts are vanity, sir; they come unasked, an' gang away without a dismissal, an' he canna help them. I'm neither gaun to say that I *think* he's your son, nor that I think he's *no* your son: sae ye needna pose me nae mair about it.'

'Hear then my determination, John: If you do not promise to me, in faith and honour, that you never will say, or insinuate such a thing again in your life, as that that boy is my natural son, I will take the keys of the church from you, and dismiss you my service.'

John pulled out the keys, and dashed them on the gravel at the reverend minister's feet. 'There are the keys o' your kirk, sir! I hae never had muckle mense o' them sin' ye entered the door o't. I hae carried them this three an thretty year, but they hae aye been like to burn a hole i' my pouch sin' ever they were turned for your admittance. Tak them again, an' gie them to wha you will, and muckle gude may he get o' them. Auld John may dee a beggar in a hay barn, or at the back of a dike, but he sall aye be master o' his ain thoughts, an' gie them vent or no, as he likes.'

He left the manse that day, and I rejoiced in the riddance; for I disdained to be kept so much under, by one who was in the bond of iniquity, and of whom there seemed no hope, as he rejoiced in his frowardness, and refused to submit to that faithful teacher, his master.

It was about this time that my reverend father preached a sermon, one sentence of which affected me most disagreeably: It was to the purport, that every unrepented sin was productive of a new sin with each breath that a man drew; and every one of these new sins added to the catalogue in the same manner. I was utterly confounded at the multitude of my transgressions; for I was sensible that there were great numbers of sins of which I had never been able thoroughly to repent, and these momentary ones, by a moderate calculation, had, I saw, long ago, amounted to a hundred and fifty thousand in the minute, and I saw no end to the series of repentances to which I had subjected myself. A life-time was nothing to enable me to accomplish the sum, and then being, for any thing I was certain of, in my state of nature, and the grace of repentance withheld from me, what was I to do, or what was to become of me? In the meantime, I went on sinning without measure; but I was still more troubled about the multitude than the magnitude of my transgressions, and the small minute ones puzzled me more than those that were more heinous, as the latter had generally some good effects in the way of punishing wicked men, froward boys, and deceitful women; and I rejoiced, even then in my early youth, at being used as a scourge in the hand of the Lord; another Jehu, a Cyrus, or a Nebuchadnezzar.[8]

On the whole, I remember that I got into great confusion relating to my sins and repentances, and knew neither where to begin nor how to proceed, and often had great fears that I was wholly without Christ, and that I would find God a consuming fire to me. I could not help running into new sins continually; but then I was mercifully dealt with, for I was often made to repent of them most heartily, by reason of bodily chastisements received on these delinquencies being discovered. I was particularly prone to lying, and I cannot but admire the mercy that has freely forgiven me all these juvenile sins. Now that I know them all to be blotted out, and that I am an accepted person, I may the more freely confess them: the truth is, that one lie always paved the way for another, from hour to hour, from day to day, and from year to year; so that I found myself constantly involved in a labyrinth of deceit, from which it was impossible to extricate myself. If I knew a person to be a godly one, I could almost have kissed his feet; but against the carnal portion of mankind, I set my face continually. I esteemed the true ministers of the gospel; but the prelatic party, and the preachers up of good works I abhorred, and to this hour I account them the worst and most heinous of all transgressors.

There was only one boy at Mr Wilson's class who kept always the upper hand of me in every part of education. I strove against him from year to year, but it was all in vain; for he was a very wicked boy, and I was convinced he had dealings with the devil. Indeed it was believed all over the country that his mother was a witch; and I was at length convinced that it was no human ingenuity that beat me with so much ease in the Latin, after I had often sat up a whole night with my reverend father, studying my lesson in all its bearings. I often read as well and sometimes better than he; but the moment Mr Wilson began to examine us, my opponent popped up above me. I determined (as I knew him for a wicked person, and one of the devil's hand-fasted children) to be revenged on him, and to humble him by some means or other. Accordingly I lost no opportunity of setting the Master against him, and succeeded several times in getting him severely beaten for faults of which he was innocent. I can hardly describe the joy that it gave to my heart to see a wicked creature suffering, for though he deserved it not for one thing, he richly deserved it for others. This may be by some people accounted a great sin in me; but I deny it, for I did it as a duty, and what a man or boy does for the right, will never be put into the sum of his transgressions.

This boy, whose name was M'Gill, was, at all his leisure hours, engaged in drawing profane pictures of beasts, men, women, houses, and trees, and, in short, of all things that his eye encountered. These profane things the Master often smiled at, and admired; therefore I began privately to try my hand likewise. I had scarcely tried above once to draw the figure of a man, ere I conceived that I had hit the very features of Mr Wilson. They were so particular, that they could not be easily mistaken, and I was so tickled and pleased with the droll likeness that I had drawn, that I laughed immoderately at it. I tried no other figure but this; and I tried it in every situation in which a man and a schoolmaster could be placed. I often wrought for hours together at this likeness, nor was it long before I made myself so much master of the outline, that I could have drawn it in any situation whatever, almost off hand. I then took M'Gill's account book of algebra home with me, and at my leisure put down a number of gross caricatures of Mr Wilson here and there, several of them in situations notoriously ludicrous. I waited the discovery of this treasure with great impatience; but the book chancing to be one that M'Gill was not using, I saw it might be long enough before I enjoyed the consummation of my grand scheme: therefore, with all the ingenuity I was master of, I brought it before our dominie's eye. But never shall I forget the rage that gleamed in the tyrant's phiz! I was actually terrified to look at him, and trembled at his voice. M'Gill was called upon, and examined relating to the obnoxious figures. He denied flatly that any of them were of his doing. But the Master inquiring at him whose they were, he could not tell, but affirmed it to be some trick. Mr Wilson at one time began, as I thought, to hesitate; but the evidence was so strong against M'Gill, that at length his solemn asseverations of innocence only proved an aggravation of his crime. There was not one in the school who had ever been known to draw a figure but himself, and on him fell the whole weight of the tyrant's vengeance. It was dreadful; and I was once in hopes that he would not leave life in the culprit. He, however, left the school for several months, refusing to return to be subjected to punishment for the faults of others, and I stood king of the class.

Matters were at last made up between M'Gill's parents and the schoolmaster, but by that time I had got the start of him, and never in my life did I exert myself so much as to keep the mastery. It was in vain; the powers of enchantment prevailed, and I was again turned down with the tear in my eye. I could think of no amends but one, and being driven to desperation, I put it in practice. I told a lie of him. I came boldly up to the master, and told him that M'Gill had in my hearing cursed him in a most shocking manner, and called him vile names. He called M'Gill, and charged him with the crime, and the proud young coxcomb was so stunned at the atrocity of the charge, that his face grew as red as crimson, and the words stuck in his throat as he feebly denied it. His guilt was manifest, and he was again flogged most nobly, and dismissed the school for ever in disgrace, as a most incorrigible vagabond.

This was a great victory gained, and I rejoiced and exulted exceedingly in it. It had, however, very nigh cost me my life; for not long thereafter, I encountered M'Gill in the fields, on which he came up and challenged me for a liar, daring me to fight him. I refused, and said that I looked on him as quite below my notice; but he would not quit me, and finally told me that he should either *lick me*, or I should *lick him*, as he had no other means of being revenged on such a scoundrel. I tried to intimidate him, but it would not do; and I believe I would have given all that I had in the world to be quit of him. He at length went so far as first to kick me, and then strike me on the face; and, being both older and stronger than he, I thought it scarcely became me to take such insults patiently. I was, nevertheless, well aware that the devilish powers of his mother would finally prevail; and either the dread of this, or the inward consciousness of having wronged him, certainly unnerved my arm, for I fought wretchedly, and was soon wholly overcome. I was so sore defeated, that I kneeled, and was going to beg his pardon; but another thought struck me momentarily, and I threw myself on my face, and inwardly begged aid from heaven; at the same time I felt as if assured that my prayer was heard, and would be answered. While I was in this humble attitude, the villain kicked me with his foot and cursed me; and I being newly encouraged, arose and encountered him once more. We had not fought long at this second turn, before I saw a man hastening toward us; on which I uttered a shout of joy, and laid on valiantly; but my very next look assured me, that the man was old John Barnet, whom I had likewise wronged all that was in my power, and between these two wicked persons I expected any thing but justice. My arm was again enfeebled, and that of my adversary prevailed. I was knocked down and mauled most grievously, and while the ruffian was kicking and cuffing me at his will and pleasure, up came old John Barnet, breathless with running, and at one blow with his open hand, levelled my opponent with the earth. 'Tak ye that, maister!' says John, 'to learn ye better breeding. Hout awa, man! an ye will fight, fight fair. Gude sauf us, ir ye a gentleman's brood, that ye will kick an' cuff a lad when he's down?'

When I heard this kind and unexpected interference, I began once more to value myself on my courage, and springing up, I made at my adversary; but John, without saying a word, bit his lip, and seizing me by the neck, threw me down. M'Gill begged of him to stand and see fair play, and suffer us to finish the battle; for, added he, 'he is a liar, and a scoundrel, and deserves ten times more than I can give him.'

'I ken he's a' that ye say, an' mair, my man,' quoth John: 'But am I sure that ye're no as bad, an' waur? It says nae muckle for ony o' ye to be tearing like tikes at ane anither here.'

John cocked his cudgel and stood between us, threatening to knock the one dead, who first offered to lift his hand against the other; but, perceiving no disposition in any of us to separate, he drove me home before him like a bullock, keeping close guard behind me, lest M'Gill had followed. I felt greatly indebted to John, yet I complained of his interference to my mother, and the old officious sinner got no thanks for his pains.

As I am writing only from recollection, so I remember of nothing farther in these early days, in the least worthy of being recorded. That I was a great, a transcendent sinner, I confess. But still I had hopes of forgiveness, because I never sinned from principle, but accident; and then I always *tried* to repent of these sins by the slump, for individually it was impossible; and though not always successful in my endeavours, I could not help that; the grace of repentance being withheld from me, I regarded myself as in no degree accountable for the failure. Moreover, there were many of the most deadly sins into which I never fell, for I dreaded those mentioned in the Revelations as excluding sins, so that I guarded against them continually. In particular, I brought myself to despise, if not to abhor, the beauty of women, looking on it as the greatest snare to which mankind are subjected, and though young men and maidens, and even old women (my mother among the rest), taxed me with being an unnatural wretch, I gloried in my acquisition; and to this day, am thankful for having escaped the most dangerous of all snares.

I kept myself also free of the sins of idolatry, and misbelief, both of a deadly nature; and, upon the whole, I think I had not then broken, that is, absolutely broken, above four out of the ten commandments; but for all that, I had more sense than to regard either my good works, or my evil deeds, as in the smallest degree influencing the eternal decrees of God concerning me, either with regard to my acceptance or reprobation. I depended entirely on the bounty of free grace, holding all the righteousness of man as filthy rags, and believing in the momentous and magnificent truth, that the more heavily loaden with transgressions, the more welcome was the believer at the throne of grace. And I have reason to believe that it was this dependence and this belief that at last ensured my acceptance there.

I come now to the most important period of my existence, the period that has modelled my character, and influenced every action of my life, without which, this detail[9] of my actions would have been as a tale that hath been told – a monotonous *farrago* – an uninteresting harangue – in short, a thing of nothing. Whereas, lo! it must now be a relation of great and terrible actions, done in the might, and by the commission of heaven. *Amen.*

Like the sinful king of Israel,[10] I had been walking softly before the Lord for a season. I had been humbled for my transgressions, and, as far as I recollect, sorry on account of their numbers and heinousness. My reverend father had been, moreover, examining me every day regarding the state of my soul, and my answers sometimes appeared to give him satisfaction, and sometimes not. As for my mother, she would harp on the subject of my faith for ever; yet, though I knew her to be a Christian, I confess that I always despised her motley instructions, nor had I any great regard for her person. If this was a crime in me, I never could help it. I confess it freely, and believe it was a judgment from heaven inflicted on her for some sin of former days, and that I had no power to have acted otherwise toward her than I did.

In this frame of mind was I, when my reverend father one morning arose from his seat, and, meeting me as I entered the room, he embraced me, and welcomed me into the community of the just upon earth. I was struck speechless, and could make no answer save by looks of surprise. My mother also came to me, kissed, and wept over me; and after showering unnumbered blessings on my head, she also welcomed me into the society of *the just made perfect*. Then each of them took me by a hand, and my reverend father explained to me how he had wrestled with God, as the patriarch of old[11] had done, not for a night, but for days and years, and that in bitterness and anguish of spirit, on my account; but that *he* had at last prevailed, and had now gained the long and earnestly desired assurance of my acceptance with the Almighty, in and through the merits and sufferings of his Son: That I was now a justified person, adopted among the number of God's children – my name written in the Lamb's book of life,[12] and that no bypast transgression, nor any future act of my own, or of other men, could be instrumental in altering the decree. 'All the powers of darkness,' added he, 'shall never be able to pluck you again out of your Redeemer's hand. And now, my son, be strong and stedfast in the truth. Set your face against sin, and sinful men, and resist even to blood, as many of the faithful of this land have done, and your reward shall be double. I am assured of your acceptance by the word and spirit of him who cannot err, and your sanctification and repentance unto life will follow in due course. Rejoice and be thankful, for you are plucked as a brand out of the burning, and now your redemption is sealed and sure.'

I wept for joy to be thus assured of my freedom from all sin, and of the impossibility of my ever again falling away from my new state. I bounded away into the fields and the woods, to pour out my spirit in prayer before the Almighty for his kindness to me: my whole frame seemed to be renewed; every nerve was buoyant with new life; I felt as if I could have flown in the air, or leaped over the tops of the trees. An exaltation of spirit lifted me, as it were, far above the earth, and the sinful creatures crawling on its surface; and I deemed myself as an eagle among the children of men, soaring on high, and looking down with pity and contempt on the grovelling creatures below.

As I thus wended my way, I beheld a young man of a mysterious appearance coming towards me. I tried to shun him, being bent on my own contemplations; but he cast himself in my way, so that I could not well avoid him; and more than that, I felt a sort of invisible power that drew me towards him, something like the force of enchantment, which I could not resist. As we approached each other, our eyes met, and I can never describe the strange sensations that thrilled through my whole frame at that impressive moment; a moment to me fraught with the most tremendous consequences; the beginning of a series of adventures which has puzzled myself, and will puzzle the world when I am no more in it. That time will now soon arrive, sooner than any one can devise who knows not the tumult of my thoughts, and the labour of my spirit; and when it hath come and passed over, when my flesh and my bones are decayed, and my soul has passed to its everlasting home, then shall the sons of men ponder on the events of my life; wonder and tremble, and tremble and wonder how such things should be.

That stranger youth and I approached each other in silence, and slowly, with our eyes fixed on each other's eyes. We approached till not more than a yard intervened between us, and then stood still and gazed, measuring each other from head to foot. What was my astonishment, on perceiving that he was the same being as myself! The clothes were the same to the smallest item. The form was the same; the apparent age; the colour of the hair; the eyes; and, as far as recollection could serve me from viewing my own features in a glass, the features too were the very same. I conceived at first, that I saw a vision, and that my guardian angel had appeared to me at this important era of my life; but this singular being read my thoughts in my looks, anticipating the very words that I was going to utter.

'You think I am your brother,' said he; 'or that I am your second self. I am indeed your brother, not according to the flesh, but in my belief of the same truths, and my assurance in the same mode of redemption, than which, I hold nothing so great or so glorious on earth.'

'Then you are an associate well adapted to my present state,' said I. 'For this time is a time of great rejoicing in spirit to me. I am on my way to return thanks to the Most High for my redemption from the bonds of sin and misery. If you will join with me heart and hand in youthful thanksgiving, then shall we two go and worship together; but if not, go your way, and I shall go mine.'

'Ah, you little know with how much pleasure I will accompany you, and join with you in your elevated devotions,' said he fervently. 'Your state is a state to be envied indeed; but I have been advised of it, and am come to be a humble disciple of yours; to be initiated into the true way of salvation by conversing with you, and perhaps by being assisted by your prayers.'

My spiritual pride being greatly elevated by this address, I began to assume the preceptor, and questioned this extraordinary youth with regard to his religious principles, telling him plainly, if he was one who expected acceptance with God at all, on account of good works, that I would hold no communion with him. He renounced these at once, with the greatest vehemence, and declared his acquiescence in my faith. I asked if he believed in the eternal and irrevocable decrees of God, regarding the salvation and condemnation of all mankind? He answered that he did so: aye, what would signify all things else that he believed, if he did not believe in that? We then went on to commune about all our points of belief; and in every thing that I suggested, he acquiesced, and, as I thought that day, often carried them to extremes, so that I had a secret dread he was advancing blasphemies. Yet he had such a way with him, and paid such a deference to all my opinions, that I was quite captivated, and, at the same time, I stood in a sort of awe of him, which I could not account for, and several times was seized with an involuntary inclination to escape from his presence, by making a sudden retreat. But he seemed constantly to anticipate my thoughts, and was sure to divert my purpose by some turn in the conversation that particularly interested me. He took care to dwell much on the theme of the impossibility of those ever falling away, who were once accepted and received into covenant with God, for he seemed to know, that in that confidence, and that trust, my whole hopes were centred.

We moved about from one place to another, until the day was wholly spent. My mind had all the while been kept in a state of agitation resembling the motion of a whirlpool, and when we came to separate, I then discovered that the purpose for which I had sought the fields had been neglected, and that I had been diverted from the worship of God, by attending to the quibbles and dogmas of this singular and unaccountable being, who seemed to have more knowledge and information than all the persons I had ever known put together.

We parted with expressions of mutual regret, and when I left him I felt a deliverance, but at the same time a certain consciousness that I was not thus to get free of him, but that he was like to be an acquaintance that was to stick to me for good or for evil. I was astonished at his acuteness and knowledge about every thing; but as for his likeness to me, that was quite unaccountable. He was the same person in every respect, but yet he was not always so; for I observed several times, when we were speaking of certain divines and their tenets, that his face assumed something of the appearance of theirs; and it struck me, that by setting his features to the mould of other people's, he entered at once into their conceptions and feelings.[13] I had been greatly flattered, and greatly interested by his conversation; whether I had been the better for it or the worse, I could not tell. I had been diverted from returning thanks to my gracious Maker for his great kindness to me, and came home as I went away, but not with the same buoyancy and lightness of heart. Well may I remember that day in which I was first received into the number, and made an heir to all the privileges of the children of God, and on which I first met this mysterious associate, who from that day forth contrived to wind himself into all my affairs, both spiritual and temporal, to this day on which I am writing the account of it. It was on the 25th day of March 1704,[14] when I had just entered the eighteenth year of my age. Whether it behoves me to bless God for the events of that day, or to deplore them, has been hid from my discernment, though I have inquired into it with fear and trembling; and I have now lost all hopes of ever discovering the true import of these events until that day when my accounts are to make up and reckon for in another world.

When I came home, I went straight into the parlour, where my mother was sitting by herself. She started to her feet, and uttered a smothered scream. 'What ails you, Robert?' cried she. 'My dear son, what is the matter with you?'

'Do you see any thing the matter with me?' said I. 'It appears that the ailment is with yourself, and either in your crazed head or your dim eyes, for there is nothing the matter with me.'

'Ah, Robert, you are ill!' cried she; 'you are very ill, my dear boy; you are quite changed; your very voice and manner are changed. Ah, Jane, haste you up to the study, and tell Mr Wringhim to come here on the instant and speak to Robert.'

'I beseech you, woman, to restrain yourself,' said I. 'If you suffer your frenzy to run away with your judgment in this manner, I will leave the house. What do you mean? I tell you, there is nothing ails me: I never was better.'

She screamed, and ran between me and the door, to bar my retreat: in the meantime my reverend father entered, and I have not forgot how he gazed, through his glasses, first at my mother, and then at me. I imagined that his eyes burnt like candles, and was afraid of him, which I suppose made my looks more unstable than they would otherwise have been.

'What is all this for?' said he. 'Mistress! Robert! What is the matter here?'

'Oh, sir, our boy!' cried my mother; 'our dear boy, Mr Wringhim! Look at him, and speak to him: he is either dying or translated, sir!'

He looked at me with a countenance of great alarm; mumbling some sentences to himself, and then taking me by the arm, as if to feel my pulse, he said, with a faltering voice, 'Something has indeed befallen you, either in body or mind, boy, for you are transformed, since the morning, that I could not have known you for the same person. Have you met with any accident?'

'No.'

'Have you seen any thing out of the ordinary course of nature?'

'No.'

'Then, Satan, I fear, has been busy with you, tempting you in no ordinary degree at this momentous crisis of your life?'

My mind turned on my associate for the day, and the idea that he might be an agent of the devil, had such an effect on me, that I could make no answer.

'I see how it is,' said he; 'you are troubled in spirit, and I have no doubt that the enemy of our salvation has been busy with you. Tell me this, has he overcome you, or has he not?'

'He has not, my dear father,' said I. 'In the strength of the Lord, I hope I have withstood him. But indeed, if he has been busy with me, I knew it not. I have been conversant this day with one stranger only, whom I took rather for an angel of light.'

'It is one of the devil's most profound wiles to appear like one,' said my mother.

'Woman, hold thy peace!' said my reverend father: 'thou pretendest to teach what thou knowest not. Tell me this, boy: Did this stranger, with whom you met, adhere to the religious principles in which I have educated you?'

'Yes, to every one of them, in their fullest latitude,' said I.

'Then he was no agent of the wicked one with whom you held converse,' said he; 'for that is the doctrine that was made to overturn the principalities and powers, the might and dominion of the kingdom of darkness. Let us pray.'

After spending about a quarter of an hour in solemn and sublime thanksgiving, this saintly man and minister of Christ Jesus, gave out that the day following should be kept by the family as a day of solemn thanksgiving, and spent in prayer and praise, on account of the calling and election of one of its members; or rather for the election of that individual being revealed on earth, as well as confirmed in heaven.

The next day was with me a day of holy exultation. It was begun by my reverend father laying his hands upon my head and blessing me, and then dedicating me to the Lord in the most awful and impressive manner. It was in no common way that he exercised this profound rite, for it was done with all the zeal and enthusiasm of a devotee to the true cause, and a champion on the side he had espoused. He used these remark-able words, which I have still treasured up in my heart: 'I give him unto Thee only, to Thee wholly, and to Thee for ever. I dedicate him unto Thee, soul, body, and spirit. Not as the wicked of this world, or the hirelings of a church profanely called by Thy name, do I dedicate this Thy servant to Thee: Not in words and form, learned by rote, and dictated by the limbs of Antichrist, but, Lord, I give him into Thy hand, as a captain putteth a sword into the hand of his sovereign, where-with to lay waste his enemies. May he be a two-edged weapon in Thy hand, and a spear coming out of Thy mouth, to destroy, and overcome, and pass over; and may the enemies of Thy church fall down before him, and be as dung to fat the land!'

From that moment, I conceived it decreed, not that I should

be a minister of the gospel, but a champion of it, to cut off the enemies of the Lord from the face of the earth; and I rejoiced in the commission, finding it more congenial to my nature to be cutting sinners off with the sword, than to be haranguing them from the pulpit, striving to produce an effect, which God, by his act of absolute predestination, had for ever rendered impracticable. The more I pondered on these things, the more I saw of the folly and inconsistency of ministers, in spending their lives, striving and remonstrating with sinners, in order to induce them to do that which they had it not in their power to do.[15] Seeing that God had from all eternity decided the fate of every individual that was to be born of woman, how vain was it in man to endeavour to save those whom their Maker had, by an unchangeable decree, doomed to destruction. I could not disbelieve the doctrine which the best of men had taught me, and toward which he made the whole of the Scriptures to bear, and yet it made the economy of the Christian world appear to me as an absolute contradiction. How much more wise would it be, thought I, to begin and cut sinners off with the sword! for till that is effected, the saints can never inherit the earth in peace. Should I be honoured as an instrument to begin this great work of purification, I should rejoice in it. But then, where had I the means, or under what direction was I to begin? There was one thing clear, I was now the Lord's, and it behoved me to bestir myself in his service. O that I had an host at my command, then would I be as a devouring fire among the workers of iniquity!

Full of these great ideas, I hurried through the city, and sought again the private path through the field and wood of Finnieston,[16] in which my reverend preceptor had the privilege of walking for study, and to which he had a key that was always at my command. Near one of the stiles, I perceived a young man sitting in a devout posture, reading on a Bible. He rose, lifted his hat, and made an obeisance to me, which I returned and walked on. I had not well crossed the stile, till it struck me I knew the face of the youth, and that he was some intimate acquaintance, to whom I ought to have spoken. I walked on, and returned, and walked on again, trying to recollect who he

was; but for my life I could not. There was, however, a fascination in his look and manner, that drew me back toward him
in spite of myself, and I resolved to go to him, if it were merely
to speak and see who he was.

I came up to him and addressed him, but he was so intent on
his book, that, though I spoke, he lifted not his eyes. I looked
on the book also, and still it seemed a Bible, having columns,
chapters, and verses; but it was in a language of which I was
wholly ignorant, and all intersected with red lines, and verses.
A sensation resembling a stroke of electricity came over me, on
first casting my eyes on that mysterious book, and I stood
motionless. He looked up, smiled, closed his book, and put it
in his bosom. 'You seem strangely affected, dear sir, by looking
on my book,' said he mildly.

'In the name of God, what book is that?' said I: 'Is it a Bible?'

'It is *my* Bible, sir,' said he; 'but I will cease reading it, for I
am glad to see you. Pray, is not this a day of holy festivity with
you?'

I stared in his face, but made no answer, for my senses were
bewildered.

'Do you not know me?' said he. 'You appear to be somehow
at a loss. Had not you and I some sweet communion and
fellowship yesterday?'

'I beg your pardon, sir,' said I. 'But surely if you are the
young gentleman with whom I spent the hours yesterday, you
have the cameleon art of changing your appearance; I never
could have recognized you.'

'My countenance changes with my studies and sensations,'
said he. 'It is a natural peculiarity in me, over which I have not
full control. If I contemplate a man's features seriously, mine
own gradually assume the very same appearance and character.
And what is more, by contemplating a face minutely, I not only
attain the same likeness, but, with the likeness, I attain the very
same ideas as well as the same mode of arranging them, so that,
you see, by looking at a person attentively, I by degrees assume
his likeness, and by assuming his likeness I attain to the possession of his most secret thoughts. This, I say, is a peculiarity
in my nature, a gift of the God that made me; but whether or

not given me for a blessing, he knows himself, and so do I. At all events, I have this privilege – I can never be mistaken of a character in whom I am interested.'

'It is a rare qualification,' replied I, 'and I would give worlds to possess it. Then, it appears, that it is needless to dissemble with you, since you can at any time extract our most secret thoughts from our bosoms. You already know my natural character?'

'Yes,' said he, 'and it is that which attaches me to you. By assuming your likeness yesterday, I became acquainted with your character, and was no less astonished at the profundity and range of your thoughts, than at the heroic magnanimity with which these were combined. And now, in addition to these, you are dedicated to the great work of the Lord; for which reasons I have resolved to attach myself as closely to you as possible, and to render you all the service of which my poor abilities are capable.'

I confess that I was greatly flattered by these compliments paid to my abilities by a youth of such superior qualifications; by one who, with a modesty and affability rare at his age, combined a height of genius and knowledge almost above human comprehension. Nevertheless, I began to assume a certain superiority of demeanour toward him, as judging it incumbent on me to do so, in order to keep up his idea of my exalted character. We conversed again till the day was near a close; and the things that he strove most to inculcate on my mind, were the infallibility of the elect, and the pre-ordination of all things that come to pass. I pretended to controvert the first of these, for the purpose of showing him the extent of my argumentative powers, and said, that 'indubitably there were degrees of sinning which would induce the Almighty to throw off the very elect.' But behold my hitherto humble and modest companion took up the argument with such warmth, that he put me not only to silence, but to absolute shame.

'Why, sir,' said he, 'by vending such an insinuation, you put discredit on the great atonement, in which you trust. Is there not enough of merit in the blood of Jesus to save thousands of worlds, if it was for these worlds that he died? Now, when you know, as you do (and as every one of the elect may know of himself), that this Saviour died for you, namely and particularly, dare you say that there is not enough of merit in his great atonement to annihilate all your sins, let them be as heinous and atrocious as they may? And, moreover, do you not acknowledge that God hath pre-ordained and decreed whatsoever comes to pass? Then, how is it that you should deem it in your power to eschew one action of your life, whether good or evil? Depend on it, the advice of the great preacher is genuine: 'What thine hand findeth to do, do it with all thy might, for none of us knows what a day may bring forth?' That is, none of us knows what is pre-ordained, but whatever is pre-ordained we *must* do, and none of these things will be laid to our charge.'

I could hardly believe that these sayings were genuine or orthodox; but I soon felt, that, instead of being a humble disciple of mine, this new acquaintance was to be my guide and director, and all under the humble guise of one stooping at my feet to learn the right. He said that he saw I was ordained to perform some great action for the cause of Jesus and his church, and he earnestly coveted being a partaker with me; but he besought of me never to think it possible for me to fall from the truth, or the favour of him who had chosen me, else that misbelief would baulk every good work to which I set my face.

There was something so flattering in all this, that I could not resist it. Still, when he took leave of me, I felt it as a great relief; and yet, before the morrow, I wearied and was impatient to see him again. We carried on our fellowship from day to day, and all the while I knew not who he was, and still my mother and reverend father kept insisting that I was an altered youth, changed in my appearance, my manners, and my whole conduct; yet something always prevented me from telling them more about my new acquaintance than I had done on the first day we met. I rejoiced in him, was proud of him, and soon could not live without him; yet, though resolved every day to disclose the whole history of my connection with him, I had it not in my power: Something always prevented me, till at length I thought no more of it, but resolved to enjoy his fascinating company in private, and by all means to keep my own with him. The resolution was vain: I set a bold face to it, but my powers were inadequate to the task; my adherent, with all the suavity imaginable, was sure to carry his point. I sometimes fumed, and sometimes shed tears at being obliged to yield to proposals against which I had at first felt every reasoning power of my soul rise in opposition; but, for all that, he never failed in carrying conviction along with him in effect, for he either forced me to acquiesce in his measures, and assent to the truth of his positions, or he put me so completely down, that I had not a word left to advance against them.

After weeks, and I may say months of intimacy, I observed, somewhat to my amazement, that we had never once prayed together; and more than that, that he had constantly led my attentions away from that duty, causing me to neglect it wholly. I thought this a bad mark of a man seemingly so much set on inculcating certain important points of religion, and resolved next day to put him to the test, and request of him to perform that sacred duty in name of us both. He objected boldly; saying there were very few people indeed, with whom he could join in prayer, and he made a point of never doing it, as he was sure they were to ask many things of which he disapproved, and that if he were to officiate himself, he was as certain to allude to many things that came not within the range of their faith. He disapproved of prayer altogether, in the manner it was generally gone about, he said. Man made it merely a selfish concern, and was constantly employed asking, asking, for every thing. Whereas it became all God's creatures to be content with their lot, and only to kneel before him in order to thank him for such benefits as he saw meet to bestow. In short, he argued with such energy, that before we parted I acquiesced, as usual, in his position, and never mentioned prayer to him any more.

Having been so frequently seen in his company, several people happened to mention the circumstance to my mother and reverend father; but at the same time had all described him differently. At length, they began to examine me with respect to the company I kept, as I absented myself from home day after day. I told them I kept company only with one young gentleman, whose whole manner of thinking on religious sub-

jects, I found so congenial with my own, that I could not live
out of his society. My mother began to lay down some of her
old hackneyed rules of faith, but I turned from hearing her with
disgust; for, after the energy of my new friend's reasoning, hers
appeared so tame I could not endure it. And I confess with
shame, that my reverend preceptor's religious dissertations
began, about this time, to lose their relish very much, and by
degrees became exceedingly tiresome to my ear. They were
so inferior, in strength and sublimity, to the most common
observations of my young friend, that in drawing a comparison
the former appeared as nothing. He, however, examined me
about many things relating to my companion, in all of which I
satisfied him, save in one: I could neither tell him who my friend
was, what was his name, nor of whom he was descended; and
I wondered at myself how I had never once adverted to such a
thing, for all the time we had been intimate.

I inquired the next day what his name was; as I said I was
often at a loss for it, when talking with him. He replied, that
there was no occasion for any one friend ever naming another,
when their society was held in private, as ours was; for his part
he had never once named me since we first met, and never
intended to do so, unless by my own request. 'But if you cannot
converse without naming me, you may call me Gil for the
present,' added he; 'and if I think proper to take another name
at any future period, it shall be with your approbation.'

'Gil!' said I; 'Have you no name but Gil? Or which of your
names is it? Your Christian or surname?'

'O, you must have a surname too, must you!' replied he,
'Very well, you may call me Gil-Martin. It is not my *Christian*
name; but it *is* a name which may serve your turn.'

'This is very strange!' said I. 'Are you ashamed of your
parents, that you refuse to give your real name?'

'I have no parents save one, whom I do not acknowledge,'
said he proudly; 'therefore, pray drop that subject, for it is a
disagreeable one. I am a being of a very peculiar temper, for
though I have servants and subjects more than I can number,
yet, to gratify a certain whim, I have left them, and retired to
this city, and for all the society it contains, you see I have

attached myself only to you. This is a secret, and I tell it you only in friendship, therefore pray let it remain one, and say not another word about the matter.'

I assented, and said no more concerning it; for it instantly struck me that this was no other than the Czar Peter of Russia,[17] having heard that he had been travelling through Europe in disguise, and I cannot say that I had not thenceforward great and mighty hopes of high preferment, as a defender and avenger of the oppressed Christian Church, under the influence of this great potentate. He had hinted as much already, as that it was more honourable, and of more avail to put down the wicked with the sword, than try to reform them, and I thought myself quite justified in supposing that he intended me for some great employment, that he had thus selected me for his companion out of all the rest in Scotland, and even pretended to learn the great truths of religion from my mouth. From that time I felt disposed to yield to such a great prince's suggestions without hesitation.

Nothing ever astonished me so much, as the uncommon powers with which he seemed invested. In our walk one day, we met with a Mr Blanchard, who was reckoned a worthy, pious divine, but quite of the moral cast,[18] who joined us; and we three walked on, and rested together in the fields. My companion did not seem to like him, but, nevertheless, regarded him frequently with deep attention, and there were several times, while he seemed contemplating him, and trying to find out his thoughts, that his face became so like Mr Blanchard's, that it was impossible to have distinguished the one from the other. The antipathy between the two was mutual, and discovered itself quite palpably in a short time. When my companion the prince was gone, Mr Blanchard asked me anent him, and I told him that he was a stranger in the city, but a very uncommon and great personage. Mr Blanchard's answer to me was as follows: 'I never saw any body I disliked so much in my life, Mr Robert; and if it be true that he is a stranger here, which I doubt, believe me he is come for no good.'

'Do you not perceive what mighty powers of mind he is

possessed of?' said I, 'and also how clear and unhesitating he is on some of the most interesting points of divinity?'

'It is for his great mental faculties that I dread him,' said he. 'It is incalculable what evil such a person as he may do, if so disposed. There is a sublimity in his ideas, with which there is to me a mixture of terror; and when he talks of religion, he does it as one that rather dreads its truths than reverences them. He, indeed, pretends great strictness of orthodoxy regarding some of the points of doctrine embraced by the reformed church; but you do not seem to perceive, that both you and he are carrying these points to a dangerous extremity. Religion is a sublime and glorious thing, the bond of society[19] on earth, and the connector of humanity with the Divine nature; but there is nothing so dangerous to man as the wresting of any of its principles, or forcing them beyond their due bounds: this is of all others the readiest way to destruction. Neither is there any thing so easily done. There is not an error into which a man can fall, which he may not press Scripture into his service as proof of the probity of, and though your boasted theologian shunned the full discussion of the subject before me, while you pressed it, I can easily see that both you and he are carrying your ideas of absolute predestination, and its concomitant appendages, to an extent that overthrows all religion and revelation together; or, at least, jumbles them into a chaos, out of which human capacity can never select what is good. Believe me, Mr Robert, the less you associate with that illustrious stranger the better, for it appears to me that your creed and his carries damnation on the very front of it.'

I was rather stunned at this; but I pretended to smile with disdain, and said, it did not become youth to control age; and, as I knew our principles differed fundamentally, it behoved us to drop the subject. He, however, would not drop it, but took both my principles and me fearfully to task, for Blanchard was an eloquent and powerful-minded old man; and, before we parted, I believe I promised to drop my new acquaintance, and was *all but* resolved to do it.

As well might I have laid my account with shunning the light of day. He was constant to me as my shadow, and by degrees he acquired such an ascendency over me, that I never was happy out of his company, nor greatly so in it. When I repeated to him all that Mr Blanchard had said, his countenance kindled with indignation and rage; and then by degrees his eyes sunk inward, his brow lowered, so that I was awed, and withdrew my eyes from looking at him. A while afterward, as I was addressing him, I chanced to look him again in the face, and the sight of him made me start violently. He had made himself so like Mr Blanchard, that I actually believed I had been addressing that gentleman, and that I had done so in some absence of mind that I could not account for. Instead of being amused at the quandary I was in, he seemed offended: indeed, he never was truly amused with any thing. And he then asked me sullenly, if I conceived such personages as he to have no other endowments than common mortals?

I said I never conceived that princes or potentates had any greater share of endowments than other men, and frequently not so much. He shook his head, and bade me think over the subject again; and there was an end of it. I certainly felt every day the more disposed to acknowledge such a superiority in him, and from all that I could gather, I had now no doubt that he was Peter of Russia. Every thing combined to warrant the supposition, and, of course, I resolved to act in conformity with the discovery I had made.

For several days the subject of Mr Blanchard's doubts and doctrines formed the theme of our discourse. My friend deprecated them most devoutly; and then again he would deplore them, and lament the great evil that such a man might do among the human race. I joined with him in allowing the evil in its fullest latitude; and, at length, after he thought he had fully prepared my nature for such a trial of its powers and abilities, he proposed calmly that we two should make away with Mr Blanchard. I was so shocked, that my bosom became as it were a void, and the beatings of my heart sounded loud and hollow in it; my breath cut, and my tongue and palate became dry and speechless. He mocked at my cowardice, and began a-reasoning on the matter with such powerful eloquence,

that before we parted, I felt fully convinced that it was my
bounden duty to slay Mr Blanchard; but my will was far, very
far from consenting to the deed.

I spent the following night without sleep, or nearly so; and
the next morning, by the time the sun arose, I was again abroad,
and in the company of my illustrious friend. The same subject
was resumed, and again he reasoned to the following purport:
That supposing me placed at the head of an army of Christian
soldiers, all bent on putting down the enemies of the church,
would I have any hesitation in destroying and rooting out these
enemies? – None surely. – Well then, when I saw and was
convinced, that here was an individual who was doing more
detriment to the church of Christ on earth, than tens of thousands of such warriors were capable of doing, was it not my
duty to cut him off, and save the elect? 'He, who would be a
champion in the cause of Christ and his Church, my brave
young friend,' added he, 'must begin early, and no man can
calculate to what an illustrious eminence small beginnings may
lead. If the man Blanchard is worthy, he is only changing his
situation for a better one; and if unworthy, it is better that one
fall, than that a thousand souls perish. Let us be up and doing
in our vocations. For me, my resolution is taken; I have but
one great aim in this world, and I never for a moment lose sight
of it.'

I was obliged to admit the force of his reasoning; for though
I cannot from memory repeat his words, his eloquence was of
that overpowering nature, that the subtility of other men sunk
before it; and there is also little doubt that the assurance I had
that these words were spoken by a great potentate, who could
raise me to the highest eminence (provided that I entered into
his extensive and decisive measures), assisted mightily in dispel-
ling my youthful scruples and qualms of conscience; and I
thought moreover, that having such a powerful back friend to
support me, I hardly needed to be afraid of the consequences. I
consented! But begged a little time to think of it. He said the
less one thought of a duty the better; and we parted.

But the most singular instance of this wonderful man's power
over my mind was, that he had as complete influence over me

by night as by day. All my dreams corresponded exactly with his suggestions; and when he was absent from me, still his arguments sunk deeper in my heart than even when he was present. I dreamed that night of a great triumph obtained, and though the whole scene was but dimly and confusedly defined in my vision, yet the overthrow and death of Mr Blanchard was the first step by which I attained the eminent station I occupied. Thus, by dreaming of the event by night, and discoursing of it by day, it soon became so familiar to my mind, that I almost conceived it as done. It was resolved on: which was the first and greatest victory gained; for there was no difficulty in finding opportunities enow of cutting off a man, who, every good day, was to be found walking by himself in private grounds. I went and heard him preach for two days, and in fact I held his tenets scarcely short of blasphemy; they were such as I had never heard before, and his congregation, which was numerous, were turning up their ears and drinking in his doctrines with the utmost delight; for O, they suited their carnal natures and self-sufficiency to a hair! He was actually holding it forth, as a fact, that 'it was every man's own blame if he was not saved!' What horrible misconstruction! And then he was alleging, and trying to prove from nature and reason, that no man ever was guilty of a sinful action, who might not have declined it had he so chosen! 'Wretched controvertist!' thought I to myself an hundred times, 'shall not the sword of the Lord be moved from its place of peace for such presumptuous and absurd testimonies as these!'

When I began to tell the prince about these false doctrines, to my astonishment I found that he had been in the church himself, and had every argument that the old divine had used *verbatim*; and he remarked on them with great concern, that these were not the tenets that corresponded with his views in society, and that he had agents in every city, and every land, exerting their powers to put them down. I asked, with great simplicity, 'Are all your subjects Christians, prince?'

'All my European subjects are, or deem themselves so,' returned he; 'and they are the most faithful and true subjects I have.'

Who could doubt, after this, that he was the Czar of Russia? I have nevertheless had reasons to doubt of his identity since that period, and which of my conjectures is right, I believe the God of heaven only knows, for I do not. I shall go on to write such things as I remember, and if any one shall ever take the trouble to read over these confessions, such a one will judge for himself. It will be observed, that since ever I fell in with this extraordinary person, I have written about him only, and I must continue to do so to the end of this memoir, as I have performed no great or interesting action in which he had not a principal share.

He came to me one day and said, 'We must not linger thus in executing what we have resolved on. We have much before our hands to perform for the benefit of mankind, both civil as well as religious. Let us do what we have to do here, and then we must wend our way to other cities, and perhaps to other countries. Mr Blanchard is to hold forth in the high church of Paisley on Sunday next, on some particularly great occasion: this must be defeated; he must not go there. As he will be busy arranging his discourses, we may expect him to be walking by himself in Finnieston Dell the greater part of Friday and Saturday. Let us go and cut him off. What is the life of a man more than the life of a lamb, or any guiltless animal? It is not half so much, especially when we consider the immensity of the mischief this old fellow is working among our fellow-creatures. Can there be any doubt that it is the duty of one consecrated to God, to cut off such a mildew?'

'I fear me, great sovereign,' said I, 'that your ideas of retribution are too sanguine, and too arbitrary for the laws of this country. I dispute not that your motives are great and high; but have you debated the consequences, and settled the result?'

'I have,' returned he, 'and hold myself amenable for the action, to the laws of God and of equity; as to the enactments of men I despise them. Fain would I see the weapon of the Lord of Hosts, begin the work of vengeance that awaits it to do!'

I could not help thinking, that I perceived a little derision of countenance on his face as he said this, nevertheless I sunk dumb before such a man, and aroused myself to the task, seeing he would not have it deferred. I approved of it in theory, but my spirit stood aloof from the practice. I saw and was convinced that the elect of God would be happier, and purer, were the wicked and unbelievers all cut off from troubling and misleading them, but if it had not been the instigations of this illustrious stranger, I should never have presumed to begin so great a work myself. Yet, though he often aroused my zeal to the highest pitch, still my heart at times shrunk from the shedding of life-blood, and it was only at the earnest and unceasing instigations of my enlightened and voluntary patron, that I at length put my hand to the conclusive work. After I said all that I could say, and all had been overborne (I remember my actions and words as well as it had been yesterday), I turned round hesitatingly, and looked up to Heaven for direction; but there was a dimness came over my eyes that I could not see. The appearance was as if there had been a veil drawn over me, so nigh that I put up my hand to feel it; and then Gil-Martin (as this great sovereign was pleased to have himself called) frowned, and asked me what I was grasping at? I knew not what to say, but answered, with fear and shame, 'I have no weapons, not one; nor know I where any are to be found.'

'The God whom thou servest will provide these,' said he; 'if thou provest worthy of the trust committed to thee.'

I looked again up into the cloudy veil that covered us, and thought I beheld golden weapons of every description let down in it, but all with their points towards me. I kneeled, and was going to stretch out my hand to take one, when my patron seized me, as I thought, by the clothes, and dragged me away with as much ease as I had been a lamb, saying, with a joyful and elevated voice, 'Come, my friend, let us depart: thou art dreaming – thou art dreaming. Rouse up all the energies of thy exalted mind, for thou art an highly-favoured one; and doubt thou not, that he whom *thou* servest, will be ever at thy right and left hand, to direct and assist thee.'

These words, but particularly the vision I had seen, of the golden weapons descending out of Heaven, inflamed my zeal to that height that I was as one beside himself; which my parents perceived that night, and made some motions toward confining me to my room. I joined in the family prayers, and then I afterwards sung a psalm and prayed by myself; and I had good reasons for believing that that small oblation of praise and prayer was not turned to sin. But there are strange things, and unaccountable agencies in nature: He only who dwells between the Cherubim can unriddle them, and to him the honour must redound for ever. *Amen.*

I felt greatly strengthened and encouraged that night, and the next morning I ran to meet my companion, out of whose eye I had now no life. He rejoiced at seeing me so forward in the great work of reformation by blood, and said many things to raise my hopes of future fame and glory; and then, producing two pistols of pure beaten gold, he held them out and proffered me the choice of one, saying, 'See what thy master hath provided thee!' I took one of them eagerly, for I perceived at once that they were two of the very weapons that were let down from Heaven in the cloudy veil, the dim tapestry of the firmament; and I said to myself, 'Surely this is the will of the Lord.'

The little splendid and enchanting piece was so perfect, so complete, and so ready for executing the will of the donor, that I now longed to use it in his service. I loaded it with my own hand, as Gil-Martin did the other, and we took our stations behind a bush of hawthorn and bramble on the verge of the wood, and almost close to the walk. My patron was so acute in all his calculations that he never mistook an event. We had not taken our stand above a minute and a half, till old Mr Blanchard appeared, coming slowly on the path. When we saw this, we cowered down, and leaned each of us a knee upon the ground, pointing the pistols through the bush, with an aim so steady, that it was impossible to miss our victim.

He came deliberately on, pausing at times so long, that we dreaded he was going to turn. Gil-Martin dreaded it, and I said I did, but wished in my heart that he might. He, however, came onward, and I will never forget the manner in which he came! No – I don't believe I ever can forget it, either in the narrow bounds of time or the ages of eternity! He was a boardly ill-shaped man, of a rude exterior, and a little bent with age; his hands were clasped behind his back, and below his coat, and he walked with a slow swinging air that was very peculiar. When he paused and looked abroad on nature, the act was highly impressive: he seemed conscious of being all alone, and conversant only with God and the elements of his creation. Never was there such a picture of human inadvertency! a man approaching step by step to the one that was to hurl him out of one existence into another, with as much ease and indifference as the ox goeth to the stall. Hideous vision, wilt thou not be gone from my mental sight! If not, let me bear with thee as I can!

When he came straight opposite to the muzzles of our pieces, Gil-Martin called out 'Eh!' with a short quick sound. The old man, without starting, turned his face and breast toward us, and looked into the wood, but looked over our heads. 'Now!' whispered my companion, and fired. But my hand refused the office, for I was not at that moment sure about becoming an assassin in the cause of Christ and his Church. I thought I heard a sweet voice behind me, whispering me to beware, and I was going to look round, when my companion exclaimed, 'Coward, we are ruined!'

I had no time for an alternative: Gil-Martin's ball had not taken effect, which was altogether wonderful, as the old man's breast was within a few yards of him. 'Hilloa!' cried Blanchard; 'what is that for, you dog!' and with that he came forward to look over the bush. I hesitated, as I said, and attempted to look behind me; but there was no time: the next step discovered two assassins lying in covert, waiting for blood. 'Coward, we are ruined!' cried my indignant friend; and that moment my piece was discharged. The effect was as might have been expected: the old man first stumbled to one side, and then fell on his back. We kept our places, and I perceived my companion's eyes gleaming with an unnatural joy. The wounded man raised himself from the bank to a sitting posture, and I beheld his eyes swimming; he, however, appeared sensible, for we heard him saying in a low and rattling voice, 'Alas, alas! whom have I offended, that they should have been driven to an act like this! Come forth and shew yourselves, that I may either forgive you before I die, or curse you in the name of the Lord.' He then fell a-groping with both hands on the ground, as if feeling for something he had lost, manifestly in the agonies of death; and, with a solemn and interrupted prayer for forgiveness, he breathed his last.

I had become rigid as a statue, whereas my associate appeared to be elevated above measure. 'Arise, thou faint-hearted one, and let us be going,' said he. 'Thou hast done well for once; but wherefore hesitate in such a cause? This is but a small beginning of so great a work as that of purging the Christian world. But the first victim is a worthy one, and more of such lights must be extinguished immediately.'

We touched not our victim, nor any thing pertaining to him, for fear of staining our hands with his blood; and the firing having brought three men within view, who were hasting towards the spot, my undaunted companion took both the pistols, and went forward as with intent to meet them, bidding me shift for myself. I ran off in a contrary direction, till I came to the foot of the Pearman Sike, and then, running up the hollow of that, I appeared on the top of the bank as if I had been another man brought in view by hearing the shots in such a place. I had a full view of a part of what passed, though not of all. I saw my companion going straight to meet the men, apparently with a pistol in every hand, waving in a careless manner. They seemed not quite clear of meeting with him, and so he went straight on, and passed between them. They looked after him, and came onward; but when they came to the old man lying stretched in his blood, then they turned and pursued my companion, though not so quickly as they might have done; and I understood that from the first they saw no more of him.

Great was the confusion that day in Glasgow. The most popular of all their preachers of morality was (what they called) murdered in cold blood, and a strict and extensive search was made for the assassin. Neither of the accomplices was found, however, that is certain, nor was either of them so much as suspected; but another man was apprehended under circumstances that warranted suspicion. This was one of the things that I witnessed in my life, which I never understood, and it surely was one of my patron's most dexterous tricks, for I must still say, what I have thought from the beginning, that like him there never was a man created. The young man who was taken up was a preacher; and it was proved that he had purchased fire arms in town, and gone out with them that morning. But the far greatest mystery of the whole was, that two of the men, out of the three who met my companion, swore, that that unfortunate preacher was the man whom they met with a pistol in each hand, fresh from the death of the old divine. The poor fellow made a confused speech himself, which there is not the least doubt was quite true; but it was laughed to scorn, and an expression of horror ran through both the hearers and jury. I heard the whole trial, and so did Gil-Martin; but we left the journeyman preacher to his fate, and from that time forth I have had no faith in the justice of criminal trials. If once a man is prejudiced on one side, he will swear any thing in support of such prejudice. I tried to expostulate with my mysterious friend on the horrid injustice of suffering this young man to die for our act, but the prince exulted in it more than the other, and said the latter was the most dangerous man of the two.

The alarm in and about Glasgow was prodigious. The country being divided into two political parties, the court and the country party, the former held meetings, issued proclamations, and offered rewards, ascribing all to the violence of party spirit, and deprecating the infernal measures of their opponents. I did not understand their political differences; but it was easy to see that the true Gospel preachers joined all on one side, and the upholders of pure morality and a blameless life on the other, so that this division proved a test to us, and it was forthwith resolved, that we two should pick out some of the leading men of this unsaintly and heterodox cabal, and cut them off one by one, as occasion should suit.

Now, the ice being broke, I felt considerable zeal in our great work, but pretended much more; and we might soon have kidnapped them all through the ingenuity of my patron, had not our next attempt miscarried, by some awkwardness or mistake of mine. The consequence was, that he was discovered fairly, and very nigh seized. I also was seen, and suspected so far, that my reverend father, my mother, and myself were examined privately. I denied all knowledge of the matter; and they held it in such a ridiculous light, and their conviction of the complete groundlessness of the suspicion was so perfect, that their testimony prevailed, and the affair was hushed. I was obliged, however, to walk circumspectly, and saw my companion the prince very seldom, who was prowling about every day, quite unconcerned about his safety. He was every day a new man, however, and needed not to be alarmed at any danger; for such a facility had he in disguising himself, that if it had not been for a pass-word which we had between us, for the purposes of recognition, I never could have known him myself.

It so happened that my reverend father was called to Edinburgh about this time, to assist with his council in settling the national affairs. At my earnest request I was permitted to accompany him, at which both my associate and I rejoiced, as we were now about to move in a new and extensive field. All this time I never knew where my illustrious friend resided. He never once invited me to call on him at his lodgings, nor did he ever come to our house, which made me sometimes to suspect, that if any of our great efforts in the cause of true religion were discovered, he intended leaving me in the lurch. Consequently, when we met in Edinburgh (for we travelled not in company) I proposed to go with him to look for lodgings, telling him at the same time what a blessed religious family my reverend instructor and I were settled in. He said he rejoiced at it, but he made a rule of never lodging in any particular house, but took these daily, or hourly, as he found it convenient, and that he never was at a loss in any circumstance.

'What a mighty trouble you put yourself to, great sovereign!' said I, 'and all, it would appear, for the purpose of seeing and knowing more and more of the human race.'

'I never go but where I have some great purpose to serve,' returned he, 'either in the advancement of my own power and dominion, or in thwarting my enemies.'

'With all due deference to your great comprehension, my illustrious friend,' said I, 'it strikes me that you can accomplish very little either the one way or the other here, in the humble and private capacity you are pleased to occupy.'

'It is your own innate modesty that prompts such a remark,' said he. 'Do you think the gaining of *you* to my service, is not an attainment worthy of being envied by the greatest potentate in Christendom? Before I had missed such a prize as the attainment of your services, I would have travelled over one half of the habitable globe.' I bowed with great humility, but at the same time how could I but feel proud and highly flattered? He continued. 'Believe me, my dear friend, for such a prize I account no effort too high. For a man who is not only dedicated to the King of Heaven, in the most solemn manner, soul, body, and spirit, but also chosen of him from the beginning, justified, sanctified, and received into a communion that never shall be broken, and from which no act of his shall ever remove him – the possession of such a man, I tell you, is worth kingdoms; because every deed that he performs, he does it with perfect safety to himself and honour to me.' I bowed again, lifting my hat, and he went on. 'I am now going to put his courage in the cause he has espoused, to a severe test – to a trial at which common nature would revolt, but he who is dedicated to be the sword of the Lord, must raise himself above common humanity. You have a father and a brother according to the flesh, what do you know of them?'

'I am sorry to say I know nothing good,' said I. 'They are reprobates, cast-aways, beings devoted to the wicked one, and, like him, workers of every species of iniquity with greediness.'

'They must both fall!' said he, with a sigh and melancholy look: 'It is decreed in the councils above, that they must both fall by your hand.'

'The God of heaven forbid it!' said I. 'They are enemies to Christ and his church, that I know and believe; but they shall live and die in their iniquity for me, and reap their guerdon when their time cometh. There my hand shall not strike.'

'The feeling is natural, and amiable,' said he; 'but you *must* think again. Whether are the bonds of carnal nature, or the bonds and vows of the Lord, strongest?'

'I will not reason with you on this head, mighty potentate,' said I, 'for whenever I do so it is but to be put down. I shall only express my determination, not to take vengeance out of the Lord's hand in this instance. It availeth not. These are men that have the mark of the beast in their foreheads and right hands; they are lost beings themselves, but have no influence over others. Let them perish in their sins; for they shall not be meddled with by me.'

'How preposterously you talk, my dear friend!' said he. 'These people are your greatest enemies; they would rejoice to see you annihilated. And now that you have taken up the Lord's cause of being avenged on *his* enemies, wherefore spare those that are your own as well as his? Besides, you ought to consider what great advantages would be derived to the cause of righteousness and truth, were the estate and riches of that opulent house in your possession, rather than in that of such as oppose the truth and all manner of holiness.'

This was a portion of the consequence of following my illustrious adviser's summary mode of procedure, that had never entered into my calculation – I disclaimed all idea of being influenced by it; however, I cannot but say that the desire of being enabled to do so much good, by the possession of these bad men's riches, made some impression on my heart, and I said I would consider of the matter. I did consider it, and that right seriously as well as frequently; and there was scarcely an hour in the day on which my resolves were not animated by my great friend, till at length I began to have a longing desire to kill my brother, in particular. Should any man ever read this scroll, he will wonder at this confession, and deem it savage and unnatural. So it appeared to me at first, but a constant thinking of an event changes every one of its features. I have done all for the best, and as I was prompted, by one who knew right and wrong much better than I did. I *had* a desire to slay him, it is true, and such a desire too as a thirsty man has to drink; but at the same time, this longing desire was mingled with a certain terror, as if I had dreaded that the drink for which I longed was mixed with deadly poison. My mind was so much weakened, or rather softened about this time, that my faith began a little to give way, and I doubted most presumptuously of the least tangible of all Christian tenets, namely, of *the infallibility of the elect*. I hardly comprehended the great work I had begun, and doubted of *my own* infallibility, or that of any created being. But I was brought over again by the unwearied diligence of my friend to repent of my backsliding, and view once more the superiority of the Almighty's counsels in its fullest latitude. *Amen*.

I prayed very much in secret about this time, and that with great fervor of spirit, as well as humility; and my satisfaction at finding all my requests granted is not to be expressed.

My illustrious friend still continuing to sound in my ears the imperious duty to which I was called, of making away with my sinful relations, and quoting many parallel actions out of the Scriptures, and the writings of the holy Fathers, of the pleasure the Lord took in such as executed his vengeance on the wicked, I was obliged to acquiesce in his measures, though with certain limitations. It was not easy to answer his arguments, and yet I was afraid that he soon perceived a leaning to his will on my part. 'If the acts of Jehu, in rooting out the whole house of his master, were ordered and approved of by the Lord,' said he, 'would it not have been more praiseworthy if one of Ahab's own sons had stood up for the cause of the God of Israel, and rooted out the sinners and their idols out of the land?'

'It would certainly,' said I. 'To our duty to God all other duties must yield.'

'Go thou then and do likewise,' said he. 'Thou art called to a high vocation; to cleanse the sanctuary of thy God in this thy native land by the shedding of blood; go thou forth then like a ruling energy, a master spirit of desolation in the dwellings of the wicked, and high shall be your reward both here and hereafter.'

My heart now panted with eagerness to look my brother in the face: On which my companion, who was never out of the way, conducted me to a small square in the suburbs of the city, where there were a number of young noblemen and gentlemen playing at a vain, idle, and sinful game, at which there was much of the language of the accursed going on; and among these blasphemers he instantly pointed out my brother to me. I

was fired with indignation at seeing him in such company, and
so employed; and I placed myself close beside him to watch all
his motions, listen to his words, and draw inferences from what
I saw and heard. In what a sink of sin was he wallowing! I
resolved to take him to task, and if he refused to be admonished,
to inflict on him some condign punishment; and knowing that
my illustrious friend and director was looking on, I resolved
to show some spirit. Accordingly, I waited until I heard him
profane his Maker's name three times, and then, my spiritual
indignation being roused above all restraint, I went up and
kicked him. Yes, I went boldly up and struck him with my foot,
and meant to have given him a more severe blow than it was
my fortune to inflict. It had, however, the effect of rousing up
his corrupt nature to quarrelling and strife, instead of taking
the chastisement of the Lord in humility and meekness. He
ran furiously against me in the choler that is always inspired by
the wicked one; but I overthrew him, by reason of impeding
the natural and rapid progress of his unholy feet, running to
destruction. I also fell slightly; but his fall proving a severe one,
he arose in wrath, and struck me with the mall which he held
in his hand, until my blood flowed copiously; and from that
moment I vowed his destruction in my heart. But I chanced to
have no weapon at that time, nor any means of inflicting due
punishment on the caitiff, which would not have been returned
double on my head, by him and his graceless associates. I mixed
among them at the suggestion of my friend, and following them
to their den of voluptuousness and sin, I strove to be admitted
among them, in hopes of finding some means of accomplishing
my great purpose, while I found myself moved by the spirit
within me so to do. But I was not only debarred, but, by the
machinations of my wicked brother and his associates, cast into
prison.

I was not sorry at being thus honoured to suffer in the cause
of righteousness, and at the hands of sinful men; and as soon
as I was alone, I betook myself to prayer, deprecating the
long-suffering of God toward such horrid sinners. My jailer
came to me, and insulted me. He was a rude unprincipled
fellow, partaking much of the loose and carnal manners of

the age; but I remembered of having read, in the Cloud of Witnesses,[20] of such men formerly, having been converted by the imprisoned saints; so I set myself, with all my heart, to bring about this man's repentance and reformation.

'Fat the deil[21] are ye yoolling an' praying that gate for, man?' said he, coming angrily in. 'I thought the days o' praying prisoners had been a' ower. We had rowth o' them aince; an' they were the poorest an' the blackest bargains that ever poor jailers saw. Gie up your crooning, or I'll pit you to an in-by place, where ye sall get plenty o't.'

'Friend,' said I, 'I am making my appeal at that bar where all human actions are seen and judged, and where you shall not be forgot, sinful as you are. Go in peace, and let me be.'

'Hae ye naebody nearer-hand hame to mak your appeal to, man?' said he; 'because an ye haena, I dread you an' me may be unco weel acquaintit by an' by?'

I then opened up the mysteries of religion to him in a clear and perspicuous manner, but particularly the great doctrine of the election of grace; and then I added, 'Now, friend, you must tell me if you pertain to this chosen number. It is in every man's power to ascertain this, and it is every man's duty to do it.'

'An' fat the better wad you be for the kenning o' this, man?' said he.

'Because, if you are one of my brethren, I will take you into sweet communion and fellowship,' returned I; 'but if you belong to the unregenerate, I have a commission to slay you.'

'The deil you hae, callant!' said he, gaping and laughing. 'An' pray now, fa was it that gae you siccan a braw commission?'

'My commission is sealed by the signet above,' said I, 'and that I will let you and all sinners know. I am dedicated to it by the most solemn vows and engagements. I am the sword of the Lord, and Famine and Pestilence are my sisters. Wo then to the wicked of this land, for they must fall down dead together, that the church may be purified!'

'Oo, foo, foo! I see how it is,' said he; 'yours is a very braw commission, but you will have the small opportunity of carrying it through here. Take my advising, and write a bit of a letter to your friends, and I will send it, for this is no place for such a great man. If you cannot steady your hand to write, as I see you have been at your great work, a word of a mouth may do; for I do assure you this is not the place at all, of any in the world, for your operations.'

The man apparently thought I was deranged in my intellect. He could not swallow such great truths at the first morsel. So I took his advice, and sent a line to my reverend father, who was not long in coming, and great was the jailer's wonderment when he saw all the great Christian noblemen of the land sign my bond of freedom.

My reverend father took this matter greatly to heart, and bestirred himself in the good cause till the transgressors were ashamed to shew their faces. My illustrious companion was not idle: I wondered that he came not to me in prison, nor at my release; but he was better employed, in stirring up the just to the execution of God's decrees; and he succeeded so well, that my brother and all his associates had nearly fallen victims to their wrath: But many were wounded, bruised, and imprisoned, and much commotion prevailed in the city. For my part, I was greatly strengthened in my resolution by the anathemas of my reverend father, who, privately (that is in a family capacity), in his prayers, gave up my father and brother, according to the flesh, to Satan, making it plain to all my senses of perception, that they were beings given up of God, to be devoured by fiends or men, at their will and pleasure, and that *whosoever* should slay them, would do God good service.

The next morning my illustrious friend met me at an early hour, and he was greatly overjoyed at hearing my sentiments now chime so much in unison with his own. I said, 'I longed for the day and the hour that I might look my brother in the face at Gilgal,[22] and visit on him the iniquity of his father and himself, for that I was now strengthened and prepared for the deed.'

'I have been watching the steps and movements of the profligate one,' said he; 'and lo, I will take you straight to his presence. Let your heart be as the heart of the lion, and your arms strong as the shekels of brass, and swift to avenge as the bolt that descendeth from Heaven, for the blood of the just and the good hath long flowed in Scotland. But already is the day of their avengement begun; the hero is at length arisen, who shall send all such as bear enmity to the true church, or trust in works of their own, to Tophet!'[23]

Thus encouraged, I followed my friend, who led me directly to the same court in which I had chastised the miscreant on the foregoing day; and behold, there was the same group again assembled. They eyed me with terror in their looks, as I walked among them and eyed them with looks of disapprobation and rebuke; and I saw that the very eye of a chosen one lifted on these children of Belial, was sufficient to dismay and put them to flight. I walked aside to my friend, who stood at a distance looking on, and he said to me, 'What thinkest thou now?' and I answered in the words of the venal prophet,[24] 'Lo now, if I had a sword into mine hand, I would even kill him.'

'Wherefore lackest thou it?' said he. 'Dost thou not see that they tremble at thy presence, knowing that the avenger of blood is among them.'

My heart was lifted up on hearing this, and again I strode into the midst of them, and eyeing them with threatening looks, they were so much confounded, that they abandoned their sinful pastime, and fled every one to his house!

This was a palpable victory gained over the wicked, and I thereby knew that the hand of the Lord was with me. My companion also exulted, and said, 'Did not I tell thee? Behold thou dost not know one half of thy might, or of the great things thou art destined to do. Come with me and I will show thee more than this, for these young men cannot subsist without the exercises of sin. I listened to their councils, and I know where they will meet again.'

Accordingly he led me a little farther to the south, and we walked aside till by degrees we saw some people begin to assemble; and in a short time we perceived the same group stripping off their clothes to make them more expert in the practice of madness and folly. Their game was begun before we approached, and so also were the oaths and cursing. I put my hands in my pockets, and walked with dignity and energy into the midst of them. It was enough: Terror and astonishment seized them. A few of them cried out against me, but their voices were soon hushed amid the murmurs of fear. One of them, in the name of the rest, then came and besought of me to grant them liberty to amuse themselves; but I refused peremptorily, dared the whole multitude so much as to touch me with one of their fingers, and dismissed them in the name of the Lord.

Again they all fled and dispersed at my eye, and I went home in triumph, escorted by my friend, and some well-meaning young Christians, who, however, had not learned to deport themselves with soberness and humility. But my ascendency over my enemies was great indeed; for wherever I appeared I was hailed with approbation, and wherever my guilty brother made his appearance, he was hooted and held in derision, till he was forced to hide his disgraceful head, and appear no more in public.

Immediately after this I was seized with a strange distemper, which neither my friends nor physicians could comprehend, and it confined me to my chamber for many days; but I knew, myself, that I was bewitched, and suspected my father's reputed concubine of the deed. I told my fears to my reverend protector, who hesitated concerning them, but I knew by his words and looks that he was conscious I was right. I generally conceived myself to be two people. When I lay in bed, I deemed there were two of us in it; when I sat up, I always beheld another person, and always in the same position from the place where I sat or stood, which was about three paces off me towards my left side. It mattered not how many or how few were present: this my second self was sure to be present in his place; and this occasioned a confusion in all my words and ideas that utterly astounded my friends, who all declared, that instead of being deranged in my intellect, they had never heard my conversation manifest so much energy or sublimity of conception; but for all that, over the singular delusion that I was two persons, my reasoning faculties had no power. The most perverse part of it was, that I rarely conceived *myself* to be any of the two persons. I thought for the most part that my companion was one of them, and my brother the other; and I found, that to be obliged to speak and answer in the character of another man, was a most awkward business at the long run.

Who can doubt, from this statement, that I was bewitched, and that my relatives were at the ground of it? The constant and unnatural persuasion that I was my brother, proved it to my own satisfaction, and must, I think, do so to every unprejudiced person. This victory of the wicked one over me kept me confined in my chamber, at Mr Millar's house, for nearly a month, until the prayers of the faithful prevailed, and I was restored. I knew it was a chastisement for my pride, because my heart was lifted up at my superiority over the enemies of the church; nevertheless, I determined to make short work with the aggressor, that the righteous might not be subjected to the effect of his diabolical arts again.

I say I was confined a month. I beg he that readeth to take note of this, that he may estimate how much the word, or even the oath, of a wicked man, is to depend on. For a month I saw no one but such as came into my room, and for all that, it will be seen, that there were plenty of the same set to attest upon oath that I saw my brother every day during that period; that I persecuted him with my presence day and night, while all the time I never saw his face, save in a delusive dream. I cannot comprehend what manœuvres my illustrious friend was playing off with them about this time; for he, having the art of personating whom he chose, had peradventure deceived them, else so many of them had never all attested the same thing. I never saw any man so steady in his friendships and attentions as he; but as he made a rule of never calling at private houses, for fear of some discovery being made of his person, so I never saw him while my malady lasted; but as soon as I grew better, I knew I had nothing ado but to attend at some of our places of meeting, to see him again. He was punctual, as usual, and I had not to wait.

My reception was precisely as I apprehended. There was no flaring, no flummery, nor bombastical pretensions, but a dignified return to my obeisance, and an immediate recurrence, in converse, to the important duties incumbent on us, in our stations, as reformers and purifiers of the Church.

'I have marked out a number of most dangerous characters in this city,' said he, 'all of whom must be cut off from cumbering the true vineyard before we leave this land. And if you bestir not yourself in the work to which you are called, I must raise up others who shall have the honour of it.'

'I am, most illustrious prince, wholly at your service,' said I. 'Show but what ought to be done, and here is the heart to dare, and the hand to execute. You pointed out my relations, according to the flesh, as brands fitted to be thrown into the burning. I approve peremptorily of the award; nay, I thirst to accomplish it; for I myself have suffered severely from their diabolical arts. When once that trial of my devotion to the faith is accomplished, then be your future operations disclosed.'

'You are free of your words and promises,' said he.

'So will I be of my deeds in the service of my master, and that shalt thou see,' said I. 'I lack not the spirit, nor the will, but I lack experience wofully; and because of that shortcoming, must bow to your suggestions.'

'Meet me here to-morrow betimes,' said he, 'and perhaps you may hear of some opportunity of displaying your zeal in the cause of righteousness.'

I met him as he desired me; and he addressed me with a hurried and joyful expression, telling me that my brother was astir, and that a few minutes ago he had seen him pass on his way to the mountain. 'The hill is wrapped in a cloud,' added he, 'and never was there such an opportunity of executing divine justice on a guilty sinner. You may trace him in the dew, and shall infallibly find him on the top of some precipice; for it is only in secret that he dares show his debased head to the sun.'

'I have no arms, else assuredly I would pursue him and discomfit him,' said I.

'Here is a small dagger,' said he; 'I have nothing of weapon-kind about me save that, but it is a potent one; and should you require it, there is nothing more ready or sure.'

'Will not you accompany me?' said I: 'Sure you will?'

'I will be with you, or near you,' said he. 'Go you on before.'

I hurried away as he directed me, and imprudently asked

some of Queensberry's guards if such and such a young man passed by them going out from the city. I was answered in the affirmative, and till then had doubted of my friend's intelligence, it was so inconsistent with a profligate's life to be so early astir. When I got the certain intelligence that my brother was before me, I fell a-running, scarcely knowing what I did; and looking several times behind me, I perceived nothing of my zealous and arbitrary friend. The consequence of this was, that by the time I reached St Anthony's well, my resolution began to give way. It was not my courage, for now that I had once shed blood in the cause of the true faith, I was exceedingly bold and ardent; but whenever I was left to myself, I was subject to sinful doubtings. These always hankered on one point: I doubted if the elect were infallible, and if the Scripture promises to them were binding in all situations and relations. I confess this, and that it was a sinful and shameful weakness in me, but my nature was subject to it, and I could not eschew it. I never doubted that I was one of the elect myself; for, besides the strong inward and spiritual conviction that I possessed, I had my kind father's assurance; and these had been revealed to him in that way and measure that they could not be doubted.

In this desponding state, I sat myself down on a stone, and bethought me of the rashness of my understanding.[25] I tried to ascertain, to my own satisfaction, whether or not I really had been commissioned of God to perpetrate these crimes in his behalf, for in the eyes, and by the laws of men, they were great and crying transgressions. While I sat pondering on these things, I was involved in a veil of white misty vapour, and looking up to heaven, I was just about to ask direction from above, when I heard as it were a still small voice close by me, which uttered some words of derision and chiding. I looked intensely in the direction whence it seemed to come, and perceived a lady, robed in white, who hasted toward me. She regarded me with a severity of look and gesture that appalled me so much, I could not address her; but she waited not for that, but coming close to my side, said, without stopping, 'Preposterous wretch! how dare you lift your eyes to heaven with such purposes in your heart? Escape homeward, and save your soul, or farewell for ever!'

These were all the words that she uttered, as far as I could ever recollect, but my spirits were kept in such a tumult that morning, that something might have escaped me. I followed her eagerly with my eyes, but in a moment she glided over the rocks above the holy well, and vanished. I persuaded myself that I had seen a vision, and that the radiant being that had addressed me was one of the good angels, or guardian spirits, commissioned by the Almighty to watch over the steps of the just. My first impulse was to follow her advice, and make my escape home; for I thought to myself, 'How is this interested[26] and mysterious foreigner, a proper judge of the actions of a free Christian?'

The thought was hardly framed, nor had I moved in a retrograde direction six steps, when I saw my illustrious friend and great adviser descending the ridge towards me with hasty and impassioned strides. My heart fainted within me; and when he came up and addressed me, I looked as one caught in a trespass. 'What hath detained thee, thou desponding trifler?' said he. 'Verily now shall the golden opportunity be lost which may never be recalled. I have traced the reprobate to his sanctuary in the cloud, and lo he is perched on the pinnacle of a precipice an hundred fathoms high. One ketch with thy foot, or toss with thy finger, shall throw him from thy sight into the foldings of the cloud, and he shall be no more seen, till found at the bottom of the cliff dashed to pieces. Make haste therefore, thou loiterer, if thou wouldst ever prosper and rise to eminence in the work of thy Lord and master.'

'I go no farther on this work,' said I, 'for I have seen a vision that has reprimanded the deed.'

'A vision?' said he: 'Was it that wench who descended from the hill?'

'The being that spake to me, and warned me of my danger, was indeed in the form of a lady,' said I.

'She also approached me and said a few words,' returned he; 'and I thought there was something mysterious in her manner.

Pray, what did she say? for the words of such a singular message, and from such a messenger, ought to be attended to. If I understood her aright, she was chiding us for our misbelief and preposterous delay.'

I recited her words, but he answered that I had been in a state of sinful doubting at the time, and it was to these doubtings she had adverted. In short, this wonderful and clear-sighted stranger soon banished all my doubts and despondency, making me utterly ashamed of them, and again I set out with him in the pursuit of my brother. He showed me the traces of his footsteps in the dew, and pointed out the spot where I should find him. 'You have nothing more to do than go softly down behind him,' said he; 'which you can do to within an ell of him, without being seen; then rush upon him, and throw him from his seat, where there is neither footing nor hold. I will go, meanwhile, and amuse his sight by some exhibition in the contrary direction, and he shall neither know nor perceive who has done him this *kind office*: for, exclusive of more weighty concerns, be assured of this, that the sooner he falls, the fewer crimes will he have to answer for, and his estate in the other world will be proportionally more tolerable, than if he spent a long unregenerate life steeped in iniquity to the loathing of the soul.'

'Nothing can be more plain or more pertinent,' said I: 'therefore I fly to perform that which is both a duty toward God and toward man!'

'You shall yet rise to great honour and preferment,' said he.

'I value it not, provided I do honour and justice to the cause of my master here,' said I.

'You shall be lord of your father's riches and demesnes,' added he.

'I disclaim and deride every selfish motive thereto relating,' said I, 'farther than as it enables me to do good.'

'Ay, but that is a great and a heavenly consideration, that *longing for ability to do good*,' said he – and as he said so, I could not help remarking a certain derisive exultation of expression which I could not comprehend; and indeed I have noted this very often in my illustrious friend, and sometimes mentioned it civilly to him, but he has never failed to disclaim it. On this occasion I said nothing, but concealing his poniard in my clothes, I hasted up the mountain, determined to execute my purpose before any misgivings should again visit me; and I never had more ado, than in keeping firm my resolution. I could not help my thoughts, and there are certain trains and classes of thoughts that have great power in enervating the mind. I thought of the awful thing of plunging a fellow creature from the top of a cliff into the dark and misty void below – of his being dashed to pieces on the protruding rocks, and of hearing his shrieks as he descended the cloud, and beheld the shagged points on which he was to alight. Then I thought of plunging a soul so abruptly into hell, or, at the best, sending it to hover on the confines of that burning abyss – of its appearance at the bar of the Almighty to receive its sentence. And then I thought, 'Will there not be a sentence pronounced against me there, by a jury of the just made perfect, and written down in the registers of heaven?'

These thoughts, I say, came upon me unasked, and instead of being able to dispel them, they mustered, upon the summit of my imagination, in thicker and stronger array: and there was another that impressed me in a very particular manner, though, I have reason to believe, not so strongly as those above written. It was this: 'What if I should fail in my first effort? Will the consequence not be that I am tumbled[27] from the top of the rock myself?' and then all the feelings anticipated, with regard to both body and soul, must happen to me! This was a spine-breaking reflection; and yet, though the probability was rather on that side, my zeal in the cause of godliness was such that it carried me on, maugre all danger and dismay.

I soon came close upon my brother, sitting on the dizzy pinnacle, with his eyes fixed stedfastly in the direction opposite to me. I descended the little green ravine behind him with my feet foremost, and every now and then raised my head, and watched his motions. His posture continued the same, until at last I came so near him I could have heard him breathe, if his face had been towards me. I laid my cap aside, and made me ready to spring upon him, and push him over. I could not for

my life accomplish it! I do not think it was that *I durst not*, for
I have always felt my courage equal to any thing in a good
cause. But I had not the heart, or something that I ought to
have had. In short, it was not done in time, as it easily might
have been. These THOUGHTS are hard enemies wherewith to
combat! And I was so grieved that I could not effect my righteous purpose, that I laid me down on my face and shed tears.
Then, again, I thought of what my great enlightened friend and
patron would say to me, and again my resolution rose indignant, and indissoluble save by blood. I arose on my right knee
and left foot, and had just begun to advance the latter forward:
the next step my great purpose had been accomplished, and the
culprit had suffered the punishment due to his crimes. But what
moved him I knew not: in the critical moment he sprung to his
feet, and dashing himself furiously against me, he overthrew
me, at the imminent peril of my life. I disencumbered myself by
main force, and fled, but he overhied me, knocked me down,
and threatened, with dreadful oaths, to throw me from the cliff.
After I was a little recovered from the stunning blow, I aroused
myself to the combat; and though I do not recollect the circumstances of that deadly scuffle very minutely, I know that I
vanquished him so far as to force him to ask my pardon, and
crave a reconciliation. I spurned at both, and left him to the
chastisements of his own wicked and corrupt heart.

My friend met me again on the hill, and derided me, in a
haughty and stern manner, for my imbecility and want of
decision. I told him how nearly I had effected my purpose, and
excused myself as well as I was able. On this, seeing me bleeding,
he advised me to swear the peace against my brother, and have
him punished in the mean time, he being the first aggressor.
I promised compliance, and we parted, for I was somewhat
ashamed of my failure, and was glad to be quit for the present
of one of whom I stood so much in awe.

When my reverend father beheld me bleeding a second time
by the hand of a brother, he was moved to the highest point of
displeasure; and, relying on his high interest and the justice of
his cause, he brought the matter at once before the courts. My
brother and I were first examined face to face. His declaration

was a mere romance: mine was not the truth; but as it was by the advice of my reverend father, and that of my illustrious friend, both of whom I knew to be sincere Christians and true believers, that I gave it, I conceived myself completely justified on that score. I said, I had gone up into the mountain early on the morning to pray, and had withdrawn myself, for entire privacy, into a little sequestered dell – had laid aside my cap, and was in the act of kneeling, when I was rudely attacked by my brother, knocked over, and nearly slain. They asked my brother if this was true. He acknowledged that it was; that I was bare-headed, and in the act of kneeling, when he ran foul of me without any intent of doing so. But the judge took him to task on the improbability of this, and put the profligate sore out of countenance. The rest of his tale told still worse, insomuch that he was laughed at by all present, for the judge remarked to him, that granting it was true that he had at first run against me on an open mountain, and overthrown me by accident, how was it, that after I had extricated myself and fled, that he had pursued, overtaken, and knocked me down a second time? Would he pretend that all that was likewise by chance? The culprit had nothing to say for himself on this head, and I shall not forget my exultation and that of my reverend father, when the sentence of the judge was delivered. It was, that my wicked brother should be thrown into prison, and tried on a criminal charge of assault and battery, with the intent of committing murder. This was a just and righteous judge, and saw things in their proper bearings, that is, he could discern between a righteous and a wicked man, and then there could be no doubt as to which of the two were acting right, and which wrong.

Had I not been sensible that a justified person could do nothing wrong, I should not have been at my ease concerning the statement I had been induced to give on this occasion. I could easily perceive, that by rooting out the weeds from the garden of the Church, I heightened the growth of righteousness; but as to the tardy way of giving false evidence on matters of such doubtful issue, I confess I saw no great propriety in it from the beginning. But I now only moved by the will and mandate of my illustrious friend: I had no peace or comfort when out of his sight, nor have I ever been able to boast of much in his presence; so true is it that a Christian's life is one of suffering.

My time was now much occupied, along with my reverend preceptor, in making ready for the approaching trial, as the prosecutors. Our counsel assured us of a complete victory, and that banishment would be the mildest award of the law on the offender. Mark how different was the result! From the shifts and ambiguities of a wicked Bench, who had a fellow-feeling of iniquity with the defenders, my suit was cast, the graceless libertine was absolved, and I was incarcerated, and bound over to keep the peace, with heavy penalties, before I was set at liberty.

I was exceedingly disgusted at this issue, and blamed the counsel of my friend to his face. He expressed great grief, and expatiated on the wickedness of our judicatories, adding, 'I see I cannot depend on you for quick and summary measures, but for your sake I shall be revenged on that wicked judge, and that you shall see in a few days.' The Lord Justice Clerk died that same week! But he died in his own house and his own bed, and by what means my friend effected it, I do not know. He would not tell me a single word of the matter, but the judge's sudden death made a great noise, and I made so many curious inquiries regarding the particulars of it, that some suspicions were like to attach to our family, of some unfair means used. For my part I know nothing, and rather think he died by the visitation of Heaven, and that my friend had foreseen it, by symptoms, and soothed me by promises of complete revenge.

It was some days before he mentioned my brother's meditated death to me again, and certainly he then found me exasperated against him personally to the highest degree. But I told him that I could not now think any more of it, owing to the late judgment of the court, by which, if my brother were missing or found dead, I would not only forfeit my life, but my friends would be ruined by the penalties.

'I suppose you know and believe in the perfect safety of your soul,' said he, 'and that that is a matter settled from the beginning of time, and now sealed and ratified both in heaven and earth?'

'I believe in it thoroughly and perfectly,' said I; 'and whenever I entertain doubts of it, I am sensible of sin and weakness.'

'Very well, so then am I,' said he. 'I think I can now divine, with all manner of certainty, what will be the high and merited guerdon of your immortal part. Hear me then farther: I give you my solemn assurance, and bond of blood, that no human hand shall ever henceforth be able to injure your life, or shed one drop of your precious blood, but it is on the condition that you walk always by my directions.'

'I will do so with cheerfulness,' said I; 'for without your enlightened counsel, I feel that I can do nothing. But as to your power of protecting my life, you must excuse me for doubting of it. Nay, were we in your own proper dominions, you could not ensure that.'

'In whatever dominion or land I am, my power accompanies me,' said he; 'and it is only against human might and human weapon that I ensure your life; on that will I keep an eye, and on that you may depend. I have never broken word or promise with you. Do you credit me?'

'Yes, I do,' said I; 'for I see you are in earnest. I believe, though I do not comprehend you.'

'Then why do you not at once challenge your brother to the field of honour? Seeing you now act without danger, cannot you also act without fear?'

'It is not fear,' returned I; 'believe me, I hardly know what fear is. It is a doubt, that on all these emergencies constantly haunts my mind, that in performing such and such actions I may fall from my upright state. This makes fratricide a fearful task.'

'This is imbecility itself,' said he. 'We have settled, and agreed on that point an hundred times. I would therefore advise that you challenge your brother to single combat. I shall ensure your safety, and he cannot refuse giving you satisfaction.'

'But then the penalties?' said I.

'We will try to evade these,' said he; 'and supposing you

should be caught, if once you are Laird of Dalcastle and Balgrennan, what are the penalties to you?'

'Might we not rather pop him off in private and quietness, as we did the deistical divine?' said I.

'The deed would be alike meritorious, either way,' said he. 'But may we not wait for years before we find an opportunity? My advice is to challenge him, as privately as you will, and there cut him off.'

'So be it then,' said I. 'When the moon is at the full, I will send for him forth to speak with one, and there will I smite him and slay him, and he shall trouble the righteous no more.'

'Then this is the very night,' said he. 'The moon is nigh to the full, and this night your brother and his sinful mates hold carousal; for there is an intended journey to-morrow. The exulting profligate leaves town, where we must remain till the time of my departure hence; and then is he safe, and must live to dishonour God, and not only destroy his own soul, but those of many others. Alack, and wo is me! The sins that he and his friends will commit this very night, will cry to heaven against us for our shameful delay! When shall our great work of cleansing the sanctuary be finished, if we proceed at this puny rate?'

'I see the deed *must* be done, then,' said I; 'and since it is so, it shall be done. I will arm myself forthwith, and from the midst of his wine and debauchery you shall call him forth to me, and there will I smite him with the edge of the sword, that our great work be not retarded.'

'If thy execution were equal to thy intent, how great a man you soon might be!' said he. 'We shall make the attempt once more; and if it fail again, why, I must use other means to bring about my high purposes relating to mankind. Home and make ready. I will go and procure what information I can regarding their motions, and will meet you in disguise twenty minutes hence, at the first turn of Hewie's lane beyond the loch.'

'I have nothing to make ready,' said I; 'for I do not choose to go home. Bring me a sword, that we may consecrate it with prayer and vows, and if I use it not to the bringing down of the wicked and profane, then may the Lord do so to me, and more also!'

We parted, and there was I left again to the multiplicity of my own thoughts for the space of twenty minutes, a thing my friend never failed in subjecting me to, and these were worse to contend with than hosts of sinful men. I prayed inwardly, that these deeds of mine might never be brought to the knowledge of men who were incapable of appreciating the high motives that led to them; and then I sung part of the 10th Psalm,[28] likewise in spirit; but for all these efforts, my sinful doubts returned, so that when my illustrious friend joined me, and proffered me the choice of two gilded rapiers, I declined accepting any of them, and began, in a very bold and energetic manner, to express my doubts regarding the justification of all the deeds of perfect men. He chided me severely, and branded me with cowardice, a thing that my nature never was subject to; and then he branded me with falsehood, and breach of the most solemn engagements both to God and man.

I was compelled to take the rapier, much against my inclination; but for all the arguments, threats, and promises that he could use, I would not consent to send a challenge to my brother by his mouth. There was one argument only that he made use of which had some weight with me, but yet it would not preponderate. He told me my brother was gone to a notorious and scandalous habitation of women, and that if I left him to himself for ever so short a space longer, it might embitter his state through ages to come. This was a trying concern to me; but I resisted it, and reverted to my doubts. On this he said that he had meant to do me honour, but since I put it out of his power, he would do the deed, and take the responsibility on himself. 'I have with sore travail procured a guardship of your life,' added he. 'For my own, I have not; but, be that as it will, I shall not be baffled in my attempts to benefit my friends without a trial. You will at all events accompany me, and see that I get justice?'

'Certes, I will do thus much,' said I; 'and wo be to him if his arm prevail against my friend and patron!'

His lip curled with a smile of contempt, which I could hardly brook; and I began to be afraid that the eminence to which I had been destined by him was already fading from my view.

And I thought what I should then do to ingratiate myself again with him, for without his countenance I had no life. 'I will be a man in act,' thought I, 'but in sentiment I will not yield, and for this he must surely admire me the more.'

As we emerged from the shadowy lane into the fair moonshine, I started so that my whole frame underwent the most chilling vibrations of surprise. I again thought I had been taken at unawares, and was conversing with another person. My friend was equipped in the Highland garb, and so completely translated into another being, that, save by his speech, all the senses of mankind could not have recognized him. I blessed myself, and asked whom it was his pleasure to personify tonight? He answered me carelessly, that it was a spark whom he meant should bear the blame of whatever might fall out to-night; and that was all that passed on the subject.

We proceeded by some stone steps at the foot of the North Loch, in hot argument all the way. I was afraid that our conversation might be overheard, for the night was calm and almost as light as day, and we saw sundry people crossing us as we advanced. But the zeal of my friend was so high, that he disregarded all danger, and continued to argue fiercely and loudly on my delinquency, as he was pleased to call it. I stood on one argument alone, which was, 'that I did not think the Scripture promises to the elect, taken in their utmost latitude, warranted the assurance that they could do no wrong; and that, therefore, it behoved every man to look well to his steps.'

There was no religious scruple that irritated my enlightened friend and master so much as this. He could not endure it. And the sentiments of our great covenanted reformers being on his side, there is not a doubt that I was wrong. He lost all patience on hearing what I advanced on this matter, and taking hold of me, he led me into a darksome booth in a confined entry; and, after a friendly but cutting reproach, he bade me remain there in secret and watch the event; 'and if I fall,' said he, 'you will not fail to avenge my death?'

I was so entirely overcome with vexation that I could make no answer, on which he left me abruptly, a prey to despair; and I saw or heard no more, till he came down to the moonlight green followed by my brother. They had quarrelled before they came within my hearing, for the first words I heard were those of my brother, who was in a state of intoxication, and he was urging a reconciliation, as was his wont on such occasions. My friend spurned at the suggestion, and dared him to the combat; and after a good deal of boastful altercation, which the turmoil of my spirits prevented me from remembering, my brother was compelled to draw his sword and stand on the defensive. It was a desperate and terrible engagement. I at first thought that the royal stranger and great champion of the faith would overcome his opponent with ease, for I considered heaven as on his side, and nothing but the arm of sinful flesh against him. But I was deceived: The sinner stood firm as a rock, while the assailant flitted about like a shadow, or rather like a spirit. I smiled inwardly, conceiving that these lightsome manœuvres were all a sham to show off his art and mastership in the exercise, and that whenever they came to close fairly, that instant my brother would be overcome. Still I was deceived: My brother's arm seemed invincible, so that the closer they fought the more palpably did it prevail. They fought round the green to the very edge of the water, and so round, till they came close up to the covert where I stood. There being no more room to shift ground, my brother then forced him to come to close quarters, on which, the former still having the decided advantage, my friend quitted his sword, and called out. I could resist no longer; so, springing from my concealment, I rushed between them with my sword drawn, and parted them as if they had been two schoolboys: then turning to my brother, I addressed him as follows: 'Wretch! miscreant! knowest thou what thou art attempting? Wouldst thou lay thine hand on the Lord's anointed, or shed his precious blood? Turn thee to me, that I may chastise thee for all thy wickedness, and not for the many injuries thou hast done to me!' To it we went, with full thirst of vengeance on every side. The duel was fierce; but the might of heaven prevailed, and not my might. The ungodly and reprobate young man fell, covered with wounds, and with curses and blasphemy in his mouth, while I escaped uninjured. Thereto his power extended not.

I will not deny, that my own immediate impressions of this affair in some degree differed from this statement. But this is precisely as my illustrious friend described it to me afterwards, and I can rely implicitly on his information, as he was at that time a looker-on, and my senses all in a state of agitation, and he could have no motive for saying what was not the positive truth.

Never till my brother was down did we perceive that there had been witnesses to the whole business. Our ears were then astounded by rude challenges of unfair play, which were quite appalling to me; but my friend laughed at them, and conducted me off in perfect safety. As to the unfairness of the transaction, I can say thus much, that my royal friend's sword was down ere ever mine was presented. But if it still be accounted unfair to take up a conqueror, and punish him in his own way, I answer: That if a man is sent on a positive mission by his master, and hath laid himself under vows to do his work, he ought not to be too nice[29] in the means of accomplishing it; and farther, I appeal to holy writ, wherein many instances are recorded of the pleasure the Lord takes in the final extinction of the wicked and profane; and this position I take to be unanswerable.

I was greatly disturbed in my mind for many days, knowing that the transaction had been witnessed, and sensible also of the perilous situation I occupied, owing to the late judgment of the court against me. But, on the contrary, I never saw my enlightened friend in such high spirits. He assured me there was no danger; and again repeated, that he warranted my life against the power of man. I thought proper, however, to remain in hiding for a week; but, as he said, to my utter amazement, the blame fell on another, who was not only accused, but pronounced guilty by the general voice, and outlawed for non-appearance! how could I doubt, after this, that the hand of heaven was aiding and abetting me? The matter was beyond my comprehension; and as for my friend, he never explained any thing that was past, but his activity and art were without a parallel.

He enjoyed our success mightily; and for his sake I enjoyed

it somewhat, but it was on account of his comfort only, for I could not for my life perceive in what degree the church was better or purer than before these deeds were done. He continued to flatter me with great things, as to honours, fame, and emolument; and, above all, with the blessing and protection of him to whom my body and soul were dedicated. But after these high promises, I got no longer peace; for he began to urge the death of my father with such an unremitting earnestness, that I found I had nothing for it but to comply. I did so; and cannot express his enthusiasm of approbation. So much did he hurry and press me in this, that I was forced to devise some of the most openly violent measures, having no alternative. Heaven spared me the deed, taking, in that instance, the vengeance in its own hand; for before my arm could effect the sanguine but meritorious act, the old man followed his son to the grave. My illustrious and zealous friend seemed to regret this somewhat; but he comforted himself with the reflection, that still I had the merit of it, having not only consented to it, but in fact effected it, for by doing the one action I had brought about both.

No sooner were the obsequies of the funeral over, than my friend and I went to Dalcastle, and took undisputed possession of the houses, lands, and effects that had been my father's; but his plate, and vast treasures of ready money, he had bestowed on a voluptuous and unworthy creature, who had lived long with him as a mistress. Fain would I have sent her after her lover, and gave my friend some hints on the occasion; but he only shook his head, and said that we must lay all selfish and interested motives out of the question.

For a long time, when I awaked in the morning, I could not believe my senses, that I was indeed the undisputed and sole proprietor of so much wealth and grandeur; and I felt so much gratified, that I immediately set about doing all the good I was able, hoping to meet with all approbation and encouragement from my friend. I was mistaken: He checked the very first impulses towards such a procedure, questioned my motives, and uniformly made them out to be wrong. There was one morning that a servant said to me, there was a lady in the back chamber who wanted to speak with me, but he could not tell me who it was, for all the old servants had left the mansion, every one on hearing of the death of the late laird, and those who had come knew none of the people in the neighbourhood. From several circumstances, I had suspicions of private confabulations with women, and refused to go to her, but bid the servant inquire what she wanted. She would not tell; she could only state the circumstances to me; so I, being sensible that a little dignity of manner became me in my elevated situation, returned for answer, that if it was business that could not be transacted by my steward, it must remain untransacted. The answer which the servant brought back was of a threatening nature. She stated that she *must* see me, and if I refused her satisfaction there, she would compel it where I should not evite her.

My friend and director appeared pleased with my dilemma, and rather advised that I should hear what the woman had to say; on which I consented, provided she would deliver her mission in his presence. She came in with manifest signs of anger and indignation, and began with a bold and direct charge against me of a shameful assault on one of her daughters; of having used the basest of means in order to lead her aside from the paths of rectitude; and on the failure of these, of having resorted to the most unqualified measures.

I denied the charge in all its bearings, assuring the dame that I had never so much as seen either of her daughters to my knowledge, far less wronged them; on which she got into great wrath, and abused me to my face as an accomplished vagabond, hypocrite, and sensualist; and she went so far as to tell me roundly, that if I did not *marry* her daughter, she would bring me to the gallows, and that in a very short time.

'Marry your daughter, honest woman!' said I, 'on the faith of a Christian, I never saw your daughter; and you may rest assured in this, that I will neither marry you nor her. Do you consider how short a time I have been in this place? How much that time has been occupied? And how there was even a *possibility* that I could have accomplished such villainies?'

'And how long does your Christian reverence suppose you have remained in this place since the late laird's death?' said she.

'That is too well known to need recapitulation,' said I: 'only a very few days, though I cannot at present specify the exact number; perhaps from thirty to forty, or so. But in all that time, certes, I have never seen either you or any of your two daughters that you talk of. You must be quite sensible of that.'

My friend shook his head three times during this short sentence, while the woman held up her hands in amazement and disgust, exclaiming, 'There goes the self-righteous one! There goes the consecrated youth, who cannot err! You, sir, know, and the world shall know of the faith that is in this most just, devout, and religious miscreant! Can you deny that you have already been in this place four months and seven days? Or that in that time you have been forbid my house twenty times? Or that you have persevered in your endeavours to effect the basest and most ungenerous of purposes? Or that you *have* attained them? hypocrite and deceiver as you are! Yes, sir; I say, dare you deny that you *have* attained your vile, selfish, and degrading purposes towards a young, innocent, and unsuspecting creature, and thereby ruined a poor widow's only hope in this world? No, you cannot look in my face, and deny aught of this.'

'The woman is raving mad!' said I. 'You, illustrious sir, know, that in the first instance, I have not yet been in this place *one* month.' My friend shook his head again, and answered me, 'You are wrong, my dear friend; you are wrong. It is indeed the space of time that the lady hath stated, to a day, since you came here, and I came with you; and I am sorry that I know for certain that you have been frequently haunting her house, and have often had private correspondence with one of the young ladies too. Of the nature of it I presume not to know.'

'You are mocking me,' said I. 'But as well may you try to reason me out of my existence, as to convince me that I have been here even one month, or that any of those things you allege against me has the shadow of truth or evidence to support it. I will swear to you, by the great God that made me; and by—'

'Hold, thou most abandoned profligate!' cried she violently, 'and do not add perjury to your other detestable crimes. Do not, for mercy's sake, any more profane that name whose attributes you have wrested and disgraced. But tell me what reparation you propose offering to my injured child?'

'I again declare, before heaven, woman, that to the best of my knowledge and recollection, I never saw your daughter. I now think I have some faint recollection of having seen your face, but where, or in what place, puzzles me quite.'

'And, why?' said she. 'Because for months and days you have been in such a state of extreme inebriety, that your time has gone over like a dream that has been forgotten. I believe, that from the day you came first to my house, you have been in a state of utter delirium, and that principally from the fumes of wine and ardent spirits.'

'It is a manifest falsehood!' said I; 'I have never, since I entered on the possession of Dalcastle, tasted wine or spirits, saving once, a few evenings ago; and, I confess to my shame, that I was led too far; but I have craved forgiveness and obtained it. I take my noble and distinguished friend there for a witness to the truth of what I assert; a man who has done more, and sacrificed more for the sake of genuine Christianity, than any this world contains. Him you will believe.'

'I hope you have attained forgiveness,' said he, seriously. 'Indeed it would be next to blasphemy to doubt it. But, of late, you have been very much addicted to intemperance. I doubt if, from the first night you tasted the delights of drunkenness, that you have ever again been in your right mind until Monday last. Doubtless you have been for a good while most diligent in your addresses to this lady's daughter.'

'This is unaccountable,' said I. 'It is impossible that I can have been doing a thing, and not doing it at the same time. But indeed, honest woman, there have several incidents occurred to me in the course of my life which persuade me I have a second self; or that there is some other being who appears in my likeness.'

Here my friend interrupted me with a sneer, and a hint that I was talking insanely; and then he added, turning to the lady, 'I know my friend Mr Colwan will do what is just and right.

Go and bring the young lady to him, that he may see her, and he will then recollect all his former amours with her.'

'I humbly beg your pardon, sir,' said I. 'But the mention of such a thing as *amours* with any woman existing, to me, is really so absurd, so far from my principles, so far from the purity of nature and frame to which I was born and consecrated, that I hold it as an insult, and regard it with contempt.'

I would have said more in reprobation of such an idea, had not my servant entered, and said, that a gentleman wanted to see me on business. Being glad of an opportunity of getting quit of my lady visitor, I ordered the servant to show him in; and forthwith a little lean gentleman, with a long aquiline nose, and a bald head, daubed all over with powder and pomatum, entered. I thought I recollected having seen him too, but could not remember his name, though he spoke to me with the greatest familiarity; at least, that sort of familiarity that an official person generally assumes. He bustled about and about, speaking to every one, but declined listening for a single moment to any. The lady offered to withdraw, but he stopped her.

'No, no, Mrs Keeler, you need not go; you need not go; you *must* not go, madam. The business I came about, concerns you – yes, that it does – Bad business yon of Walker's? Eh? Could not help it – did all I could, Mr Wringhim. Done your business. Have it all cut and dry here, sir – No, this is not it – Have it among them, though – I'm at a little loss for your name, sir (addressing my friend) – seen you very often, though – exceedingly often – quite well acquainted with you.'

'No, sir, you are not,' said my friend, sternly. The intruder never regarded him; never so much as lifted his eyes from his bundle of law papers, among which he was bustling with great hurry and importance, but went on—

'*Im*possible! Have seen a face very like it, then – what did you say your name was, sir? – very like it indeed. Is it not the young laird who was murdered whom you resemble so much?'

Here Mrs Keeler uttered a scream, which so much startled me, that it seems I grew pale. And on looking at my friend's face, there was something struck me so forcibly in the likeness between him and my late brother, that I had very nearly fainted. The woman exclaimed, that it was my brother's spirit that stood beside me.

'Impossible!' exclaimed the attorney; 'at least I hope not, else his signature is not worth a pin. There is some balance due on yon business, madam. Do you wish your account? because I have it here, ready discharged, and it does not suit letting such things lie over. This business of Mr Colwan's will be a severe one on you, madam – rather a severe one.'

'What business of mine, if it be your will, sir,' said I. 'For my part I never engaged you in business of any sort, less or more.' He never regarded me, but went on. 'You may appeal, though: Yes, yes, there are such things as appeals for the refractory. Here it is, gentlemen, here they are all together. Here is, in the first place, sir, your power of attorney, regularly warranted, sealed, and signed with your own hand.'

'I declare solemnly that I never signed that document,' said I.

'Ay, ay, the system of denial is not a bad one in general,' said my attorney; 'but at present there is no occasion for it. You do not deny your own hand?'

'I deny every thing connected with the business,' cried I; 'I disclaim it *in toto*, and declare that I know no more about it than the child unborn.'

'That is exceedingly good!' exclaimed he; 'I like your pertinacity vastly! I have three of your letters, and three of your signatures; that part is all settled, and I hope so is the whole affair; for here is the original grant to your father, which he has never thought proper to put in requisition. Simple gentleman! But here have I, Lawyer Linkum, in one hundredth part of the time that any other notary, writer, attorney, or writer to the signet in Britain, would have done it, procured the signature of his Majesty's commissioner, and thereby confirmed the charter to you and your house, sir, for ever and ever – Begging your pardon, madam.' The lady, as well as myself, tried several times to interrupt the loquacity of Linkum, but in vain: he only raised his hand with a quick flourish, and went on:

'Here it is: "JAMES, by the grace of God, King of Great Britain, France, and Ireland, to his right trusty cousin, sendeth greeting: And whereas his right leal and trust-worthy cousin, George Colwan, of Dalcastle and Balgrennan, hath suffered great losses, and undergone much hardship, on behalf of his Majesty's rights and titles; he therefore, for himself, and as prince and steward of Scotland, and by the consent of his right trusty cousins and councillors, hereby grants to the said George Colwan, his heirs and assignees whatsomever, heritably and irrevocably, all and haill the lands and others underwritten: *To wit*, All and haill, the five merk land of Kipplerig; the five pound land of Easter Knockward, with all the towers, fortalices, manor-places, houses, biggings, yards, orchards, tofts, crofts, mills, woods, fishings, mosses, muirs, meadows, commonties, pasturages, coals, coal-heughs, tenants, tenantries, services of free tenants, annexes, connexes, dependencies, parts, pendicles, and pertinents of the same whatsomever; to be peaceably brooked, joysed, set, used, and disposed of by him and his aboves, as specified, heritably and irrevocably, in all time coming: And, in testimony thereof, His Majesty, for himself, and as prince and steward of Scotland, with the advice and consent of his foresaids, knowledge, proper motive, and kingly power, makes, erects, creates, unites, annexes, and incorporates, the whole lands above mentioned in an haill and free barony, by all the rights, miethes, and marches thereof, old and divided, as the same lies, in length and breadth, in houses, biggings, mills, multures, hawking, hunting, fishing; with court, plaint, herezeld, fock, fork, sack, sock, thole, thame, vert, wraik, waith, wair, venison, outfang thief, infang thief, pit and gallows, and all and sundry other commodities. Given at our Court of Whitehall, &c. &c. God save the King.

Compositio 5 lib. 13. 8.

Registrate 26th September, 1687."[30]

'See, madam, here are ten signatures of privy councillors of that year, and here are other ten of the present year, with his Grace the Duke of Queensberry at the head. All right – See here it is, sir – all right – done your work. So you see, madam, this gentleman is the true and sole heritor of all the land that your father possesses, with all the rents thereof for the last twenty years, and upwards – Fine job for my employers! – sorry on your account, madam – can't help it.'

I was again going to disclaim all interest or connection in the matter, but my friend stopped me; and the plaints and lamentations of the dame became so overpowering, that they put an end to all farther colloquy; but Lawyer Linkum followed me, and stated his great outlay, and the important services he had rendered me, until I was obliged to subscribe an order to him for £100 on my banker.

I was now glad to retire with my friend, and ask seriously for some explanation of all this. It was in the highest degree unsatisfactory. He confirmed all that had been stated to me; assuring me, that I had not only been assiduous in my endeavours to seduce a young lady of great beauty, which it seemed I had effected, but that I had taken counsel, and got this supposed, old, false, and forged grant, raked up and new signed, to ruin the young lady's family quite, so as to throw her entirely on myself for protection, and be wholly at my will.

This was to me wholly incomprehensible. I could have freely made oath to the contrary of every particular. Yet the evidences were against me, and of a nature not to be denied. Here I must confess, that, highly as I disapproved of the love of women, and all intimacies and connections with the sex, I felt a sort of indefinite pleasure, an ungracious delight in having a beautiful woman solely at my disposal. But I thought of her spiritual good in the meantime. My friend spoke of my backslidings with concern; requesting me to make sure of my forgiveness, and to forsake them; and then he added some words of sweet comfort. But from this time forth I began to be sick at times of my existence. I had heart-burnings, longings, and yearnings, that would not be satisfied; and I seemed hardly to be an accountable creature; being thus in the habit of executing transactions of the utmost moment, without being sensible that I did them. I was a being incomprehensible to myself. Either I had a second self, who transacted business in my likeness, or else my body was at times possessed by a spirit over which it had no controul, and of whose actions my own soul was wholly unconscious.

This was an anomaly not to be accounted for by any philosophy of mine, and I was many times, in contemplating it, excited to terrors and mental torments hardly describable. To be in a state of consciousness and unconsciousness, at the same time, in the same body and same spirit, was impossible. I was under the greatest anxiety, dreading some change would take place momently in my nature; for of dates I could make nothing: one-half, or two-thirds of my time, seemed to me to be totally lost. I often, about this time, prayed with great fervour, and lamented my hopeless condition, especially in being liable to the commission of crimes, which I was not sensible of, and could not eschew. And I confess, notwithstanding the promises on which I had been taught to rely, I began to have secret terrors, that the great enemy of man's salvation was exercising powers over me, that might eventually lead to my ruin. These were but temporary and sinful fears, but they added greatly to my unhappiness.

The worst thing of all was, what hitherto I had never felt, and, as yet, durst not confess to myself, that the presence of my illustrious and devoted friend was becoming irksome to me. When I was by myself, I breathed freer, and my step was lighter; but, when he approached, a pang went to my heart, and, in his company, I moved and acted as if under a load that I could hardly endure. What a state to be in! And yet to shake him off was impossible – we were incorporated together – identified with one another, as it were, and the power was not in me to separate myself from him. I still knew nothing who he was, farther than that he was a potentate of some foreign land, bent on establishing some pure and genuine doctrines of Christianity, hitherto only half understood, and less than half exercised. Of this I could have no doubts, after all that he had said, done, and suffered in the cause. But, alongst with this, I was also certain, that he was possessed of some supernatural power, of the source of which I was wholly ignorant. That a man could be a Christian, and at the same time a powerful necromancer, appeared inconsistent, and adverse to every principle taught in our church; and from this I was led to believe, that he inherited his powers from on high, for I could not doubt either of the soundness of his principles, or that he accomplished things impossible to account for.

Thus was I sojourning in the midst of a chaos of confusion. I looked back on my bypast life with pain, as one looks back on a perilous journey, in which he has attained his end, without gaining any advantage either to himself, or others; and I looked forward, as on a darksome waste, full of repulsive and terrific shapes, pitfalls, and precipices, to which there was no definite bourne, and from which I turned with disgust. With my riches, my unhappiness was increased tenfold; and here, with another great acquisition of property, for which I had pleaded, and which I had gained in a dream, my miseries and difficulties were increasing. My principal feeling, about this time, was an insatiable longing for something that I cannot describe or denominate properly, unless I say it was for *utter oblivion* that I longed. I desired to sleep; but it was for a deeper and longer sleep, than that in which the senses were nightly steeped. I longed to be at rest and quiet, and close my eyes on the past and the future alike, as far as this frail life was concerned. But what had been formerly and finally settled in the counsels above, I presumed not to call in question.

In this state of irritation and misery, was I dragging on an existence, disgusted with all around me, and in particular with my mother, who, with all her love and anxiety, had such an insufferable mode of manifesting them, that she had by this time rendered herself exceedingly obnoxious to me. The very sound of her voice at a distance, went to my heart like an arrow, and made all my nerves to shrink; and as for the beautiful young lady of whom they told me I had been so much enamoured, I shunned all intercourse with her or hers, as I would have done with the devil. I read some of their letters and burnt them, but refused to see either the young lady or her mother, on any account.

About this time it was, that my worthy and reverend parent came with one of his elders to see my mother and myself. His presence always brought joy with it into our family, for my mother was uplifted, and I had so few who cared for me, or for whom I cared, that I felt rather gratified at seeing him. My illustrious friend was also much more attached to him, than any other person (except myself), for their religious principles tallied in every point, and their conversation was interesting, serious, and sublime. Being anxious to entertain well and highly the man to whom I had been so much indebted, and knowing that with all his integrity and righteousness, he disdained not the good things of this life, I brought from the late laird's well-stored cellars, various fragrant and salubrious wines, and we drank and became merry, and I found that my miseries and overpowering calamities, passed away over my head like a shower that is driven by the wind. I became elevated and happy, and welcomed my guests an hundred times; and then I joined them in religious conversation, with a zeal and enthusiasm which I had not often experienced, and which made all their hearts rejoice, so that I said to myself, 'Surely every gift of God is a blessing, and ought to be used with liberality and thankfulness.'

The next day I waked from a profound and feverish sleep, and called for something to drink. There was a servant answered whom I had never seen before, and he was clad in my servant's clothes and livery. I asked for Andrew Handyside, the servant who had waited at table the night before; but the man answered with a stare and a smile.

'What do you mean, sirrah,' said I. 'Pray what do you here? or what are you pleased to laugh at? I desire you to go about your business, and send me up Handyside. I want him to bring me something to drink.'

'Ye sanna want a drink, maister,' said the fellow: 'Tak a hearty ane, and see if it will wauken ye up something, sae that ye dinna ca' for ghaists through your sleep. Surely ye haena forgotten that Andrew Handyside has been in his grave these six months?'

This was a stunning blow to me. I could not answer farther, but sunk back on my pillow as if I had been a lump of lead, refusing to take a drink or any thing else at the fellow's hand, who seemed thus mocking me with so grave a face. The man seemed sorry, and grieved at my being offended, but I ordered

him away, and continued sullen and thoughtful. Could I have
again been for a season in utter oblivion to myself, and trans-
acting business which I neither approved of, nor had any connection with! I tried to recollect something in which I might
have been engaged, but nothing was pourtrayed on my mind
subsequent to the parting with my friends at a late hour the
evening before. The evening before it certainly was: but if so,
how came it, that Andrew Handyside, who served at table that
evening, should have been in his grave six months! This was a
circumstance somewhat equivocal; therefore, being afraid to
arise lest accusations of I knew not what might come against
me, I was obliged to call once more in order to come at what
intelligence I could. The same fellow appeared to receive my
orders as before, and I set about examining him with regard to
particulars. He told me his name was Scrape; that I hired him
myself; of whom I hired him; and at whose recommendation. I
smiled, and nodded so as to let the knave see I understood he
was telling me a chain of falsehoods, but did not choose to
begin with any violent asseverations to the contrary.

'And where is my noble friend and companion?' said I. 'How
has he been engaged in the interim?'

'I dinna ken him, sir,' said Scrape; 'but have heard it said,
that the strange mysterious person that attended you, him that
the maist part of folks countit uncanny, had gane awa wi' a Mr
Ringan o' Glasko last year, and had never returned.'

I thanked the Lord in my heart for this intelligence, hoping
that the illustrious stranger had returned to his own land and
people, and that I should thenceforth be rid of his controlling
and appalling presence. 'And where is my mother?' said I. The
man's breath cut short, and he looked at me without returning
any answer. 'I ask you where my mother is?' said I.

'God only knows, and not I, where she is,' returned he. 'He
knows where her soul is, and as for her body, if you dinna ken
something o' it, I suppose nae man alive does.'

'What do you mean, you knave?' said I. 'What dark hints are
these you are throwing out? Tell me precisely and distinctly
what you know of my mother?'

'It is unco queer o' ye to forget, or pretend to forget every thing that gate, the day, sir,' said he. 'I'm sure you heard enough about it yestreen; an' I can tell you, there are some gayan ill-faurd stories gaun about that business. But as the thing is to be tried afore the circuit lords, it wad be far wrang to say either this or that to influence the public mind; it is best just to let justice tak its swee. I hae naething to say, sir. Ye hae been a good enough maister to me, and paid my wages regularly, but ye hae muckle need to be innocent, for there are some heavy accusations rising against you.'

'I fear no accusations of man,' said I, 'as long as I can justify my cause in the sight of Heaven; and that I can do this I am well aware. Go you and bring me some wine and water, and some other clothes than these gaudy and glaring ones.'

I took a cup of wine and water; put on my black clothes, and walked out. For all the perplexity that surrounded me, I felt my spirits considerably buoyant. It appeared that I was rid of the two greatest bars to my happiness, by what agency I knew not. My mother, it seemed, was gone, who had become a grievous thorn in my side of late, and my great companion and counsellor, who tyrannized over every spontaneous movement of my heart, had likewise taken himself off. This last was an unspeakable relief; for I found that for a long season I had only been able to act by the motions of his mysterious mind and spirit. I therefore thanked God for my deliverance, and strode through my woods with a daring and heroic step; with independence in my eye, and freedom swinging in my right hand.

At the extremity of the Colwan wood, I perceived a figure approaching me with slow and dignified motion. The moment that I beheld it, my whole frame received a shock as if the ground on which I walked had sunk suddenly below me. Yet, at that moment, I knew not who it was; it was the air and motion of some one that I dreaded, and from whom I would gladly have escaped; but this I even had not power to attempt. It came slowly onward, and I advanced as slowly to meet it; yet when we came within speech, I still knew not who it was. It bore the figure, air, and features of my late brother, I thought, exactly; yet in all these there were traits so forbidding, so mixed with an appearance of misery, chagrin, and despair, that I still shrunk from the view, not knowing on whose face I looked. But when the being spoke, both my mental and bodily frame received another shock more terrible than the first, for it was the voice of the great personage I had so long denominated my friend, of whom I had deemed myself for ever freed, and whose presence and counsels I now dreaded more than hell. It was his voice, but so altered – I shall never forget it till my dying day. Nay, I can scarce conceive it possible that any earthly sounds could be so discordant, so repulsive to every feeling of a human soul, as the tones of the voice that grated on my ear at that moment. They were the sounds of the pit, wheezed through a grated cranny, or seemed so to my distempered imagination.

'So! Thou shudderest at my approach now, dost thou?' said he. 'Is this all the gratitude that you deign for an attachment of which the annals of the world furnish no parallel? An attach-ment which has caused me to forego power and dominion, might, homage, conquest and adulation, all that I might gain one highly valued and sanctified spirit, to my great and true principles of reformation among mankind. Wherein have I offended? What have I done for evil, or what have I not done for your good, that you would thus shun my presence?'

'Great and magnificent prince,' said I humbly, 'let me request of you to abandon a poor worthless wight to his own wayward fortune, and return to the dominion of your people. I am unworthy of the sacrifices you have made for my sake; and after all your efforts, I do not feel that you have rendered me either more virtuous or more happy. For the sake of that which is estimable in human nature, depart from me to your own home, before you render me a being either altogether above, or below the rest of my fellow creatures. Let me plod on towards heaven and happiness in my own way, like those that have gone before me, and I promise to stick fast by the great principles which you have so strenuously inculcated, on condition that you depart and leave me for ever.'

'Sooner shall you make the mother abandon the child of her bosom; nay, sooner cause the shadow to relinquish the substance, than separate me from your side. Our beings are amalgamated, as it were, and consociated in one, and never shall I depart from this country until I can carry you in triumph with me.'

I can in nowise describe the effect this appalling speech had on me. It was like the announcement of death to one who had of late deemed himself free, if not of something worse than death, and of longer continuance. There was I doomed to remain in misery, subjugated, soul and body, to one whose presence was become more intolerable to me than ought on earth could compensate: And at that moment, when he beheld the anguish of my soul, he could not conceal that he enjoyed it. I was troubled for an answer, for which he was waiting: it became incumbent on me to say something after such a protestation of attachment; and, in some degree to shake the validity of it, I asked, with great simplicity, where he had been all this while?

'Your crimes and your extravagancies forced me from your side for a season,' said he; 'but now that I hope the day of grace is returned, I am again drawn towards you by an affection that has neither bounds nor interest; an affection for which I receive not even the poor return of gratitude, and which seems to have its radical sources in fascination. I have been far, far abroad, and have seen much, and transacted much, since I last spoke with you. During that space, I grievously suspect that you have been guilty of great crimes and misdemeanours, crimes that would have sunk an unregenerated person to perdition; but as I knew it to be only a temporary falling off, a specimen of that liberty by which the chosen and elected ones are made free, I closed my eyes on the wilful debasement of our principles, knowing that the transgressions could never be accounted to your charge, and that in good time you would come to your senses, and throw the whole weight of your crimes on the shoulders that had voluntarily stooped to receive the load.'

'Certainly I will,' said I, 'as I and all the justified have a good right to do. But what crimes? What misdemeanours and transgressions do you talk about? For my part, I am conscious of none, and am utterly amazed at insinuations which I do not comprehend.'

'You have certainly been left to yourself for a season,'

returned he, 'having gone on rather like a person in a delirium, than a Christian in his sober senses. You are accused of having made away with your mother privately; as also of the death of a beautiful young lady, whose affections you had seduced.'

'It is an intolerable and monstrous falsehood!' cried I, interrupting him; 'I never laid a hand on a woman to take away her life, and have even shunned their society from my childhood: I know nothing of my mother's exit, nor of that young lady's whom you mention – Nothing whatever.'

'I hope it is so,' said he. 'But it seems there are some strong presumptuous proofs against you, and I came to warn you this day that a precognition is in progress, and that unless you are perfectly convinced, not only of your innocence, but of your ability to prove it, it will be the safest course for you to abscond, and let the trial go on without you.'

'Never shall it be said that I shrunk from such a trial as this,' said I. 'It would give grounds for suspicions of guilt that never had existence, even in thought. I will go and show myself in every public place, that no slanderous tongue may wag against me. I have shed the blood of sinners, but of these deaths I am guiltless; therefore, I will face every tribunal, and put all my accusers down.'

'Asseveration will avail you but little,' answered he, composedly: 'It is, however, justifiable in its place, although to me it signifies nothing, who know too well that you *did* commit both crimes, in your own person, and with your own hands. Far be it from me to betray you; indeed, I would rather endeavour to palliate the offences; for though adverse to nature, I can prove them not to be so to the cause of pure Christianity, by the mode of which we have approved of it, and which we wish to promulgate.'

'If this that you tell me be true,' said I, 'then is it as true that I have two souls, which take possession of my bodily frame by turns, the one being all unconscious of what the other performs; for as sure as I have at this moment a spirit within me, fashioned and destined to eternal felicity, as sure am I utterly ignorant of the crimes you now lay to my charge.'

'Your supposition may be true in effect,' said he. 'We are all

subjected to two distinct natures[31] in the same person. I myself
have suffered grievously in that way. The spirit that now directs
my energies is not that with which I was endowed at my creation. It is changed within me, and so is my whole nature. My
former days were those of grandeur and felicity. But, would
you believe it? *I was not then a Christian.* Now I am. I have
been converted to its truths by passing through the fire, and
since my final conversion, my misery has been extreme. You
complain that I have not been able to render you more happy
than you were. Alas! do you expect it in the difficult and exter-
minating career which you have begun. I, however, promise
you this – a portion of the only happiness which I enjoy, sublime
in its motions, and splendid in its attainments – I will place you
on the right hand of my throne, and show you the grandeur of
my domains, and the felicity of my millions of true professors.'

I was once more humbled before this mighty potentate, and
promised to be ruled wholly by his directions, although at that
moment my nature shrunk from the concessions, and my soul
longed rather to be inclosed in the deeps of the sea, or involved
once more in utter oblivion. I was like Daniel in the den of
lions, without his faith in divine support, and wholly at their
mercy. I felt as one round whose body a deadly snake is twisted,
which continues to hold him in its fangs, without injuring him,
farther than in moving its scaly infernal folds with exulting
delight, to let its victim feel to whose power he has subjected
himself; and thus did I for a space drag an existence from
day to day, in utter weariness and helplessness; at one time
worshipping with great fervour of spirit, and at other times so
wholly left to myself, as to work all manner of vices and follies
with greediness. In these my enlightened friend never accompanied me, but I always observed that he was the first to lead
me to every one of them, and then leave me in the lurch. The
next day, after these my fallings off, he never failed to reprove
me gently, blaming me for my venial transgressions; but then
he had the art of reconciling all, by reverting to my justified
and infallible state, which I found to prove a delightful healing
salve for every sore.

But, of all my troubles, this was the chief: I was every day and every hour assailed with accusations of deeds of which I was wholly ignorant; of acts of cruelty, injustice, defamation, and deceit; of pieces of business which I could not be made to comprehend; with law-suits, details, arrestments of judgment, and a thousand interminable quibbles from the mouth of my loquacious and conceited attorney. So miserable was my life rendered by these continued attacks, that I was often obliged to lock myself up for days together, never seeing any person save my man Samuel Scrape, who was a very honest blunt fellow, a staunch Cameronian, but withal very little conversant in religious matters. He said he came from a place called Penpunt, which I thought a name so ludicrous, that I called him by the name of his native village, an appellation of which he was very proud, and answered every thing with more civility and perspicuity when I denominated him Penpunt, than Samuel, his own Christian name. Of this peasant was I obliged to make a companion on sundry occasions, and strange indeed were the details which he gave me concerning myself, and the ideas of the country people concerning me. I took down a few of these in writing, to put off the time, and here leave them on record to show how the best and greatest actions are misconstrued among sinful and ignorant men.

'You say, Samuel, that I hired you myself – that I have been a good enough master to you, and have paid you your weekly wages punctually. Now, how is it that you say this, knowing, as you do, that I never hired you, and never paid you a sixpence of wages in the whole course of my life, excepting this last month?'

'Ye may as weel say, master, that water's no water, or that stanes are no stanes. But that's just your gate, an' it is a great pity aye to do a thing an' profess the clean contrair. Weel then, since you havena paid me ony wages, an' I can prove day and date when I was hired, an' came hame to your service, will you be sae kind as to pay me now? That's the best way o' curing a man o' the mortal disease o' leasing-making that I ken o'.'

'I should think that Penpunt and Cameronian principles, would not admit of a man taking twice payment for the same article.'

'In sic a case as this, sir, it disna hinge upon principles, but a piece o' good manners; an' I can tell you that at sic a crisis, a Cameronian is a gayan weel-bred man. He's driven to this, that he maun either make a breach in his friend's good name, or in his purse; an' O, sir, whilk o' thae, think you, is the most precious? For instance, an a Galloway drover had comed to the town o' Penpunt, an' said to a Cameronian (the folk's a' Cameronians there), "Sir, I want to buy your cow." "Vera weel," says the Cameronian, "I just want to sell the cow, sae gie me twenty punds Scots, an' take her w'ye." It's a bargain. The drover takes away the cow, an' gies the Cameronian his twenty pund Scots. But after that, he meets him again on the white sands, amang a' the drovers an' dealers o' the land, an' the Gallowayman, he says to the Cameronian, afore a' thae witnesses, "Come, Master Whiggam,[32] I hae never paid you for yon bit useless cow, that I bought, I'll pay her the day, but you maun mind the luck-penny; there's muckle need for't" – or something to that purpose. The Cameronian then turns out to be a civil man, an' canna bide to make the man baith a feele an' liar at the same time, afore a' his associates; an' therefore he pits his principles aff at the side, to be a kind o' sleepin partner, as it war, an' brings up his good breeding to stand at the counter: he pockets the money, gies the Galloway drover time o' day, an' comes his way. An' wha's to blame? *Man mind yoursel* is the first commandment. A Cameronian's principles never came atween him an' his purse, nor sanna in the present case; for as I canna bide to make you out a leear, I'll thank you for my wages.'

'Well, you shall have them, Samuel, if you declare to me that I hired you myself in this same person, and bargained with you with this same tongue, and voice, with which I speak to you just now.'

'That I do declare, unless ye hae twa persons o' the same appearance, and twa tongues to the same voice. But, od saif us, sir, do you ken what the auld wives o' the clachan say about you?'

'How should I, when no one repeats it to me?'

'Oo, I trow it's a' stuff – folk shouldna heed what's said by auld crazy kimmers. But there are some o' them weel kend for witches too; an' they say – lord have a care o' us! – they say the deil's often seen gaun sidie for sidie w'ye, whiles in ae shape, an' whiles in another. An' they say that he whiles takes your ain shape, or else enters into you, and then you turn a deil yoursel.'

I was so astounded at this terrible idea that had gone abroad, regarding my fellowship with the prince of darkness, that I could make no answer to the fellow's information, but sat like one in a stupor; and if it had not been for my well-founded faith, and conviction that I was a chosen and elected one before the world was made, I should at that moment have given into the popular belief, and fallen into the sin of despondency; but I was preserved from such a fatal error by an inward and unseen supporter. Still the insinuation was so like what I felt myself, that I was greatly awed and confounded.

The poor fellow observed this, and tried to do away the impression by some farther sage remarks of his own.

'Hout, dear sir, it is balderdash, there's nae doubt o't. It is the crownhead o' absurdity to tak in the havers o' auld wives for gospel. I told them that my master was a peeous man, an' a sensible man; an' for praying, that he could ding auld Mac-millan himself.[33] "Sae could the deil," they said, "when he liket, either at preaching or praying, if these war to answer his ain ends." "Na, na," says I, "but he's a strick believer in a' the truths o' Christianity, my master." They said, sae was Satan, for that he was the firmest believer in a' the truths of Christianity that was out o' heaven; an' that, sin' the Revolution that the gospel had turned sae rife, he had been often driven to the shift o' preaching it himsel, for the purpose o' getting some wrang tenets introduced into it, and thereby turning it into blasphemy and ridicule.'

I confess, to my shame, that I was so overcome by this jumble of nonsense, that a chillness came over me, and in spite of all my efforts to shake off the impression it had made, I fell into a faint. Samuel soon brought me to myself, and after a deep draught of wine and water, I was greatly revived, and felt my spirit rise above the sphere of vulgar conceptions, and the restrained views of unregenerate men. The shrewd but loquacious fellow, perceiving this, tried to make some amends for the pain he had occasioned to me, by the following story, which I noted down, and which was brought on by a conversation to the following purport:

'Now, Penpunt, you may tell me all that passed between you and the wives of the clachan. I am better of that stomach qualm, with which I am sometimes seized, and shall be much amused by hearing the sentiments of noted witches regarding myself and my connections.'

'Weel, you see, sir, I says to them, "It will be lang afore the deil intermeddle wi' as serious a professor, and as fervent a prayer as my master, for gin he gets the upper hand o' sickan men, wha's to be safe?" An', what think ye they said, sir? There was ane Lucky Shaw set up her lang lantern chafts, an' answered me, an' a' the rest shanned and noddit in assent an' approbation: "Ye silly, sauchless, Cameronian cuif!" quo she, "is that a' that ye ken about the wiles and doings o' the prince o' the air, that rules an' works in the bairns of disobedience? Gin ever he observes a proud professor, wha has mae than ordinary pretensions to a divine calling, and that reards and prays till the very howlets learn his preambles, *that's* the man Auld Simmie fixes on to mak a dishclout o'. He canna get rest in hell, if he sees a man, or a set of men o' this stamp, an' when he sets fairly to wark, it is seldom that he disna bring them round till his ain measures by hook or by crook. Then, O it is a grand prize for him, an' a proud deil he is, when he gangs hame to his ain ha', wi' a batch o' the souls o' sic strenuous professors on his back. Ay, I trow, auld Ingleby, the Liverpool packman, never came up Glasco street wi' prouder pomp, when he had ten horse-laids afore him o' Flanders lace, an' Hollin lawn, an' silks an' satins frae the eastern Indians, than Satan wad strodge into hell with a pack-laid o' the souls o' proud professors on his braid shoulders. Ha, ha, ha! I think I see how the auld thief wad be gaun through his gizened dominions, crying his wares, in derision, 'Wha will buy a fresh, cauler divine, a bouzy bishop, a fasting zealot, or a piping priest? For a' their prayers an' their praises, their aumuses, an' their penances, their whinings, their

howlings, their rantings, an' their ravings, here they come at
last! Behold the end! Here go the rare and precious wares! A
fat professor for a bodle, an' a lean ane for half a merk!'" I
declare, I trembled at the auld hag's ravings, but the lave o' the
kimmers applauded the sayings as sacred truths. An' then Lucky
went on: "There are many wolves in sheep's claithing, among
us, my man; mony deils aneath the masks o' zealous professors,
roaming about in kirks and meeting-houses o' the land. It was
but the year afore the last, that the people o' the town o'
Auchtermuchty grew so rigidly righteous, that the meanest hind
among them became a shining light in ither towns an' parishes.
There was nought to be heard, neither night nor day, but
preaching, praying, argumentation, an' catechizing in a' the
famous town o' Auchtermuchty. The young men wooed their
sweethearts out o' the Song o' Solomon, an' the girls returned
answers in strings o' verses out o' the Psalms. At the lint-
swinglings, they said questions round; and read chapters, and
sang hymns at bridals; auld and young prayed in their dreams,
an' prophesied in their sleep, till the deils in the farrest nooks
o' hell were alarmed, and moved to commotion. Gin it hadna
been an auld carl, Robin Ruthven, Auchtermuchty wad at that
time hae been ruined and lost for ever. But Robin was a cunning
man, an' had rather mae wits than his ain, for he had been in
the hands o' the fairies when he was young, an' a' kinds o'
spirits were visible to his een, an' their language as familiar to
him as his ain mother tongue. Robin was sitting on the side o'
the West Lowmond, ae still gloomy night in September, when
he saw a bridal[34] o' corbie craws coming east the lift, just on
the edge o' the gloaming. The moment that Robin saw them,
he kenned, by their movements, that they were craws o' some
ither warld than this; so he signed himself, and crap into the
middle o' his bourock. The corbie craws came a' an' sat down
round about him, an' they poukit their black sooty wings, an'
spread them out to the breeze to cool; and Robin heard ae
corbie speaking, an' another answering him; and the tane said
to the tither: 'Where will the ravens find a prey the night?' 'On
the lean crazy souls o' Auchtermuchty,' quo the tither. 'I fear
they will be o'er weel wrappit up in the warm flannens o' faith,

an' clouted wi' the dirty duds o' repentance, for us to mak a meal o',' quo the first. 'Whaten vile sounds are these that I hear coming bumming up the hill?' 'O these are the hymns and praises o' the auld wives and creeshy louns o' Auchtermuchty, wha are gaun crooning their way to heaven; an' gin it warna for the shame o' being beat, we might let our great enemy tak them. For sic a prize as he will hae! Heaven, forsooth! What shall we think o' heaven, if it is to be filled wi' vermin like thae, amang whom there is mair poverty and pollution, than I can name.' 'No matter for that,' said the first, 'we cannot have our power set at defiance; though we should put them in the thief's hole, we must catch them, and catch them with their own bait too. Come all to church to-morrow, and I'll let you hear how I'll gull the saints of Auchtermuchty. In the mean time, there is a feast on the Sidlaw hills to-night, below the hill of Macbeth – Mount, Diabolus, and fly.'[35] Then, with loud croaking and crowing, the bridal of corbies again scaled the dusky air, and left Robin Ruthven in the middle of his cairn.

' "The next day the congregation met in the kirk of Auchtermuchty, but the minister made not his appearance. The elders ran out and in, making inquiries; but they could learn nothing, save that the minister was missing. They ordered the clerk to sing a part of the 119th Psalm, until they saw if the minister would cast up. The clerk did as he was ordered, and by the time he reached the 77th verse, a strange divine entered the church, by the *western door*,[36] and advanced solemnly up to the pulpit. The eyes of all the congregation were riveted on the sublime stranger, who was clothed in a robe of black sackcloth, that flowed all around him, and trailed far behind, and they weened him an angel, come to exhort them, in disguise. He read out his text from the Prophecies of Ezekiel,[37] which consisted of these singular words: 'I will overturn, overturn, overturn it; and it shall be no more, until he come, whose right it is, and I will give it him.'

' "From these words he preached such a sermon as never was heard by human ears, at least never by ears of Auchtermuchty. It was a true, sterling, gospel sermon – it was striking, sublime, and awful in the extreme. He finally made out the IT, mentioned

in the text, to mean, properly and positively, the notable town
of Auchtermuchty. He proved all the people in it, to their
perfect satisfaction, to be in the gall of bitterness and bond of
iniquity, and he assured them, that God would overturn them,
their principles, and professions; and that they should be no
more, until the devil, the town's greatest enemy, came, and then
it should be given unto him for a prey, for it was his right, and
to him it belonged, if there was not forthwith a radical change
made in all their opinions and modes of worship.

'"The inhabitants of Auchtermuchty were electrified – they
were charmed; they were actually raving mad about the grand
and sublime truths delivered to them, by this eloquent and
impressive preacher of Christianity. 'He is a prophet of the
Lord,' said one, 'sent to warn us, as Jonah was sent to the Nin-
evites.' 'O, he is an angel sent from heaven, to instruct this great
city,' said another, 'for no man ever uttered truths so sublime
before.' The good people of Auchtermuchty were in perfect
raptures with the preacher, who had thus sent them to hell by
the slump, tag, rag, and bobtail! Nothing in the world delights
a truly religious people so much, as consigning them to eternal
damnation. They wondered after the preacher – they crowded
together, and spoke of his sermon with admiration, and still as
they conversed, the wonder and the admiration increased; so
that honest Robin Ruthven's words would not be listened to.
It was in vain that he told them he heard a raven speaking, and
another raven answering him: the people laughed him to scorn,
and kicked him out of their assemblies, as a one who spoke evil
of dignities; and they called him a warlock, an' a daft body, to
think to mak language out o' the crouping o' craws.

'"The sublime preacher could not be heard of, although all
the country was sought for him, even to the minutest corner of
St Johnston and Dundee; but as he had announced another
sermon on the same text, on a certain day, all the inhabitants of
that populous country, far and near, flocked to Auchtermuchty.
Cupar, Newburgh, and Strathmiglo, turned out men, women,
and children. Perth and Dundee gave their thousands; and from
the East Nook of Fife to the foot of the Grampian hills, there
was nothing but running and riding that morning to Auchter-

muchty. The kirk would not hold the thousandth part of them. A splendid tent was erected on the brae north of the town, and round that the countless congregation assembled. When they were all waiting anxiously for the great preacher, behold, Robin Ruthven set up his head in the tent, and warned his countrymen to beware of the doctrines they were about to hear, for he could prove, to their satisfaction, that they were all false, and tended to their destruction!

' "The whole multitude raised a cry of indignation against Robin, and dragged him from the tent, the elders rebuking him, and the multitude threatening to resort to stronger measures; and though he told them a plain and unsophisticated tale of the black corbies, he was only derided. The great preacher appeared once more, and went through his two discourses with increased energy and approbation. All who heard him were amazed, and many of them went into fits, writhing and foaming in a state of the most horrid agitation. Robin Ruthven sat on the outskirts of the great assembly, listening with the rest, and perceived what they, in the height of their enthusiasm, perceived not – the ruinous tendency of the tenets so sublimely inculcated. Robin kenned the voice of his friend the corby-craw again, and was sure he could not be wrang: sae when public worship was finished, a' the elders an' a' the gentry flocked about the great preacher, as he stood on the green brae in the sight of the hale congregation, an' a' war alike anxious to pay him some mark o' respect. Robin Ruthven came in amang the thrang, to try to effect what he had promised; and, with the greatest readiness and simplicity, just took haud o' the side an' wide gown, an' in sight of a' present, held it aside as high as the preacher's knee, and behold, there was a pair o' cloven feet! The auld thief was fairly catched in the very height o' his proud conquest, an' put down by an auld carl. He could feign nae mair, but gnashing on Robin wi' his teeth, he dartit into the air like a fiery dragon, an' keust a reid rainbow our the taps o' the Lowmonds.

' "A' the auld wives an' weavers o' Auchtermuchty fell down flat wi' affright, an' betook them to their prayers aince again, for they saw the dreadfu' danger they had escapit, an' frae that day to this it is a hard matter to gar an Auchtermuchty man listen to a sermon at a', an' a harder ane still to gar him applaud ane, for he thinks aye that he sees the cloven foot peeping out frae aneath ilka sentence.

' "Now, this is a true story, my man," quo the auld wife; "an' whenever you are doubtfu' of a man, take auld Robin Ruthven's plan, an' look for the cloven foot, for it's a thing that winna weel hide; an' it appears whiles where ane wadna think o't. It will keek out frae aneath the parson's gown, the lawyer's wig, and the Cameronian's blue bannet; but still there is a gouden rule[38] whereby to detect it, an' that never, never fails." The auld witch didna gie me the rule, an' though I hae heard tell o't often an' often, shame fa' me an I ken what it is! But ye will ken it well, an' it wad be nae the waur of a trial on some o' your friends, maybe; for they say there's a certain gentleman seen walking wi' you whiles, that, wherever he sets his foot, the grass withers as gin it war scoudered wi' a het ern. His presence be about us! What's the matter wi' you, master? Are ye gaun to take the calm o' the stamock again?'

The truth is, that the clown's absurd story, with the still more ridiculous application, made me sick at heart a second time. It was not because I thought my illustrious friend was the devil, or that I took a fool's idle tale as a counterbalance to divine revelation, that had assured me of my justification in the sight of God before the existence of time. But, in short, it gave me a view of my own state, at which I shuddered, as indeed I now always did, when the image of my devoted friend and ruler presented itself to my mind. I often communed with my heart on this, and wondered how a connection, that had the well-being of mankind solely in view, could be productive of fruits so bitter. I then went to try my works by the Saviour's golden rule, as my servant had put it into my head to do; and, behold, not one of them would stand the test. I had shed blood on a ground on which I could not admit that any man had a right to shed mine; and I began to doubt the motives of my adviser once more, not that they were intentionally bad, but that his was some great mind led astray by enthusiasm, or some overpowering passion.

He seemed to comprehend every one of these motions of my heart, for his manner towards me altered every day. It first became any thing but agreeable, then supercilious, and finally, intolerable; so that I resolved to shake him off, cost what it would, even though I should be reduced to beg my bread in a foreign land. To do it at home was impossible, as he held my life in his hands, to sell it whenever he had a mind; and besides, his ascendancy over me was as complete as that of a huntsman over his dogs. I was even so weak, as, the next time I met with him, to look stedfastly at his foot, to see if it was not cloven into two hoofs. It was the foot of a gentleman, in every respect, so far as appearances went, but the form of his counsels was somewhat equivocal, and if not double, they were amazingly crooked.

But, if I had taken my measures to abscond and fly from my native place, in order to free myself of this tormenting, intolerant, and bloody reformer, he had likewise taken his to expel me, or throw me into the hands of justice. It seems, that about this time, I was haunted by some spies connected with my late father and brother, of whom the mistress of the former was one. My brother's death had been witnessed by two individuals; indeed, I always had an impression that it was witnessed by more than one, having some faint recollection of hearing voices and challenges close beside me; and this woman had searched about until she found these people; but, as I shrewdly suspected, not without the assistance of the only person in my secret – my own warm and devoted friend. I say this, because I found that he had them concealed in the neighbourhood, and then took me again and again where I was fully exposed to their view, without being aware. One time in particular, on pretence of gratifying my revenge on that base woman, he knew so well where she lay concealed, that he led me to her, and left me to the mercy of two viragos, who had very nigh taken my life. My time of residence at Dalcastle was wearing to a crisis. I could no longer live with my tyrant, who haunted me like my shadow; and besides, it seems there were proofs of murder leading against me from all quarters. Of part of these I deemed myself quite free, but the world deemed otherwise; and how the matter would have gone, God only knows, for, the case never having undergone a judicial trial, I do not. It perhaps, however, behoves me here to relate all that I know of it, and it is simply this:

On the first of June 1712 (well may I remember the day), I was sitting locked in my secret chamber, in a state of the utmost despondency, revolving in my mind what I ought to do to be free of my persecutors, and wishing myself a worm, or a moth, that I might be crushed and at rest, when behold Samuel entered, with eyes like to start out of his head, exclaiming, 'For God's sake, master, fly and hide yourself, for your mother's found, an' as sure as you're a living soul, the blame is gaun to fa' on you!'

'My mother found!' said I. 'And, pray, where has she been all this while?' In the mean time, I was terribly discomposed at the thoughts of her return.

'Been, sir! Been? Why, she has been where ye pat her, it seems – lying buried in the sands o' the linn. I can tell you, ye will see her a frightsome figure, sic as I never wish to see again. An' the young lady is found too, sir: an' it is said the devil – I beg pardon sir, *your friend*, I mean – it is said your *friend* has made the discovery, an' the folk are away to raise officers, an' they will be here in an hour or two at the farthest, sir; an' sae you hae not a minute to lose, for there's proof, sir, strong proof, an' sworn proof, that ye were last seen wi' them baith; sae, unless ye can gie a' the better an account o' baith yoursel an' them, either hide, or flee for your bare life.'

'I will neither hide nor fly,' said I; 'for I am as guiltless of the blood of these women as the child unborn.'

'The country disna think sae, master; an' I can assure you, that should evidence fail, you run a risk o' being torn limb frae limb. They are bringing the corpse here, to gar ye touch them baith afore witnesses,[39] an' plenty o' witnesses there will be!'

'They shall not bring them here,' cried I, shocked beyond measure at the experiment about to be made: 'Go, instantly, and debar them from entering my gate with their bloated and mangled carcases.'

'The body of your own mother, sir!' said the fellow emphatically. I was in terrible agitation; and, being driven to my wit's end, I got up and strode furiously round and round the room.

Samuel wist not what to do, but I saw by his staring he deemed me doubly guilty. A tap came to the chamber door: we both started like guilty creatures; and as for Samuel, his hairs stood all on end with alarm, so that when I motioned to him, he could scarcely advance to open the door. He did so at length, and who should enter but my illustrious friend, manifestly in the utmost state of alarm. The moment that Samuel admitted him, the former made his escape by the prince's side as he entered, seemingly in a state of distraction. I was little better, when I saw this dreaded personage enter my chamber, which he had never before attempted; and being unable to ask his errand, I suppose I stood and gazed on him like a statue.

'I come with sad and tormenting tidings to you, my beloved and ungrateful friend,' said he; 'but having only a minute left to save your life, I have come to attempt it. There is a mob coming towards you with two dead bodies, which will place you in circumstances disagreeable enough: but that is not the worst, for of that you may be able to clear yourself. At this moment there is a party of officers, with a Justiciary warrant from Edinburgh, surrounding the house, and about to begin the search of it, for you. If you fall into their hands, you are inevitably lost; for I have been making earnest inquiries, and find that every thing is in train for your ruin.'

'Ay, and who has been the cause of all this?' said I, with great bitterness. But he stopped me short, adding, 'There is no time for such reflections at present: I gave you my word of honour that your life should be safe from the hand of man. So it shall, if the power remain with me to save it. I am come to redeem my pledge, and to save your life by the sacrifice of my own. Here – Not one word of expostulation, change habits with me, and you may then pass by the officers, and guards, and even through the approaching mob, with the most perfect temerity. There is a virtue in this garb, and instead of offering to detain you, they shall pay you obeisance. Make haste, and leave this place for the present, flying where you best may, and if I escape from these dangers that surround me, I will endeavour to find you out, and bring you what intelligence I am able.'

I put on his green frock coat, buff belt, and a sort of a

turban that he always wore on his head, somewhat resembling a bishop's mitre: he drew his hand thrice across my face, and I withdrew as he continued to urge me. My hall door and postern gate were both strongly guarded, and there were sundry armed people within, searching the closets; but all of them made way for me, and lifted their caps as I passed by them. Only one superior officer accosted me, asking if I had seen the culprit? I knew not what answer to make, but chanced to say, with great truth and propriety, 'He is safe enough.' The man beckoned with a smile, as much as to say, 'Thank you, sir, that is quite sufficient'; and I walked deliberately away.

I had not well left the gate, till, hearing a great noise coming from the deep glen toward the east, I turned that way, deeming myself quite secure in this my new disguise, to see what it was, and if matters were as had been described to me. There I met a great mob, sure enough, coming with two dead bodies stretched on boards, and decently covered with white sheets. I would fain have examined their appearance, had I not perceived the apparent fury in the looks of the men, and judged from that how much more safe it was for me not to intermeddle in the affray. I cannot tell how it was, but I felt a strange and unwonted delight in viewing this scene, and a certain pride of heart in being supposed the perpetrator of the unnatural crimes laid to my charge. This was a feeling quite new to me; and if there were virtues in the robes of the illustrious foreigner, who had without all dispute preserved my life at this time – I say, if there was any inherent virtue in these robes of his, as he had suggested, this was one of their effects, that they turned my heart towards that which was evil, horrible, and disgustful.

I mixed with the mob to hear what they were saying. Every tongue was engaged in loading me with the most opprobrious epithets! One called me a monster of nature; another an incarnate devil; and another a creature made to be cursed in time and eternity. I retired from them, and winded my way southward, comforting myself with the assurance, that so mankind had used and persecuted the greatest fathers and apostles of the Christian church, and that their vile opprobrium could not alter the counsels of heaven concerning me.

On going over that rising ground called Dorington Moor, I could not help turning round and taking a look of Dalcastle. I had little doubt that it would be my last look, and nearly as little ambition that it should not. I thought how high my hopes of happiness and advancement had been on entering that mansion, and taking possession of its rich and extensive domains, and how miserably I had been disappointed. On the contrary, I had experienced nothing but chagrin, disgust, and terror; and I now consoled myself with the hope that I should henceforth shake myself free of the chains of my great tormentor, and for that privilege was I willing to encounter any earthly distress. I could not help perceiving, that I was now on a path which was likely to lead me into a species of distress hitherto unknown, and hardly dreamed of by me, and that was total destitution. For all the riches I had been possessed of a few hours previous to this, I found that here I was turned out of my lordly possessions without a single merk, or the power of lifting and commanding the smallest sum, without being thereby discovered and seized. Had it been possible for me to have escaped in my own clothes, I had a considerable sum secreted in these, but, by the sudden change, I was left without a coin for present necessity. But I had hope in heaven, knowing that the just man would not be left destitute; and that though many troubles surrounded him, he would at last be set free from them all. I was possessed of strong and brilliant parts, and a liberal education; and though I had somehow unaccountably suffered my theological qualifications to fall into desuetude, since my acquaintance with the ablest and most rigid of all theologians, I had nevertheless hopes that, by preaching up redemption by grace, pre-ordination, and eternal purpose, I should yet be enabled to benefit mankind in some country, and rise to high distinction.

These were some of the thoughts by which I consoled myself as I posted on my way southward, avoiding the towns and villages, and falling into the cross ways that led from each of the great roads passing east and west, to another. I lodged the first night in the house of a country weaver, into which I stepped at a late hour, quite overcome with hunger and fatigue, having travelled not less than thirty miles from my late home. The man received me ungraciously, telling me of a gentleman's house at no great distance, and of an inn a little farther away; but I said I delighted more in the society of a man like him, than that of any gentleman of the land, for my concerns were with the poor of this world, it being easier for a camel to go through the eye of a needle, than for a rich man to enter into the kingdom of heaven. The weaver's wife, who sat with a child on her knee, and had not hitherto opened her mouth, hearing me speak in that serious and religious style, stirred up the fire, with her one hand; then drawing a chair near it, she said, 'Come awa, honest lad, in by here; sin' it be sae that you belang to Him wha gies us a' that we hae, it is but right that you should share a part. You are a stranger, it is true, but *them* that winna entertain a stranger will never entertain an angel unawares.'

I never was apt to be taken with the simplicity of nature; in general I despised it; but, owing to my circumstances at the time, I was deeply affected by the manner of this poor woman's welcome. The weaver continued in a churlish mood throughout the evening, apparently dissatisfied with what his wife had done in entertaining me, and spoke to her in a manner so crusty that I thought proper to rebuke him, for the woman was comely in her person, and virtuous in her conversation; but the weaver her husband was large of make, ill-favoured, and pestilent; therefore did I take him severely to task for the tenor of his conduct; but the man was froward, and answered me rudely, with sneering and derision, and, in the height of his caprice, he said to his wife, 'Whan focks are sae keen of a chance o' entertaining angels, gudewife, it wad maybe be worth their while to tak tent what kind o' angels they are. It wadna wonder me vera muckle an ye had entertained your friend the deil the night, for aw thought aw fand a saur o' reek an' brimstane about him. *He's* nane o' the best o' angels, an' focks winna hae muckle credit by entertaining him.'

Certainly, in the assured state I was in, I had as little reason to be alarmed at mention being made of the devil as any person on earth: of late, however, I felt that the reverse was the case, and that any allusion to my great enemy, moved me exceedingly. The weaver's speech had such an effect on me, that both he and his wife were alarmed at my looks. The latter thought I was angry, and chided her husband gently for his rudeness; but the weaver himself rather seemed to be confirmed in his opinion that I was the devil, for he looked round like a startled roe-buck, and immediately betook him to the family Bible.

I know not whether it was on purpose to prove my identity or not, but I think he was going to desire me either to read a certain portion of Scripture that he had sought out, or to make family worship, had not the conversation at that instant taken another turn; for the weaver, not knowing how to address me, abruptly asked my name, as he was about to put the Bible into my hands. Never having considered myself in the light of a malefactor, but rather as a champion in the cause of truth, and finding myself perfectly safe under my disguise, I had never once thought of the utility of changing my name, and when the man asked me, I hesitated; but being compelled to say something, I said my name was Cowan. The man stared at me, and then at his wife, with a look that spoke a knowledge of something alarming or mysterious.

'Ha! Cowan?' said he. 'That's most extrordinar! Not Colwan, I hope?'

'No: Cowan is my sirname,' said I. 'But why not Colwan, there being so little difference in the sound?'

'I was feared ye might be that waratch that the deil has taen the possession o', an' eggit him on to kill baith his father an' his mother, his only brother, an' his sweetheart,' said he; 'an' to say the truth, I'm no that sure about you yet, for I see you're gaun wi' arms on ye.'

'Not I, honest man,' said I; 'I carry no arms; a man conscious of his innocence and uprightness of heart, needs not to carry arms in his defence now.'

'Ay, ay, maister,' said he; 'an' pray what div ye ca' this bit windlestrae that's appearing here?' With that he pointed to something on the inside of the breast of my frock-coat. I looked at it, and there certainly was the gilded haft of a poniard, the same weapon I had seen and handled before, and which I knew my illustrious companion always carried about with him; but till that moment I knew not that I was in possession of it. I drew it out: a more dangerous or insidious looking weapon could not be conceived. The weaver and his wife were both frightened, the latter in particular; and she being my friend, and I dependant on their hospitality, for that night, I said, 'I declare I knew not that I carried this small rapier, which has been in my coat by chance, and not by any design of mine. But lest you should think that I meditate any mischief to any under this roof, I give it into your hands, requesting of you to lock it by till to-morrow, or when I shall next want it.'

The woman seemed rather glad to get hold of it; and, taking it from me, she went into a kind of pantry out of my sight, and locked the weapon up; and then the discourse went on.

'There cannot be such a thing in reality,' said I, 'as the story you were mentioning just now, of a man whose name resembles mine.'

'It's likely that you ken a wee better about the story than I do, maister,' said he, 'suppose you do leave the L out of your name. An' yet I think sic a waratch, an' a murderer, wad hae taen a name wi' some gritter difference in the sound. But the story is just that true, that there were twa o' the Queen's officers here nae mair than an hour ago, in pursuit o' the vagabond, for they gat some intelligence that he had fled this gate; yet they said he had been last seen wi' black claes on, an' they supposed he was clad in black. His ain servant is wi' them, for the purpose o' kennin the scoundrel, an' they're galloping through the country like madmen. I hope in God they'll get him, an' rack his neck for him!'

I could not say *Amen* to the weaver's prayer, and therefore tried to compose myself as well as I could, and made some religious comment on the causes of the nation's depravity. But suspecting that my potent friend had betrayed my flight and disguise, to save his life, I was very uneasy, and gave myself up for lost. I said prayers in the family, with the tenor of which the wife was delighted, but the weaver still dissatisfied; and, after a supper of the most homely fare, he tried to start an argument with me, proving, that every thing for which I had interceded in my prayer, was irrelevant to man's present state.

But I, being weary and distressed in mind, shunned the contest, and requested a couch whereon to repose.

I was conducted into the other end of the house, among looms, treadles, pirns, and confusion without end; and there, in a sort of box, was I shut up for my night's repose, for the weaver, as he left me, cautiously turned the key of my apartment, and left me to shift for myself among the looms, determined that I should escape from the house with nothing. After he and his wife and children were crowded into their den, I heard the two mates contending furiously about me in suppressed voices, the one maintaining the probability that I was the murderer, and the other proving the impossibility of it. The husband, however, said as much as let me understand, that he had locked me up on purpose to bring the military, or officers of justice, to seize me. I was in the utmost perplexity, yet, for all that, and the imminent danger I was in, I fell asleep, and a more troubled and tormenting sleep never enchained a mortal frame. I had such dreams that they will not bear repetition, and early in the morning I awaked, feverish, and parched with thirst.

I went to call mine host, that he might let me out to the open air, but before doing so, I thought it necessary to put on some clothes. In attempting to do this, a circumstance arrested my attention (for which I could in nowise account, which to this day I cannot unriddle, nor shall I ever be able to comprehend it while I live) – the frock and turban, which had furnished my disguise on the preceding day, were both removed, and my own black coat and cocked hat laid down in their place. At first I thought I was in a dream, and felt the weaver's beam, web, and treadle-strings with my hands, to convince myself that I was awake. I was certainly awake; and there was the door locked firm and fast as it was the evening before. I carried my own black coat to the small window, and examined it. It was my own in verity; and the sums of money, that I had concealed in case of any emergency, remained untouched. I trembled with astonishment; and on my return from the small window, went doiting in amongst the weaver's looms, till I entangled myself, and could not get out again without working great deray

amongst the coarse linen threads that stood in warp from one
end of the apartment unto the other. I had no knife whereby to
cut the cords of this wicked man, and therefore was obliged to
call out lustily for assistance. The weaver came half-naked,
unlocked the door, and, setting in his head and long neck,
accosted me thus:

'What now, Mr Satan? What for are ye roaring that gate?
Are you fawn inna little hell, instead o' the big muckil ane? Deil
be in your reistit trams! What for have ye abscondit yoursel
into ma leddy's wab for?'

'Friend, I beg your pardon,' said I: 'I wanted to be at the
light, and have somehow unfortunately involved myself in the
intricacies of your web, from which I cannot get clear without
doing you a great injury. Pray do, lend your experienced hand
to extricate me.'

'May aw the pearls o' damnation[40] light on your silly snout,
an I dinna estricat ye weel enough! Ye ditit, donnart, deil's burd
that ye be! what made ye gang howkin in there to be a poor
man's ruin? Come out, ye vile rag-of-a-muffin, or I gar ye come
out wi' mair shame and disgrace, an' fewer haill banes in your
body.'

My feet had slipped down through the double warpings of a
web, and not being able to reach the ground with them (there
being a small pit below), I rode upon a number of yielding
threads, and there being nothing else that I could reach, to
extricate myself was impossible. I was utterly powerless; and
besides, the yarn and cords hurt me very much. For all that, the
destructive weaver seized a loom-spoke, and began a-beating
me most unmercifully, while, entangled as I was, I could do
nothing but shout aloud for mercy, or assistance, whichever
chanced to be within hearing. The latter, at length, made its
appearance, in the form of the weaver's wife, in the same state
of dishabille with himself, who instantly interfered, and that
most strenuously, on my behalf. Before her arrival, however, I
had made a desperate effort to throw myself out of the entangle-
ment I was in; for the weaver continued repeating his blows
and cursing me so, that I determined to get out of his meshes
at any risk. This effect made my case worse; for my feet being

wrapt among the nether threads, as I threw myself from my saddle on the upper ones, my feet brought the others up through these, and I hung with my head down, and my feet as firm as they had been in a vice. The predicament of the web being thereby increased, the weaver's wrath was doubled in proportion, and he laid on without mercy.

At this critical juncture the wife arrived, and without hesitation rushed before her offended lord, withholding his hand from injuring me farther, although then it was uplifted along with the loom-spoke in overbearing ire. 'Dear Johnny! I think ye be gaen dementit this morning. Be quiet, my dear, an' dinna begin a Boddel Brigg[41] business in your ain house. What for ir ye persecutin' a servant o' the Lord's that gate, an' pitting the life out o' him wi' his head down an' his heels up?'

'Had ye said a servant o' the deil's, Nans, ye wad hae been nearer the nail, for gin he binna the auld ane himsel, he's gayan sib till him. There, didna I lock him in on purpose to bring the military on him; an' in place o' that, hasna he keepit me in a sleep a' this while as deep as death? An' here do I find him abscondit like a speeder i' the mids o' my leddy's wab, an' me dreamin' a' the night that I had the deil i' my house, an' that he was clapper-clawin me ayont the loom. Have at you, ye brunstane thief!' and, in spite of the good woman's struggles, he lent me another severe blow.

'Now, Johnny Dods, my man! O Johnny Dods, think if that be like a Christian, and ane o' the heroes o' Boddel Brigg, to entertain a stranger, an' then bind him in a web wi' his head down, an' mell him to death! O Johnny Dods, think what you are about! Slack a pin, an' let the good honest religious lad out.'

The weaver was rather overcome, but still stood to his point that I was the deil, though in better temper; and as he slackened the web to release me, he remarked, half laughing, 'Wha wad hae thought that John Dods should hae escapit a' the snares an' dangers that circumfauldit him, an' at last should hae weaved a net to catch the deil.'

The wife released me soon, and carefully whispered me, at the same time, that it would be as well for me to dress and be going. I was not long in obeying, and dressed myself in my black clothes, hardly knowing what I did, what to think, or whither to betake myself. I was sore hurt by the blows of the desperate ruffian; and, what was worse, my ankle was so much strained, that I could hardly set my foot to the ground. I was obliged to apply to the weaver once more, to see if I could learn any thing about my clothes, or how the change was effected. 'Sir,' said I, 'how comes it that you have robbed me of my clothes, and put these down in their place over night?'

'Ha! thae claes? Me pit down thae claes!' said he, gaping with astonishment, and touching the clothes with the point of his forefinger; 'I never saw them afore, as I have death to meet wi': So help me God!'

He strode into the work-house where I slept, to satisfy himself that my clothes were not there, and returned perfectly aghast with consternation. 'The doors were baith fast lockit,' said he. 'I could hae defied a rat either to hae gotten out or in. My dream has been true! My dream has been true! The Lord judge between thee and me; but, in his name, I charge you to depart out o' this house; an', gin it be your will, dinna tak the braidside o't w'ye, but gang quietly out at the door wi' your face foremost. Wife, let nought o' this enchanter's remain i' the house, to be a curse, an' a snare to us; gang an' bring him his gildit weapon, an' may the Lord protect a' his ain against its hellish an' deadly point!'

The wife went to seek my poniard, trembling so excessively that she could hardly walk, and shortly after, we heard a feeble scream from the pantry. The weapon had disappeared with the clothes, though under double lock and key; and the terror of the good people having now reached a disgusting extremity, I thought proper to make a sudden retreat, followed by the weaver's anathemas.

My state both of body and mind was now truly deplorable. I was hungry, wounded, and lame; an outcast and a vagabond in society; my life sought after with avidity, and all for doing that to which I was predestined by him who fore-ordains whatever comes to pass. I knew not whither to betake me. I had purposed going into England, and there making some use of the classical education I had received, but my lameness rendered this impracticable for the present. I was therefore obliged to turn my face towards Edinburgh, where I was little known – where concealment was more practicable than by skulking in the country, and where I might turn my mind to something that was great and good. I had a little money, both Scots and English, now in my possession, but not one friend in the whole world on whom I could rely. One devoted friend, it is true, I had, but he was become my greatest terror. To escape from him, I now felt that I would willingly travel to the farthest corners of the world, and be subjected to every deprivation; but after the certainty of what had taken place last night, after I had travelled thirty miles by secret and bye-ways, I saw not how escape from him was possible.

Miserable, forlorn, and dreading every person that I saw, either behind or before me, I hasted on towards Edinburgh, taking all the bye and unfrequented paths; and the third night after I left the weaver's house, I reached the West Port, without meeting with any thing remarkable. Being exceedingly fatigued and lame, I took lodgings in the first house I entered, and for these I was to pay two groats a-week, and to board and sleep with a young man who wanted a companion to make his rent easier. I liked this; having found from experience, that the great personage who had attached himself to me, and was now become my greatest terror among many surrounding evils, generally haunted me when I was alone, keeping aloof from all other society.

My fellow lodger came home in the evening, and was glad at my coming. His name was Linton, and I changed mine to Elliot. He was a flippant unstable being, one to whom nothing appeared a difficulty, in his own estimation, but who could effect very little, after all. He was what is called by some a compositor, in the Queen's printing house, then conducted by a Mr James Watson.[42] In the course of our conversation that night, I told him that I was a first-rate classical scholar, and would gladly turn my attention to some business wherein my education might avail me something; and that there was nothing would delight me so much as an engagement in the Queen's printing office. Linton made no difficulty in bringing about that arrangement. His answer was, 'Oo, gud sir, you are the very man we want. Gud bless your breast and your buttons, sir! Ay, that's neither here nor there – That's all very well – Ha-ha-ha – A byeword in the house, sir. But, as I was saying, you are the very *man* we want – You will get any money you like to ask, sir – *Any* money you like, sir. God bless your buttons! – That's settled – All done – Settled, settled – I'll do it, I'll do it – No more about it; no more about it. Settled, settled.'

The next day I went with him to the office, and he presented me to Mr Watson as the most wonderful genius and scholar ever known. His recommendation had little sway with Mr Watson, who only smiled at Linton's extravagancies, as one does at the prattle of an infant. I sauntered about the printing office for the space of two or three hours, during which time Watson bustled about with green spectacles on his nose, and took no heed of me. But seeing that I still lingered, he addressed me at length, in a civil gentlemanly way, and inquired concerning my views. I satisfied him with all my answers, in particular those to his questions about the Latin and Greek languages; but when he came to ask testimonials of my character and acquirements, and found that I could produce none, he viewed me with a jealous eye, and said he dreaded I was some ne'er-do-weel, run from my parents or guardians, and he did not chuse to employ any such. I said my parents were both dead; and that being thereby deprived of the means of following out my education, it behoved me to apply to some business in which my education might be of some use to me. He said he would take me into the office, and pay me according to the business I performed, and the manner in which I deported myself; but he could take no man into her Majesty's printing office upon a regular engagement, who could not produce the most respectable references with regard to morals.

I could not but despise the man in my heart who laid such a stress upon morals, leaving grace out of the question; and viewed it as a deplorable instance of human depravity and self conceit; but for all that, I was obliged to accept of his terms, for I had an inward thirst and longing to distinguish myself in the great cause of religion, and I thought if once I could print my own works, how I would astonish mankind, and confound their self wisdom and their esteemed morality – blow up the idea of any dependence on good works, and *morality*, forsooth! And I weened that I might thus get me a name even higher than if I had been made a general of the Czar Peter's troops against the infidels.

I attended the office some hours every day, but got not much encouragement, though I was eager to learn every thing, and could soon have set types considerably well. It was here that I first conceived the idea of writing this journal, and having it printed, and applied to Mr Watson to print it for me, telling him it was a religious parable such as the Pilgrim's Progress. He advised me to print it close, and make it a pamphlet, and then if it did not sell, it would not cost me much; but that religious pamphlets, especially if they had a shade of allegory in them, were the very rage of the day. I put my work to the press, and wrote early and late; and encouraging my companion to work at odd hours, and on Sundays, before the press-work of the second sheet was begun, we had the work all in types, corrected, and a clean copy thrown off for farther revisal. The first sheet was wrought off; and I never shall forget how my heart exulted when at the printing house this day, I saw what numbers of my works were to go abroad among mankind, and I determined with myself that I would not put the Border name of Elliot, which I had assumed, to the work.

Thus far have my History and Confessions been carried.

I must now furnish my Christian readers with a key to the process, management, and winding up of the whole matter; which I propose, by the assistance of God, to limit to a very few pages.

Chesters, July 27, 1712. – My hopes and prospects are a wreck. My precious journal is lost! consigned to the flames! My enemy hath found me out, and there is no hope of peace or rest for me on this side the grave.

In the beginning of the last week, my fellow lodger came home, running in a great panic, and told me a story of the devil having appeared twice in the printing house, assisting the workmen at the printing of my book, and that some of them had been frightened out of their wits. That the story was told to Mr Watson, who till that time had never paid any attention to the treatise, but who, out of curiosity, began and read a part of it, and thereupon flew into a great rage, called my work a medley of lies and blasphemy, and ordered the whole to be consigned to the flames, blaming his foreman, and all connected with the press, for letting a work go so far, that was enough to bring down the vengeance of heaven on the concern.

If ever I shed tears through perfect bitterness of spirit it was at that time, but I hope it was more for the ignorance and folly of my countrymen than the overthrow of my own hopes. But my attention was suddenly aroused to other matters, by Linton mentioning that it was said by some in the office the devil had inquired for me.

'Surely you are not such a fool,' said I, 'as to believe that the devil really was in the printing office?'

'Oo, gud bless you sir! saw him myself, gave him a nod, and good-day. Rather a gentlemanly personage – Green Circassian hunting coat and turban – Like a foreigner – Has the power of vanishing in one moment though – Rather a suspicious circumstance that. Otherwise, his appearance not much against him.'

If the former intelligence thrilled me with grief, this did so with terror. I perceived who the personage was that had visited the printing house in order to further the progress of my work; and at the approach of every person to our lodgings, I from that instant trembled every bone, lest it should be my elevated and dreaded friend. I could not say I had ever received an office at his hand that was not friendly, yet these offices had been of a strange tendency; and the horror with which I now regarded him was unaccountable to myself. It was beyond description, conception, or the soul of man to bear. I took my printed sheets, the only copy of my unfinished work existing; and, on pretence of going straight to Mr Watson's office, decamped from my lodgings at Portsburgh a little before the fall of evening, and took the road towards England.

As soon as I got clear of the city, I ran with a velocity I knew not before I had been capable of. I flew out the way towards Dalkeith so swiftly, that I often lost sight of the ground, and I said to myself, 'O that I had the wings of a dove,[43] that I might fly to the farthest corners of the earth, to hide me from those against whom I have no power to stand!'

I travelled all that night and the next morning, exerting myself beyond my power; and about noon the following day I went into a yeoman's house, the name of which was Ellanshaws, and requested of the people a couch of any sort to lie down on, for I was ill, and could not proceed on my journey. They showed me to a stable-loft where there were two beds, on one of which I laid me down; and, falling into a sound sleep, I did not awake till the evening, that other three men came from the fields to sleep in the same place, one of whom lay down beside me, at which I was exceedingly glad. They fell all sound asleep, and I was terribly alarmed at a conversation I overheard somewhere outside the stable. I could not make out a sentence, but trembled to think I knew one of the voices at least, and rather than not be mistaken, I would that any man had run me through with a sword. I fell into a cold sweat, and once thought of instantly putting hand to my own life, as my only means of relief (May the rash and sinful thought be in mercy forgiven!), when I heard as it were two persons at the door, contending, as I thought, about their right and interest in me. That the one was forcibly preventing the admission of the other, I could hear distinctly, and their language was mixed with something dreadful and mysterious. In an agony of terror, I awakened my snoring companion with great difficulty, and asked him, in a low whisper, who these were at the door? The man lay silent, and listening, till fairly awake, and then asked if I had heard any thing? I said I had heard strange voices contending at the door.

'Then I can tell you, lad, it has been something neither good nor canny,' said he: 'It's no for naething that our horses are snorking that gate.'

For the first time, I remarked that the animals were snorting and rearing as if they wished to break through the house. The man called to them by their names, and ordered them to be quiet; but they raged still the more furiously. He then roused his drowsy companions, who were alike alarmed at the panic of the horses, all of them declaring that they had never seen either Mause or Jolly start in their lives before. My bed-fellow and another then ventured down the ladder, and I heard one of them then saying, 'Lord be wi' us! What can be i' the house? The sweat's rinning off the poor beasts like water.'

They agreed to sally out together, and if possible to reach the kitchen and bring a light. I was glad at this, but not so much so when I heard the one man saying to the other, in a whisper, 'I wish that stranger man may be canny enough.'

'God kens!' said the other: 'It doesnae look unco weel.'

The lad in the other bed, hearing this, set up his head in manifest affright as the other two departed for the kitchen; and, I believe, he would have been glad to have been in their company. This lad was next the ladder, at which I was extremely glad, for had he not been there, the world should not have induced me to wait the return of these two men. They were not well gone, before I heard another distinctly enter the stable, and come towards the ladder. The lad who was sitting up in his bed, intent on the watch, called out, 'Wha's that there? Walker, is that you? Purdie, I say, is it you?'

The darkling intruder paused for a few moments, and then came towards the foot of the ladder. The horses broke loose, and snorting and neighing for terror, raged through the house. In all my life I never heard so frightful a commotion. The being that occasioned it all, now began to mount the ladder toward our loft, on which the lad in the bed next the ladder sprung from his couch, crying out, 'the L—d A—y preserve us! what can it be?' With that he sped across the loft, and by my bed, praying lustily all the way; and, throwing himself from the other end of the loft into a manger, he darted, naked as he was, through among the furious horses, and making the door, that stood open, in a moment he vanished and left me in the lurch. Powerless with terror, and calling out fearfully, I tried to follow his example; but not knowing the situation of the places with regard to one another, I missed the manger, and fell on the pavement in one of the stalls. I was both stunned and lamed on the knee; but terror prevailing, I got up and tried to escape. It was out of my power; for there were divisions and cross divisions in the house, and mad horses smashing every thing before them, so that I knew not so much as on what side of the house the door was. Two or three times was I knocked down by the animals, but all the while I never stinted crying out with all my power. At length, I was seized by the throat and hair of the head, and dragged away, I wist not whither. My voice was now laid, and all my powers, both mental and bodily, totally overcome; and I remember no more till I found myself lying naked on the kitchen table of the farm house, and something like a horse's rug thrown over me. The only hint that I got from the people of the house on coming to myself was, that my absence would be good company; and that they had got me in a woful state, one which they did not chuse to describe, or hear described.

As soon as day-light appeared, I was packed about my business, with the hisses and execrations of the yeoman's family, who viewed me as a being to be shunned, ascribing to me the visitations of that unholy night. Again was I on my way southward, as lonely, hopeless, and degraded a being as was to be found on life's weary round. As I limped out the way, I wept, thinking of what I might have been, and what I really had become: of my high and flourishing hopes, when I set out as the avenger of God on the sinful children of men; of all that I had dared for the exaltation and progress of the truth; and it was with great difficulty that my faith remained unshaken, yet was I preserved from that sin, and comforted myself with the certainty, that the believer's progress through life is one of warfare and suffering.

My case was indeed a pitiable one. I was lame, hungry, fatigued, and my resources on the very eve of being exhausted. Yet these were but secondary miseries, and hardly worthy of a thought, compared with those I suffered inwardly. I not only looked around me with terror at every one that approached, but I was become a terror to myself; or rather, my body and soul were become terrors to each other; and, had it been possible, I felt as if they would have gone to war. I dared not look at my face in a glass, for I shuddered at my own image and likeness. I dreaded the dawning, and trembled at the approach of night, nor was there one thing in nature that afforded me the least delight.

In this deplorable state of body and mind, was I jogging on towards the Tweed, by the side of the small river called Ellan, when, just at the narrowest part of the glen, whom should I meet full in the face, but the very being in all the universe of God I would the most gladly have shunned. I had no power to fly from him, neither durst I, for the spirit within me, accuse him of falsehood, and renounce his fellowship. I stood before him like a condemned criminal, staring him in the face, ready to be winded, twisted, and tormented as he pleased. He regarded me with a sad and solemn look. How changed was now that majestic countenance, to one of haggard despair – changed in all save the extraordinary likeness to my late brother, a resemblance which misfortune and despair tended only to heighten. There were no kind greetings passed between us at meeting, like those which pass between the men of the world; he looked on me with eyes that froze the currents of my blood, but spoke not, till I assumed as much courage as to articulate – 'You here! I hope you have brought me tidings of comfort?'

'Tidings of despair!' said he. 'But such tidings as the timid and the ungrateful deserve, and have reason to expect. You are an outlaw, and a vagabond in your country, and a high reward is offered for your apprehension. The enraged populace have burnt your house, and all that is within it; and the farmers on the land bless themselves at being rid of you. So fare it with every one who puts his hand to the great work of man's restoration to freedom, and draweth back, contemning the light that is within him! Your enormities caused me to leave you to yourself for a season, and you see what the issue has been. You have given some evil ones power over you, who long to devour you, both soul and body, and it has required all my power and influence to save you. Had it not been for my hand, you had been torn in pieces last night; but for once I prevailed. We must leave this land forthwith, for here there is neither peace, safety, nor comfort for us. Do you now, and here, pledge yourself to one who has so often saved your life, and has put his own at stake to do so? Do you pledge yourself that you will henceforth be guided by my counsel, and follow me whithersoever I chuse to lead?'

'I have always been swayed by your counsel,' said I, 'and for your sake, principally, am I sorry, that all our measures have proved abortive. But I hope still to be useful in my native isle, therefore let me plead that your highness will abandon a poor despised and outcast wretch to his fate, and betake you to your realms, where your presence cannot but be greatly wanted.'

'Would that I could do so!' said he wofully. 'But to talk of that is to talk of an impossibility. I am wedded to you so closely, that I feel as if I were the same person. Our essences are one, our bodies and spirits being united, so, that I am drawn towards you as by magnetism, and wherever you are, there must my presence be with you.'

Perceiving how this assurance affected me, he began to chide me most bitterly for my ingratitude; and then he assumed such looks, that it was impossible for me longer to bear them; therefore I staggered out the way, begging and beseeching of him to give me up to my fate, and hardly knowing what I said; for it struck me, that, with all his assumed appearance of misery and wretchedness, there were traits of exultation in his hideous countenance, manifesting a secret and inward joy at my utter despair.

It was long before I durst look over my shoulder, but when I did so, I perceived this ruined and debased potentate coming slowly on the same path, and I prayed that the lord would hide me in the bowels of the earth, or depths of the sea. When I crossed the Tweed, I perceived him still a little behind me; and my despair being then at its height, I cursed the time I first met with such a tormentor; though, on a little recollection it occurred, that it was at that blessed time when I was solemnly dedicated to the Lord, and assured of my final election, and confirmation, by an eternal decree never to be annulled. This being my sole and only comfort, I recalled my curse upon the time, and repented me of my rashness.

After crossing the Tweed, I saw no more of my persecutor that day, and had hopes that he had left me for a season; but, alas, what hope was there of my relief after the declaration I had so lately heard! I took up my lodgings that night in a small miserable inn in the village of Ancrum, of which the people seemed alike poor and ignorant. Before going to bed, I asked if it was customary with them to have family worship of evenings? The man answered, that they were so hard set with the world, they often could not get time, but if I would be so kind as officiate they would be much obliged to me. I accepted the invitation, being afraid to go to rest lest the commotions of the foregoing night might be renewed, and continued the worship as long as in decency I could. The poor people thanked me, hoped my prayers would be heard both on their account and my own, seemed much taken with my abilities, and wondered how a man of my powerful eloquence chanced to be wandering about in a condition so forlorn. I said I was a poor student of theology, on my way to Oxford. They stared at one another with expressions of wonder, disappointment, and fear. I afterwards came to learn, that the term *theology* was by them quite misunderstood, and that they had some crude conceptions that nothing was taught at Oxford but the *black arts*, which ridiculous idea prevailed over all the south of Scotland. For the present I could not understand what the people meant, and less so, when the man asked me, with deep concern, 'If I was serious in my intentions of going to Oxford? He hoped not, and that I would be better guided.'

I said my education wanted finishing – but he remarked, that the Oxford arts were a bad finish for a religious man's education. Finally, I requested him to sleep with me, or in my room all the night, as I wanted some serious and religious conversation with him, and likewise to convince him that the study of the fine arts, though not absolutely necessary, were not incompatible with the character of a Christian divine. He shook his head, and wondered how I could call them *fine arts* – hoped I did not mean to convince him by any ocular demonstration, and at length reluctantly condescended to sleep with me, and let the lass and wife sleep together for one night. I believe he would have declined it, had it not been some hints from his wife, stating, that it was a good arrangement, by which I understood there were only two beds in the house, and that when I was preferred to the lass's bed, she had one to shift for.

The landlord and I accordingly retired to our homely bed, and conversed for some time about indifferent matters, till he fell sound asleep. Not so with me: I had that within which would not suffer me to close my eyes; and about the dead of night, I again heard the same noises and contention begin outside the house, as I had heard the night before; and again I heard it was about a sovereign and peculiar right in me. At one time the noise was on the top of the house, straight above our bed, as if the one party were breaking through the roof, and the other forcibly preventing it; at another time it was at the door, and at a third time at the window; but still mine host lay sound by my side, and did not waken. I was seized with terrors indefinable, and prayed fervently, but did not attempt rousing my sleeping companion until I saw if no better could be done. The women, however, were alarmed, and, rushing into our apartment, exclaimed that all the devils in hell were besieging the house. Then, indeed, the landlord awoke, and it was time for him, for the tumult had increased to such a degree, that it shook the house to its foundations, being louder and more furious than I could have conceived the heat of battle to be when the volleys of artillery are mixed with groans, shouts, and blasphemous cursing. It thundered and lightened; and there were screams, groans, laughter, and execrations, all intermingled.

I lay trembling and bathed in a cold perspiration, but was soon obliged to bestir myself, the inmates attacking me one after the other.

'O, Tam Douglas! Tam Douglas! haste ye an' rise out fra-yont that incarnal devil!' cried the wife: 'Ye are in ayont the auld ane himsel, for our lass Tibbie saw his cloven cloots last night.'

'Lord forbid!' roared Tam Douglas, and darted over the bed like a flying fish. Then, hearing the unearthly tumult with which he was surrounded, he returned to the side of the bed, and addressed me thus, with long and fearful intervals:

'If ye be the deil, rise up, an' depart in peace out o' this house – afore the bedstrae take kindling about ye, an' than it'll maybe be the waur for ye – Get up – an' gang awa out amang your cronies, like a good – lad – There's nae body here wishes you ony ill – D'ye hear me?'

'Friend,' said I, 'no Christian would turn out a fellow creature on such a night as this, and in the midst of such a commotion of the villagers.'

'Na, if ye be a mortal man,' said he, 'which I rather think, from the use you made of the holy book – Nane o' your practical jokes on strangers an' honest foks. These are some o' your Oxford tricks, an' I'll thank you to be ower wi' them. – Gracious heaven, they are brikkin through the house at a' the four corners at the same time!'

The lass Tibby, seeing the innkeeper was not going to prevail with me to rise, flew toward the bed in desperation, and seizing me by the waist, soon landed me on the floor, saying: 'Be ye deil, be ye chiel, ye's no lie there till baith the house an' us be swallowed up!'

Her master and mistress applauding the deed, I was obliged to attempt dressing myself, a task to which my powers were quite inadequate in the state I was in, but I was readily assisted by every one of the three; and as soon as they got my clothes thrust on in a loose way, they shut their eyes lest they should see what might drive them distracted, and thrust me out to the street, cursing me, and calling on the fiends to take their prey and begone.

The scene that ensued is neither to be described, nor believed, if it were. I was momently surrounded by a number of hideous fiends, who gnashed on me with their teeth, and clenched their crimson paws in my face; and at the same instant I was seized by the collar of my coat behind, by my dreaded and devoted friend, who pushed me on, and with his gilded rapier waving and brandishing around me, defended me against all their united attacks. Horrible as my assailants were in appearance (and they had all monstrous shapes), I felt that I would rather have fallen into their hands, than be thus led away captive by my defender at his will and pleasure, without having the right or power to say my life, or any part of my will, was my own. I could not even thank him for his potent guardianship, but hung down my head, and moved on I knew not whither, like a criminal led to execution, and still the infernal combat continued, till about the dawning, at which time I looked up, and all the fiends were expelled but one, who kept at a distance; and still my persecutor and defender pushed me by the neck before him.

At length he desired me to sit down and take some rest, with which I complied, for I had great need of it, and wanted the power to withstand what he desired. There, for a whole morning did he detain me, tormenting me with reflections on the past, and pointing out the horrors of the future, until a thousand times I wished myself non-existent. 'I have attached myself to your wayward fortune,' said he; 'and it has been my ruin as well as thine. Ungrateful as you are, I cannot give you up to be devoured; but this is a life that it is impossible to brook longer. Since our hopes are blasted in this world, and all our schemes of grandeur overthrown; and since our everlasting destiny is settled by a decree which no act of ours can invalidate, let us fall by our own hands, or by the hands of each other; die like heroes; and, throwing off this frame of dross and corruption, mingle with the pure ethereal essence of existence, from which we derived our being.'

I shuddered at a view of the dreadful alternative, yet was obliged to confess that in my present circumstances existence was not to be borne. It was in vain that I reasoned on the sinfulness of the deed, and on its damning nature; he made me condemn myself out of my own mouth, by allowing the absolute nature of justifying grace, and the impossibility of the elect ever falling from the faith, or the glorious end to which they were called; and then he said, this granted, self-destruction was the act of a hero, and none but a coward would shrink from it, to suffer a hundred times more every day and night that passed over his head.

I said I was still contented to be that coward; and all that I

begged of him was, to leave me to my fortune for a season, and
to the just judgment of my creator; but he said his word and
honour were engaged on my behoof, and these, in such a case,
were not to be violated. 'If you will not pity yourself, have pity
on me,' added he: 'turn your eyes on me, and behold to what
I am reduced.'

Involuntarily did I turn round at the request, and caught a
half glance of his features. May no eye destined to reflect the
beauties of the New Jerusalem inward upon the beatific soul,
behold such a sight as mine then beheld! My immortal spirit,
blood, and bones, were all withered at the blasting sight; and I
arose and withdrew, with groanings which the pangs of death
shall never wring from me.

Not daring to look behind me, I crept on my way, and that
night reached this hamlet on the Scottish border; and being
grown reckless of danger, and hardened to scenes of horror, I
took up my lodging with a poor hind, who is a widower, and
who could only accommodate me with a bed of rushes at his
fire-side. At midnight I heard some strange sounds, too much
resembling those to which I had of late been inured; but they
kept at a distance, and I was soon persuaded that there was a
power protected that house superior to those that contended
for, or had the mastery over me. Overjoyed at finding such an
asylum, I remained in the humble cot. This is the third day I have
lived under the roof, freed of my hellish assailants, spending my
time in prayer, and writing out this my journal, which I have
fashioned to stick in with my printed work, and to which I
intend to add portions while I remain in this pilgrimage state,
which, I find too well, cannot be long.

August 3, 1712. – This morning the hind has brought me
word from Redesdale, whither he had been for coals, that a
stranger gentleman had been traversing that country, making
the most earnest inquiries after me, or one of the same appearance; and from the description that he brought of this stranger,
I could easily perceive who it was. Rejoicing that my tormentor
has lost traces of me for once, I am making haste to leave my
asylum, on pretence of following this stranger, but in reality to
conceal myself still more completely from his search. Perhaps

this may be the last sentence ever I am destined to write. If so, farewell Christian reader! May God grant to thee a happier destiny than has been allotted to me here on earth, and the same assurance of acceptance above! *Amen.*

Ault-Righ, [44] *August* 24, 1712. – Here am I, set down on the open moor to add one sentence more to my woful journal; and then, farewell all beneath the sun!

On leaving the hind's cottage on the Border, I hasted to the north-west, because in that quarter I perceived the highest and wildest hills before me. As I crossed the mountains above Hawick, I exchanged clothes with a poor homely shepherd, whom I found lying on a hill side, singing to himself some woful love ditty. He was glad of the change, and proud of his saintly apparel; and I was no less delighted with mine, by which I now supposed myself completely disguised; and I found moreover that in this garb of a common shepherd I was made welcome in every house. I slept the first night in a farm-house nigh to the church of Roberton, without hearing or seeing aught extraordinary; yet I observed next morning that all the servants kept aloof from me, and regarded me with looks of aversion. The next night I came to this house, where the farmer engaged me as a shepherd; and finding him a kind, worthy, and religious man, I accepted of his terms with great gladness. I had not, however, gone many times to the sheep, before all the rest of the shepherds told my master, that I knew nothing about herding, and begged of him to dismiss me. He perceived too well the truth of their intelligence; but being much taken with my learning, and religious conversation, he would not put me away, but set me to herd his cattle.

It was lucky for me, that before I came here, a report had prevailed, perhaps for an age, that this farm-house was haunted at certain seasons by a ghost. I say it was lucky for me, for I had not been in it many days before the same appalling noises began to prevail around me about midnight, often continuing till near the dawning. Still they kept aloof, and without doors; for this gentleman's house, like the cottage I was in formerly, seemed to be a sanctuary from all demoniacal power. He appears to be a good man and a just, and mocks at the idea of supernatural agency, and he either does not hear these persecuting spirits, or will not acknowledge it, though of late he appears much perturbed.

The consternation of the menials has been extreme. They ascribe all to the ghost, and tell frightful stories of murders having been committed there long ago. Of late, however, they are beginning to suspect that it is I that am haunted; and as I have never given them any satisfactory account of myself, they are whispering that I am a murderer, and haunted by the spirits of those I have slain.

August 30. – This day I have been informed, that I am to be banished the dwelling-house by night, and to sleep in an out-house by myself, to try if the family can get any rest when freed of my presence. I have peremptorily refused acquiescence, on which my master's brother struck me, and kicked me with his foot. My body being quite exhausted by suffering, I am grown weak and feeble both in mind and bodily frame, and actually unable to resent any insult or injury. I am the child of earthly misery and despair, if ever there was one existent. My master is still my friend; but there are so many masters here, and every one of them alike harsh to me, that I wish myself in my grave every hour of the day. If I am driven from the family sanctuary by night, I know I shall be torn in pieces before morning; and then who will deign or dare to gather up my mangled limbs, and give them honoured burial.

My last hour is arrived: I see my tormentor once more approaching me in this wild. Oh, that the earth would swallow me up, or the hill fall and cover me! Farewell for ever!

September 7, 1712. – My devoted, princely, but sanguine friend, has been with me again and again. My time is expired, and I find a relief beyond measure, for he has fully convinced me that no act of mine can mar the eternal counsel, or in the smallest degree alter or extenuate one event which was decreed before the foundations of the world were laid. He said he had watched over me with the greatest anxiety, but perceiving my rooted aversion towards him, he had forborn troubling me with his presence. But now, seeing that I was certainly to be driven from my sanctuary that night, and that there would be a number of infernals watching to make a prey of my body, he came to caution me not to despair, for that he would protect me at all risks, if the power remained with him. He then repeated an ejaculatory prayer, which I was to pronounce, if in great extremity. I objected to the words as equivocal, and susceptible of being rendered in a meaning perfectly dreadful; but he reasoned against this, and all reasoning with him is to no purpose. He said he did not ask me to repeat the words, unless greatly straitened; and that I saw his strength and power giving way, and when perhaps nothing else could save me.

The dreaded hour of night arrived; and, as he said, I was expelled from the family residence, and ordered to a byre, or cow-house, that stood parallel with the dwelling-house behind, where, on a divot loft, my humble bedstead stood, and the cattle grunted and puffed below me. How unlike the splendid halls of Dalcastle! And to what I am now reduced, let the reflecting reader judge. Lord, thou knowest all that I have done for thy cause on earth! Why then art thou laying thy hand so sore upon me? Why hast thou set me as a butt of thy malice? But thy will must be done! Thou wilt repay me in a better world. *Amen.*

September 8. – My first night of trial in this place is overpast! Would that it were the last that I should ever see in this detested world! If the horrors of hell are equal to those I have suffered, eternity will be of short duration there, for no created energy can support them for one single month, or week. I have been buffeted as never living creature was. My vitals have all been torn, and every faculty and feeling of my soul racked, and tormented into callous insensibility. I was even hung by the locks over a yawning chasm, to which I could perceive no bottom, and then – not till then, did I repeat the tremendous prayer! – I was instantly at liberty; and what I now am, the Almighty knows! *Amen.*

September 18, 1712. – Still am I living, though liker to a vision than a human being; but this is my last day of mortal existence. Unable to resist any longer, I pledged myself to my devoted friend, that on this day we should die together, and trust to the charity of the children of men for a grave. I am solemnly pledged; and though I dared to repent, I am aware he will not be gainsaid, for he is raging with despair at his fallen and decayed majesty, and there is some miserable comfort in the idea that my tormentor shall fall with me. Farewell, world,[45] with all thy miseries; for comforts or enjoyments hast thou none! Farewell, woman, whom I have despised and shunned; and man, whom I have hated; whom, nevertheless, I desire to leave in charity! And thou, sun, bright emblem of a far brighter effulgence, I bid farewell to thee also! I do not now take my last look of thee, for to thy glorious orb shall a poor suicide's last earthly look be raised. But, ah! who is yon that I see approaching furiously – his stern face blackened with horrid despair! My hour is at hand. – Almighty God, what is this that I am about to do! The hour of repentance is past, and now my fate is inevitable. – *Amen, for ever!* I will now seal up my little book, and conceal it; and cursed be he who trieth to alter or amend!

END OF THE MEMOIR

What can this work be? Sure, you will say, it must be an allegory; or (as the writer calls it) a religious PARABLE, showing the dreadful danger of self-righteousness? I cannot tell. Attend to the sequel: which is a thing so extraordinary, so unprecedented, and so far out of the common course of human events, that if there were not hundreds of living witnesses to attest the truth of it, I would not bid any rational being believe it.

In the first place, take the following extract from an authentic letter,[1] published in *Blackwood's Magazine* for *August*, 1823.

'On the top of a wild height called Cowanscroft, where the lands of three proprietors meet all at one point, there has been for long and many years the grave of a suicide marked out by a stone standing at the head, and another at the feet. Often have I stood musing over it myself, when a shepherd on one of the farms, of which it formed the extreme boundary, and thinking what could induce a young man, who had scarcely reached the prime of life, to brave his Maker, and rush into his presence by an act of his own erring hand, and one so unnatural and preposterous. But it never once occurred to me, as an object of curiosity, to dig up the mouldering bones of the culprit, which I considered as the most revolting of all objects. The thing was, however, done last month, and a discovery made of one of the greatest natural phenomena that I have heard of in this country.

'The little traditionary history that remains of this unfortunate youth, is altogether a singular one. He was not a native of the place, nor would he ever tell from what place he came; but he was remarkable for a deep, thoughtful, and sullen disposition. There was nothing against his character that any body knew of here, and he had been a considerable time in the place. The last service he was in was with a Mr Anderson of Eltrive (Ault-Righ, *the King's burn*), who died about 100 years ago, and who had hired him during the summer to herd a stock of young cattle in Eltrive Hope. It happened one day in the month of September, that James Anderson,[2] his master's son, went with this young man to the Hope to divert himself. The herd had his dinner along with him, and about one o'clock, when the boy proposed going home, the former pressed him very hard to stay and take share of his dinner; but the boy refused, for fear his parents might be alarmed about him, and said he *would* go home: on which the herd said to him, 'Then, if ye winna stay with me, James, ye may depend on't I'll cut my throat afore ye come back again.'

'I have heard it likewise reported, but only by one person, that there had been some things stolen out of his master's house a good while before, and that the boy had discovered a silver knife and fork, that was a part of the stolen property, in the herd's possession that day, and that it was this discovery that drove him to despair.

'The boy did not return to the Hope that afternoon; and, before evening, a man coming in at the pass called *The Hart Loup*, with a drove of lambs, on the way for Edinburgh, perceived something like a man standing in a strange frightful position at the side of one of Eldinhope hay-ricks. The driver's attention was riveted on this strange uncouth figure, and as the drove-road passed at no great distance from the spot, he first called, but receiving no answer, he went up to the spot, and behold it was the above-mentioned young man, who had hung himself in the hay-rope that was tying down the rick.

'This was accounted a great wonder; and every one said, if the devil had not assisted him it was impossible the thing could have been done; for, in general, these ropes are so brittle, being made of green hay, that they will scarcely bear to be bound over the rick. And the more to horrify the good people of this neighbourhood, the driver said, when he first came in view, *he could almost give his oath* that he saw two people busily engaged at the hay-rick, going round it and round it, and he thought they were dressing it.

'If this asseveration approximated at all to truth, it makes this evident at least, that the unfortunate young man had hanged himself after the man with the lambs came in view. He was, however, quite dead when he cut him down. He had fastened two of the old hay-ropes at the bottom of the rick on one side (indeed they are all fastened so when first laid on), so that he had nothing to do but to loosen two of the ends on the other side. These he had tied in a knot round his neck, and then slackening his knees, and letting himself down gradually, till the hay-rope bore all his weight, he had contrived to put an end to his existence in that way. Now the fact is, that if you try all the ropes that are thrown over all the outfield hay-ricks in Scotland, there is not one among a thousand of them will hang a colley dog; so that the manner of this wretch's death was rather a singular circumstance.

'Early next morning, Mr Anderson's servants went reluctantly away, and, taking an old blanket with them for a winding sheet, they rolled up the body of the deceased, first in his own plaid, letting the hay-rope still remain about his neck, and then rolling the old blanket over all, they bore the loathed remains away to the distance of three miles or so, on spokes, to the top of Cowan's-Croft, at the very point where the Duke of Buccleuch's land, the Laird of Drummelzier's, and Lord Napier's, meet,[3] and there they buried him, with all that he had on and about him, silver knife and fork and altogether. Thus far went tradition, and no one ever disputed one jot of the disgusting oral tale.

'A nephew of that Mr Anderson's who was with the hapless youth that day he died, says, that, as far as he can gather from the relations of friends that he remembers, and of that same uncle in particular, it is one hundred and five years next month (that is September, 1823) since that event happened; and I think it likely that this gentleman's information is correct. But sundry other people, much older than he, whom I have consulted, pretend that it is six or seven years more. They say they have heard that Mr James Anderson was then a boy ten years of age; that he lived to an old age, upwards of fourscore, and it is two and forty years since he died. Whichever way it may be, it was about that period some way, of that there is no doubt.

'It so happened, that two young men, William Shiel[4] and W. Sword, were out, on an adjoining height, this summer, casting peats, and it came into their heads to open this grave in the wilderness, and see if there were any of the bones of the suicide of former ages and centuries remaining. They did so, but opened only one half of the grave, beginning at the head and about the middle at the same time. It was not long till they came upon the old blanket – I think they said not much more than a foot from the surface. They tore that open, and there was the hay-rope lying stretched down alongst his breast, so fresh that they saw at first sight that it was made of *risp*, a sort of long sword-grass that grows about marshes and the sides of lakes. One of the young men seized the rope and pulled by it, but the old enchantment of the devil remained – it would not break; and so he pulled and pulled at it, till behold the body came up into a sitting posture, with a broad blue bonnet on its head, and its plaid around it, all as fresh as that day it was laid in! I never heard of a preservation so wonderful, if it be true as was related to me, for still I have not had the curiosity to go and view the body myself. The features were all so plain, that an acquaintance might easily have known him. One of the lads gripped the face of the corpse with his finger and thumb, and the cheeks felt quite soft and fleshy, but the dimples remained and did not spring out again. He had fine yellow hair, about nine inches long; but not a hair of it could they pull out till they cut part of it off with a knife. They also cut off some portions of his clothes, which were all quite fresh, and distributed them among their acquaintances, sending a portion to me, among the rest, to keep as natural curiosities. Several gentlemen have in a manner forced me to give them fragments of these enchanted garments: I have, however, retained a small portion for you,[5] which I send along with this, being a piece of his plaid, and another of his waistcoat breast, which you will see are still as fresh as that day they were laid in the grave.

'His broad blue bonnet was sent to Edinburgh several weeks ago, to the great regret of some gentlemen connected with the land, who wished to have it for a keep-sake. For my part, fond as I am of blue bonnets, and broad ones in particular, I declare I durst not have worn that one. There was nothing of the silver knife and fork discovered, that I heard of, nor was it very likely it should: but it would appear he had been very near run of cash, which I daresay had been the cause of his utter despair; for, on searching his pockets, nothing was found but three old Scots halfpennies. These young men meeting with another shepherd afterwards, his curiosity was so much excited that they went and digged up the curious remains a second time, which was a pity, as it is likely that by these exposures to the air, and from the impossibility of burying it up again as closely as it was before, the flesh will now fall to dust.'

The letter from which the above is an extract, is signed JAMES HOGG, and dated from Altrive Lake, *August 1st*, 1823. It bears the stamp of authenticity in every line; yet, so often had I been hoaxed by the ingenious fancies displayed in that Magazine, that when this relation met my eye, I did not believe it; but from the moment that I perused it, I half formed the resolution of investigating these wonderful remains personally, if any such existed; for, in the immediate vicinity of the scene, as I supposed, I knew of more attractive metal than the dilapidated remains of mouldering suicides.

Accordingly, having some business in Edinburgh in September last, and being obliged to wait a few days for the arrival of a friend from London, I took that opportunity to pay a visit to my townsman and fellow collegian, Mr L—t of C—d, advocate.[6] I mentioned to him Hogg's letter, asking him if the statement was founded at all on truth. His answer was, 'I suppose so. For my part I never doubted the thing, having been told that there has been a deal of talking about it up in the Forest for some time past. But, God knows! Hogg has imposed as ingenious lies on the public ere now.'

I said, if it was within reach, I should like exceedingly to visit both the Shepherd and the Scots mummy he had described. Mr L—t assented at the first proposal, saying he had no objections to take a ride that length with me, and make the fellow produce his credentials: That we would have a delightful jaunt through a romantic and now classical country, and some good sport into the bargain, provided he could procure a horse for me, from his father-in-law, next day. He sent up to a Mr L—w to inquire, who returned for answer, that there was an excellent pony at my service, and that he himself would accompany us, being obliged to attend a great sheep fair at Thirlestane; and that he was certain the Shepherd would be there likewise.

Mr L—t said that was the very man we wanted to make our party complete; and at an early hour next morning we started for the ewe fair of Thirlestane, taking Blackwood's Magazine for August along with us. We rode through the ancient royal burgh of Selkirk, halted and corned our horses at a romantic village, nigh to some deep linns on the Ettrick, and reached the market ground at Thirlestane-green a little before mid-day. We soon found Hogg, standing near the *foot* of the market, as he called it, beside a great drove of *paulies*, a species of stock that I never heard of before. They were small sheep, striped on the backs with red chalk. Mr L—t introduced me to him as a great wool-stapler,[7] come to raise the price of that article; but he eyed me with distrust, and turning his back on us, answered, 'I hae sell'd mine.'

I followed, and shewing him the above-quoted letter, said I was exceedingly curious to have a look of these singular remains he had so ingeniously described; but he only answered me with the remark, that 'It was a queer fancy for a woo-stapler to tak.'

His two friends then requested him to accompany us to the spot, and to take some of his shepherds with us to assist in raising the body; but he spurned at the idea, saying, 'Od bless ye, lad! I hae ither matters to mind. I hae a' thae paulies to sell, an' a' yon Highland stotts down on the green every ane; an' then I hae ten scores o' yowes to buy after, an' if I canna first sell my ain stock, I canna buy nae ither body's. I hae mair ado than I can manage the day, foreby ganging to houk up hunder-year-auld banes.'

Finding that we could make nothing of him, we left him with his *paulies*, Highland stotts, grey jacket, and broad blue bonnet, to go in search of some other guide. L—w soon found one, for he seemed acquainted with every person in the fair. We got a fine old shepherd, named W—m B—e, a great original, and a very obliging and civil man, who asked no conditions but that we should not speak of it, because he did not wish it to come to his master's ears, that he had been engaged in *sic a profane thing*. We promised strict secrecy; and accompanied by another farmer, Mr S—t, and old B—e, we proceeded to the grave, which B—e described as about a mile and a half distant from the market ground.[8]

We went into a shepherd's cot to get a drink of milk, when I read to our guide Mr Hogg's description, asking him if he thought it correct? He said there was hardly a bit o't correct, for the grave was not on the hill of Cowan's-Croft, nor yet on the point where three lairds' lands met, but on the top of a hill called the Faw-Law, where there was no land that was not the Duke of Buccleuch's within a quarter of a mile. He added that it was a wonder how the poet could be mistaken there, who once herded the very ground where the grave is, and saw both hills from his own window. Mr L—w testified great surprise at such a singular blunder, as also how the body came *not* to be buried at the meeting of three or four lairds' lands, which had always been customary in the south of Scotland. Our guide said he had always heard it reported, that the Eltrive men, with Mr David Anderson at their head, had risen before day on the

Monday morning, it having been on the Sabbath day that the man *put down* himself; and that they set out with the intention of burying him on Cowan's-Croft, where three marches met at a point. But it having been an invariable rule to bury such *lost sinners* before the rising of the sun, these five men were overtaken by day-light, as they passed the house of Berry-Knowe; and by the time they reached the top of the Faw-Law, the sun was beginning to skair the east. On this they laid down the body, and digged a deep grave with all expedition; but when they had done, it was too short, and the body being stiff, it would not go down, on which Mr David Anderson looking to the east, and perceiving that the sun would be up on them in a few minutes, set his foot on the suicide's brow, and tramped down his head into the grave with his iron-heeled shoe, until his nose and skull crashed again, and at the same time uttered a terrible curse on the wretch who had disgraced the family, and given them all this trouble. This anecdote, our guide said, he had heard when a boy, from the mouth of Robert Laidlaw, one of the five men who buried the body.

We soon reached the spot, and I confess I felt a singular sensation, when I saw the grey stone[9] standing at the head, and another at the feet, and the one half of the grave manifestly new digged, and closed up again as had been described. I could still scarcely deem the thing to be a reality, for the ground did not appear to be wet, but a kind of dry rotten moss. On looking around, we found some fragments of clothes, some teeth, and part of a pocket-book, which had not been returned into the grave, when the body had been last raised, for it had been twice raised before this, but only from the loins upward.

To work we fell with two spades, and soon cleared away the whole of the covering. The part of the grave that had been opened before, was filled with mossy mortar, which impeded us exceedingly, and entirely prevented a proper investigation of the fore parts of the body. I will describe every thing as I saw it before four respectable witnesses, whose names I shall publish at large if permitted. A number of the bones came up separately; for with the constant flow of liquid stuff into the deep grave, we could not see to preserve them in their places. At length great

loads of coarse clothes, blanketing, plaiding, &c. appeared; we
tried to lift these regularly up, and on doing so, part of a
skeleton came up, but no flesh, save a little that was hanging in
dark flitters about the spine, but which had no consistence; it
was merely the appearance of flesh without the substance. The
head was wanting; and I being very anxious to possess the skull,
the search was renewed among the mortar and rags. We first
found a part of the scalp, with the long hair firm on it; which,
on being cleaned, is neither black nor fair, but of a darkish
dusk, the most common of any other colour. Soon afterwards
we found the skull, but it was not complete. A spade had
damaged it, and one of the temple quarters was wanting. I am
no phrenologist, not knowing one organ from another, but I
thought the skull of that wretched man no study. If it was
particular for any thing, it was for a smooth, almost perfect
rotundity, with only a little protuberance above the vent of
the ear.[10]

When we came to that part of the grave that had never
been opened before, the appearance of every thing was quite
different. There the remains lay under a close vault of moss,
and within a vacant space; and I suppose, by the digging in the
former part of the grave, that part had been deepened, and
drawn the moisture away from this part, for here all was perfect.
The breeches still suited the thigh, the stocking the leg, and the
garters were wrapt as neatly and as firm below the knee as if
they had been newly tied. The shoes were all opened in the
seams, the hemp having decayed, but the soles, upper leathers,
and wooden heels, which were made of birch, were all as fresh
as any of those we wore. There was one thing I could not help
remarking, that in the inside of one of the shoes there was a
layer of cow's dung, about one eighth of an inch thick, and in
the hollow of the sole fully one fourth of an inch. It was firm,
green, and fresh; and proved that he had been working in a
byre. His clothes were all of a singular ancient cut, and no less
singular in their texture. Their durability certainly would have
been prodigious; for in thickness, coarseness, and strength, I
never saw any cloth in the smallest degree to equal them. His
coat was a frock coat, of a yellowish drab colour, with wide

sleeves. It is tweeled, milled, and thicker than a carpet. I cut off two of the skirts and brought them with me. His vest was of striped serge, such as I have often seen worn by country people. It was lined and backed with white stuff. The breeches were a sort of striped plaiding, which I never saw worn, but which our guide assured us was very common in the country once, though. from the old clothes which he had seen remaining of it, he judged that it could not be less than 200 years since it was in fashion. His garters were of worsted, and striped with black or blue; his stockings gray, and wanting the feet. I brought samples of all along with me. I have likewise now got possession of the bonnet, which puzzles me most of all. It is not conformable with the rest of the dress. It is neither a broad bonnet, nor a Border bonnet; for there is an open behind, for tying, which no genuine Border bonnet, I am told, ever had. It seems to have been a Highland bonnet, worn in a flat way like a scone on the crown, such as is sometimes still seen in the west of Scotland. All the limbs, from the loins to the toes, seemed perfect and entire, but they could not bear handling. Before we got them returned again into the grave, they were all shaken to pieces, except the thighs, which continued to retain a kind of flabby form.

All his clothes that were sewed with linen yarn were lying in separate portions, the thread having rotten; but such as were sewed with worsted remained perfectly firm and sound. Among such a confusion, we had hard work to find out all his pockets, and our guide supposed, that, after all, we did not find above the half of them. In his vest pocket was a long clasp knife, very sharp; the haft was thin, and the scales shone as if there had been silver inside. Mr Sc—t took it with him, and presented it to his neighbour, Mr R—n of W—n L—e, who still has it in his possession.[11] We found a comb, a gimblet, a vial, a small neat square board, a pair of plated knee-buckles, and several samples of cloth of different kinds, rolled neatly up within one another. At length, while we were busy on the search, Mr L—t picked up a leathern case, which seemed to have been wrapped round and round by some ribbon, or cord, that had been rotten from it, for the swaddling marks still remained. Both L—w

and B—e called out that 'it was the tobacco spleuchan, and a
well-filled ane too'; but on opening it out, we found, to our
great astonishment, that it contained *a printed pamphlet*. We
were all curious to see what sort of a pamphlet such a person
would read; what it could contain that he seemed to have had
such a care about? for the slough in which it was rolled, was
fine chamois leather; what colour it had been, could not be
known. But the pamphlet was wrapped so close together, and
so damp, rotten, and yellow, that it seemed one solid piece. We
all concluded, from some words that we could make out, that
it was a religious tract, but that it would be impossible to make
any thing of it. Mr L—w remarked that it was a great pity if a
few sentences could not be made out, for that it was a question
what might be contained in that little book; and then he
requested Mr L—t to give it to me, as he had so many things
of literature and law to attend to, that he would never think
more of it. He replied, that either of us were heartily welcome
to it, for that he had thought of returning it into the grave, if
he could have made out but a line or two, to have seen what
was its tendency.

'Grave, man!' exclaimed L—w, who speaks excellent strong
broad Scots: 'My truly, but ye grave weel! I wad esteem the
contents o' that spleuchan as the most precious treasure. I'll tell
you what it is, sir: I hae often wondered how it was that this
man's corpse has been miraculously preserved frae decay, a
hunder times langer than ony other body's, or than even a
tanner's. But now I could wager a guinea, it has been for the
preservation o' that little book. And Lord kens what may be
in't! It will maybe reveal some mystery that mankind disna ken
naething about yet.'

'If there be any mysteries in it,' returned the other, 'it is not
for your handling, my dear friend, who are too much taken up
about mysteries already.' And with these words he presented
the mysterious pamphlet to me. With very little trouble, save
that of a thorough drying, I unrolled it all with ease, and found
the very tract which I have here ventured to lay before the
public, part of it in small bad print, and the remainder in
manuscript. The title page is written, and is as follows:

THE PRIVATE MEMOIRS
AND CONFESSIONS
OF A JUSTIFIED SINNER:

WRITTEN BY HIMSELF.

FIDELI CERTA MERCES.[12]

And, alongst the head, it is the same as given in the present edition of the work. I altered the title to *A Self-justified Sinner*, but my booksellers did not approve of it; and there being a curse pronounced by the writer on him that should dare to alter or amend, I have let it stand as it is. Should it be thought to attach discredit to any received principle of our church, I am blameless. The printed part ends at page 183, and the rest is in a fine old hand, extremely small and close. I have ordered the printer to procure a fac-simile of it, to be bound in with the volume.

With regard to the work itself, I dare not venture a judgment, for I do not understand it. I believe no person, man or woman, will ever peruse it with the same attention that I have done, and yet I confess that I do not comprehend the writer's drift. It is certainly impossible that these scenes could ever have occurred, that he describes as having himself transacted. I think it *may be* possible that he had some hand in the death of his brother, and yet I am disposed greatly to doubt it; and the numerous distorted traditions, &c. which remain of that event, may be attributable to the work having been printed and burnt, and of course the story known to all the printers, with their families and gossips. That the young Laird of Dalcastle came by a violent death, there remains no doubt; but that this wretch slew him, there is to me a good deal. However, allowing this to have been the case, I account all the rest either dreaming or madness; or, as he says to Mr Watson, a religious parable, on purpose to illustrate something scarcely tangible, but to which he seems to have attached great weight. Were the relation at all consistent with reason, it corresponds so minutely with traditionary facts, that it could scarcely have missed to have been received as authentic; but in this day, and with the present generation, it will not go down, that a man should be daily tempted by the devil, in the semblance of a fellow-creature; and at length lured to self-destruction, in the hopes that this same fiend and tormentor was to suffer and fall along with him. It was a bold theme for an allegory, and would have suited that age well had it been taken up by one fully qualified for the task, which this writer was not. In short, we must either conceive him not only the greatest fool, but the greatest wretch, on whom was ever stamped the form of humanity; or, that he was a religious maniac, who wrote and wrote about a deluded creature, till he arrived at that height of madness, that he believed himself the very object whom he had been all along describing. And in order to escape from an ideal tormentor, committed that act for which, according to the tenets he embraced, there was no remission, and which consigned his memory and his name to everlasting detestation.

FINIS

MARION'S JOCK

There wad aiblins nane o'you ken Marion. She lived i' the Dod-Shiel, and had a callant to the lang piper, him that Squire Ridley's man beat at the Peel-hill meeting. Weel, you see, he was a gilliegaupy of a callant, gayan like the dad o' him; for Marion said he wad hae eaten a horse ahint the saddle; and as her shieling wasna unco weel stored o' meat, she had ill getting him mainteened; till at the lang and the last it just came to this pass, that whenever Jock was i' the house, it was a constant battle atween Marion and him. Jock fought to be at meat, and Marion to keep him frae it, and mony hard clouts and claws there passed. They wad hae foughten about a haggis, or a new kirning o' butter, for a hale hour, and the battle generally endit in Jock's getting a good share o' ilka thing. When he had fairly gained the possession, by whatever means, he feasted with the greatest satisfaction, licking his large ruddy lips, and looking all about him with eyes of the utmost benevolence. Marion railed all the while that the poor lad was enjoying himself, without any mercy and restraint, and there wasna a vile name under the sun that had ony signification of a glutton in it, that she didna ca' him by. Jock took the bite wi' the buffet – he heard a' the ill names, and munched away. Oh, how his heart did rejoice o'er a fat lunch o' beef, a good haggis, or even a cog o' milk brose! Poor fellow! such things were his joy and delight. So he snapped them up, and in two or three hours after he was as ready for another battle as ever.[1]

This was a terrible life to lead. Times grew aye the langer the waur; and Marion was obliged to hire poor Jock to Goodman Niddery, to herd his kye and his pet sheep. Jock had nae

thoughts at a' o' ganging to sic a job at first; but Marion tauld
him ilka day o' the fat beef, the huge kebbucks, and the parridge
sae thick that a horn spoon wadna delve into them, till he
grew impatient for the term-day. That day came at length, and
Marion went away hame wi' her son to introduce him. The
road was gayan lang, and Jock's crappin began to craw. He
speered a hunder times about the meat at Goodman Niddery's
house, and every answer that Marion gae was better than the
last, till Jock believed he was gaun hame to a continual feast. It
was a delightful thought, for the craving appetite within him
was come to a great height. They reached the place, and went
into the kitchen. Jock's een were instantly on the look-out; but
they didna need to range far. Above the fire there hung two
sides of bacon, more than three inches deep of fat, besides many
other meaner objects: the hind legs of bullocks, sheep, and deer,
were also there; but these were withered, black, and sapless in
appearance. Jock thought the very substance was dried out o'
them. But the bacon! How it made Jock smack his lips! It was
so juicy, that even the brown skin on the outside of it was all
standing thick o' eebright beaming drops like morning dew.
Jock was established at Goodman Niddery's: he would not have
flitted again and left these two sides of bacon hanging there for
an estate. Marion perceived well where the sum of his desires
was fixed, and trembled for fear of an instant attack. Well might
she; for Jock had a large dirk or sheathed knife (a very useful
weapon) that he wore, and that he took twice out of its place,
looked at its edge, and then at the enormous bacon ham, which
was more than three inches deep of solid fat, with the rich drops
of juice standing upon the skin. Jock drew his knife on his
sandal, then on the edge of a wooden table that stood beside
him, examined the weapon's edge again, and again fixed his
green eyes on the bacon. 'What do the people mean,' thought
he to himself, 'that they do not instantly slice down a portion
of that glorious meat, and fry it on the coals? Would they but
give me orders to do it – would they even give me the least hint,
how slashingly I would obey!'

    None of them had the good sense to give Jock ony sic orders.
He was two or three times on the very point of helping himself,

and at last got up on his feet, it was believed, for the sole purpose of making an attack on the bacon ham, when, behold, in came Goodman Niddery!

'There's your master, sirrah!' whispered Marion; 'haste ye and whup aff your bonnet.'

Jock looked at him. There was something very severe and forbidding in his countenance; so Jock's courage failed him, and he even took aff his bonnet, and sat down with that in his one hand and the drawn knife in the other. Marion's heart was greatly relieved, and she now ventured on a little conversation.

'I hae brought you hame my lad, Goodman, and I hope he'll be a good servant to you.'

'I coudna say, Marion: gin he be as gude as you ca'd him, he'll do. I think he looks like ane that winna be behind at his bicker.'

'Ay, weel I wat, Goodman, and that's true; and I wadna wish it were otherwise. Slaw at the meat, slaw at the wark, ye ken.'

'That is a good hint o' my mother's!' thinks Jock to himsel: 'What though I should show the auld niggard a sample? The folk o' this house surely hae nae common sense.'

The dinner was now, however, set down on the kitchen-table. The goodman sat at the head, the servants in a row on each side, and Jock and his mother at the foot. The goodwife stood behind her servants, and gave all their portions. The dinner that day consisted of broad bannocks, as hard as horn, a pail of thin sour milk, called whig, and a portion of a large kebbuck positively as dry as wood. Jock was exceedingly dissatisfied, and could not but admire the utter stupidity of the people, and their total want of all proper distinction. He thought it wonderful that rational creatures should not know what was good for them. He munched, and munched, and gnawed at the hard bread and cheese, till his jaws were sore; but he never once looked at the food before him; but leaning his cheek on his hand to rest his wearied grinders somewhat at every bite he took, and every splash of the sour shilpy milk that he lapped in, he lifted his eyes to the fat bacon ham with the juice standing on it in clear bells.

Marion wished herself fairly out of the house, for she perceived there would be an outbreak; and to prepare the good
people for whatever might happen, she said before going away,
'Now, goodwife, my callant's banes are green, and he's a fast
growing twig: I want to ken if he will get plenty o'meat here.'

'I winna answer for that, Marion; he shall fare as the lave
fare; but he's may-be no very easily served. There are some
misleared servants wha think they never get enough.'

'Tell me this thing, then, goodwife; will he see enough?'

'Ay; I shall answer for that part o't.'

'Then I shall answer for the rest, goodwife.'

Jock had by this time given up contending with the timber
cheese, and the blue sour milk, and, taking a lug of a bannock
in his hand, the size of a shoe sole, he went away and sat down
at the fireside, where he had a full view of the bacon ham, three
inches thick of fat, with the dew standing on its brown skin.

The withered bread swallowed rather the better of this
delicious sight; so Jock chewed and looked, and looked and
chewed, till his mother entered into the security mentioned.
'That is a capital hint,' thought Jock; 'I shall verify my good
mother's cautionry, for I can stand this nae langer.' He sprang
up on a seat, sliced off a large flitch of bacon, and had it on the
coals before one had time to pronounce a word; and then
turning his back to it, and his face to the company, he stood
with his drawn dirk, quite determined to defend his prey.

The goodwife spoke first up. 'Gudeness have a care o' us! see
to the menseless tike!' cried she. 'I declare the creature has na
the breeding o'a whalp!'

Jock was well used to such kind of epithets; so he bore this
and some more with the utmost suavity, still, however, keeping
his ground.

Goodman Niddery grinned, and his hands shook with anger,
as if struck with a palsy; but for some reason or other he did
not interfere. The servants were like to burst with laughter; and
Jock kept the goodwife at bay with his drawn knife, till his slice
was roasted; and then, laying it flat on his dry piece of bread,
he walked out to the field to enjoy it more at leisure. Marion
went away home; and the goodman and goodwife both deter-

mined to be revenged on Jock, and to make him pay dear for his audacity.

Jock gave several long looks after Marion as she vanished on Kettlemoor but he had left no kind of meat in her shieling when he came away, else it was likely he would have followed his mother home again. He was still smacking his lips after his rich repast, and he had seen too much good stuff about the house of his new master to leave it at once; so he was even fain to bid Marion good bye in his heart, wipe the filial tear from his eye, poor man, and try to reconcile himself to his new situation.

'Do you carry aye that lang gully knife about wi'you, master cow-herd, or how do they ca'ye?' said his master, when they next met after the adventure of the bacon.

'I hae aye carried it yet,' said Jock, with great innocence; 'and a gay gude whittle it is.'

'Ye maun gie that up,' said Niddery; 'we dinna suffer chaps like you to carry sic weapons about our house.'

Jock fixed his green eyes on his master's face. He could hardly believe him to be serious; still there was something in his look he did not like; so he put his knife deeper into his pocket, drew one step back, and, putting his under row of teeth in front of those above, waited the issue of such an unreasonable demand.

'Come, come; give it up I say. Give it to me; I'll dispose of it for you.'

'I'll see you at the bottom o' the place my mother speaks about whiles,' thought Jock to himself, 'afore I gie my gully either to you or ony that belangs to you.' He still kept his former position, however, and the same kind of look at his master's face, only his een grew rather greener.

'Won't you give it up, you stubborn thief? Then I will take it, and give you a good drubbing into the bargain.'

When Jock heard this, he pulled out his knife. 'That is a good lad to do as you are bidden,' said his master. But Jock, instead of delivering up his knife, drew it from the sheath, which he returned to his pocket. 'Now I sal only say this,' said he; 'the first man that tries to take my ain knife frae me – he may do it – but he shall get the length o't in his monyplies first.' So saying, he drew back his hand with a sudden jerk.

Goodman Niddery gave such a start that he actually leaped off the ground, and holding up both his hands, exclaimed, 'What a savage we have got here! what a Satan!' And without speaking another word, he ran away to the house, and left Jock standing with his drawn knife in his hand.

The goodman's stomach burned with revenge against Jock; so that night he sent him supperless to bed, out of requital for the affair of the fat bacon; and next day the poor boy was set down to a very scanty breakfast, which was not fair. His eye turning invariably to one delicious object, the goodman perceived well what was passing in his heart; and, on some pretence, first sent away all the servants, and then the goodwife. He next rose up himself, with his staff in his hand, and, going slowly away into the little parlour, said, as he went through the kitchen, 'What can be become o' a' the folk?' and with that entered the dark door that opened in a corner. He made as though he had shut the door; but he turned about within it and peeped back.

The moment that he vanished was the watchword for Jock: he sprang from his seat at the bottom of the table, and, mounting a form, began to whang away at the bacon ham. Some invidious bone, or hard object of some sort, coming unfortunately in contact with the edge of his knife, his progress was greatly obstructed; and though he cut and sawed with all his might, before he succeeded in separating a piece of about two pounds' weight from the main body, his master had rushed on him from his concealment, and, by one blow of his staff, laid him flat on the floor. The stroke was a sore one, for it was given with extreme good-will, and deprived Jock of sensibility for the time being. He and his form both came down with a great rumble, but the knife remained buried in the fat bacon ham; and the inveterate goodman was not satisfied with felling the poor lad, but kicked him, and laid on him with his stick after he was down. The goodwife at length came running, and put a stop to this cruelty; and fearing the boy was murdered, and that they would be hanged for it, she got assistance, and soon brought Jock again to himself.

Jock had been accustomed to fight for his meat, and in some

measure laid his account with it; so that, on the whole, he took his broken head as little to heart as could have been expected, certainly less than any other boy of the same age would have done. It was only a little more rough than he had been prepared to look for; but had he succeeded in his enterprise, he would not have been ill-content. The goodwife and her maids had laid him on a kitchen bed and bathed his temples; and on recovering from stupefaction, the first thing he did was to examine his pockets to see if he had his gully. Alack! there was nothing but the empty sheath. Then he *did* lose the field, and fell a blubbering and crying. The goodwife thought he was ill, and tried to soothe him by giving him some meat. He took the meat of course, but his heart was inconsolable; till, just when busy with his morsel, his eye chanced to travel to the old place, as if by instinct, and there he beheld the haft of his valued knife, sticking in the bacon ham, its blade being buried deep in sappy treasures. He sprang over the bed, and traversing the floor with staggering steps, mounted a form, and stretched forth his hand to possess himself again of his gully.

'Aih! Gudeness have a care o'us!' cried the goodwife: 'saw ever ony body the like o'that? The creature's bacon mad! Goodman! Goodman, come here!'

Jock, however, extricated his knife and fled, though he could scarcely well walk. Some of the maids averred that he at the same time slid a corner of the ham into his pocket; but it is probable they belied him, for Jock had been munching in the bed but the moment before.

He then went out to his cows, weak as he was. He had six cows, some mischievous calves, and ten sheep to herd; and he determined to take good care of these, as also, now that he had got his knife again, not to want his share of the good things about the house, of which he saw there was abundance. However, several days came and went, and Jock was so closely watched by his master and mistress all the time he was in the house, that he could get nothing but his own scanty portion. What was more, Jock was obliged every day to drive his charge far a-field, and remain with them from morn till evening. He got a few porridge in the morning, and a hard bannock and a bottle of sour milk to carry along with him for his dinner.[2] This miserable meal was often despatched before eleven o'clock, so that poor Jock had to spend the rest of the day in fasting, and contriving grand methods of obtaining some good meat in future.

There was one thing very teasing: he had a small shieling, which some former herd had built, and plenty of sticks to burn for the gathering or cutting. He had thus a fire every day, without any thing to roast on it. Jock sat over it often in the most profound contemplation, thinking how delightfully a slice of bacon would fry on it; how he would lay the slice on his hard bannock, and how the juice would ooze out of it! Never was there a man who had richer prospects than Jock had: still his happiness lay only in perspective. But experience teaches man wisdom, and wisdom points out to him many expedients.

Among Jock's pet sheep there was one fat ewe-lamb, the flower of the flock, which the goodwife and the goodman both loved and valued above all the rest. She was as beautiful and playful as innocence itself, and, withal, as fat as she could lie in her skin. There was one rueful day, and a hungry one, that Jock had sat long over his little fire of sticks, pondering on the joys of fat flesh. He went out to turn his mischievous calves, whose nebs were never out of an ill deed, and at that time they had strayed into the middle of a cornfield. As bad luck would have it, by the way he perceived this dawted ewe-lamb lying asleep in the sun; and, out of mere frolic, as any other boy would have done, he flew on above her and tried if he could hold her down. After hard struggling he mastered her, took her between his feet, stroked her snowy fleece and soft downy cheek, and ever, as he patted her, repeated these words, 'O but ye be a bonny beast!'

The lamb, however, was not much at her ease; she struggled a little now and then; but finding that it availed not, she gave it over; and seeing her comrades feeding near her, she uttered some piteous bleats. They could afford her no assistance; but they answered her in the same tremulous key. After patting her a good while, Jock began to handle her breast and ribs, and found that she was, in good earnest, as fat as pork. This was a ticklish experiment for the innocent lamb. Jock was seized with certain inward longings, and yearnings that would not be repressed. He hesitated long, long, and sometimes his pity awoke; but there was another natural feeling that proved the stronger of the two; so Jock at length took out his long knife and unsheathed it. Next he opened the fleece on the lamb's throat till its bonny white skin was laid bare, and not a hair of wool to intervene between it and the point of his knife. He was again seized with deep remorse, as he contemplated the lamb's harmless and helpless look; so he wept aloud, and tried to put his knife again into its sheath; but he could not.

To make a long tale short, Jock took away the lamb's life, and that not in the most gentle or experienced way. She made no resistance, and only uttered one bleat. 'Poor beast!' said Jock; 'I dare say ye like this very ill, but I canna help it. Ye are suffering for a' your bits o' ill done deeds now.'

The day of full fruition and happiness for Jock was now arrived. Before evening he had roasted and eaten the kidneys, and almost the whole of the draught or pluck. His heart rejoiced within him, for never was there more delicious food. But the worst of it was, that the devils of calves were going all the while in the middle of a cornfield, which his master saw from the house, and sent one running all the way to turn them. The man had also orders to 'waken the dirty blackguard callant if he was sleeping, and gie him his licks.'

Jock was otherwise employed; but, as luck would have it, the man did not come into his hut, nor discover his heinous crime; for Jock met him among the corn, and took a drubbing with all proper decorum.

But dangers and suspicions encompassed poor Jock now on every side. He sat down to supper at the bottom of the board with the rest of the servants, but he could not eat a single morsel. His eyes were not fixed on the bacon ham as usual, and moreover, they had quite lost that sharp green gleam for which they were so remarkable. These were circumstances not to be overlooked by the sharp eyes of his master and mistress.

'What's the matter wi' the bit dirty callant the night?' said the latter. 'What ails you, sirrah, that you hae nae ta'en your supper? Are you weel eneugh?'

Jock wasna ill, he said; but he could not enter into particulars about the matter any farther. The goodman said, he feared the blade had been stealing, for he did not kythe like ane that had been fasting a' day; but after the goodwife and he had examined the hams, kebbucks, beef-barrel, meal-girnel, and every place about the house, they could discern nothing a-missing, and gave up farther search; but not suspicion.

Jock trembled lest the fat lamb might be missed in the morning when he drove out his flock; but it was never remarked that the lamb was a-wanting. He took very little breakfast, but drove his kine and sheep, and the devils of calves, away to the far field, and hasted to his wee housie. He borrowed a coal every day from a poor woman, who lived in a cot at the road-side, to kindle his fire, and that day she noticed, what none else had done, that his coat was all sparked over with blood, and asked him of the reason. Jock was rather startled by the query, and gave her a very suspicious look, but no other answer.

'I fear ye hae been battling wi' some o' your neighbours?' said she.

This was a great relief for Jock's heart. 'Ay, just that,' said he, and went away with his coal.

What a day of feasting Jock had! He sliced and roasted, and roasted and ate till he could hardly walk. Once when the calves were going into a mischief, which they were never out of, he tried to run, but he could not run a foot; so he was obliged to lie down and roll himself on the ground, take a sleep, and then proceed to work again.

There was nutrition in the very steams that issued from Jock's hut; the winds that blew over it carried health and savoury delight over a great extent of country. A poor hungry boy that herded a few lean cows on an adjoining farm, chancing to come into the track of this delicious breeze, became at once like a statue. He durst not move a step for fear of losing the delicious scent; and there he stood with his one foot before the other, his chin on his right shoulder, his eyes shut, and his mouth open, his nose being pointed straight to Jock's wee housie. The breeze

still grew richer, till at last it led him as straight as if there had
been a hook in his nose to Jock's shieling; so he popped in, and
found Jock at the sublime employment of cooking and eating.
The boy gaped and stared at the mangled body of the lamb,
and at the rich repast that was going on; but he was a very
ignorant and stupid boy, and could not comprehend any thing;
so Jock fed him with a good fat piece well roasted, and let him
go again to his lean cows.

Jock looked very plump and thriving-like that night; his
appearance was quite sleek, somewhat resembling that of a
young voluptuary; and, to lull suspicion, he tried to take some
supper; but not one bite or sup was he able to swallow. The
goodwife, having by that time satisfied herself that nothing
was stolen, became concerned about Jock, and wanted him to
swallow some physic, which he peremptorily refused to do.

'How can the puir thing tak ony meat?' said she. 'He's a'
swalled i' the belly. Indeed I rather suspect that he's swalled
o'er the hale body.'

The next morning, as Jock took out his drove, the goodman
was standing at the road-side to look at them. Jock's heart grew
cold, as well it might, when the goodman called out to him,
'Callant, what hae you made o' the gude lamb?'

'Is she no there?' said Jock, after a long pause, for he was so
much astounded that he could not speak at the first.

'Is she no there!' cried the goodman again in great wrath,
imitating Jock's voice. 'If ye binna blind, ye may see that. But I
can tell you, my man, gin ye hae letten ought happen to that
lamb, ye had better never hae been born.'

'What can be comed o' the beast?' said Jock. 'I had better
look the house, she's may be stayed in by herself.'

Jock didna wait for an order, but, glad to be a little farther
off from his master, he ran back and looked in the fold and
sheep-house, and every nettle bush around them, as he had
been looking for a lost knife.

'I can see naething o' her,' said he, as he came slounging
back, hanging his head, and keeping aloof from the goodman,
who still carried his long pike-staff in his hand.

'But I'll mak you see her, and find her baith, hang-dog!' said he; 'or deil be in my fingers an I dinna twist your neck about. Are you sure you had her yestreen?'

O yes! Jock was sure he had her yestreen. The women were examined if they had observed her as they milked the cows: they could not tell. None of them had seen her; but they could not say she was not there. All was in commotion about the steading, for the loss of the dawted pet-lamb, which was a favourite with every one of the family.

Jock drove his cattle and nine sheep to the field – roasted a good collop or two of his concealed treasure, and snapped them up, but found that they did not relish so well as formerly; for now that his strong appetite for fat flesh was somewhat allayed, yea, even fed to loathing, he wished the lamb alive again: he began, moreover, to be in great bodily fear; and to provide against the probability of any discovery being made, he lifted the mangled remains of his prey, and conveyed them into an adjoining wood, where he covered them carefully up with withered leaves, and laid thorns above them. 'Now,' said Jock, as he left the thicket, 'let them find that out wha can.'

The goodman went to all the herds around, inquiring after his lamb; but could hear no intelligence of her till he came to the cottage of poor Bessie, the old woman that had furnished Jock with a coal every day. When he put the question to her, the rock and the lint fell out of Bessie's hand, and she sat a while quite motionless.

'What war ye saying, goodman? War ye saying ye had lost your bonnie pet-lamb?'

'Even sae, Bessie.'

'Then, goodman, I fear you will never see her living again. What kind o' callant is that ye hae gotten? He's rather a suspicious-looking chap. I tentit his claes a' spairged wi' blude the tither day, and baith this and some days bygane he has brought in his dinner to me, saying that he dought nae eat it.'

Goodman Niddery could make no answer to this, but sat for a while grumphing and groaning, as some late events passed over his mind; particularly how Jock's belly was swollen, and how he could not take any supper. But yet the idea that the boy had killed his favourite, and eaten her, was hardly admissible:

the deed was so atrocious he could not conceive any human being capable of it, strong as circumstances were against his carnivorous herd. He went away with hurried and impatient steps to Jock's wee house, his old colley dog trotting before him, and his long pike-staff in his hand. Jock eyed him at a distance, and kept out of his path, pretending to be engaged in turning the calves to a right pasture, and running and threshing them with a long goad; for though they were not in any mischief then, he knew that they would soon be in some.

The goodman no sooner set his nose within Jock's shieling than he was convinced some horrid deed had been done. It smelled like a cook's larder; and, moreover, his old dog, who had a very good scent, was scraping among the ashes, and picking up fragments of something which he seemed very much to enjoy. Jock did not know what to do when he saw how matters stood, yet he still had hopes that nothing would appear to criminate him. The worst thing that he saw was the stupid hungered boy on the adjoining farm coming wading through the corn. He had left his dirty lean kine picking up the very roots of the grass, and had come snouking away in hopes of getting another fat bit for his impoverished stomach. But when he saw Goodman Niddery come out of the cot with impassioned strides, he turned and ran through the strong corn with his whole might, always jumping up as he proceeded.

The goodman called angrily on his old dog to come after him, but he would not come, for he was working with his nose and fore-feet among Jock's perfumed ashes with great industry; so the goodman turned back into the house, and hit him over the back with his long pike-staff, which made him glad to give over, and come out about his business; and away the two went to reconnoitre further.

As soon as the old dog was fairly a-field again he took up the very track by which Jock had carried the carcass that morning, and went as straight as a line to the hidden treasure in the thicket. The goodman took off the thorns, and removed the leaves, and there found all that remained of his favourite and beautiful pet-lamb. Her throat was all cut and mangled, her mouth open, and her tongue hanging out, and about one half of her whole body a-wanting. The goodman shed tears of grief, and wept and growled with rage over the mangled form, and forthwith resolved (which was hardly commendable) to seize Jock, and bring him to that very spot and cut his throat.

Jock might have escaped with perfect safety, had he had the sense or foresight to have run off as soon as he saw his master enter the wood; but there seems to be an infatuation that directs the actions of some men. Jock did not fly, but went about and about, turning his kine one while, his nine sheep another, and always between hands winning a pelt at one of the ill-conditioned calves, till his incensed master returned from the fatal discovery, and came up to him. There was one excuse for him; he was not sure if the carcass had been found, for he could not see for the wood whether or not his master went to the very place, and he never thought of the sagacity of the dog.

When Goodman Niddery first left the wood he was half running, and his knees were plaiting under him with the anticipation of horrid revenge. Jock did not much like his gait; so he kept always the herd of cows, and the sheep too, betwixt himself and this half-running master of his. But the goodman was too cunning for poor Jock; he changed his step into a very slow careless walk, and went into the middle of the herd of cows, pretending to be whistling a tune, although it was in fact no tune, but merely a concatenation of tremulous notes on C sharp, without the least fall of harmony. He turned about this cow and the other cow, watching Jock all the while with the tail of his eye, and trilling his hateful whistle. Jock still kept a due distance. At length the goodman called to him, 'Callant, come hither, like a man, and help me to wear this cow against the ditch. I want to get haud o' her.'

Jock hesitated. He did not like to come within stroke of his master's long stick, neither did he know on what pretence absolutely to refuse his bidding; so he stood still, and it was impossible to know by his looks whether he was going to comply or run off altogether. His master dreaded the latter, and called to him in a still kinder manner, until Jock at last unfortunately yielded. The two wore the cow, and wore the cow, up against the ditch, until the one was close upon her one side, and the other upon her other. 'Chproo! hawkie! chproo, my bonnie cow!' cried the goodman, spreading out his arms, with his pike-staff clenched fast in his right hand; then springing by the cow in a moment, he flew upon Jock, crying out, with the voice of a demon, 'D—n you, rascal! but I'll do for you now!'

Jock wheeled about to make his escape, and would have beaten his master hollow, had he been fairly started, or time-ously apprised of his dreadful danger; but ere he had run four or five steps the pike-staff came over the links of his neck with such a blow, that it laid him flat on his face in a mire. The goodman then seized him by the cuff of the neck with the one hand, and by the hair of his head with the other, and said, with a triumphant and malicious laugh, 'Now, get up, and come away wi' me, my braw lad, and I'll let you see sic a sight as you never saw. I'll let you see a wally-dy sight! Get up, like a good cannie lad!'

As he said this, he pulled Jock by the hair, and kicked him with his foot, until he obliged him to rise, and in that guise he led him away to the wood. He had a hold of his rough weather-beaten hair with the one hand, and with the other he heaved the cudgel over him; and as they went, the following was some of the discourse that passed between them.

'Come away, now, my fine lad. Are nae ye a braw, honest, good callant? Do nae ye think ye deserve something that's unco good frae me? Eh? Ay, ye surely deserve something better nor ordinar'; and ye shall hae it too.' (Then a kick on the posteriors, or a lounder with the staff.) 'Come your ways, like a sonsy, brave callant, and I'll let you see a bonny thing and a braw thing in yon brake o' the wood, ye ken.'

Jock cried so piteously that, if his master had not had a heart of stone, he would have relented, and not continued in his fatal purpose; but he only grew the longer the more furious.

'O let me gang! let me gang! let me gang!' cried Jock. 'Let me gang! let me gang! for it wasna me. I dinna ken naething about it at a'!'

'Ye dinna ken naething about what, my puir man?'

'About yon bit sheep i' the wood, ye ken.'

'You rascal! you rogue! you villain! you have confessed that you kend about it, when I wasna speiring ony sic question at you. You hound! you dog! you savage wolf that you are! Mother of God! but I will do for you! You whelp! you dog! you scoundrel! come along here.' (Another hard blow.) 'Tell me now, my precious lad, an ye war gaun to be killed, as ye ken something about killing, whether would you choose to have your throat cut, or to have your feet tied and be skinned alive?'

'O dinna kill me! dinna kill me!' cried poor Jock. 'My dear master, dinna kill me, for I canna brook it. Oh, oh! an ye kill me I'll tell my mother, that will I; and what will Marion say t'ye, when she has nane but me? Oh, master, dinna kill me, and I'll never do the like o't again!'

'Nay, I shall take warrant for that: you shall never do the like o't again!'

In this melancholy and heart-breaking manner he dragged him on all the way by the rough towsy head, kicking him one while, and beating him another, till he brought him to the very spot where the mangled remains of the pet-lamb were lying. It was a blasting sight for poor Jock, especially as it doubled his master's rage and stern revenge, and these were, in all conscience, high enough wrought before. He twined the hapless culprit round by the hair, and knocked him with his fist, for he had dropped the staff to enable him to force Jock to the place of sacrifice; and he swore by many an awful oath, that if it should cost him his life, he would do to Jock as he had done to that innocent lamb.

With that he threw him on the ground, and got above him with his knees; and Jock having by that time lost all hope of moving his ruthless master by tears or prayers, began a-struggling with the force which desperation sometimes gives, and fought with such success that it was with difficulty his master could manage him.

It was very much like a battle between an inveterate terrier and a bull-dog; but, in spite of all that Jock could do, the goodman got out his knife. It was not, however, one like Jock's, for it had a folding blade, and was very hard to open, and the effecting of this was no easy task, for he could not get both his hands to it. In this last desperate struggle, Jock got hold of his master's cheek with his left hand, and his nails being very long, he held it so strait that he was like to tear it off. His master capered up with his head, holding it back the full length of Jock's arm; yet still being unable to extricate his cheek from Jock's hold, he raised up his knife in his right hand, in order to open it with his teeth, and, in the first place, to cut off Jock's hand, and his head afterwards. He was holding down Jock with his right knee and his left hand; and while in the awkward capering attitude of opening his knife, his face was turned nearly straight up, and his eyes had quite lost sight of his victim. Jock held up his master's cheek, and squeezed it still the more, which considerably impeded his progress in getting the knife open; and, at that important moment, Jock whipped out his own knife, his old dangerous friend, and struck it into the goodman's belly to the haft. The moment he received the wound he sprang up as if he had been going to fly into the air, uttered a loud roar, and fell back above the dead pet-lamb.

Lord, how Jock ran! He was all bespattered with blood, some of it his own, and some of it his master's; wanted the bonnet, and had the bloody knife in his hand; and was, without all doubt, a wild frightsome-looking boy. As he sped through the wood, he heard the groans and howls of his master in the agonies of death behind him. Every one of them added to Jock's swiftness, till it actually became beyond the speed of mortal man. If it be true that love lends a pair of wings, fear, mortal fear, lends two pair. There is nought in life I regret so much as that I did not see Jock in this flight; it must have been such an extraordinary one. There was poor Jock flying with the speed of a fox from all the world, and yet still flying into the world. He had no home, no kindred to whom he durst now retreat, no hold of any thing in nature, save of his own life and his good whittle; and he was alike unwilling to part with either of these. The last time he was seen was by two women on Kirtle-common. He appeared sore bespent, but was still running on with all his might.

The goodman was found before the evening, but only lived

to tell how he had come by his end. All his friends and servants were raised, and sent in pursuit of Jock. How he eluded them no man knows; but from that day Marion's Jock[3] has never been more seen or heard of in this land.

JOHN GRAY O' MIDDLEHOLM

There was once a man of great note, of little wit, some cunning, and inexhaustible good nature, who lived in the wretched village of Middleholm, on the border of Tiviotdale, to whom the strangest lot befell, that ever happened to a poor man before. He was a weaver to his trade, and a feuar; about six feet four inches in height; wore a black coat with horn buttons of the same colour, each of them twice as broad and thick as a modern lady's gold watch. This coat had wide sleeves, but no collar, and was all clouted about the elbows and armpits, and moreover the tails of it met, if not actually overlapped each other, a little above his knee. He always wore a bonnet, and always the same bonnet, for ought that any one could distinguish. It was neither a broad nor a round bonnet, a Highland bonnet nor a Lowland bonnet, a large bonnet nor a small bonnet; nevertheless, it was a bonnet, and a very singular one too, for it was a *long bonnet*, shaped exactly like a miller's meal-scoop. He was altogether a singular figure, and a far more singular man. Who has not heard of John Gray, weaver and feuar in Middleholm?

John had a garden, which was a middling good one, and would have been better, had it been well sorted; he had likewise a cow that was a very little, and a very bad one; but he had a wife that was the worst of all. She was what an author would call a half-witted inconsiderate woman; but the Middleholm wives defined her better, for they called her 'a tawpie, and an even-down haverel'. Of course John's purse was very light, and it would never throw against the wind; his meals were spare and irregular, and his cheek-bones looked as if they would peep through the face. It is impossible for a man to be in this state without knowing the value of money, or at least regretting the want of it. His belly whispers to him every hour of the day, that it would be a good thing to have; and when parched with drought of an evening, and neighbours are going into the ale-house to enjoy their crack and their evening draught, how killing the reflection, that not one penny is to spare! It even increases a man's thirst, drying the very glands of his mouth to a cinder – It makes him feel more hungry, and creates a sort of void, either in idea or in the stomach, which it is next to impossible to fill up. Such power over the internal feelings has this same emptiness of the purse.

John had all these feelings most keenly in his way; for his sides were so long, and so lank, and enclosed in such a bound of space, that it was no easy matter to fill it up. Now, it being a grand position in philosophy, that no space within the earth's atmosphere can remain a void, owing to the intolerable pressure of air, amounting to the inconceivable weight of fifteen pounds on every square inch, it may well be conceived what an insuffer-able column pressed constantly on John's spacious tube. Noth-ing gave John so much uneasiness as the constant suggestions of this invidious column of air.

There was but one thing on earth that could counter-work this pressure of elemental fluid, and keep it up to its proper sphere, and that was money. This was a grand discovery made by John, which Bacon himself never thought on, or thought of only to be completely mistaken. That sage says, 'The state of all things here is, to extenuate, and turn things to be more pneumatical and rare; and not to retrograde from pneumatical to that which is dense.' How absurd! It is evident that Mr Bacon had never been a feuar in Middleholm.

John's system was exactly the reverse of this, and it was the right one. He conceived, and felt, that the tangible part of the body ought always to prevail over the pneumatical; and then, as to the means of accomplishing this, he discovered that money, money alone, was the equivalent power that could equiponder-ate in such a case. But as to the means of procuring this great universal anodyne, that puzzled John more than the great dis-covery itself.[1]

Every man, however, has some prospects, or at least some hopes, of increasing his stock of this material. John had his hopes of doing so too; but no man, or woman either, will guess on what these hopes were founded. It could not possibly be by the profits of his weaving, at least with such a wife as he had; for John's proficiency in that useful art was far short of what was expected of a country weaver in those days. He could work a pair of blankets, or a grey plaid; but beyond that his science reached not. When any customer offered him a linen web, however coarse, or a brace of table-cloths, he modestly declined them, by assuring the goodwife, 'that his loom didna answer thae kind o' things, and when fo'k teuk in things that didna answer their looms, they whiles fashed them mair than if they had keepit them out.' It could not be by the profits of the miserable feu that he hoped to make money, for the produce of that was annually consumed before it came half to maturity. He had no rich friends; and his live stock consisted of, a small lean cow, two wretched-looking cats, a young one and an old one; six homely half-naked daughters, one son, and his wife, Tibby Stott.

But it is hard for a man to give up the idea of advancing somewhat in life, either by hook or by crook. To stand still, and stagnate as it were, or yield to a retrograde motion, are among the last things that the human mind assents to. John's never assented to any such thing. Notwithstanding all these disadvantages that marshalled against him, he had long-cherished and brilliant hopes of making rich; and that by the simplest and most natural way in the world, namely, by finding a purse, or *a pose*, as he more emphatically called it.

Was not John the true philosopher of nature? What others illustrated by theory, he exemplified in practice; namely, that the mind must grasp at something before. John longed exceedingly to have money – every other method of attaining it seemed fairly out of his reach, save this; and on this he fixed with avidity, and enjoyed the prospect as much as one does who believes he must fall heir to an estate. He knew all the folks in the kingdom that had got forward in life by finding poses; but the greatest curiosity of all was, that he never believed money to be made in any other way. John never saw money made by industry in his life; there was never any made at Middleholm, neither in his days nor those of any other man, and what he had never seen exemplified he could not calculate on: so that, whenever he heard of a man in the neighbourhood who had advanced his fortune rapidly, John uniformly attributed it to his good fortune in having found a pose.

But it was truly amazing, how many of these he believed to be lying hid all over the country, especially in the vicinity of the old abbeys. And John reasoned in this manner: 'The monks and the abbots amassed all the money in the country; they had the superiority of all the lands, and all the wealth, and all the rents at their control. Then, on the approach of any marauding army, it was well known that they went always out and hid their enormous wealth in the fields, from whence a great part of it was never again lifted.' And then there was all the fields of battle, with which the Border counties abound, concerning which fields John argued in this way: 'Suppose now there were 20,000 English and 15,000 Scots met on a field; there might be mony mae, and there might be fewer; but, supposing there were so many, every one of these would hide his purse before he came into the battle, because he kend weel, that if he were either woundit or taen prisoner, he wad soon be strippit o' that. In ony o' thae cases, when it was hidden, he could get it again; whereas, if he was killed, it was o' nae mair use to him, an' was as weel there as in the hands o' his enemies. There was then 35,000 purses, or poses rather, a' hid in a very sma' bounds. An' then, to consider how many great battles war foughten a' o'er the country, an' often too when the tae party was laden wi' spulzie.' In short, John believed that all these Border districts were lined with poses, and that we every day walked over immense sums of old sterling coinage.

He had several times visited the fields of Philliphaugh,[2] of Middlestead, and Ancrum Moor; and on each of these he had delved a great deal, looking for poses; but, as he simply and good-naturedly remarked, never chanced to light on the right spot. For all that he was nothing discouraged, but every year grew more and more intent on realizing some of these hidden treasures.

He had heard of a large sum of money that was hid in a castle of Liddesdale, and another at Tamleuchar Cross; and of these two he talked so long, and so intently, that he resolved at last to go and dig, first for the one treasure, and then for the other. So one evening he got some mattocks ready, and prepared for his journey, being resolved to set out the next morning.

But that night he had a singular dream, or rather a vision, that deterred him. The narrative must be given in John's own words, as it has doubtless never been so well told by any other person. No one else could be so affected by the circumstances, and when the heart is affected, the language, however diffuse, has something in it that approximates to nature.

'I was lying in my bed, close yerkit against the stock; for my wife, poor creature! had tae o' the weans in ayont her, an' they war a' sniffin an' sleepin; an' there was I, lying thinking and thinking what I wad do wi' a' my money aince I had it howkit up; when, ere ever I wist, in comes an auld grey-headit man close to my bed-side. He was clad in a grey gown, like the auld monks lang syne; but he had nae cross hingin at his breast; an' he lookit me i' the face, an' says to me, says he, "John Gray o' Middleholm, do you ken me?" "Na, honest man," quo I; "how should I ken you?"

' "But I ken you, John Gray; an' I hae often been by your side, an' heard what ye war sayin, an' kend what ye war thinkin, an' seen what ye war doing, when ye didna see me. Ye're a very poor man, John Gray."

' "Ye needna tell me that, honest man; there needs nae apparition come frae the dead to tell me that."

' "An' ye hae a very ill wife, John Gray, an' a set o' ill-bred menseless bairns. Now, how many o' them will ye gie me, an' I'll mak ye rich? Will ye gie me Tibby Stott hersel?"

' "Weel I wat, honest man, she wad be better wi' ony body than me; but I can never gie away auld Tibby Stott, ill as she is, against her will. She has lien sae lang by my side, an' sleepit i' my bosom, that she's turned like a second nature to me; an', I trow, we maun just tak the gude wi' the ill, an' fight thegither as lang as our heads wag aboon the ground, though mony a sair heart an' hungry wame she has gart me dree.' He then named o'er a' the bairns to me, ane by ane, an' pledd an' fleeched me for this an' the tither ane; but, after a' he could say, an' a' the promises he could make, I wadna condescend to part wi' ane o' my bairns."

'"John Gray o' Middleholm," quo' he, "ye're a great fool; I kend ay ye were a fool; an' a' the country kens it as weel as me; but ye're no just sae ill as I thought you had been. How do you propose to maintain a' thae tawpies, young an' auld?"

'"Aye, that's the question, friend," quo I; "an' it's easier to speer than answer it. But I hae a plan i' my head for that too; yet I dinna ken how far it may be advisable to tell you a' about it."

'"O poor daft Jock Gray o' Middleholm!" quo he; "ye're that lazy ye winna work, an' ye're that stupid that ye hae married a wife that canna work, an' ye hae gotten a bike o' gillygawpie weans, that ye're breedin up like a wheen brute beasts; and the hale o' ye can neither work nor want; an' ye're gaun away the morn to mine the auld Castle o' Hermitage, an' carry away the mighty spoils that are hidden there. An' then ye're gaun away to Tamleuchar Cross,

> To houk the pots o' goud, that lie
> Atween the wat grund an' the dry,
> Where grows the weirdest an' the warst o' weeds,
> Where the horse never steps, an' the lamb never feeds.[3]

But, John Gray o' Middleholm, you'll never finger a plack o' thae twa poses, for the deil keeps the taen, an' me the tither."

'"Eh! gudesooth, friend, an that be the case, I fear I may drink to them. But wha are ye, an it may be speer'd?"

'"I am ane that kens a' the secrets o' a' the hidden poses in Scotland; an' I'm a great friend to you, John Gray o' Middleholm."

'"I'm unco glad to hear it, man; troth am I! I'm right blithe to hear it! Then, there shall be houkin an' shoolin, countin and coupin ower!"

' "Nane where ye trow; for ye're but a short-sightit carle; an' the warst faut that ye hae – ye're daft, John Gray. But, if ye'll be ruled by me, I'll tell you where ye'll find a pose that will mak you a rich man for the langest day ye hae to live. Gang ye away down to the town o' Kelso, an' tak a line frae the end o' the auld brigg to the north neuk o' the abbey, an' exactly at the middle step you will find a comically shapen stane; raise ye up that when nae body sees, an' there you will find an auld yettlin oon-pan filled fu' o' goud an' siller to the very ee."

' "But, friend, I never was at Kelso, and I never saw either the brigg or the abbey-kirk; an' how am I to find the stane? an', ower an' aboon a', gin I fa' to an' houk up the fok's streets, what will they say to me?"

' "Weel, weel, tak your ain way, John Gray; I hae tauld ye. But ye're daft, poor man; there, ye're gaun away to mine a' the vaults o' the biggest castle o' Liddesdale, an' then ye're gaun to trench a hale hillside at Tamleuchar, a' upon mere chance. An' here, I tell you where the pose is lying, an' ye'll no be at the pains to gang an' turn ower ae stane an' lift it. Ye're clean daft, John Gray o' Middleholm; but I hae tauld ye, sae tak your ain daft gate." An' wi' that the auld body elyed away, an' left me. I was sae grieved that he had gane away in a pet, for he was the very kind o' man I wantit, that I hollo'd, an' called after him, as loud as I could, to come back. But, gude sauf us a'! at that moment, my wife, Tibby Stott, poor creature! wakened me; for I was roaring through my sleep, an' the hale had been a dream.'

John was terribly puzzled next day, and knew not which way to proceed. He did not like to go to hand-gripes with the devil, after such a warning as he had got, and therefore he judged it as safe to delay storming his Castle of Hermitage, till he considered the matter more maturely. On the other hand, it was rather ungenerous to go and seize on his friend's treasure at the Cross of Tamleuchar, after such a friendly visit; and he feare likewise, that the finding of it was very uncertain; yet h not know but this might be some malicious spirit, w was to put him by getting the money. And as to K never thought of it before; and it took such a long time to train his ideas to any subject, that he never once thought of going there: so all the schemes were postponed for some time.

'A while after that,' says John, 'I was sitting at my loom, an' I was workin an' workin, an' thinkin an' thinkin, how to get ane o' thae hidden poses. "I maun either hae a pose soon," says I to mysel, "or else I maun dee o' hunger; an' Tibby Stott, poor creature! she maun dee o' hunger; an' a' my innocent bairns maun dee o' hunger, afore I get them up to do for theirsels." Thae war heavy concerns on me, an' I was sair dung down. When, or ever I wist, in comes my auld friend, the grey-headit monk. "John Gray o' Middleholm," quo he; "do you ken me?" "Ay, that I do, honest man; an' weel too! Right blithe am I to see your face again, for I was unco vexed when ye gaed away an' left me sae cuttily afore."

'"Ye're a daft man, John Gray, that's the truth o' the matter; but ye hae some good points about ye, an' I'm your friend. Ye say, ye dinna ken Kelso, nor the place where the pose is lying: now, if ye'll gang wi' me, I'll let you see the very place, an' the very stane that the money is lying aneath; an' if ye winna be at the pains to turn it ower and take the pose, I'll e'en gie it to some ither body; I hae tauld ye, John Gray o' Middleholm."

'"Dinna gie it to nae other body, an⁴ it be your will, honest man," quo I; I says till him, "An' I's gang w'ye, fit for fit, when ye like." Sae up I gets, just as I was workin at the loom, wi' my leather apron on, an' a rash o' loom needles in my cuff; an' it wasna a rap till we were at Kelso, where I soon saw the situation o' the town, an' the brigg, an' the auld abbey. Then he takes me to a stane, a queer three-neukit stane, just like a cockit hat. "Now," says he, "John Gray o' Middleholm, the siller's in aneath this; but it winna be very easily raised; put ye a mark on it, till ye get mattocks an' a convenient time, for I maunna be seen here." I first thought o' leaving my apron on it, but thinking that wad bring a' the fock o' the town, I took ane o' the loom needles to stick in beside it, thinking naebody wad notice that. Bless me! friend, quo I, this is the saftest an' the smoothest stane that ever I fand in my life; it is surely made o' chalk; an' wi' that, I rammed ane o' the loom needles down

through the middle o' the stane into the very head. But I hadna'
weel done that, afore there was sic yells an' cries rase out frae
aneath the stane, as gin a' the devils o' hell had been broken
loose on me; an' the blood sprang frae the chalk stane; an' it
spoutit on my hands, an' it spoutit on my face, till I was frightit
out o' my wits! Sae I bang'd up, an' ran for bare life; but sic a
fa' as I got! I had almost broken my neck. Where think ye I had
been a' the time, but lyin' sound sleepin' i' my bed; an' instead
o' rinning the needle into the three-neukit stane, I had rammed
it to the head in the haunch o' Tibby Stott, poor creature. Then
there was sic a whillibalu as never was heard! An' she threepit,
an' insistit on me, that I was ettling to murder her. 'Dear Tibby
Stott, woman," quo' I; "Tibby," says I to her, "If I had been
ettling to murder you, wadna' I hae run the loom needle into
some other part than where I did? It will be lang or ye murder
there, Tibby Stott, especially wi' a loom needle."

'I had now gotten Kelso sae completely i' my head, that away
I sets again, to see, at least, if the town was set the same way as
I had seen it in my vision. I fand every thing the same; the brig,
the auld abbey, an' the three-neukit stane shapit like a cockit
hat, mid-way between them; but I coudna' get it houkit, for the
fo'k were a' gaun asteer, an' ay this ane was spying an' looking
at me, an' the tither ane was spying an' looking at me. Sae I
hides my mattocks in a corner o' the auld abbey-kirk, an' down
I gaes to saunter a while about the water side, to see if the
Kelso fo'k wad settle within their ain doors, an' mind their ain
business. I hadna' been lang at the water side, till I sees a hare
sitting sleeping in her den. Now, thinks I, that wad be a good
dinner for Tibby an' the bairns, an' me. Sae I slides away very
cunningly, never letting wit that I saw her; but I had my ee
gledgin' out at the tae side; an' as soon as I wan fornent her, I
threw mysel' on aboon her a' my length. Then she waw'd, an'
she scream'd, an' she sprawled, till I thought she wad win away
frae me; but at length I grippit her by the throat. "Ye auld
bitch, that ye are," quo' I; "I's do for ye now. But, wi' that, the
hare gae me sic a drive wi' a' her four feet at ance, that she gart
me flee aff frae aboon her like a drake into the hard stanes at
the water side, till I was amaist fell'd. An' there I lay groaning;

an' the hare she lay i' the bit screamin. Pity my case! where had I been a' the time, but sound sleepin' i' my ain bed? An' instead o' catchin' a hare, I had catch'd naething but auld Tibby Stott, poor creature; an' had amaist smothered her an' choakit her into the bargain.

'I was really excessively grieved this time; but what could I help it? I ran an' lightit a candle; an' I thought my heart should hae broken, when the poor thing got up on her bare knees, an' beggit me to spare her life. "Dear Tibby Stott!" quo' I; "Tibby, my woman," I says to her, "It will be the last thing that ever I'll think of to harm your life, poor creature!" says I.

'"Na, na, but John, I heard ye ca' me an awfu' like name for a man to ca' his wife; an' ye said that ye wad do for me now."

'"Tibby Stott, my woman," quo I; "I'm really sorry for what has happened; but ye maun forgie me, for in faith an' troth I thought ye war a hare."

'"A hare! Na na, John, that winna gang down – Had ye said ye thought I was a mare, I might hae excused ye. I'm sure there wad hae been far less difference in size wi' the tane as the tither."

'Tibby Stott's no that far wrang there, thinks I to mysel, horn daft as she is.

'"But, John, what did ye tak me for the ither night, when ye stickit me wi' a loom needle into the bane?"

'"Indeed, Tibby, I'm amaist ashamed to say it; but I thought ye war a three-neukit stane, i' the shape of a cockit hat."'

When Tibby Stott heard this, she drew quietly to her clothes, and hastened out of the house. She was now quite alarmed, thinking that her husband had lost his reason; and, running to one of the neighbouring cottages, she awakened the family, and related to them her tale of dismay; informing them, that her husband had, in the first place, mistaken her for a three-cornered stone, and had stabbed her through the haunch with a loom needle. This relation only excited their merriment; but when she told them, that a few minutes ago he had mistaken her for a hare, and getting above her, had seized her by the throat, trying to worry her for one, it made them look aghast, and they all acquiesced in the belief, that John had been bitten by a mad dog, and was now seized with the malady; and that, when he tried to worry his wife for a hare, he had believed himself to be a dog, a never failing symptom of the distemper. Their whole concern now was, how to get the poor children out of the house; for they dreaded, that on the return of his fit, he might mistake them all for hares crouching in their dens, and worry every one of them. Two honest weavers therefore volunteered their services to go and reconnoitre, and to try if possible to get out the unfortunate children.

Now it so happened, that John was curiously engaged at the very time that these men went to the window, which was productive of another mistake, and put the villagers into the most dreadful dismay. As soon as he observed that Tibby Stott stayed so long away from her bed, he suspected that she had left the house; and, on rising to search for her, he soon found his conjecture too true. This he regretted, thinking that she would make fools both of herself and him, a thing which John accounted very common for wives to do, as the man had no better experience; and, not doubting but that his presence would be likely to make things worse, he awoke the eldest girl, whose name was *Grace* (the most unappropriate one that could have been bestowed), and desired her to go and bring back her mother. At first she refused to move, grumbling excessively, and bidding her father go himself; but John, at last, by dint of expostulation, getting her to comply, she requested him to bring her some clothes, and her stockings and shoes from beyond the fire. John called her a good girl, and ran, naked as he was, to bring her apparel. The clothes he found as she directed him, and hastening to the form beyond the fire to bring her stockings and shoes, he set down the lamp and lifted them. The stockings being tied together by a pair of long red garters, John found that he could not carry them all conveniently, so he took the clothes and the shoes in one hand, the lamp in the other, and the staniraw stockings and red garters, in his hurry, he took in his teeth. In this most equivocal situation was John first discovered by the two men as they peeped in at the window, on which they fled with precipitation, while their breasts were throbbing with horror.

When they returned to the house which they had lately left, they found a number of the villagers assembled, all gaping in dismay at the news, that *the lang weaver*, as they always stiled John Gray, was gone mad, and had tried to worry his wife for a hare. Scarcely had they swallowed this uncommon accident, when the two men entered; and the additional horror of the party may hardly be described, when they told what they had seen. 'Mercy on us a', sirs!' cried they, 'what will be done? John Gray has worried ane o' the lasses already; an' we saw him wi' our een, rinning up an' down the house naked, wi' her claes a' torn i' the tae hand, an' her heart, liver, and thrapple in his teeth, an' his een glancin' like candles!' The women uttered an involuntary scream; the men groaned in spirit; and the Rev. John Mathews, the Antiburgher[5] minister of the village, who had likewise been called up, and had joined the group, proposed that they should say prayers. The motion was agreed to without a division; the minister became a mouth, as he termed it, to the party, and did not fail to remember the malady of the lang weaver, and the danger to which his children were exposed.

While they were yet in the midst of their devotions, the amiable Grace Gray entered, inquiring for her mother; but, after many interrogations, both by the minister and others, the villagers remained in uncertainty with regard to the state of John's malady until it was day. But then, on his appearance, coming in a hurried manner toward the house to seek his wife and daughter, there was such a dispersion! He ran, and she ran,[6] and there was no one ran faster than the Antiburgher minister, who escaped praying, as he flew, that the Lord would make his feet as the feet of hinds upon the mountains. However, the whole fracas of John's hydrophobia ended without any thing very remarkable, save these: that Tibby Stott asked her daughter with great earnestness, 'Whilk o' them it was that was worried? an' hoped in God that it wasna' little Crouchy.' This was a poor decrepid, insignificant child, who was however her mother's darling, and whose loss would have been more regretted by her than all the rest of the family put together. The other remarkable circumstance was, that the story had spread so rapidly, that it never could be recalled or again assimilated to the truth, and it is frequently related as a fact over all the south country to this day, among the peasantry. Many a time have I heard it, and shuddered at the story; and I am sure many, into whose hand these tales may fall, have likewise heard the woful relation, that a weaver in Middleholm was once bit by his own terrier, and that five years afterwards, he went mad, and tried to worry his wife, who escaped; but that he succeeded in worrying his daughter, and on the neighbours assembling and breaking into the house, that he was found in the horrible guise in which the two men had described him.

John continued to be eyed with dark and lurking suspicion for some time; but he cared very little about such vulgar mistakes, for his mind was more and more taken up about finding poses. This reiterated vision of the old gray-headed monk, the town of Kelso, the bridge, the abbey, and the three-neukit stane like a cockit hat, had now taken full and ample possession of his brain, that he thought of it all day, and by night again visited it in his dreams. Often had he been there in idea, and, as he believed, in spirit, while his mortal part was lying dormant at the wrong side of Tibby Stott; but, at the long and the last, he resolved to go there in person, and, at all events, to see if the town was the same as had been represented to him in his visions.

Accordingly John set out, one morning early in the spring, on his way to the town of Kelso; but he would neither tell his wife, nor any one about Middleholm, where he was going, or what he was going about. He went as he was, with his staff in his hand, and his long bonnet on his head, without any of his mattocks for digging or heaving up broad stones, although he knew that purses were generally hid below them. Therefore John felt as disconsolate by the way, as a parish-minister does who goes from home to preach without a sermon in his pocket, or like a warrior going out to battle without his armour or weapons. He had, besides, but very little money in his pocket; only a few halfpence, and these he found could be but ill spared at home; and the only hope he had, was in the great sum of money that lay hid beneath the three-neukit stane like a cocket-hat, which stane, he knew, lay exactly mid-way between the end of the bridge and the north corner of the abbey.

John arrived at the lovely town of Kelso a little before the going down of the sun, and immediately set out about surveying the premises; but, to his great disappointment, he found that nothing was the same as it had been shown to him in his dream. The town and the abbey were both on the wrong side of the river, and he scarcely felt convinced that it was the same place. Moreover, the middle space between the end of the bridge and the abbey it was impossible to fix on, owing to some houses that interrupted the line. However, he looked narrowly and patiently all the way, from the one to the other, for the three-cornered stone, often stopping to scrape away the dust with his hands or feet from the sides of every broad one, to ascertain its exact form. He found many broadish stones, and some that inclined a little to a triangular form, but none of them like the one he had dreamed of; though there were some that he felt a strong inclination to raise up, merely that he might see what was below them.

But the more he looked, the better was he convinced, that the middle space between the abbey and the bridge was occupied by an old low-roofed house, within which the three-cornered stone, and the pose of course, behoved to be. Four or five times, in the course of his investigations, did John draw near to the door of this house, and every time stood hesitating whether or not he should enter; but, as he had resolved to tell his errand to no one living, not for fear of being laughed at, but for fear any one should come between him and the pose, he declined going in.

Not having enough of money to procure himself a night's lodging at an inn, he went and bought a pennyworth of bread at a baker's shop, that he might not be chargeable to any one; and, going down to the side of the river, he made a hearty supper on his roll, drinking a little pure water to it. It was here that John, to his infinite pleasure, first discovered a similarity between his vision and the existing scene. For, be it remembered, that, in one of his dreams, he went down to the side of the River Tweed to while away the time, and there discovered a hare sitting in her form. He now remembered having seen this very scene in his dream, which he now looked on, all in the same arrangement, and thenceforward felt a conviction, that this vision would not go for nothing. He then went into a narrow street that stretched to the eastward, as he described it, and went on till he heard the well-known sound of the jangling of weavers' treadles. As the proverb goes, 'Birds of a feather, flock ay thegither'; into that house John went, and asked the privilege of a bed, telling them, he himself was a poor weaver, who had come a long journey, in hopes to recover a large sum of money in the town, but not having as yet been successful, he had not wherewith to pay his night's lodging at an inn. The honest people made him very welcome, for the people of that beautiful town, from the highest to the lowest, are noted for a spirit of benevolence. But they tried in vain to pry into his business, and to learn who the creditor was from whom he expected to recover the sum of money. John, on the other hand, was very inquisitive of his host about the old abbey – what sort of people the monks were – how they were dressed, and if they had much money – what they did with it on a sudden invasion by the English? and, in particular, *Where he supposed to be exactly the middle space between the bridge and the abbey?* The man answered all his queries civilly; and, though he sometimes suspected his guest of a little derangement in intellect, gave him what information he could on these abstruse points; manifesting all the while, however, a disposition rather to enter into a debate about some of the modern tenets of religion. This John avoided as much as possible; for, though John was an Antiburgher, he knew little more about the matter, save that his sect was right and all the rest of the world wrong, which was quite sufficient for him; but, finding that the Kelso weaver was not disposed so readily to admit this, he waved the engagement from time to time, and always introduced the more interesting and not less mysterious subject, of purses hidden in the earth.

Next morning John was early astir, and busily engaged in search of the three-cornered stone; but still with the same success; and ever and anon his investigations brought him to the door of the low-roofed ancient house before mentioned, which he still surveyed with a wistful look, as if desirous to enter. The occupier of this old mansion was a cobler, a man stricken in years, who had a stall in the one end of it, while his wife and daughter kept a small fruit-shop in the other, and by these means earned a decent livelihood. This cobler, being a very industrious man, was at his work both late and early, and had noted all John's motions the evening before, as well as that morning. Curious to know what were the stranger's motives in prying so much about his door, he went out and accosted him, just as he was in the act of stooping to clean the dust away from the sides of a broad stone to see what shape it was. As he spoke, John turned round his head and looked at him; but he was so amazed at the figure he saw, that he could not articulate a syllable. 'What's the matter w'ye, friend?' said the cobler; 'or what is it you hae lost?' John still could not speak a word; but there he stuck, with his one knee leaning on the ground, his muddy hands hanging at a distance from his body, like a man going to leap, his head turned round, and his mouth open, gaping on this apparition of a cobler. The latter, at once conceiving that he had addressed a maniac, stood and gazed at him in silence and pity. John was the first who broke silence, and certainly his address had not the effect of removing the cobler's apprehensions. 'The warld be a wastle us![7] friend, is this you?' said John. 'There's nae doubt o't ata', man,' returned the cobler; 'this is *me*, as sure as that is *you*; but wha either you or me is, I fancy me or you disna very weel ken.' 'Honest man, do you no ken me?' said John; 'tell me honestly, did you never see my face afore?' 'Why,' said the cobler, 'I now think I have seen it before; but where, I do not recollect.' 'Was it in the night-time or the day-time that you saw me?' said John. 'Certainly, never in the night-time,' returned the cobler. 'Then I fancy I am wrang,' said John; 'I'm forgetting mysel', an' no thinkin what I'm speakin about; but I aux your pardon.' 'O there's nae offence, honest friend,' quoth the cobler; 'no ae grain: It is only a sma' mistake; you thought it was *me*, and I thought it was *you*, an' it seems it turns out to be neither the one nor the other.'[8] The cobler's wit was lost upon John, who again sunk into silence and gazed; for he saw that this ancient cobler was the very individual person that had appeared to him in his sleep, and told him of the treasure. And, still to approximate the vision closer to reality, the cobler wore a large three-cocked hat on his head. John was in utter consternation, and knew not what to make of it. He saw that it was not a three-neukit stane which the cobler wore on his head, and though very like one in colour, yet that it had once been felt. Still the hat had such a striking resemblance to the stone which John had so often seen in his vision, that he was satisfied the one was represented by the other. He saw there was something extraordinary in the case, and something that boded him luck; but how to solve this mystery of the three-neukit stane and the cockit hat, John was greatly at a loss. He had no doubt that he had found the cue[9] to the treasure; for he had found this cockit hat exactly mid-way between the bridge and the north corner of the abbey, as nearly as he could judge or measure. It was not indeed a three-neukit stane, but it was very like one; and at any rate, it was the very thing, shape, and size, and all, that he had dreamed about, and under which he had been assured the gold was hid. Above all, here was the very person, in form, voice, size, and feature, whose image had appeared to him in his sleep, and had held repeated conversations with him on the subject of the hidden pose; but then, what was there below the hat save the cobler, and he could not possibly be a pan full of gold and silver? The coincidence was however too striking to be passed over without scrutiny. Even the wisest of men would have been struck with it, and have tried to find out some solution; and curious would I be to know what a wise man, in such a case, would have thought of the matter.

John, as I said, was the philosopher of nature, and always fixed on the most obvious and simple solutions, in determining on effects from their general causes. He first asked of the cobler a sight of his hat; which being granted, he looked inside of it; but perceiving that there was neither money nor lining of any sort there, he returned it, saying, it was a curious hat. He then asked the cobler, seriously, if he had never swallowed any gold. The other said, he had not to his knowledge. 'At least,' said John; 'you certainly could not swallow any very large quantity? Very weel, then, frien'; if ye'll be sae gude as to stand a wee bit

back.' The cobler did so; and John, marking the precise spot
where he had been standing, and on which he had first seen him
in his real corporeal being, went directly to procure mattocks to
dig with, thinking it would to a certainty be below that spot,
and of course virtually covered by the hat at the time he first
saw its ample and triangular form.

He soon got a pick and spade, and fell to digging on the side
of the narrow street with all expedition, to the great amusement
of the old cobler, who, for fear of incurring blame from his
townsmen, went into his stall, and awaited the issue of this
singular adventure.

Poor John was hungry, and the column of air was become so
oppressive on him, that he felt as if his life depended on his
success, and wrought with no ordinary exertion. The pit waxed
in its dimensions, and deepened exceedingly. He first came to
sand, and then to loam, at which time his hopes ran very high,
for he found two or three small bones, which he was sure had
once formed a part of the body of some immensely rich abbot;
and finally, he came to a stiff, almost an impenetrable till.
Nevertheless he continued to dig, until the town's people, beginning to move about as the morning advanced, gathered about
him, and asked him what he meant? He desired them to mind
their own business, and let him mind his; and on this the first
comers went away, thinking he was a man employed in re-
pairing the street; but it was not long ere two town officers
arrived, and forced him to desist, threatening, that if he refused
to comply, and to fill up the hole exactly as he found it, they
would carry him to prison, and have him punished. John was
forced to yield, and once more abandon his golden dream. He
filled up the pit with evident marks of chagrin and disappointment, some averring that they even saw the tears dropping from
his eyes, and mixing with the gravel. He had now nothing for
it, but to return as he came, and apply to the wretched loom
once more. He even knew not where he was to procure a
breakfast, and still less how Tibby Stott, poor creature! and the
children, were breakfasting at home. The officers asked him
whence he came, and what he wanted; but he refused to satisfy

them; and after he had made the street as it was, and to their satisfaction, they left him.

There was something so whimsical in all that the cobler had witnessed, that he determined, if possible, to find out something of the man's meaning. He dreaded that he was a little deranged in his intellects; still there was a harmless simplicity about the stranger that interested him; and he thought he discerned glimpses of shrewdness that could not possibly be inherent in an ideot. Accordingly, as soon as the crowd had dispersed, and John had lifted his plaid and staff, and blown his nose two or three times, as he took a last look of the bridge and the old abbey, the cobler went out to him, addressed him with kindness, and beseeched him to go in, and take share of his breakfast.

Thankfully did John accept of the invitation, and seldom has a man done more justice to his entertainer's hospitality, than our hero did that morning. After despatching a bowlfull of good oat meal parritch, washed down with a bottle of brisk treacle ale, the cobler's daughter presented them with a large cut of broiled salmon. This rich and solid fare answering John's complaint exceedingly well, he set to it with so much generous avidity, that the cobler restrained himself, and suffered his guest to realize the greater part of it. The delightful sensations excited by this repast raised John's heart a little above his late disappointment, and even before the salmon was finished, he had begun to converse with some spirit. But his sphere of conversation was rather of a circumscribed nature, being confined to one object, namely, that of poses hidden in the earth, with its collateral branches. He asked the cobler what sort of men the monks were, who had lived in that grand abbey – Of the abbots that governed them – The sources of their great riches, and how they disposed of these on any invasion by the English.

There was no subject on which the cobler loved more to converse, having himself come of that race, and, as he assured John, the sixth in descent from the last abbot and a lady of high quality; he, and his forebears so far back, having been the fruits of a Christmas confession; and that, had the establishment still continued, he would in all likelihood have at that day been abbot himself. He showed John an old charter on emblazoned vellum, granted by Malcolm the fourth to the abbey of Kelso, on the removal of the Cistertian Monks from Selkirk to that place; and he talked so long on the customs and usages of the monks, the manner of lives they led, their fasts, holidays, and pilgrimages, that John never thought to be so weary of monachism; no mention having ever been made of their poses, in all this lengthened discourse.

After breakfast, the cobler pledged John in a bumper of brandy, and then handed his guest another, which John took with a blushing smile, and after holding it up between him and the light to enjoy its pure dark colour, he drank to the good health of the cobler; and, as the greatest blessing on earth that he could think of, wished he might find a good pose.

The cobler, thinking he now had his guest in the proper key, asked him to explain to him, if he pleased, the motives of his procedure that morning and last night? John laughed with a sly leer, bit his lip, and looking at the women who were bustling but and ben, at length told his host, that if he was to tell him that, he must tell him by himself; on which they went into the stall, and after John had desired the cobler to shut the door, he addressed him as follows:

'Now, ye see, friend, ye're sic an honest kind man, that I canna refuse to tell you ony thing; an' for that cause, I'll tell you the plain truth; but, as I ken you will think me a great fool, I'll neither tell you my name, nor my wife's name, nor the name o' the place where I bide; but it is a wee bit out o' Kelso; no very far; I can gang hame to my dinner. Ye maun just let that satisfy you on that score. Weel, ye see, disna I dream ae night, that there's an auld oon-pan, fu' o' gold an' silver, hidden aneath a queer shapen stane, exactly mid-way atween the end o' your brig an' the north neuk o' the auld abbey there; an' I dreamed it sae aft, that I could get nae rest; for troth it was like to mislead me, an' pit me by mysel a' thegither. To sickan a height did the fleegary rin in my imagination (hee, hee, hee! Is the door closs, think ye?), that I mistook the stane that was happin the pose, and, meaning to pit a mark in it to ken it by (Will naebody hear us, think ye?), disna I rin a lang sharp bodkin into the head i' the wrang side o' my wife, poor creature! till I e'en gart her skirl like a gait, an' amaist[10] fleyed her out o' her wits. An' there was ae night after that, she ran a greater risk still. Sae, troth, just to prevent me frae fa'ing till her wi' a pick an' a spade some night, an' to see gin it wad help me to ony better blink o' rest, I was fain to come to Kelso yestreen, to see if there was sic a thing or no. An' this morning, when you and I first met, for reasons that I needna an' canna weel explain, I thought I had found the very spot. Now, that's the main truth, an' I daresay you will think me a great fool.'

The cobler, who was mightily amused by this statement of facts, answered as follows: 'A man, my good friend, may act foolishly at a time, an' yet no be a'thegither a fool. To be a fool, you see, is to – is to – In short, it's to be a fool – a born fool like. But it is a Gallic word[11] that, an' has mony meanings. Now, dreaming disna make a man a fool; but it makes him a fool sae far, that he may play the fool in his dream. He may rise in his sleep, an' play the fool; but if he dinna play the fool after he wakens, he canna just be ca'd an absolute fool. But it is the fool, who, after he has dreamed, takes a' his dreams for reality. At least, it is acting very foolishly to do that.' 'I thought your speech wad land there,' said John. 'No, but stay till I explain mysel',' said the cobler. 'O, ye needna fash, the thing's plain enough,' said John; 'I maun think about setting awa' hame.' 'Stop a wee bit, man,' said the cobler, taking hold of John's coat as he was rising, 'I hae a queer story to tell you about a purse afore ye gang away, that will explain the matter wi' mair clearness an' precision than a' the learning an' logic that I'm master o'.

'It is ower true, what I maun tell you, honest man, that I am very ill for dreaming mysel, an' mony a wild unsonsy dream I hae had; an' the mair I strave against it, I grew aye the waur. When I was a young child, there was hardly a night that I didna' dream I was a monk, an' confessing some ane or ither o' the bonny lasses an' wives about Kelso. An' sic tales as I thought they tauld me! Then, when I saw them again sittin' i' the kirk, wi' their douse decent faces, I couldna' get their confessions out o' my mind, gude forgie me! an' I had some kind o' inklin'

about my heart, that they were a' true. There was the folly o'
the thing! Then I had nae sooner closed my een the neist night
than I was a monk again, and hard engaged at the auld business.
There was ane Bess Kelly, a fine sponkin' lass, that a' the lads
were like to gang wudd about; I'm sure I confessed Bess mair
nor a hunder times i' my sleep, an' mony was the sin I pardoned
till her.' John chuckled, and grinned, and made every now and
then a long neck by the cobler, to see if the door was close
enough shut; but when he reached thus far, John rose, passed
him, and felt the latch, and though the door was shut, he gave
it a push with his shoulder, to make it, if possible, go a little
closer. 'Friend, I can tell you,' said John; 'there may be here
that ken, an' here that dinna ken; but that's a very queer story.
So you always dreamed you were a monk?' 'So often,' said the
cobler, 'that the idea became familiar to me; and even in the
day time, I often deemed myself one.' 'So did I,' said John, 'it
became familiar to me too, and I thought you a monk both by
night and by day.' The cobler stared at John, and thought him
mad in good earnest; but the latter, feeling that he was going
to divulge more perhaps than prudence and caution with regard
to hidden poses warranted, corrected himself by saying, that he
thought he resembled one of that order, in his grave, decent
appearance, which was all he meant to say. The cobler then
went on.

'Weel, I'm no yet come to the story I was gaun to tell you. I
had sic a dream last night, as I hae nae had these twenty
years; and, I think, I never had sic a queer dream in my life.
An' then it was sae like your ain, too; for it was about a hidden
purse.' 'Aye aye, man!' said John, 'Gude sauf us! what was't?
but stop a wee till I see if the door be close steekit.' John again
felt the door, gave it another push, and then sat down, with
open mouth and ears, to drink in the story of the cobler's
dream.

'I was as usual a monk, and had gane out after vespers to
take a walk by the side o' the Tweed; an' as I was gaun down
by the boat-pool foot, I sees an ill-faur'd-looking carle, something like yoursel', sitting eating a roll, an' he'd a living hare
lying beside him that he had catched in her den.' 'Hout, friend!'

said John, 'but did you really dream that?' 'In very deed I did,' said the cobler, 'why do you doubt it?' 'Because, friend,' said John, 'they may be here that ken, an' here that dinna ken; but that's a very queer dream indeed.' 'There's nae doubt o't,' said the cobler; 'but stay till you hear it out. Weel, I says to the carle (he was very like you), friend, will you sell your hare? "Hout na'," quo' he, "you palmer bodies are a' poor, ye hae nae sae muckle siller atween you an' poverty as wad buy my hare. Ye're a very poor man, monk, for a' the rich confessions ye hae made, an' ye're a daft man, that's waur; but, an ye wad like to be rich, I can tell you where you will get plenty o' goud an' siller." I thankit the carle, an' said there were few that wadna' like to be richer than they were, an' I had nae objections at a' to the thing. "Weel, weel," quo' he; "he that hides kens best where to seek; but there was mony ane i' the days o' langsyne, wha haid weel, but never wan back to howk again. Gang ye your ways west the country the morn, an' spier for a place they ca' Middleholm; an' when ye come there, speer for a man they ca' John Gray. Gang ye into his garden, an' ye will find thirteen apple-trees in it, six at the head, an' six at the foot, an' ane in the middle."' 'Hout friend!' said John, interrupting him, 'but are ye no joking? did you really dream that?' 'As sure as yon sun is in the heaven, I did,' said the cobler; 'why should you doubt it?' 'Because ye see, friend,' said John, 'they are here that ken, an' here that dinna ken; but, let me tell you, that's a very queer dream indeed. Weel, what did the fearsome carle say mair?'

' "Gang ye into that garden," quo' he, "an' begin at the auld apple-tree in the middle, an' howk deep in the yird below that tree, an' you will find an auld pan filled fu' o' money to the ee. When ye hae disposed o' that, if ye like to gang back to that man's garden, an' howk weel, you will find a pose o' reid goud aneath every apple-tree that's in it." Now, wadnae ye hae reckoned me as a fool if I had taen a' this for truth? an' thought I was acting very foolishly, if I had gane away into the west country, asking for a place an' a man that perhaps hae nae existence? To hae gane about, as our school rhyme says, spearing for

"The town that ne'er was framed,
An' the man that ne'er was named,
The tree that never grew,
An' the bird that never flew." '[12]

'O there's nae doubt o' the thing, friend, it wad hae been great nonsense – there's nae doubt o't at a'. But yet, for a' that, it's the queerest dream, ae way an' a' ways, that I ever heard i' my life; an' I hae a great mind to gang an' speer after the place an' the man mysel'. If I get as good a breakfast, an' as good a dram, as I did for the last pose I howkit, my labour winna' be lost a' thegither.'

The cobler laughed, and wished John all manner of success; and the latter parted from him with many professions of esteem; and, in higher spirits than ever he was before, he went straight home to Tibby Stott and Middleholm, and prepared next morning to begin and root up the old apple-tree in the middle of the garden. Now, there were exactly thirteen trees in it, as the cobler said; a circumstance of which the owner was not aware till that very night when he returned from Kelso.

Poor Tibby Stott was right glad to see her husband again, for the report in the village was, that he had run away mad; and, as the country people were in terrible alarm about that time for mad dogs, and pursuing and killing them every day, Tibby dreaded that poor John would be shot, or sticked with long forks, like the rest. She viewed him at first with a jealous eye; but, on seeing him so good-humoured and kind to the children and herself, she became quite reconciled to him, and wept for joy, poor creature! at getting him back again; for she found she would have been utterly helpless without him, although ten times a-day she called him *a cool-the-loom*. John told her how he had travelled to Kelso, and spent a day and a night there on some important business, and had only wared one penny; and, among other things, how he had learned to cultivate his garden so as to make it produce great riches.

Next morning, as soon as it was day, John began a digging at one side of the old apple-tree, but he was terribly impeded

by roots, and came very ill speed. Some of these he cut, and
digged in below others; for he found, that when they were cut,
they impeded his progress nearly as much as before. By the time
the villagers rose, John had made a large pit; but then the alarm
began, and spread like wild-fire, that the lang weaver was come
home again madder than ever, and had been working all night
digging a grave in his garden, which every one suspected he
meant for Tibby Stott. The pit that he had made, by chance,
bore an exact resemblance to a grave, and great was the buzz
in the village of Middleholm that morning. The people gathered
around him, at first looking cautiously over the garden wall;
but at last they came close about him, every man with his staff
in his hand, and asked him how he did, and what he was
engaged in. John said he had been away down the country,
inquiring by what means to improve his garden, and he had
been instructed to prune the roots of his apple-trees in place of
the branches; for that they had run to wood below the earth,
which had been the cause of their growing wild and barren.
The villagers knew not what to make of this, it was so unlike
any thing that the lang weaver had ever done before; so they
continued to hang over him, and watch his progress, with all
manner of attention. John saw this would never do, for they
would discover all; and then there were so many who would
be for sharing the money along with him, that a small share
might only fall to him; and, moreover, if they told the lord of
the manor, he would claim it altogether.

John had a good deal of low cunning; and, as he had now
got very deep on one side of the tree, in order to mislead the
villagers, he took a wheelbarrow, and hurled a kind of sour
dung that had been accumulating around his cow-house for
years, with which he crammed the pit that he had made below
the tree, and, after covering it over with the mould, he tramped
it down.[13] His neighbours then went away and left him, convinced that he had got some new chimera into his head about
gardening, which would turn out a piece of folly at the last.
John was now left to prosecute his grand research quietly; save
that Tibby Stott never ceased intreating him 'to mind his loom

an' let the trees alane.' John answered with great rationality, 'sae I will, Tibby, my woman, I will mind the loom; but ye ken a man maun do ae thing afore anither.'

Towards the evening, Mr Mathews, the minister, went into the garden to *get a crack wi' John*, and see his new scheme of gardening. John had now got to a considerable depth on the south side of the tree, and not much regarding the tame moral remarks, or the threadbare puns of his pastor (these two little amiable characteristics of the Calvinistical[14] divine), was plying at his task with all his might, for still as he grew more hungry his exertions increased; and just at that precious instant, his spade rattled along the surface of a broad stone. 'John,' said the minister, 'What have you got there, John?' 'I fancy I'm come to the solid rock now, sir,' said John, 'I needna' howk nae deeper here.' 'John, give me the mattock, John,' said the minister; 'I propine,[15] that it would be nothing inconsistent with prudence and propriety to investigate this matter a little. This garden, as I understand, was planted by four friars of the order of St Benedict, who were the first founders of this village; and these people had sometimes great riches, John. Give me the mattock, John, and if I succeed in raising that stone, I shall claim all that is below it.' 'I wad maybe contest that point wi' your worship,' said John; 'for I can tell you what you will find below it.' 'And pray, what would I find below it, John?' said the Antiburgher minister. 'Just yird an' stane to the centre o' the globe,' said John; 'an' sic a pit wad spoil my bit garden.' 'Why, you are grown a wit, John,' said the divine, 'as well as a gardener. That answer is very good; nevertheless, give me the mattock, John.'

The minister might as well have asked John's heart's blood. He determined to keep hold of his spade, and likewise the possession of his pit; yet he did not wish to fight the minister. So, turning his face to him, and keeping his spade behind his back, he said to him, 'Hout na', sir, ye dinna ken how to handle spades an' shools, gin it be nae maybe the shool o' the word to delve into our hearts an' souls wi'.' 'There's more strength than propriety in that remark, John,' said the minister. 'But I can tell you, sir,' continued John, with a readiness that was not

customary with him, 'the hale secret o' the stane. Thae monk
bodies were good gardeners, an' they laid aye a braid stane
aneath the roots o' ilka fruit-tree that they plantit, to keep the
bits o' tendrils frae gripping down to the cauld till, whilk wad
soon spoil the tree.' 'Why, John, I have heard of such an experiment, indeed; and I suspect you have guessed nearer to the truth
than might have been gathered from the tenor of the foregoing
chapter of your life, John; it is therefore vain for a man to waste
his strength for nought. A good evening to you, John.' 'Gude
e'en, gude e'en to your Reverence,' said John, as he turned
about in his hole, chuckling and laughing with delight; and
when the Antiburgher minister was fairly out at the gate, he
nodded his head, and said to himself, 'Now, if I hae nae mumpit
the minister, my name's no John Gray o' Middleholm. Thae
gospel bodies want to hae a finger in ilka ane's pye, but they
manna hae things a' their ain gate neither. O there's nae set o'
men on the face o' the yird, as keen o' siller as the ministers!
Ane wad think, to hear them preach, that they held the warld
quite at the staff's end; but a' the time they're nibblin nibblin
at it just like a trout at a worm, or a hare at a kailstock. He
thought to hae my pose! Let him haud him wi' his steepin' –
screw'd as it is off the backs an' the meltiths o' mony a poor
body.'

John took hold of a stone hammer, and gave the broad stone
a smash on the one side. As he struck, the stone tottered, and
John heard distinctly, something that jingled below it. The very
hairs of his head stood upright, he was in such agitation! the
hammer dropped from his hand, and he jumped out of the pit,
gazed all around him, and then ran towards the house, impelled
by some inward feeling to communicate his good fortune to his
partner; but by the way reflection whispered in his ear, that
Tibby Stott, poor creature! was not the person calculated for
keeping such an important secret. This set him back to his pose;
which, in trembling anxiety, he resolved to survey; and, cleaning
all the earth from above the stone, he heaved it up, and there
beheld . . .

It must not here be told what John beheld. It would be too
much for the reader's happiness to bear. He must be left to

conjecture what it was that John discovered below that broad stone, and it is two to one he will guess wrong, for all that he has heard about it, and for as plain as matters have been made to him. John let the stone sink down again – took the wheel-barrow and filled the pit full of wet straw, which he judged better than dung; then, covering it over with earth, he went into his supper of thin bleared sowins, amid his confused and noisy family, all quarrelling about their portions; and finally, to his bed with Tibby Stott.

That night, John drew nearer to Tibby than usual, and put his arm around her neck. 'Wow, John, hinny!' quoth she, 'what means a' this kindness the night?' 'Tibby Stott, my woman Tibby,' said John, 'I hae a secret to tell you; but ye're to promise, an' swear to me, that ye're never to let it to the tap o' your tongue, as lang as ye hae life, afore ony body but mysel.' Tibby promised all that John desired her, and she repeated as many oaths after him as he chose, eager to learn this great secret; and John, after affecting great hesitation and scruples, addressed her as follows:

'Tibby Stott, do ye ken what was the matter wi' me, when I was last sae unweel?' 'Na, John, I didna ken then, nor ken I yet.' 'But I kend, Tibby Stott; and there's no anither in this world kens, or ever maun ken, but yoursel. I was very ill then, Tibby; an' I was in a very queer way. Ay, I was waur than ony body thought! But do you ken how I got better, Tibby?' 'Indeed, I dinna ken that nouther, John.' 'But I'll tell you, Tibby. I was brought to bed o' twa black birds; an' I hae them keepin concealed i' the house; an' they're twa ill spirits, far waur than cockatrices. Now, if this war kend, I wad be hanged, an' ye wad be burnt at the stake for a witch; therefore, keep the secret as you value both our lives. An' Tibby, ye maun never gang to look for thae twa birds, for if ever ye find them, they'll flee away wi' you to an ill place; an' mind ye an' dinna gang to be telling this to ony living flesh, Tibby Stott.'

'Na, na, John; sin' ye bid me, I sall never tak the tale o'er the tap o' my tongue. But, oh! alak! an wae's me! what's to come o' us? Ye hae gart a' my flesh girrel, John; to think that ever my gudeman sude hae been made a mither! an' then to think

what he's mither to! Mither o' twa deils! The Lord have a care
o' us, John! wad it no be better to let the twa imps flee away,
or get Mr Mathews to lair them?'

'But tent me here, Tibby Stott, my woman, Tibby, they're
sent for gude luck –'

'It can only be deil's luck, at the best, John; an' his can never
be good luck.'

'The best o' a' luck, Tibby; for I can tell you, we'll never
want as lang as they are in the house. They'll bring me siller
when I like, an' what I like; an' a' that ye hae to do, is to haud
your tongue, an' ye'll find the good o't; but if ever ye let this
secret escape you, we're ruined hip and thigh for ever.'

Tibby promised again for the sake of the money; but the
next morning before she swept her house, she ran in unto a
neighbouring gossip, and addressed her as follows:

'Wow, Jean, I hae gotten a screed o' unco news sin' I last saw
you! I trow ye didna ken that we had a crying i' this town the
tither week?'

'I wat, Tibby, I never heard o' sic a thing afore.'

'Aye, but atween you an' me, there's a pair o' braw twins
come to the warl, though nane o' the best-hued anes that may
be. But they'll be snug-keepit anes, an' weel-tochered anes, and
weel keepit out o' sight, as maiden's bairns should be. Aye,
Jean, my dow; but an ye kend wha's the mither o' them, your
een wad stand i' back water wi' laughin!'[16]

'What? Hout fie Tibby! I wat weel it isna Bess Bobagain, the
Antiburgher minister's housekeeper?'

'Waur nor that yet; an' that wad hae been ill eneuch. But ye
see the thing maunna be tauld; or else ye maun swear never to
tell it again, as lang as ye live.'

'Me tell it again! Nah! It is weel kend I never tauld a secret
i' my life. Ane may safely trust me wi' ony thing. My father,
honest man, used to say to me, even when I was but a wee
toddlin thing, that he had sae muckle to lippen to me, that he
could hae trustit me wi' a housefu' o' untelled millstanes. The
thing that's bred i' the bane, winna easily ding out o' the flesh.
When I was sae trusty then, what should I be now?'

'Aye, to be sure, there's a great deal in that. It says muckle for ane, when ane's pawrent can trust ane, sae as to do as ane likes i' ane's house. My father wad never trust me wi' a boddle; but mony a time he said I wad be a good poor man's wife, for that the best thing ony body could do for a poor man, was to gie him employment, an' I was the ane that wad haud mine busy for the maist part o' the four and twenty hours. But for a' my father's far-seen good sense, I hae had eneuch ado wi' John Gray, for though he's nae bad hand when he's on the loom, it is nae easy matter to keep him at the batt. But that's a' away frae our story. Sin your father could trust you sae far, I think I may trust you too, only ye're to say *as sure as death*, you will never tell it again.'

Jane complied, as was most likely, for the sake of this mysterious and scandalous story, as she deemed it to be, and after every precaution on the part of Tibby Stott, her gossip was entrusted with the whole. It would be endless to recount all the promises that were stipulated for, made, and broken at Middleholm, in the course of that day. Suffice it, that before night, every one, both old and young in the village, knew that the lang weaver had been *brought to bed o' twa black craws*.

This was too ridiculous a story to be believed, even by the ignorant inhabitants of that ancient village; and, as John shrewdly anticipated, they only laughed at John Gray's crazy wife. It proved however to him, that it would never do to trust his helpmate with the secret of finding hidden poses, and that whatever money he drew from such funds, it behoved him to ascribe it to the generosity of the two black birds.

So John arose one moonlight night, while others slept, went into his garden, and removing the wet straw, he again lifted up the broad stone, and took from under it the valuable treasure of which he had formerly made discovery. This was neither less nor more than the very thing he had always been told of, both by the vision of the cobler in his dream, and by the cobler himself; namely, an old pan filled with coins, of a date and reign John knew nothing about. Nearly one fourth of the whole bulk was made up of broad pieces of gold, but very thin, enclosed in one side of the pan; the rest was all silver, in a considerable state of decay. There were likewise among the gold, four rude square coins, about a quarter of an inch in thickness, and nearly the weight of a dollar each. John emptied them into a bag, and marched straight to Edinburgh with his treasure; where, after a great deal of manœuvring, he sold the whole for the miserable sum of £213:12:6, being the exact value of the metal (as the man assured him) to a scruple. John got his payment in gold and silver, for he would have nothing to do with bank notes, and brought the whole home with him. He knew nothing about putting money out at interest; and, still in fear lest he should be discovered, he hid it in the corner of his chest, resolved to live well on it till it was done, and then dig up another tree, take the pose from below it, and sell, and spend that in course; and so on: for John knew perfectly well, that he had a dozen of poses more to begin to, when the first was done.

Thenceforward, John's meals became somewhat more plentiful, but improved nothing in quality. He had been so long used to a life of poverty, that parsimony was become natural to him, and it was but seldom that he applied to the two birds for assistance. He could not rest however until he digged below one other tree, that he might have some guess what the extent of his treasure was, and what he had to depend on.

He accordingly began, and digged all round the next, and in beneath it, until the pits on each side met below the stem of the tree at a great depth, so that every one of the downward roots were cut; but for all that he could do, he could find no treasure whatever, and was obliged to give up the scrutiny considerably disappointed. Having, however, discovered, in the former adventure, that the removal of a part of the immense quantity of miry sour dung, from about his cow-house, had been attended with some conveniences, he likewise filled up this latter pit with a farther portion of that, and again betook himself to his loom and his twa black craws.

The next year, to the astonishment of all, but more particularly to John himself, who had never once calculated on such an event, these two trees, after being literally covered over with healthy blossoms, bore such a load of fruit as never had been witnessed in that country. Almost every branch required a prop to prevent it being torn from the tree, by the increasing weight.

John pulled the apples always as they ripened, and sent a quantity down every week by the carrier to his friend, the Cobler of Kelso, whose wife and daughter, it will be remembered, kept a fruit shop in one end of his dwelling. At the close of the year, when John went down to settle with his old friend, and the three-cocked hat, the latter paid him gratefully £7, 10s. for the produce of these two trees, and thanked him for his credit; not forgetting to treat him at breakfast with a cut of broiled salmon and a glass of brandy.

John, perceiving that this was good interest for a few wheel-barrows full of sour mire, followed the same mode with all his apple-trees, and planted more, so that in the course of a few years, the cobler paid him annually from 30 to 45 pounds Sterling for fruit, a great sum in those days; and thus was the cobler's extraordinary dream thoroughly fulfilled, not alone with regard to the main pose in the old pan, but that below every tree of the garden.

John now lived comfortably, with his family, all the days of his life, and there were no lasses had such trim and elegant cockernonies in all the Antiburgher meeting-house of Middle-holm as the daughters of the lang weaver. But Tibby Stott, poor creature! believed till her dying-day, that their wealth was supplied by the twa mysterious black craws, whose place of concealment she never found out, nor ever sought after.

Glossary

aboon above
ae one
ahint behind
aiblins perhaps
aith oath
an if
anent concerning
art and part legal phrase for
    collusion
asteer astir
Auld Simmie the Devil
aumuses alms

batt place, beat
bells bubbles
between hands at intervals
bicker beaker, bowl
bike swarm
bit place, position
bleared thin
boardly burly
bodle copper coin
bourock cottage, hovel, bothy
bow-kail cabbage
braidside the whole side
braird first shoots of a grain or
    grass crop
brigg bridge
brose a dish of oatmeal
brunstane brimstone
bumming humming, droning

but and ben front and back of a
    two-roomed cottage, to and
    fro

calm qualm
canny shrewd, skilful, pleasant,
    prudent, steady
carle fellow
cast dig peat, throw out or off,
    swarm (of bees)
cast-away unregenerate or
    reprobate person
cast up turn up
cauler freshly caught
cause legal case or hearing
chafts jaws
chaperon gentleman's cap or
    hood
chiel child, person
clachan village
cloot hoof
clout patch or mend, strike
cockernonie woman's cap
cool-the-loom lazybones
corant running or gliding dance
corbie craw raven, crow
coupin knocking or falling over
cracks talks
crappin stomach
creeshy greasy
crying birth

cuif fool
cutty short, abrupt

dawted cherished, spoilt
dee do, die
deray disarray, mess
detail an account
devil's burd offspring of the Devil
ding hit, beat
ditit muddled
divot turf
doiting stumbling
donnart stupid
dought nae wasn't able to
dow dove
draught animal's entrails
dree the weird suffer the fate
drink to them kiss them goodbye
dung doitrified stupefied

ee eye
elyed vanished
ettling trying
even-down haverel complete
    fool
evite avoid

fash bother
faut fault
feele fool
feu, feuar a tenure of land, and
    the renter of that land, under
    feudal law
flannen flannel
fleeched implored
fleegary bauble
fley frighten
fornent opposite
focks, foks folks
forby apart from
fra-yont from beyond
fraze flowery or flattering speech

gait goat
gart me dree made me suffer
gate way
gayan, gey fairly, very
gillygawpie foolish person
gin if
girrel shudder
gizened dried-up
gledgin' squinting
goodman, goodwife heads of a
    household, a tenant farmer
    and his wife
goud gold
gowk fool, cuckoo
gully large knife

haill whole
hand-fasted hands tied
haud hold, keep
hawkie cow
hind farm hand
hinny honey
hoad road a mess
Hollin lawn Holland linen
howk dig
howlet owl
How's-tey-ca'-him what d'you
    call him

ilka each
ill-faurd ill-favoured
ill wife bad wife

jaud jade
jerkin bodice
juggs pillory

kailstock cabbage stalk
kebbuck cheese
keek peep
ketch thrust
keust cast

kimmers womenfolk
kirning a churning
kye cows
kythe show, look

laid flattened (as of crops)
lair lay, exorcize
land tenement
lang long
lave the rest
lead a proof argue a proof in law
leasing-making lying, slander
leear liar
libelled stated, charged or indicted
lien lain
lift sky
links stretch of grass, golf course
lint-swingling flax-beating
lippen trust
lounder to hit
loup leap
luck-penny sum of money
   handed back by a seller
Lucky a name for a landlady or
   senior female
lug flap, ear

mae more
margin marginal note, clue
meal-girnel meal chest
mell strike a hammer blow
meltith a meal
mense sense, respect, honour
merk silvery coin
misleared greedy, uncouth
moniplies guts, one of a cow's
   stomachs
muckle much
mumpit tricked

neb nose
neuk nook, corner

oo-pan for baking bread
overhied overtook
ower over, too much

parrige porridge
pelt a blow
pennyworth revenge
pirn spool, bobbin
pit put
plack copper coin
pluck an animal's liver, heart
   and lungs
poukit plucked
pretend claim

raip rope
reard roar
rede advise
reid red
rigging ridge, roof
rip vile fellow
rock and lint spinner's distaff
   and flax
rowth plenty

sanna shan't
sauchless senseless, naive
saur savour, smell
scoudered scorched
session the kirk session of
   minister and elders
shan make a wry face
shekel coin, unit of measurement
shieling cottage, hut
shilpy stale
shoolin' shovelling
sib kin
sic such
side low-hanging
sidie for sidie side by side
siller silver
skair scour

skirl screech
slack-a-pin relax (slacken the web)
slough skin
slounging slouching
slump, by the in total
smoored smothered
snouking sniffing
sowins steeped oatmeal
spairged spattered, splashed
speer ask
spleuchan pouch
sponkin' flashing, sparkling
spulzie plunder
stane stone
staniraw dyed red
steekit shut
steepin' stipend
stott bullock
strae straw
strodge strut
superiority feudal entitlement to a piece of land
swee sway
swire a hollow

tae the one
take tent pay attention
tawpie silly person
tentit noticed
term-day quarter-day, when hirings were settled
threepit made out, argued
throng busy

tike dog
till hard clay
tolbooth prison, town hall
toom kists empty chests
tweeled twilled

unco very, highly, strange
unsonsy unlucky, unwholesome, ugly

wally-dy woeful
wame stomach
waratch wretch
wared spent
waur worse
wear manoeuvre, an animal or a boat
weirdest most ominous
well-tochered bringing a good dowry
wheen a few
whiles at times
whittle knife
windlestrae straw
wudd mad

yelloch yell
yerkit against the stock forced against the edge of the box-bed
yestreen yesterday evening
yettlin cast-iron
yird earth
yowes ewes

Notes

CONFESSIONS OF A JUSTIFIED SINNER
THE EDITOR'S NARRATIVE

1. *Dalcastle*: Located in the West of Scotland. Hogg's principal city was Scotland's capital city of Edinburgh, but much of the action of the novel takes place in the West. The novel, published anonymously, was dedicated, 'respectfuly inscribed', to a virtuous Lord Provost of Glasgow, William Smith. In order to strengthen his incognito, Hogg felt that it might be worth presenting himself as 'a Glasgow Literateur'.

2. *monitors*: A word that works hard in Hogg's writings, where it can mean recorders, observers, examples, warnings and admonitions, critics and editors.

3. *Reformation principles*: Promulgated by Luther, Calvin and, in Scotland, John Knox. The Scottish Reformation settlement brought the Presbyterian form of church government, with its refusal of bishops. Adherents of the Stuart monarchy and episcopate would one day contribute to the Jacobite coup attempts that followed the 'Glorious Revolution' of 1688 and the establishment of a new court and a Whig ascendancy. The mention of a 'court party', at this point in the novel, suggests the Royalists of the Restoration period. The expression also suggests here an opposition of town and country.

4. *the Amorite, the Hittite, and the Girgashite*: Inhabitants of the land of Canaan, ousted by the Israelites.

5. *held*: An earlier use of the word.

6. *regenerated person*: Or justified person – one of the elect, the just, the born-again, saved from before birth, and, according to the ultra-Calvinist, 'antinomian' view of their condition, beyond the constraints of morality. Election (or adoption) and predestination were constituents of justification by faith, as opposed to works, or good deeds.

7. *separation complete*: In 1820, four years before the publication
    of the novel, Hogg embarked on a successful marriage to a pious
    wife, of evangelical and, eventually, Free Kirk sympathies. The
    domestic arrangements that ensued for Dalcastle and his lady
    resemble those devised a few years earlier by his friend John
    Ballantyne, for himself and his wife, at his house of Harmony
    Hall by the Firth of Forth. In the wicked words of John Gibson
    Lockhart, there was a private wing, the accesses to which 'were
    so narrow that it was physically impossible for the handsome
    and portly lady who bore his name to force her person through
    any one of them' (*Electric Shepherd*, pp. 183–4).

8. *civil wars*: The struggles between Presbyterians and Royalists that
    arose for both Scotland and England in the mid-seventeenth cen-
    tury. The story of Scotland's Covenanters began with the National
    Covenant of 1638 and the Solemn League and Covenant of 1643.
    These saw the Scots as a chosen people, the new Israel, and
    affirmed the Presbyterian faith. The second tried to impose it on
    England, by cementing an alliance with the Parliamentary oppo-
    sition to Charles I. During 'the killing time', God's own were
    hunted in the South of Scotland by Charles II's dragoons. At other
    times, some of the King's supporters were fined and expropriated.

9. *twelve*: The error in arithmetic may be meant as Rabina's.

10. *Moabite*: A Biblical tribe, enemies of Israel.

11. *extremity*: The passage refers to the complex, coat-turning poli-
    tics that led up to the Act of Union of 1707, a politics charac-
    terized by the *Oxford Companion to Scottish History* (2001,
    p. 605) as 'tortuous' and 'kaleidoscopic'. The 'famous session'
    appears to be the 1703 session of the Scottish Parliament, where
    the Duke of Queensberry, who had moved from James II to
    William III, was Queen Anne's representative, or Lord Com-
    missioner. The Jacobite Cavalier party, then gaining ground, was
    opposed by the governing Court party of the day, which was also
    opposed to the Country party. The first Duke of Argyll, overlord
    of the Campbells, was an upholder of the 1688 revolution, and
    the foremost Presbyterian leader. He was alleged by Jacobites to
    have died, in 1703, of 'bruises received in a brothel' (*Collected
    Works* edn., p. 217). Hogg's friend David Brewster invented the
    kaleidoscope, and his novel has been thought 'kaleidoscopic'.

12. *tennis*: Real tennis seems to be meant (*CW*).

13. *hardly bested*: Hard-pressed. The expression occurs in the medi-
    eval poem about William Wallace by Harry the Minstrel, a
    modernization of which delighted the young Hogg.

14.   *regiment*: Recruited from the Covenanting population of the South-West. Cameronians were ultra-Presbyterians, led at the outset by Richard Cameron, who was killed in 1680.

15.   *human merit*: The mere virtue of the castaway, or unregenerate Christian.

16.   *verses*: From the seventeenth-century metrical Psalms of David (109).

17.   *demure*: The word is used in the novel to suggest a solemnly reserved puritan demeanour, in which, as here, meekness may play little part.

18.   *Grey-Friars*: A celebrated kirk, where the National Covenant was signed.

19.   *darkness*: In his essay 'Nature's Magic Lantern', Hogg recounts a similar experience of his own. His concern with optical illusion owed something to his friend, the eminent 'man of science', David Brewster. Hogg was interested in 'refracted' light.

20.   *fellows*: Hogg himself took a superstitious view of children born out of wedlock. Seven out of ten natural children were 'not like other people', in some way 'misshapen' or 'perverse'. A daughter, and perhaps two, were fathered by him out of wedlock. See *Electric Shepherd*, pp. 60–61.

21.   *promise*: God's promise to the chosen, their salvation secured by Christ's atonement.

22.   *Duke of Melfort*: Hogg has in mind a historical personage, whose son is the Thomas Drummond of the novel. The real Thomas Drummond fought for the Jacobites in 1715, and has been considered a source for Hogg's story 'The Adventures of Captain John Lochy'.

23.   *cue*: 'Cue' for 'clue' is found in 'John Gray o' Middleholm'.

24.   *hung up*: Mrs Mary ('Lucky') McKinnon, the keeper of an Edinburgh brothel where a murder was committed, was defended in court by Francis Jeffrey, editor of the Whig *Edinburgh Review*, unjustly tried, and hanged before a crowd of 20,000 on 23 April 1823: see the *CW* edition and *Electric Shepherd*.

25.   *satisfaction*: A sentiment Hogg ascribes to himself in his *Memoir*, p. 134: a liar at Hogg's expense 'will gang to hell that's aye some comfort'.

26.   *wore*: 'Wear' can mean manoeuvre or direct, as in the case of a boat or a beast. 'Marion's Jock' uses it with reference to a cow.

27.   *Gil-Martin*: A Gaelic name for a fox, and a name in Gaelic folklore for a shape-changing trickster (*CW*, p. 226). Gil-Moules is a dark god in Hogg's play *All-Hallow Eve*.

PRIVATE MEMOIRS AND CONFESSIONS

OF A SINNER

1. *Scottish worthies*: A proverbial expression. John Howie's long-lived Covenanting commemoration, *Scots Worthies*, appeared in 1774.

2. *Single Catechism*: The Shorter Catechism, made known to Hogg at Ettrick school, seems to be meant. With the metrical Psalms of David, a main feature of his intermittent early education and of the national curriculum.

3. *covenant*: God's covenant with the favoured few.

4. *heavens*: This tribute to God's creation comes close to the wording of a speech by Friar Bacon in Hogg's novel *The Three Perils of Man*, which appeared a year before the *Confessions* (*Electric Shepherd*, p. 210). According to his friend Sydney Smith, the Parliamentary Reformer Francis Jeffrey felt that the Creation had been seriously mishandled ('Damn the solar system! bad light – planets too distant – pestered with comets') and that he himself could have done a lot better (see Alan Bell's *Sydney Smith*, 1980, p. 46).

5. *red-letter side*: Red lines or letters can be hellish in Hogg. Those whose names are suitably inscribed in the book of life (Revelation 21:27) will be permitted to enter the New Jerusalem.

6. *cast of grace*: 'Cast' could mean a look, a chance, a lucky stroke, the throw of a dice or of a fishing line, a religious conversion. Later in the novel it is used of a legal case to mean 'thrown out'. Further senses are supplied in the glossary.

7. *Melchizedek*: King of Salem, a priest sometimes associated with Christ.

8. *Jehu, a Cyrus, or a Nebuchadnezzar*: Masterful Old Testament kings.

9. *detail*: Account.

10. *sinful king of Israel*: Ahab.

11. *patriarch of old*: Jacob.

12. *the Lamb's book of life*: See Note 5.

13. *feelings*: Hogg's interest in likeness and 'unstable' looks was evident several years earlier, in his journal the *Spy*, where he writes of the 'abominable propensity' whereby, by 'contemplating a person's features minutely, modelling my own after the same manner as nearly as possible, and putting my body into the same posture which seems most familiar to them, I can ascertain

the compass of their minds and thoughts'. Meanwhile, in the novel, Bessy Gillies bids people to beware of 'likeness'. See also Gil-Martin's impending account of the 'peculiarity in my nature', and the Introduction to this edition.

14. *the 25th day of March 1704*: P. D. Garside (CW) notes that this is the date of the Feast of the Annunciation, which commemorates the Angel Gabriel's announcement to Mary of her motherhood of the Messiah.

15. *power to do*: A central contradiction of predestinarian Christianity, in which repentance was at once enjoined and prevented.

16. *Finnieston*: Now part of Glasgow.

17. *Czar Peter of Russia*: Whose travels in Western Europe took him in 1698 to England, where, at Deptford, he studied shipbuilding.

18. *of the moral cast*: Blanchard is condemned by the sinner as a believer in the efficacy of good works, as opposed to salvation by faith, and accounted deistical.

19. *bond of society*: Sentiments expressed by Hogg in his *Lay Sermons* of 1834, CW, p. 83: 'Wo to him who would weaken the bonds with which true Christianity connects us with Heaven and with one another!' His sermons nevertheless inveigh against 'deistical reformers', whose views are treated as tantamount to atheism.

20. *the Cloud of Witnesses*: A Covenanting martyrology of 1714.

21. *Fat the deil*: Hogg liked to imitate Highlanders' English, both in and out of print.

22. *Gilgal*: Joshua's camp, an Israelite stronghold. See 1 Samuel 15 for some exemplary carnage.

23. *Tophet*: Hell; the name, too, of an ominous site near Jerusalem.

24. *the venal prophet*: Balaam. Belial was a name for the Devil, or for a fiend, and 'children of Belial' is a name from Deuteronomy that is applied in Covenanter fiction to Royalist persecutors of the faithful.

25. *the rashness of my understanding*: First edition. The 1947 and 1969 editions give 'undertaking'. The CW edition quotes Isaiah 32:4: 'The heart also of the rash shall understand knowledge . . .'

26. *interested*: Biased, or designing.

27. *tumbled*: Hogg tumbled down Ben More (unscathed) in 1811, according to the *Spy* (CW, pp. 401, 440–43).

28. *10th Psalm*: A plea to God for vengeance on the wicked.

29. *too nice*: The Machiavellian precept whereby the end justifies the means appears to go unmentioned in Hogg.

30. *26th September, 1687*: An accurate burlesque of the style of

ancient charters. 'All and haill' means 'in all'. Tofts are home-
steads, coal-heughs pits. 'Brooked' means possessed, as does
'joysed'. Miethes are boundaries, multures a duty on milling
grain. Among the other feudalities, 'sack' and 'sock' relate to the
rights of lordship, while 'outfang thief' and 'infang thief' relate,
respectively, to a lord's right to pursue a robber beyond the lord's
jurisdiction and to arrest him on his land. 'Right trusty cousin'
is 'right trust cousin' in the first edition and in CW.

31. *two distinct natures*: Duality had scarcely become a domestic
feature in the Scotland of Hogg's earlier years, but it would
appear that it became quite common to speak in this way. Hogg's
contemporary Henry Cockburn, a man of very different outlook,
wrote, in his *Life* of Francis Jeffrey (2 vols, 1852, Vol. I, p. 200),
of a fellow lawyer, John Clerk: 'It is difficult to describe a person
whose conditions in repose and in action, that is, in his private
and in his professional life, almost amounted to the possession
of two natures.' Hogg and Cockburn spoke the Scots that Jeffrey,
a lover of Scotland, wanted to shed. Elsewhere in the volume
(p.48), Cockburn says that Jeffrey was nevertheless 'familiar with
the writers in that classic Scotch, of which much is good old
English, from Gavin Douglas to Burns. He saw the genius of
Scott, and Wilson, and Hogg, and Galt, and others, elicited by
the rich mines of latent character and history with which their
country abounds.' The judgement is supported by the story that
follows about the saints of Auchtermuchty.

32. *Whiggam*: A West of Scotland Presbyterian (*cf* Whiggamore,
considered ancestral to the name Whig). Penpunt is in Nithsdale,
Dumfriesshire.

33. *Macmillan*: In 1706, John Macmillan became the leader of the
Cameronians, who then became Macmillanites.

34. *bridal*: An obscure word, perhaps prompted by the 'bridal' that
precedes it. It may mean the V-shape or bridle shape of a forma-
tion of birds. Corbie crows are ravens. Black birds can be hellish
in Hogg, who alludes here to Scott's, and the tradition's, ballad
of the two conversing, man-eating corbies. John Gray o' Middleholm dreams that he has given birth to two evil-spirited black
crows.

35. *Mount, Diabolus, and fly*: A name for Satan, from John Bunyan.
The cry is heard in a pawkie ballad which has been attributed to
Hogg: the Warlock o' Aikwood, Michael Scott, flies on a bad
black horse to Paris and blasts its towers. The cry is also heard
in a version of the story given in Walter Scott's notes of 1830 to

The Lay of the Last Minstrel. In this version the French have been committing piracy.

36. *western door*: The opposite end of a pre-Reformation church to the sanctum of the altar.

37. *Prophecies of Ezekiel*: Israel is to be overturned for its impurities by Nebuchadnezzar, at God's will. The 119th Psalm, longest of the Psalms, celebrates obedience to God's will.

38. *gouden rule*: The injunction in the Sermon on the Mount to do as you would be done by has been known as the Golden Rule.

39. *witnesses*: A reference to the idea that a murderer's touch will cause the corpse in question to bleed. Hogg's poem 'The Pedlar' has the idea.

40. *pearls o' damnation*: A play on words ('pearls' for 'perils') similar to other writers' word-plays at Hogg's expense which occurred at this time: Walter Scott and Hogg's *Blackwood's* friends punned on his name and on the names of two of his novels (his *Three Perils of Man* and *of Woman*, pearls produced by the Swine of Ettrick).

41. *Boddel Brigg*: In 1679, the Covenanters were defeated at Bothwell Bridge.

42. *Mr James Watson*: Became in 1711 one of the Queen's Printers in Scotland. He was a publisher of theology and of religious allegory – of John Bunyan's *Holy War*. The sinner's narrative has been seen by some as an anti-type or 'dark inversion' of *Pilgrim's Progress* (*CW*, p. 245). Certain of Hogg's writings were seen by himself as allegories.

43. *the wings of a dove*: Psalms 55:6 and 68:13, a cry of the period, heard in De Quincey's *Confessions of an English Opium-Eater* (1822, Penguin 1971, p. 69).

44. *Ault-Righ*: A Gaelic derivation for Altrive, the farm where Hogg spent most of his adult life. He points out here that the Gaelic word means the King's Burn.

45. *Farewell, world*: Such farewells are a feature of Covenanter testaments, and were associated with delivery from the scaffold. The parting words of notable people, under sentence of death, were a convention which appears to have influenced Hogg's novel. Two testaments by, or ghosted for, malefactors may have served him: *The Confession of Nicol Muschet of Boghall* (1818) and the *Life of David Haggart* (1821). Muschet murdered his wife in the valley below the summit of Arthur's Seat in Edinburgh and in the vicinity of Robert Wringhim's struggle with his brother. Haggart's account was of interest at *Blackwood's*, and his name

was coupled with Hogg's in the magazine's symposium, the 'Noctes Ambrosianae'. The account is editorially framed, as Robert Wringhim's is, and there are holograph notes by Cockburn in the British Library copy which call it a pack of lies.

THE EDITOR'S NARRATIVE

1. *letter*: Most of this letter to the editor follows.
2. *James Anderson*: Anderson was a name well known to Hogg. A James Anderson was once a tenant at Altrive, and a man of that name was said to have taught Hogg his letters.
3. *meet*: There was a belief that suicides were buried at boundaries of this sort.
4. *William Shiel*: A shepherd, remembered for having taken part in the opening of the suicide's grave.
5. *you*: William Blackwood. Hogg is writing to a journal about a strange Border event, and is disposed, at this point, to guess that shortage of money may have occasioned the suicide's despair.
6. *advocate*: John Gibson Lockhart of Chiefswood is meant. Lockhart, Scott's son-in-law, joins the expedition to see the corpse, together with the poet William Laidlaw, who was Scott's secretary, and others.
7. *wool-stapler*: Buyer of wool. Hogg said that he once mistook Wordsworth for a horse-dealer of the same surname.
8. *market ground*: The initials used here refer to local worthies who cannot be firmly identified. Beattie was an Ettrick name. John Beattie was the Ettrick schoolmaster, like his father before him. His daughter Mary married Hogg's brother William. A Margaret Beattie bore a child who may have been Hogg's.
9. *stone*: A cairn of stones now stands (in customary fashion) near the summit of Fall Law.
10. *above the vent of the ear*: For phrenologists, the site of the destructive faculty.
11. *possession*: A Wilton Lodge was inhabited at this time by a gentleman scholar, another James Anderson.
12. *Fideli certa merces*: A sure reward for the faithful.

MARION'S JOCK

1. *as ever*: In Hogg's novel of 1822, *The Three Perils of Man*, the tale of Marion's Jock is told by the Laird of Peatstacknowe in the course of a storytelling competition. Later in the novel Jock

is revealed to be a delinquent Tam Craik, 'the Deil's Tam', a carnivore, with the green eyes of a cannibal. The novel depicts a medieval chivalry, a siege of the English in Roxburgh Castle, and an expedition to the wizard Michael Scott's nearby castle of Aikwood, where magic breaks out, shapes are changed, human beings doubled and devoured. The company includes the beguiling Border knight Charlie and the maid Delany.

2. *dinner*: Jock's shieling life resembles that of Hogg in his herding days, as recalled in his *Memoir*, where a bottle of sweet milk is itemized. Sour milk, says the story slyly, is called whig.

3. *Marion's Jock*: In *The Three Perils of Man* (1972 edn., p. 232) Michael Scott – who is derived from the historical personage of that name, a world-famous thirteenth-century philosopher, an enemy, as it happens, of the black arts – offers a symbolic interpretation of the tale. He informs the company that the maid Delany 'is the favourite lamb' whom the teller of the tale 'wishes you to kill and feast on in the same delicious manner as did the hero of his tale; and I am the goodman whom you are to stick afterwards, and fairly make your escape'.

JOHN GRAY O' MIDDLEHOLM

1. *great discovery itself*: The distinction between the material and the pneumatic, no doubt assailable in science, nevertheless reflects the interest in scientific experiment that often shows itself in Hogg's flights of fancy. These included a trip to the Moon. The quotation from Bacon comes from the *Sylva Sylvarum* of 1627.

2. *Philliphaugh*: Montrose's Royalist army was defeated at Philiphaugh near Selkirk in 1645.

3. *feeds*: Versions of the riddles quoted in the story are to be found in Robert Chambers's *Popular Rhymes of Scotland* (3rd ed., 1847, pp. 27–8, 37–42, 322). This collection first appeared, in part, in 1826, and Hogg was in touch with Chambers that year, concerning the collection. Chambers's book refers to Hogg's *Winter Evening Tales* (1820), where the present tale first appeared, and to the business of lucky dreams and digs. Treasure-trove as revealed to the dreamer is a feature of Scottish folklore, and a story similar to the one Hogg tells is recounted by Chambers. Some of the material in his collection would seem to have been shared with Hogg over a period of years. In 1813 Hogg told the publisher Constable: 'I have for many years been col-

lecting the rural and traditionary tales of Scotland and I have of late been writing them over again and new-modelling them.' The 'cottagers of Scotland' had furnished him with this material, parts of which had appeared in his magazine the *Spy* and were to appear in *Winter Evening Tales*. But it is also the case that his own adventures had furnished the material, according to his journalist friends, who claimed to have heard the stories from him, orally, many's the time. Having tired of the 'hackneyed' designation of 'the Ettrick Shepherd', Hogg fancied signing the rural and traditionary series of tales proposed to Constable with the lairdly name of J. H. Craig of Douglas (see *CW* edn., p. xv). It would be a little hard to believe that a laird had written 'John Gray o' Middleholm'. This, too, is a tale of the country kind, with something of the anti-clerical fabliau about it. But it would be equally hard to think of it as the work of a rural innocent. Hogg has remodelled, and sophisticated, what had come to him from the cottages, and from Chambers.

4. *an it be*: The 1820 edition has: 'an' it be'. See pp. 251 and 257 ('an ye') for a similar adjustment.

5. *Antiburgher*: The Presbyterian Seceders left the Church of Scotland in 1733. This Seceder minister was a member of the Anti-Burgher synod, formed in 1747, which rejected the religious oath imposed on local authority office-holders.

6. *ran*: Hogg was a runner, in life, and a connoisseur of running. Marion's Jock runs, and so does Connel of Dee, another of his incarnations, in a poem published in *Winter Evening Tales*, where 'he ran, and he ran' (*CW*, p. 418). Indeed, 'it may not be said that he ran, for he flew.'

7. *warld be a wastle us*: Keep us from wordly cares.

8. *the one nor the other*: This colloquy of doubles, with its stress on the uncertainty, the who's who, of the human personality, anticipates the engagement with duality soon to be pursued in the *Confessions*.

9. *cue*: See *Confessions*, the editor's opening narrative, Note 23.

10. *amaist*: The 1820 edition has 'was amaist'.

11. *Gallic word*: The Gaelic word *fuil* appears to have been taken from the English.

12. *flew*: For a version of this impressive rhyme see Chambers. The Chambers version is said (*CW*, p. 570–71) to have been a description of the coat of arms of the city of Glasgow, taken from the seals of the Bishop of Glasgow.

13. *tramped it down*: Luke 13 has Jesus' parable about the good

effect of digging about, and dunging, a fig tree (*CW*, p. 569), a parable of repentance. In the *Confessions* David Anderson 'tramped down' the sinner's head into his grave, as the sun rose.

14. *Calvinistical*: The word is used with a disapproval that might appear to side with the countryside, with the folk, as against a theoretical and self-seeking priesthood, and with a dominant meaning of the *Confessions*.

15. *propine*: Possibly a mistake for 'propone', meaning to advance a legal argument.

16. *wi' laughin*: You'd cry with laughter.

READ MORE IN PENGUIN

In every corner of the world, on every subject under the sun, Penguin represents quality and variety – the very best in publishing today.

For complete information about books available from Penguin – including Puffins, Penguin Classics and Arkana – and how to order them, write to us at the appropriate address below. Please note that for copyright reasons the selection of books varies from country to country.

In the United Kingdom: Please write to *Dept. EP, Penguin Books Ltd, Bath Road, Harmondsworth, West Drayton, Middlesex UB7 0DA*

In the United States: Please write to *Consumer Services, Penguin Putnam Inc., 405 Murray Hill Parkway, East Rutherford, New Jersey 07073-2136.* VISA and MasterCard holders call 1-800-631-8571 to order Penguin titles

In Canada: Please write to *Penguin Books Canada Ltd, 10 Alcorn Avenue, Suite 300, Toronto, Ontario M4V 3B2*

In Australia: Please write to *Penguin Books Australia Ltd, 487 Maroondah Highway, Ringwood, Victoria 3134*

In New Zealand: Please write to *Penguin Books (NZ) Ltd, Private Bag 102902, North Shore Mail Centre, Auckland 10*

In India: Please write to *Penguin Books India Pvt Ltd, 11 Community Centre, Panchsheel Park, New Delhi 110017*

In the Netherlands: Please write to *Penguin Books Netherlands bv, Postbus 3507, NL-1001 AH Amsterdam*

In Germany: Please write to *Penguin Books Deutschland GmbH, Metzlerstrasse 26, 60594 Frankfurt am Main*

In Spain: Please write to *Penguin Books S. A., Bravo Murillo 19, 1°B, 28015 Madrid*

In Italy: Please write to *Penguin Italia s.r.l., Via Vittorio Emanuele 45/a, 20094 Corsico, Milano*

In France: Please write to *Penguin France, 12, Rue Prosper Ferradou, 31700 Blagnac*

In Japan: Please write to *Penguin Books Japan Ltd, Iidabashi KM-Bldg, 2-23-9 Koraku, Bunkyo-Ku, Tokyo 112-0004*

In South Africa: Please write to *Penguin Books South Africa (Pty) Ltd, P.O. Box 751093, Gardenview, 2047 Johannesburg*

PENGUIN CLASSICS

A JOURNAL OF THE PLAGUE YEAR
DANIEL DEFOE

'It was a most surprising thing, to see those Streets, which were usually so thronged, now grown desolate'

In 1665 the Great Plague swept through London, claiming nearly 100,000 lives. In *A Journal*, written nearly sixty years later, Defoe vividly chronicled the progress of the epidemic. We follow his fictional narrator through a city transformed: the streets and alleyways deserted; the houses of death with crosses daubed on their doors; the dead-carts on their way to the pits. And he recounts the horrifying stories of the citizens he encounters, as fear, isolation and hysteria take hold. *A Journal* is both a fascinating historical document and a supreme work of imaginative reconstruction.

This edition contains a new introduction, an appendix on the Plague, a topographical index and maps of contemporary London, and reproduces Anthony Burgess's original introduction.

'The most reliable and comprehensive account of the Great Plague that we possess' Anthony Burgess

'Within the texture of Defoe's prose London becomes a living and suffering being' Peter Ackroyd

Edited with an introduction by Cynthia Wall

PENGUIN CLASSICS

MOLL FLANDERS DANIEL DEFOE

'I grew as impudent a Thief, and as dexterous as ever *Moll Cut-Purse* was'

Born and abandoned in Newgate Prison, Moll Flanders is forced to make her own way in life. She duly embarks on a career that includes husband-hunting, incest, bigamy, prostitution and pick-pocketing, until her crimes eventually catch up with her. One of the earliest and most vivid female narrators in the history of the English novel, Moll recounts her adventures with irresistible wit and candour – and enough guile that the reader is left uncertain whether she is ultimately a redeemed sinner or a successful opportunist.

Based on the first edition of 1722, this volume includes a chronology, notes on currency, and maps of London and Virginia in the late seventeenth century.

Edited with an introduction and notes by David Blewett

PENGUIN CLASSICS

THE LIFE AND OPINIONS OF TRISTRAM SHANDY, GENTLEMAN   LAURENCE STERNE

'L—d! said my mother, what is all this story about? –
A COCK and a BULL, said Yorick – and one of the best of its kind I ever heard'

Laurence Sterne's great masterpiece of bawdy humour and rich satire defies any attempt to categorize it. Part novel, part digression, its gloriously disordered narrative interweaves the birth and life of the unfortunate 'hero' Tristram Shandy, the eccentric philosophy of his father Walter, the amours and military obsessions of Uncle Toby, and a host of other characters, including Dr Slop, Corporal Trim and the parson Yorick. A joyful celebration of the endless possibilities of the art of fiction, *Tristram Shandy* is also a wry demonstration of its limitations.

The text and notes of this volume are based on the acclaimed Florida Edition, with a critical introduction by Melvyn New and Christopher Ricks's introductory essay from the first Penguin Classics edition of the novel.

'The excellent Florida *Tristram Shandy* . . . will be the definitive edition' *Studies in English Literature*

'The book that I would never tire of . . . Sterne was about 250 years ahead of his time' Roy Porter

THE FLORIDA EDITION
Edited by Melvyn New and Joan New

PENGUIN CLASSICS

BLEAK HOUSE   CHARLES DICKENS

'Jarndyce and Jarndyce has passed into a joke. That is the only good that has ever come of it'

As the interminable case of Jarndyce and Jarndyce grinds its way through the Court of Chancery, it draws together a disparate group of people: Ada and Richard Clare, whose inheritance is gradually being devoured by legal costs; Esther Summerson, a ward of court, whose parentage is a source of deepening mystery; the menacing lawyer Tulkinghorn; the determined sleuth Inspector Bucket; and even Jo, the destitute little crossing-sweeper. A savage, but often comic, indictment of a society that is rotten to the core, *Bleak House* is one Dickens's most ambitious novels, with a range that extends from the drawing rooms of the aristocracy to the poorest of London slums.

This edition follows the first edition in book form of 1853. Terry Eagleton's preface examines characterization and considers *Bleak House* as an early work of detective fiction.

'Perhaps his best novel . . . when Dickens wrote *Bleak House* he had grown up' G. K. Chesterton

'One of the finest of all English satires' Terry Eagleton

Edited with an introduction and notes by Nicola Bradbury and with a new preface by Terry Eagleton

PENGUIN CLASSICS

THE DIARY OF A NOBODY
GEORGE AND WEEDON GROSSMITH

'I fail to see – because I do not happen to be a "Somebody" – why my diary should not be interesting'

Mr Pooter is a man of modest ambitions, content with his ordinary life. Yet he always seems to be troubled by disagreeable tradesmen, impertinent young office clerks and wayward friends, not to mention his devil-may-care son Lupin's unsuitable choice of bride. Try as he might, he cannot avoid life's embarrassing mishaps. In the bumbling, absurd yet ultimately endearing figure of Pooter, the Grossmiths created an immortal comic character and a superb satire on the snobberies of middle-class suburbia – one which also sends up late Victorian crazes for Aestheticism, spiritualism and bicycling, as well as the fashion for publishing diaries by anybody and everybody.

This edition contains the original illustrations by Weedon Grossmith, further reading and an introduction by Ed Glinert discussing the novel's initial serialization in *Punch*, reactions to Pooter, the growth of suburbs and the figure of Mrs Pooter.

'The jewel at the heart of English comic literature' William Trevor

'The funniest book in the world' Evelyn Waugh

Edited with an introduction and notes by Ed Glinert

PENGUIN CLASSICS

FAR FROM THE MADDING CROWD
THOMAS HARDY

'I *hate* to be thought men's property in that way'

Independent and spirited Bathsheba Everdene has come to Weatherbury to take up her position as a farmer on the largest estate in the area. Her bold presence draws three very different suitors: the gentleman-farmer Boldwood, soldier-seducer Sergeant Troy and the devoted shepherd Gabriel Oak. Each, in contrasting ways, unsettles her decisions and complicates her life, and tragedy ensues, threatening the stability of the whole community. The first of his works set in Wessex, Hardy's novel of swift passion and slow courtship is imbued with his evocative descriptions of rural life and landscapes, and with unflinching honesty about sexual relationships.

This edition, based on Hardy's original 1874 manuscript, is the complete novel he never saw published, and restores its full candour and innovation. Rosemarie Morgan's introduction discusses the history of its publication, and the biblical and classical allusions that permeate the novel.

'Wonderful . . . a landscape which satisfies every stir of the imagination and which ravishes the senses' Ronald Blythe

Edited with an introduction and notes by Rosemarie Morgan and Shannon Russell

PENGUIN CLASSICS

THE PICTURE OF DORIAN GRAY   OSCAR WILDE

'The horror, whatever it was, had not yet entirely spoiled that marvellous beauty'

Enthralled by his own exquisite portrait, Dorian Gray exchanges his soul for eternal youth and beauty. Influenced by his friend Lord Henry Wotton, he is drawn into a corrupt double life: indulging his desires in secret while remaining a gentleman in the eyes of polite society. Only his portrait bears the traces of his decadence. *The Picture of Dorian Gray* was a *succès de scandale*. Early readers were shocked by its hints at unspeakable sins, and the book was later used as evidence against Wilde at the Old Bailey in 1895.

This definitive edition includes a selection of contemporary reviews condemning the novel's immorality, and the introduction to the first Penguin Classics edition by Peter Ackroyd.

Edited with an introduction and notes by Robert Mighall